THE BOMB QUEST

The Bomb Quest is published under Reverie, a sectionalized division under Di Angelo Publications, Inc.

Reverie is an imprint of Di Angelo Publications.
Copyright 2025.
All rights reserved.
Printed in the United States of America.

Di Angelo Publications
Los Angeles, California

Library of Congress
The Bomb Quest
ISBN: 978-1-962603-26-3
Paperback

Words: David Kent
Cover Design: Savina Mayeur
Interior Design: Kimberly James
Editor: Hollie S. McKay

Downloadable via www.dapbooks.shop and other e-book retailers.

For educational, business, and bulk orders, contact sales@diangelopublications.com.

1. Fiction --- Thrillers --- Historical
2. Fiction --- Historical --- 20th Century --- Post World War II
3. Fiction --- Action & Adventure

THE BOMB QUEST

DAVID KENT

*To my father whose love and extreme patience allowed
me to blossom.
To Prem Rawat whose message gives me confidence and strength.
To my daughter Rachel whose far too early departure from this
Earth inspired me to finish the book.
To my wife Raquel whose steadfast faith and belief in me has kept
me on the right path.*

CHAPTER 1

Day 1 in Japan

Joshua's eyes flew open as the airplane's wheels hit the runway at Narita Airport, Tokyo, Japan. The words of his grandfather, Nathaniel Meister, a World War II bombardier, came flooding back as they did every time Joshua awakened.

"Grandson, I have something to tell you."

"What is that, Grampa?"

"The whole world knows that on August 6, 1945, the U.S. dropped an atomic bomb on Hiroshima, Japan. On August 9, 1945, we dropped another atomic bomb on Nagasaki. On August 15, the Japanese surrendered. But what the world doesn't know is that on August 12, 1945, we dropped a hydrogen bomb on Tokyo that didn't go off. And now I want you to find it."

"What, Grampa? How do you know that?"

"Because I am the one who dropped the bomb."

"And you want me to find it?"

"Yes, grandson. I want you to find it."

"Seriously?"

"Yes."

And so began Joshua's mission or quest or wild goose chase or something. *Is this all a dream, or is this real? Did the U.S. drop a hydrogen bomb on Tokyo just before the end of World War II?* Joshua wondered. *Did it not go off? Is it still there?*

Joshua sighed in frustration. How maddening it was not to have answers to the questions that mattered most. Here he was, in Japan, beginning his quest to locate an unexploded hydrogen bomb from World War II.

One thing was certain—actually, two. First, Joshua had worked for the CIA, so he knew if the CIA or another agency found out there was a bomb in Tokyo Bay, there'd be agents on their way by now. Second, someone with bad intent had found out about the bomb, and they were also enroute, likely with a team. This was something he suspected based on an undeniable gut feeling.

Great. Both groups would kill him if they found him, but not before torturing him for information. Joshua shuddered at the thought of electrodes and other unspeakable methods they would use. Yet, he had no choice because the world didn't need a hydrogen bomb falling into the wrong hands. Also, Joshua's grandfather had chosen him, so now this mission was his crusade, his defining moment, his duty, no matter how short his life might be as a result. Still, the comparison to the Crusaders wasn't comforting—they hadn't fared too well.

Joshua's father, David Meister, had drilled into him that doing one's duty was the true mark of a man, no matter the consequences. That is why David Meister had been awarded the Air Force Cross and two purple hearts for what he did in Vietnam. His grandfather Nathaniel, too, was awarded the Medal of Honor for his bravery after being captured by and escaping from the Nazis.

A lot to live up to indeed. Aside from that legacy staring at him and the fact that he didn't want to let his grandfather down, Joshua was in too deep to back out now because he knew too much. If he quit now and his grandfather subsequently spilled the beans, the CIA would silence them both. The original goal of serving humanity by safely disposing of the bomb, while a noble goal, was superseded by the raw reality of a certain demise if he quit or failed. No choice but to trudge on.

As the aircraft taxied to the gate, Joshua's unease grew. His mind flitted to the key dates that ended World War II. Well, the three official dates, he corrected himself. Only in his secret world did a fourth date matter: August 12, 1945, when a hydrogen bomb was dropped on Tokyo, a truth the world didn't know.

Joshua had to find the bomb to assure himself that the world would never know the truth about the mission on August 12th, and for the world to never suffer the effects if the bomb were to fall into the wrong hands—a distinct possibility. And in no small measure, the truth would give his grandfather peace near the end of his life, and that meant more to Joshua than his lofty aspiration vis-à-vis the world.

Pulling a folded piece of paper from his pocket, Joshua stared at it for the 500th time. It bore his grandfather's military orders, with his notes scrawled on the back about the war's final days. Those words were etched into Joshua's memory, a haunting guide to his perilous quest:

— 6 August 1945 | Hiroshima | 1st atomic bomb; 146,000 dead
— 9 August 1945 | Nagasaki | 2nd atomic bomb; 30,000 dead
— 12 August 1945 | Tokyo | 1st hydrogen bomb; 0 dead thus far
— 15 August 1945 | Japanese surrender

The conversation with his grandfather, Col. Nathaniel Meister, that accompanied the scribblings on the order would also be etched into Joshua's consciousness forever.

"What, Grampa? You're saying that Tokyo was the target for the United States' first hydrogen bomb?"

"Yes. The Imperial Palace in Tokyo was the specific target for the

world's first hydrogen bomb, but like I said, it didn't explode. I want you to go and find it."

"Me? Why me?" Joshua wanted to know.

"Because you are the only one I trust to do it, Joshua. Only you."

Just me, huh, Grampa? Thanks, thought Joshua, feeling a measure of pride at being chosen while wishing he had not. Again, his gut feeling was that others were somehow aware of the presence of the unexploded hydrogen bomb, and they were about to be, or were already, racing to claim the deadliest weapon on Earth. That thought sent his heart pounding again, leaving him feeling both terrified and utterly alone. How prescient that thought was.

Was it even true? Could his grandfather's story be just that—a story? Joshua couldn't shake the nagging doubt. Being trusted by his grandfather to complete his most important task meant the world to Joshua, but was he risking torture and death for nothing more than an old veteran's pipe dream? There was only one way to find, out and here he was about to do it.

Nathaniel used to trust Joshua to ride his bike to the corner store and buy him two packs of Lucky Strikes and two packs of unfiltered Pall Malls, and to keep the change. If Joshua were to back out now, such a pussy move would prove he couldn't be trusted to do his duty, and Joshua was not having that. Diving in Tokyo Bay was the only way to demonstrate to his only living relative he was worthy of being trusted, pipe dream or not.

CHAPTER 2

Joshua Meister was born in Marshall, Michigan, in February of 2000 and displayed an early aptitude for languages. Joshua's mother, Lucia Flores, had emigrated from Zaragoza, in the northern region of Spain, with her parents when she was two. The Flores family settled in Chicago where, while in college at the University of Chicago, Lucia met David.

David Meister was attending a seminar on Agent Orange that Lucia's favorite professor had organized. Their eyes connected, and sparks flew—David was riveted by Lucia's blue eyes just as she was by his. Despite David being almost twenty years older than Lucia, it was love at first sight. David began commuting from Detroit to Chicago to court Lucia. Her father, Raul, was not happy at first but soon accepted David because his actions showed that he cherished and would honor Lucia.

Once they were married, they chose Marshall because it was halfway between Detroit and Chicago and because the nearby city of Battle Creek had a large VA facility. Lucia started a non-profit to help young Latinas who had children very early learn how to stand on their own two feet and become independent. David rose to be head of the Battle Creek VA facility, creating many programs to treat veterans with what came to be known as post-traumatic stress syndrome.

Growing up in a household where Spanish was commonly

spoken, by age two Joshua was fluent in both English and Spanish. At Mommy's Day Out, a German-speaking caregiver introduced him to German, and within a month, Joshua was speaking some German too.

Being an only child had both advantages and disadvantages. Joshua never lacked toys or games, and he played with other little kids from the neighborhood as well as children from all over the world. Yet when they would leave, Joshua found himself alone again, which left him feeling rather empty. To cope with his loneliness, Joshua stayed active by playing all kinds of team sports. He was especially good at soccer, being fast and well-coordinated. Joshua enjoyed the camaraderie while listening to lots of different languages.

Joshua's language skills continued to grow by watching movies in other languages, and by the time he enrolled at the University of Michigan, he spoke four: English, Spanish, German, and French. Joshua planned to learn Mandarin, Cantonese, and Arabic in college, choosing international relations as his major with hopes of working for the UN or a multinational corporation.

While passionate about languages, Joshua also felt a deep sense of duty to serve his country, influenced by his family's strong military history. His father and three brothers had served in Vietnam, with only two returning. The brothers who had died were always solemnly toasted at holiday dinners, their folded flags permanently displayed on the mantle. His family's proud military service extended all the way back to the Revolutionary War.

Although Joshua was drawn to continue this tradition—and although he was a damned good shot—he did not like killing. Wounding a deer on his first hunt, watching it twitch, and then having to track it down as it struggled to live, left a lasting impression on him.

One cold winter day during his senior year at the University of Michigan, with COVID and remote classes finally behind him, Joshua was heading across campus to a World War II history class when two official-looking men stopped him. Both wore black overcoats, black suits, white shirts, and black ties—images that made Joshua smile as he thought of the old movie *Men in Black*.

"Excuse me. Are you Joshua Meister?" one of the men wanted to know.

Joshua stopped walking and looked at the men. "Yes, I am," he replied. "How can I help you?"

The men pulled out business cards embossed with "C.I.A." at the top. They certainly looked like government agents: short hair, fit, with neatly polished shoes. The first agent spoke again in a friendly tone, glancing at the World War II history book Joshua was carrying.

"I see that you're studying history, young man. We are recruiters for the government, specifically looking for candidates to work for the CIA. We've had our eyes on you since you recited the Pledge of Allegiance in four languages in high school," the agent recalled. "How many do you speak now, Joshua?"

"I more or less speak six now, sir," Joshua answered. "And I'm studying one more."

"Tell us, if you will," the man continued, "what have you been studying in college?"

Joshua thought for a second, since he'd kept his multiple language skills more or less to himself once he started at Michigan. Then he spoke: "I've been focusing on international trade while learning Mandarin and Cantonese, and my Arabic is coming along. So, as I said: six plus, I guess."

The men looked at each other, obviously impressed. "How well is your Arabic coming along?"

Joshua smiled a bit. "Pretty good, I'd say, but I have a ways to go. I've been putting most of my time into becoming fluent in Chinese because, for one thing, there are more of them than anyone else. Also, they're our biggest trading partner and our biggest competitor."

The CIA agents nodded and smiled in unison. "You're right about all of that," agreed the first agent.

Then the second agent spoke again. "What are your plans for work after you graduate?"

Joshua turned to face him. "Not sure, sir. Maybe law school, maybe a year of traveling, maybe even get a job," he finished, chuckling.

Everyone was smiling now.

"Your father and grandfather proved through their military service that they're strong patriots, and we hope the same sense of duty has been imbued in you. That's why we tracked you down on campus today. We'd like for you to come to Langley in May for an all-expenses-paid weekend, Joshua, to check it out," offered Agent One. "We could use someone with your language skills, so if you're inclined to serve your country, call this number and a visit will be arranged."

Agent One handed Joshua his business card.

"Thank you, sirs. I'll think about it and let you know." Joshua felt proud about the offer and felt the need to salute.

"That sounds fine, Joshua. Enjoy the rest of your senior year and get back to us if you're interested," concluded Agent Two.

"Oh, sirs. Yes, sirs. I'll do that," replied Joshua, looking at the card. "Have a nice day, gentlemen." He immediately felt stupid for saying that and flushed red, hoping they didn't notice.

"We will," said Agent Two over his shoulder as they turned to walk away. "We look forward to hearing from you soon."

One moment I'm walking to a World War II history class and the next I'm being recruited by the CIA, Joshua thought, his pulse pounding with excitement. "Fuckin' A!" he shouted aloud, now jumping up and down as he ran toward class. *Serving our country at the CIA is perfect for me—and I wouldn't be carrying a rifle trying to kill other human beings. That's very okay by me too.*

CHAPTER 3

Joshua's quest to find an unexploded hydrogen bomb began on March 15, 2025. The bomb, named *Payback*, was meant to be dropped on the Imperial Palace in Tokyo on August 12, 1945, as revenge for Pearl Harbor. However, the bombardier—Joshua's grandfather, Nathaniel Meister—released the bomb early, and it landed unexploded in Tokyo Bay. Nathaniel had explained to him that he chose to release the bomb prematurely because he questioned the mission's morality. With hundreds of thousands already dead from the atomic bombings of Hiroshima and Nagasaki, he believed a hydrogen bomb detonation over Tokyo would have killed over a million civilians.

Joshua could see, in his mind's eye, the image of his grandfather telling him the story:

"Why are you crying, Grampa?" Joshua wanted to know as he moved closer to Nathaniel.

"Because I feel guilty for not doing my job, grandson," confessed Nathaniel.

Joshua gazed intently at his grandfather, riveted by what he was hearing. Nathaniel cut a tall silhouette for a man born in 1925. He still had a full head of gray hair cut Army short on the sides, a flat stomach, piercing blue eyes, and a very firm handshake. Nathaniel's thumb and first finger on his right hand were yellow from holding countless thousands of cigarettes, as were his teeth—of which he still had them all. Unlike many old men, Nathaniel was always perfectly shaved, his clothes sharply pressed, with the smell of Brut aftershave emanating forth, somewhat countering the cigarette odor.

Nathaniel's room was a shrine to discipline and a life well-lived in service. His uniform hung proudly in the open closet, pressed to perfection, brass buttons gleaming under the soft overhead light. Framed medals and commendations lined the walls in precise formation, not a single one askew, each telling a story of battles fought and victories earned. On his nightstand, a neatly folded American flag sat beside a photo of his younger self—standing tall, eyes sharp, jaw set with purpose. His bed was made with military precision, corners tucked so tight you could bounce a coin off the sheets. Even in the quiet hum of the nursing home, the old colonel carried himself with the rigid grace of a man who had never once allowed disorder to take root.

"But you saved the lives of more than a million people by not following orders, didn't you, Grampa?" Joshua prodded gently, reaching out his hand to touch Nathaniel's shoulder.

"Yes, I did," agreed Nathaniel, the tears starting to dry, his halted breath beginning to normalize. "And for that I am eternally grateful. I'm not sure I could have survived the weight of a million souls pressing down on me."

"Then you did the right thing at the time, didn't you, Grampa?" Joshua reassured him.

"Yes, but I am still tortured by the fact that never before and never after did I disobey an order. That still weighs on me, grandson. Weighs on me heavily," admitted Nathaniel, his anguished voice trailing off as he turned away.

"If you had to do it over again, Grampa, what would you do?"

Nathaniel turned back around, cleared his throat, and announced with conviction, "If given the choice, I would do the same damned thing again, grandson."

Joshua looked around the tiny room and again noticed the bed, perfectly made with the corners tucked in military style. Joshua had been taught the same way to make a bed by his father, who also practiced impeccable personal style. There was a framed photo of Nathaniel and six men standing next to a World War II bomber on the wall over his small desk, and a second photo of him with his four sons at a campsite above the bed. On the neatly arranged desk sat a notebook, a ruler, and a calendar opened to March 2025. The dark gray day, with rain beating on the window, added to the somber mood.

Joshua knew there were very few men with the mettle of his grandfather. His faith in the man was why Joshua took on the quest to find and extract the hydrogen bomb from Tokyo Bay, where it had lain for nearly 80 years. Joshua reflected on how the world would be drastically different had the bomb, a hundred times more powerful than its atomic predecessors, exploded over Tokyo. He also felt he owed a duty to mankind to rid the world of the danger it posed. Nathaniel thought about that alternate reality every day.

As Joshua walked toward baggage claim, he once again couldn't shake the feeling that time was of the essence. He suspected, for reasons he couldn't identify, that he wasn't alone in his quest. He unfolded the paper again, which had the mission's military orders printed on the front and his grandfather's handwritten notes on the back.

35° 36' 1.012" N

139° 52' 0.512" E

These numbers supposedly represented the intersection

of the latitudinal and longitudinal lines that marked the spot where the bomb hit Tokyo Bay—coordinates kept secret since 1945. Joshua recalled how Grampa Nate had extracted the old yellow document from a box of papers and held the wrinkled sheet in his gnarled but still steady hands, gazing intently at what was written there. After a moment of introspection, Nathaniel handed the paper to Joshua.

On the front was typed:

12 August 1945
Operation: Cherry Blossom
Mission: Payback
Authorization: Army Chief of Staff Approval
Target: Tokyo—Emperor's Palace
Special Instructions: Bombs Away

The faint remnants of U.S. Army Air Force stamps on the paperwork, along with his unwavering belief in his grandfather, were the final push Joshua needed to come to Tokyo. Again, he was certain that time really was of the essence; that for some reason, the bomb had to be found now—if there really was a bomb to be found. Joshua shuddered involuntarily, the hair rising on his neck. He couldn't shake the eerie feeling that if he didn't find and retrieve the bomb now, someone with bad intentions would find it and use it. For reasons he couldn't pinpoint, Joshua was certain that some evil someone would do anything, even kill, to find and gain control of the bomb. The irony of dying for a bomb that maybe didn't exist made him smile wryly. If his parents were still alive, they would be proud: *"Joshua Meister, killed in pursuit of a phantom bomb."*

Joshua took this occasion to run through a mental checklist of the factors that brought him to Japan. He couldn't be 100 percent sure Nathaniel's story was true. After all, the man was 99 years old and could very well be losing it. Yet, to concoct such a fantastic tale and recruit Joshua to pursue it was too cruel a joke for his grandfather to play—and besides, the old paperwork supported the story's truth. Determined, he spat out, "Fuck it; onward!"

After departing the aircraft, Joshua checked out Narita Airport. Thoroughly modern in design and efficient—traits that ran through all of Tokyo, he would soon discover, since everything was rebuilt after the devastation of World War II. Joshua breathed deeply, his shoulders relaxing a little; a slight comfort came over him as he studied the people and surroundings. Most were much shorter than him, and everyone bowed slightly but respectfully, quite often.

There were large observation decks for plane watchers, and the signs were in English, with different colors identifying various terminals. Joshua had no trouble finding his way to a train station linked to the airport. An employee told him the train would drop him off a block from the Hilton Hotel. Very organized. Very efficient. Very polite people.

Joshua continued his ruminations during the train trip into downtown Tokyo. He briefly considered informing his former CIA boss about his mission but decided against it out of respect for his grandfather, and for his own safety too. The more people who knew, the more likely something would screw up. *Loose lips sink ships,* his grandmother used to say. He didn't want the authorities to have a reason to grab his grandfather and lock him away in some far-off prison—and there was no telling what they'd do to a former employee if they found out about the mission.

Joshua was tortured by the fact that he still wasn't sure if there was anything in the water at the coordinates he'd been given. As he grabbed his bag and headed for the hotel, he realized he was completely alone; he knew no one in Japan and spoke no Japanese. Joshua had bought a book of common phrases but had mostly slept during the flight. To make matters worse, he hadn't converted any dollars to yen and had missed the chance to do so at the airport. *Hopefully the hotel will have some yen for me to exchange.*

What else was he forgetting? Was the equipment he'd ordered to be shipped to the hotel already there? Had he ordered everything he needed to dive in Tokyo Bay? Joshua couldn't afford to forget any details. Too much was riding on his thorough, complete attention to everything—everything. Not usually his strong suit. Joshua caught a glimpse of himself in the lobby mirror and was unhappy, though not surprised, by how he looked. Although he was barely 25 years old, and by most accounts a handsome, fit six-foot-two, 200-pound, blue-eyed man, the stress he was under was apparent. His eyes had bags under them, and his heart was pounding; anxiety had now replaced the comfort he felt earlier. Joshua pulled his shoulders back and tried to stand up straight, but the effort was largely in vain. His drawn, anxious look from the travels and the weight of the quest betrayed him.

CHAPTER 4

Thinking back to the plane ride, Joshua remembered glancing at the woman seated next to him on the flight to Japan, suspecting she was Chinese. His suspicion was confirmed when she spoke in Mandarin before takeoff, mentioning she was on her way home to Shanghai, connecting through Tokyo. Her name was Lisha ("Sweet"), and she was tiny and pretty with big dark eyes. They spoke to each other in Chinese during the flight, and talking with her brightened his spirits, reminding him of his college days at Michigan, studying Chinese while his love, Mei Lei Ho, studied English.

As he waited to check in at the hotel, Joshua couldn't help but think of Mei Lei. She was also tiny—four-foot-eleven and 41 kilos, not a milligram more, she would say. She had jet-black hair down to her waist and sparkling dark brown eyes. They made quite the couple when walking together: the tall and the short of it, as it were. Joshua always had to be careful not to hit her in the head with his elbows when they stood side by side.

Mei Lei was exceedingly smart and witty but controlled and rigid, too. Proof of her rigidity was her not responding to any of the hundred or so emails and texts he sent after she went home. When Mei Lei told Joshua the relationship was over, she meant it. The great wall of China was real, at least as far as Joshua was concerned.

Was she back in Hong Kong, running the family business, or pursuing a PhD somewhere? He missed her and regretted the cultural divide that had kept them apart. Despite their love for each other, Mei Lei had never been willing to cross the line into a physical relationship, fearing it would bring shame to her family.

Except for the one time when she did.

When Christmas break arrived, Mei Lei prepared to leave, never to return, and Joshua was to take her to the airport the next day. They went to their favorite dim sum spot for dinner, a small restaurant on the north side of Ann Arbor, where Mei Lei unexpectedly ordered a beer. One beer led to another, and Joshua found the courage to kiss her. He forced himself not to dwell on the details of that night, content now with the memory that they had spent it together before she left for Hong Kong.

In spite of having finally breached the Great Wall of Mei Lei, she made it clear there would be no contact once she left. And there wasn't. Looking back, Joshua realized he still had deep feelings for Mei Lei but understood, at least partly, that cultural barriers prevented any future connection.

He sighed, shrugged his shoulders, and turned his attention to the challenge of finding a boat to rent—then having to transport his equipment to it. Too much to carry in one load. Two trips would increase the risk of drawing attention, but oh well. *Oh well indeed,* he thought, as his pulse quickened and a cold, scared feeling took root in his stomach.

Joshua didn't want anyone in Japan to notice him; being unseen and operating in the shadows was his ally. However, being a tall gaijin was the opposite of anonymity. Being noticed could lead to questions—like why anyone would want to dive in Tokyo Bay. Joshua shook his head, trying to dismiss his concern. Focusing now on the job at hand, he decided to scout the bay.

He Googled "boats for rent" and had an Uber driver take him to a marina. There, he approached the harbor master, asking in Google-supplied Japanese to rent a boat for a photo shoot. The man handed him a paper with a phone number. Joshua called it.

A female voice answered, and though he didn't understand most of what she said, he responded in Japanese with another phrase he had practiced: "My name is Joshua. Do you speak English?"

"No, but hold on, please."

Joshua only understood the Japanese word for "no," spelled "no" with a line over the "o" but pronounced differently. Since she hadn't hung up, he waited.

"Hello," greeted a male voice in English. "My name is Hosaki. I am the owner. How can I help you today?"

"Thank you for taking my call," Joshua responded politely, remembering his manners. "I want to rent a boat to scout out possible locations for a movie shoot."

"Okay. I have a boat I can rent to you. Do you have experience driving a boat?" Mr. Hosaki wanted to know.

"Yes, sir. Thank you very much," assured Joshua. "I have papers to show you that I'm qualified to safely drive your boat. Plus, I'll put down a big deposit."

"Okay. We're at the entrance of Pier 5. My name is on the door, number 105."

Using Google Translate to read the characters, Joshua knew he could find the place. He headed toward Pier 5, excitement rising, quickening his step—careful not to run and draw attention.

Soon, Pier 4 came into view, then Pier 5. He scanned the slips: 102, 103, 104—and there it was, 105. Four power boats of various sizes were moored outside, all Sea Rays, made in America. The sight of the familiar boats made Joshua breathe easier; he'd learned to pilot Sea Rays as a kid on Lake Michigan.

Joshua climbed the neatly painted stairs and knocked on a metal door. After a few seconds, a young Japanese man in a Grateful Dead T-shirt appeared. They both bowed slightly as the man opened the door and motioned for him to enter. Inside, an older woman sat at an oak roll-top desk with a computer and adding machine. Joshua bowed respectfully and waited.

"Are you the man who wanted to rent a boat to scout out possible movie locations?" asked a voice in Japanese-accented English from the back of the office.

"Yes, sir. I'm Joshua Meister, and I want to rent a boat for a week to scout locations."

"Do you have experience piloting a boat in an ocean harbor, Mr. Joshua?" came the question, as a small man in his fifties wearing bifocals stepped forward. They bowed again.

"Yes, sir, as I mentioned on the phone, I do. Here are my papers from the United States Coast Guard showing my experience and certification."

Mr. Hosaki took the papers and studied them carefully.

"Very good, Mr. Joshua. Obey the harbor markers and stay out of the way of the container ships at all times. Do you understand?"

Bowing again, Joshua confirmed, "Yes, sir, I'll obey the rules of the harbor and take care of your equipment."

Mr. Hosaki bowed and pointed toward the door, leading the way to the slips.

"Here she is, Mr. Joshua. What do you think?" he asked, pointing at one of the biggest boats.

The boat was a 24-foot center console Sea Ray with a 300-horsepower Suzuki engine. Joshua was elated; his shoulders visibly relaxed. This boat was big enough, fast enough, and had sufficient storage to hide his scuba gear. He took a deep breath.

Mr. Hosaki handed Joshua the key. "Good luck with your movie mission, Mr. Joshua. When you're done each day, please bring the boat back to its slip and we'll fill it with gasoline so it'll be ready for you the next day."

Joshua was about to cast off when the woman from the desk—the bookkeeper and probably the wife—came scurrying out, waving papers. Nearly out of breath, she flailed her arms and scolded Mr. Hosaki.

"Sorry, Mr. Joshua. I forgot to have you sign the contract," Mr. Hosaki squeaked, embarrassed. He took the papers from the woman, bowed again, and handed them to Joshua. Joshua scribbled his name, bowed again, and returned the papers.

"Did you get my credit card information, Mr. Hosaki?" Joshua asked.

Mr. Hosaki put his hands on his head. "Oh no. Very sorry. I forgot that, too."

Joshua handed over his Visa. The bookkeeper muttered to herself, then returned moments later with a receipt. Relieved, Joshua started the engine. Mr. Hosaki cast off the lines. After final mutual bows, Joshua breathed deeply, trying to calm down. His hands and legs were shaking as he carefully reversed the boat out of the slip and eased her up to 25 knots, heading toward his grandfather's coordinates. Once he cleared the marina, his breathing returned to normal, and he quit shaking. *That was weird,* thought Joshua. *I've never been so scared I shook. Just glad I didn't pee myself too.*

After 30 minutes, following the arrow on his phone, he arrived at the location. He confirmed it with his map app, then turned on the fish finder. The device showed smooth ocean contours and a depth of 65 feet.

Mission one complete. Joshua fired up the engine and headed to a parking lot about a mile away that had a slip for his boat. *Thank God for Google.* He parked the boat, congratulating himself on his plan to secretly load the diving gear there. An Uber took him back to the hotel, where he loaded a baggage cart with all the gear and returned to the taxi area. A minivan appeared.

The minivan dropped him at the lot without issue. Joshua's heart pounded again as he moved everything to the boat, then breathed a sigh of relief once it was all secured in the lockers. Starting the engine, he backed out. Heart pounding again.

Jesus, I'm paranoid, he realized. *Scared of being found out. Step two complete and undetected. Thank God.*

The water was smooth. As the sun began to set, it cast long, shimmering silver reflections on the bay. Joshua felt safe and serene in the land of the rising sun. He had hoped to begin searching right away but decided to wait for a full search tomorrow, using today for reconnaissance. Mr. Hosaki was waiting by the slip.

"How did the boat perform for you today?" he asked.

"It performed flawlessly, Mr. Hosaki. You have a very nice boat," said Joshua, content.

"Did you find any good locations for the film?"

Joshua flinched. *Man, I'm on edge.* Then he remembered what he'd told them that morning. "Oh, no. Nothing stood out. But I hope something will jump out at me in the next few days."

"Just be careful," warned Mr. Hosaki. "There are many rocks and sandbars that have damaged more than one boat."

"Thank you, Mr. Hosaki," Joshua said, bowing slightly. "I'll be very mindful."

"What time will you return tomorrow?"

"I hope to be here by 7:00 a.m. for an early start."

"That will be fine. The boat will be fueled and ready."

"Is it okay to leave my camera equipment on board overnight?" Joshua asked, taking a small risk.

"Yes, of course. Your equipment will be safe here."

"Thank you again, Mr. Hosaki, for your kindness and concern," Joshua said. He knew leaving the gear on board was risky, but hauling it back through the Hilton lobby was worse.

It was 20:00. He could hardly wait to get back to his room to call his grandfather. Realizing he hadn't eaten since landing, he found a sushi place. Unable to read the characters, he just pointed at the menu. The smell of squid and noodles filled the elevator. *Food first, then Grampa.*

He dialed. 11:00 hours in St. Louis—perfect.

"Colonel Nathaniel Meister speaking. Who is calling?" came his grandfather's voice.

"It's me, Grampa. Joshua, calling from Tokyo."

A sigh of relief came from the other end. "Joshua, my boy! I've been waiting two days for your call. And how about that, you called right on time."

"Well, Grampa, it takes two days to get here. But I made it, and the equipment did too," Joshua explained, ignoring the joke.

"Glad to hear it. Did you make it to the harbor?"

"Yes, sir. I rented a 24-foot Sea Ray for a week."

"You didn't tell them why you were renting it, did you?"

"No, of course not. I said I was scouting film locations."

Joshua could almost see Nathaniel's smile. "Excellent. Did you go to the spot?"

"I sure did. Used my phone to punch in the coordinates, GPS

took me right there. The boat has a fish finder. When I arrived, I checked the ocean floor."

"Oh yeah?" Nathaniel asked, excited. "What did it show?"

"About 65 feet deep with a gentle slope."

"Any chance it showed the outline of a big bomb?"

Joshua hadn't thought of that. "No, Grampa. But tomorrow I'll crisscross with the fish finder and see if I get lucky. Good news is, if the bomb's there, it's within safe diving depth."

"Well, that is good news. I've often wondered if the impact would have carried the bomb deep enough to bury itself."

"Good point. Didn't you say it looked like an oversized fat cigar?"

"Yes, about six feet in diameter and ten feet long. It wouldn't roll much, even on a hill, because of poles sticking out on both ends."

"That's what I thought. Still, if it landed upside down, the impact might've snapped off the poles and it could've rolled to the deepest part—120 feet—too deep for me."

"Are you backing out, grandson?" Nathaniel asked, peeved.

"No, Grampa, I'm not. I'm just saying the safe depth is 100 feet, not 120. I hope it didn't roll, because I'll be diving alone."

"You're right. I'm not asking you to kill yourself. I'd rather it lay there 80 more years than lose you."

"I know. Thanks. I like the idea of scanning with the fish finder. Besides, the odds of it landing upside down and rolling are pretty small."

Nathaniel nodded on the other end. "Going back out in the morning?"

"Yes, 7:00 a.m. I hid the gear on the boat. I'll put a couple fishing poles out for cover."

"Call me tomorrow. I'm getting real excited."

"Me too. Love you, Grampa."

"For the first time ever: love you too, Joshua. Goodbye." Afterward, Nathaniel worried again. Had he done right by sending Joshua? He reasoned that the benefit to mankind was worth the risk, though his stomach churned at the thought.

Back in his hotel room, Joshua was too excited to sleep. *I bet Betsy's thinking of me right now,* he mused, dialing.

"Hello?"

"Hi, Bets, it's me, calling from Japan."

"Hi, Mo," Betty's voice flows in, sweet as ever. "I was just thinking of you, my Mo."

"Oh yeah? What were you thinking?"

"Nothing I can say over the phone, big guy."

"Ooh, that sounds inviting. I wish I had time to hear what your hand's doing—but I have no time now," Joshua said. "Anyway, I rented a boat and I'm diving tomorrow."

"Be careful. There are sharks. Also, you're on speaker."

"Oh, you little vixen. I'll be careful." He wasn't worried about sharks—he was thinking of her hands.

"Okay. Miss you."

"Miss you too. Bye."

Betsy was a good girl, a nurse he'd met at the nursing home, sun-kissed and sandy blonde, with a heart full of kindness and a spine of quiet steel. She was kind even to the gruff old men. Through his mind's eye, he saw her: the very picture of a good Midwestern girl, still in shape from cheerleading. She'd once confided that at 14, her breasts grew too large for gymnastics—not a problem for Joshua. Her blondish hair fell down when she was on top of him, green eyes bright.

After hanging up, he tried to focus on the work at hand—but had to handle something else first.

Eventually, he set thoughts of Betsy aside. He needed two scuba tanks; one wasn't enough, especially for a deep dive. Maybe Mr. Hosaki knew where to rent them.

As with all divers, Joshua's life depended on his watch's accuracy, to ensure a safe ascent with enough oxygen to avoid drowning or the bends. Diving alone was never recommended, but there was no choice. He hoped the bomb was at 65 feet, not 120.

Still, there was risk. He wasn't that experienced a diver, and had only dived in the clear waters of the Caymans and Cancun—not the cold, murky depths of Tokyo Bay. Thinking positively but battling apprehension, Joshua hoped, as his grandfather suggested, that the fish finder would bring luck in finding *Payback*.

Payback for Pearl Harbor.

CHAPTER 5

Day 2 in Japan

Joshua woke up feeling refreshed and ready to attack the new day. He had slept surprisingly well and carried an overall positive feeling as he reflected on the past ten days. Ten days ago, he had walked into CIA headquarters in Langley, Virginia, as usual, around 8:20 a.m. Joshua liked his job—the intellectual exercise of piecing together and making sense of conversations, often coded, was challenging and fun.

Analysts were expected to arrive by 8:00 a.m. for the morning meeting, but Joshua was rarely there on time. He often stayed up late playing video games—Fortnite was his favorite—and he'd never been an early riser, not since adolescence anyway.

Joshua dreaded the thought of facing his boss, retired Marine Col. Mac Sanders, who he knew was a stickler for timeliness. However, he figured his stellar analytical and multi-language skills made up for his habitual tardiness. The CIA's version of Colonel Sanders was fat and did not have flowing white hair; instead, he wore a flat-top, shaved tight. Nor did he have a white suit or any facial hair.

Joshua smiled at this mental caricature. Colonel Sanders was not at all charming, unlike the Kentucky Fried Chicken mascot. Rather, white spittle would form at the edges of his mouth in a most disgusting way whenever he lectured the analysts—which made seats at the back of the room the most desired. The Colonel had bad digestion and was always in a foul mood, considering the analysts under him to be slackers. His gravelly voice seemed to penetrate the walls, giving everyone the shivers.

Colonel Sanders—no jokes, please—had served the country for 32 years, largely handling logistics, making sure men and materials showed up where needed. To hear him talk about it, however, you'd think he had personally won all the wars in Iraq and Afghanistan with his uncanny insight and bravery. No one asked how brave he'd been while signing orders at Camp Pendleton to supply the troops on the ground in Kandahar. Oh well.

Rumor had it that when the U.S. pulled out of Afghanistan, Colonel Sanders was the one who decided to use the civilian airport rather than the secure U.S. base at Bagram Airfield. That genius move led to his sudden retirement from the Marines and reassignment to the CIA.

Not that the morning meetings mattered much to Joshua, who worked as an analyst in Sanders' division, specializing in translating languages—Arabic and Chinese mostly, but also some German, French, and Spanish. The meetings usually focused on deadlines and budgets—not Joshua's concern.

His true specialty was listening to and translating the various dialects of Arabic, a skill that had secured him the job after the CIA recruiters at Michigan encouraged him to learn it. As he rode the elevator, he hoped to avoid, but nonetheless braced himself for, the inevitable encounter with "Old Iron Pants."

The door opened and—shit—who was standing there? The Colonel glared at Joshua, then at his watch, and grunted, "You're late again, Meister, so you're fired! Get your shit and be out of here by oh-eight-hundred-thirty hours!"

"Come on, Colonel, the Beltway traffic was really backed up

today," Joshua pleaded, his legs weakening, voice cracking.

"I told you I would not tolerate anyone under my command being late, son," shouted Sanders, forehead veins bulging, spittle foaming at the corners of his mouth.

"But I have been better lately, Colonel. Shoot, this is the first time this week I've been late. Look," Joshua added, searching for something positive, "I even contributed to the morning meetings both yesterday and the day before. And how about my stellar work, for which I've received many awards and recognitions?"

"That's just too fucking bad, Meister," was the Colonel's emphatic, sarcastic response. "I've warned you a million times about being here at oh-eight-hundred. I even sent an email last week. And as to your awards—so what? How many sand niggers have you locked up? None. So get the fuck out and don't ever come back." He pointed first at Joshua, then at the door.

Joshua was stunned. He felt helpless, unable to think of anything further to say as he watched the fat fuck waddle down the hallway. Now pissed, he thought about how he might turn the tables on the cocksucker—but no ideas, and no one to turn to, came to mind.

Now what? Joshua wanted to follow the old fuck and cold-cock him upside the back of his fat, wrinkled, flat-top head. He was triple pissed because, in his mind, he really had tried lately to be on time. But he stood there stunned and numb, weakness flooding his entire body, unable to move.

Joshua dragged his feet in shame as he shuffled back to his area. A few amigos stopped by as he packed the few personal items scattered around his desk. "Hey, man. You'll find something. Stay in touch," encouraged his friend Stuart, another translator.

"Sure," replied Joshua, knowing he wouldn't.

He turned in his I.D. badge at the security desk and walked out to his car. *What the fuck am I going to do now?* he wondered, shoulders slumped, stomach churning. He had no immediate family—his parents were gone, and he had no siblings. The only person left was his father's father, Nathaniel Meister.

The last time they'd seen each other was at Joshua's dad's funeral, just after graduation three years ago. David had died from cancer caused by Agent Orange exposure, and his mother, Lucia, had died years earlier in a tragic car wreck. Nathaniel, now in a nursing home, was Joshua's last living relative, and staff recently told him that while Nathaniel was still in remarkably good health, at 99 he might not have much time left.

His grandfather's dwindling time, combined with Joshua's sudden abundance of it, made a road trip to St. Louis sound ideal. But Jesus, Joshua never expected to hear the story Nathaniel told him—nor that he'd end up traveling halfway around the world looking for a lost, deadly hydrogen bomb.

"My mind is willing, but my body disagrees," Nathaniel had said when Joshua invited him to D.C. a year earlier. Nathaniel dreamed of visiting the Smithsonian flight museum and paying respects at Arlington, but flying was no longer an option.

Nathaniel Meister had been a B-26 bombardier during World War II, serving on the German front. He flew 23 missions, survived being shot down, captured by Nazis, and escaping. He was the only member of his crew to make it back through enemy lines.

Late one night after a family gathering, Nathaniel told Joshua how Nazi anti-aircraft gunners used American soldiers' parachutes for target practice. He'd flown through plenty of flak but said floating under a parachute was like being a sitting duck—or a "floating duck," as he put it.

Nathaniel often filled in for wounded or killed crewmates, even once piloting a B-26 to safety when the pilot was killed and the co-pilot badly hurt. Landing in a muddy field earned him the Distinguished Service Medal. On another mission, he'd watched a wing gunner sucked out of the fuselage after a flak hit—a sight that haunted him.

But nothing compared to the terror of being shot at while descending by parachute. Six men had bailed out of the doomed bomber, and Nathaniel could see the ack-ack muzzle flashes and hear the shells screaming toward them as they fell.

"My chute didn't deploy right away, so I was about a thousand feet below everybody else that night," Nathaniel recalled. "First, I could see the flashes, then hear the pop, pop, pop of the guns. Then the shells howled like demons from hell—boom, boom, boom—shrapnel flying everywhere, cutting guys to pieces."

"What did you do?"

"Well, I pulled out my .45 and started shooting back at those bastards."

"Did you hit anybody?"

"No, probably not. I was up about 5,000 feet, and .45s are only good to about 50. I couldn't hit shit. But I was good at math, which is why the military made me a bombardier." Nathaniel smiled faintly. "If I'd been better at shooting, I might've been that wing gunner sucked out."

"What happened to the other guys?"

"Once they saw me firing at the ack-ack guns, some started shooting too. It seemed the Nazi gunners had done this before—they'd shoot for a while, wait for us to drift lower, then open up again."

"Why do you think that was?"

"The shells were timed to explode at certain altitudes. Those fuckers would wait till we floated into the kill zone, then let fly."

"That doesn't seem very fair."

"Fair? Do you know what war is, boy? It's to kill everything that moves and destroy everything else—by any and all means possible," Nathaniel said, voice hard.

"But Grampa, you made it back," Joshua said gently.

"Yes, somehow," Nathaniel replied, quiet.

"How about your buddies?"

"All killed but me. I saw one blown apart by a direct hit, a couple whose chutes were shredded. Mine was hit too."

"What happened?"

Nathaniel took a long drag on his Lucky Strike, flicked ashes onto the dewy grass, and looked away.

"I got hit in the shoulder. My chute had two big-ass holes blown through it. That shrapnel burns. Set my flight suit on fire. I was trying to put it out when I realized I was going down too fast."

"Is that when you bent over and kissed your ass goodbye?"

"Grandson, you're a real smartass sometimes. That'll get you in trouble—or maybe save your Tweety Bird ass. You don't know the half of it," Nathaniel growled.

Joshua realized he'd crossed a line. Nathaniel gave him a dark look and stomped inside. That was many years ago. Now, heading to St. Louis, Joshua reflected on how his mouth often put him in harm's way. He'd been fired, lost girlfriends, been in fights—sometimes in six languages—because he couldn't shut up.

Though many of those times were his fault, some weren't.

Being bright and quick-witted was a virtue. He more often than not held his tongue when he could have said something mean. But sometimes, as his grandfather noted, he was a smartass, and out came unfiltered comments that weren't well received. To keep the neon in the tube, a friend at the CIA taught him to box, and he often worked out frustrations on the heavy bag in his apartment.

Then, Joshua thought of Mei Lei Ho, a woman he met at Michigan's language lab. Intrigued by her beauty, he approached her speaking Mandarin, but she shut him down with an icy look. Undeterred, he discreetly followed her out—he'd learned not to directly stalk after a painful encounter with a jealous boyfriend.

Though he lost her that night, Joshua spent days looking for her, hoping to catch a glimpse at Sari Hill dorm. He eventually saw a shadow in a lit window and spent days gazing up, hoping she'd notice.

Was it her cold rejection that made him determined to bridge the gap? No, not really. Was it her beauty? Absolutely. Her perfect, petite frame? Yes. His mother had been small, dark-haired, and beautiful too. But it ran deeper. Joshua sensed there was far more to Mei Lei than met the eye.

For weeks, he kept up his quiet watch, without success. Then one day, from behind him, a woman spoke in Mandarin.

"Do you like to eat dim sum?"

Joshua spun around. There she was.

"Yes, I like to eat dim sum," he answered in Mandarin.

"What is your name?"

He'd told her six weeks ago, but giving her the benefit of the doubt, he said, "Joshua Meister. What's yours?"

"Mei Lei Ho. Where did you learn Mandarin?"

"From Babel online and Chinese martial arts movies."

"Oh, how American of you," she smiled, wrinkling her nose.

It didn't sound like a compliment, but given the prize, Joshua took it in stride.

"Why did you come to the U.S.?"

"To learn English and study American ways," she said, easily hitting the softball he pitched.

On a roll, Joshua pressed on. "What have you learned about American ways?"

Looking straight at him, piercing his thin defenses, Mei Lei said flatly, "I've learned some Americans don't respect silence as a sign to be left alone."

Ouch. That stung. Embarrassed but feeling he had nothing to lose, Joshua shot back, "Then why talk to me today?"

Her answer was blunt. "I was tired of making late-night trips to the lab and seeing you outside my window every day. Now do you understand why?"

Ouch again. He paused, grateful she didn't have Bruce Lee there to chop him in half.

Determined to recover, he changed tactics. "Where's good dim sum around here?"

"Nowhere. But my friends and I are cooking Saturday. You're invited."

"I'd be delighted. But I don't even know your name."

She turned slightly pink. "My name is Mei Lei Ho. And I know you're Joshua Meister."

"How?"

"You just told me. And it's on your notebook."

"Oh. Right." Feeling stupid and puzzled by this turnaround, he had to know. "Given how much I've apparently annoyed you, why ask me now?" He hoped for a good sign. But no.

"Because you speak Chinese, and I need someone to accompany me."

Deflated, he nodded. "Okay. I'll meet you at your dorm. Thanks for the invite."

"No response, just, 'I will see you tonight.'"

A group dinner was better than nothing. He hoped Saturday wouldn't turn into a showdown with Bruce Lee.

CHAPTER 6

Joshua pushed thoughts of Mei Lei aside as he neared the nursing home. He knew he needed to devote all his focus to his grandfather. Joshua had called ahead to let the staff know he was coming, but his throat tightened and a lump rose when they told him that sometimes Grampa couldn't recall his name—that he was slipping mentally, though still physically strong. *Wow. First, I lose my parents, now my grandfather?* A wave of loneliness and abandonment seized him, casting a dark shadow over his outlook on life. Tears ran down his face.

Trying to feel better, Joshua hoped his grandfather would tell him more war stories. Sometimes Grampa Nate would, sometimes he wouldn't.

Joshua always thought the Army Air Corps had been cruel to send his grandfather to fight the Japanese after being shot down over Germany. He recalled how Nathaniel had told him about initially avoiding capture, having landed behind enemy lines. Nathaniel would always stare off into the distance, clenching his fists as he remembered his buddies the German gunners picked off one by one.

"The gunners nearly killed me, too," Nathaniel recalled of that night.

"As I was descending, after I emptied my .45 shooting back at them, the gun batteries zeroed in on me. The concussion from exploding shells swung my chute left and right as I came down," Nathaniel recounted, waving his hands side to side, reliving it. "I looked around and saw I was the only one left. Two other guys were still floating down—both dead. I tried to maneuver behind the closest one to use him as a shield. But hell, I was no pilot. I couldn't fly a parachute for shit."

"But Grampa, didn't you land a B-26 after the pilot was killed and the co-pilot wounded?" Joshua encouraged.

"Yeah, sure, I did that. But it wasn't pretty, and I had a coach on the ground. I'd never jumped out of an airplane before. In flight school, we only jumped off a 60-foot tower. They told us: pull the left cord to go left, the right to go right, or both to slow down. But none of that shit worked—my chute was full of holes, I had a shrapnel wound, and I was coming down fast."

"I guess you wanted to pull both cords then, didn't you?" As soon as he said it, Joshua regretted opening his mouth.

"Hell no. I didn't want to slow down—I was getting shot at! You sure say some dumbass things sometimes, grandson," Nathaniel groused, shooting him a withering look.

"But actually," Nathaniel continued, "pulling either cord just spun me in circles. With ack-ack exploding all around, plus soldiers taking potshots, I figured I was a goner."

"How is it they didn't get you?"

"One of the shells exploded so close I could feel the heat. It ripped a bigger hole in my canopy. Shrapnel hit my shoulder and set my flight jacket on fire. I started dropping almost like freefall. I looked down and thought *for sure* I was going to die when I hit."

"What did the ground look like?"

"Hard and coming up fast, you moron. Jesus, Joshua—you really test a man's patience."

Trying to recover, Joshua tried another angle. "No, I mean, was it woods, farmland, or what?"

"Boy, you ask some really stupid fucking questions. I wasn't admiring the scenery. I was making my peace with God."

Feeling stupid, Joshua stayed silent, hoping his grandfather would keep going.

"Next thing I knew, I was drowning. I'd landed in a pond, twenty feet underwater, up to my armpits in muck with the chute settling over my head," Nathaniel said. "Turns out those lousy bastards were taking turns shooting at me. But because I fell so fast, they couldn't adjust their guns. Probably figured the impact would kill me anyway."

Joshua wanted to ask what his grandfather thought about God's answer to his prayers at that point but checked himself. Instead, he tried, "So how did you get out of the pond?"

"When the canopy settled, there was an air pocket above me. I had some air to breathe while I wriggled out of the muck. Somehow, I swam up and paddled to shore. The water cushioned my fall—no broken bones. But I had no idea where I was, where the enemy was, or how to get back to our guys."

"What did you do then?"

"I looked up at the moon and kind of knew where I was in Germany. As it moved west, I headed that way."

"Did you see people?"

"Nope, thank God. Not right away. Locals didn't treat downed flyboys too good. But I didn't see troops either. Just farmland, woods, and fences."

He continued, "I figured if I traveled at night and hid in the day, I might make it. I was so damn mad at those flak gunners I wanted to find them and give them a few shots of their own."

"Did you find any flak batteries?"

DAVID KENT

"No—probably for the best," Nathaniel admitted, nodding at the thought. "I traveled all night, heading west, avoiding lights, crossing roads quick and quiet."

"What about when the sun came up?"

"When it was close to sunrise, I buried myself in haystacks or tucked up against fence rows or under downed trees."

"Then you'd sleep all day and move at night?"

Fixing him with a sharp look only someone who's truly seen death can give, Nathaniel replied slowly, "No. It wasn't like finding a nice warm bed at the Holiday Inn. I was scared, hungry, wounded, and thirsty. Too much so to sleep. For two days, I waited until the sun was low, then headed out again."

"How long till you reached our troops?"

"I didn't reach them right away," Nathaniel said. "On the third night, I thought I was close—artillery shells were louder. I headed toward the flashes. But fuck me if I didn't walk right into where a squad of Nazis had bedded down."

"What happened?"

"I tried to sneak away, but a voice said in English, 'Get on your knees and put your hands up, Amerikaner.'"

"Shit," I thought. *I'm fucked.* I dropped to my knees, raised my hands."

"And were you fucked, Grampa?" Joshua pressed, leaning in.

"Yes," Nathaniel admitted, head low. "The noise woke the others. They all gathered around, took turns bashing me with rifle butts, laughing as they turned the snow red with my blood."

"The commander, an SS officer, ordered them to tie my hands behind my back. I still have the scars," Nathaniel said, showing Joshua his gnarled wrists.

"Jesus, Grampa, that's awful."

"They stood me up and marched me east, stabbing me with

bayonets to hurry me along. I figured they'd interrogate me, then I'd be tortured and dead."

"You have scars there too?"

"Oh shit, yes. Look," he said, lifting his shirt to show his back. "Looks like a pin cushion, doesn't it?"

"It sure the fuck does, Grampa—fucking awful."

Seeing his grandfather's scarred back, Joshua understood why some veterans were bitter enough to justify dropping atomic bombs on a beaten Japan. Hesitantly, he asked, "Were you scared?"

"Sure. Not of dying, but of being tortured first."

After a long march, they arrived at a makeshift prison camp guarded by Jeeps. Nathaniel noticed an opening in the fence and thought to escape. A British soldier tried first, got stuck, and was bayoneted. Filled with rage, Nathaniel kicked the guard, knocked him out, and grabbed his machine gun. As he crawled through the hole, bullets struck the men shielding him.

Once out, he ran for the woods, but the Nazis knew the land better and soon came after him.

"What happened then?"

"They were catching up. I hunkered behind a fallen tree, waiting for them to overrun me. Tried to make my peace with God again. But God had other plans, Joshua," Nathaniel said with pride. "Just as they were about to find me, all hell broke loose over the hills—artillery and mortars everywhere."

"So I stood up, figured I might as well go down like the Alamo. But those four fuckers turned to look at the shells and I mowed them down. *Fuck you motherfuckers!*"

Nathaniel turned away, completely lost in the memory.

"By then, I was beyond pissed. Didn't care if I lived. I grabbed their guns and snuck back to the camp. Saw some flyboys near the fence. Helped two through and gave them weapons."

"Three of us had guns now. We took off into the woods where some Nazis were milling about. They didn't know we were armed, so when they stepped into a clearing, we cut them down."

"The bombardment was still going, so we ran toward it, hoping it was Allied fire. I lost the others. When day broke, I hid until dark."

"I walked and ran all night. Then I heard what I thought was an American Jeep. As I crossed an open field, hugging the edge, I went toward it."

"Were they surprised to see you?"

"Surprised? Hell, *I* was surprised when I heard German. I couldn't have been more than fifteen feet away. I dropped right there. They were looking at a captured Jeep, talking."

"Did you shoot them? Hijack the Jeep?"

Joshua felt his face burn as Nathaniel gave him *the look*.

"No, son. This wasn't a movie. I didn't know how many there were or what they had. Plus, I was almost out of ammo. So I crawled backward until I couldn't hear them, then snuck around."

"You did make it to our side though?"

"Sure did. After two more nights hustling through barbed wire and avoiding mines. The artillery was deafening. Then I heard Tommy guns and M-1s. Figured Germans didn't have those, but knew either side might shoot me."

"I shimmied up a pine to get a look. Saw muzzle flashes four or five miles off. Decided to wait and let our boys come."

"They did—but it was a hell of a firefight. I stayed in that tree maybe thirty hours. Bullets everywhere. Germans retreating, P-51s strafing, artillery hammering the woods."

"Grampa, must've been ironic—being shot at from the air again, this time by your own guys."

God, Joshua thought. *I stuck my foot in my mouth again.* Nathaniel didn't even look at him, just turned away.

"I'm sorry, Grampa. Was just trying to joke."

"Well boy, it wasn't goddamn funny then or now. And it wasn't ironic. I could've been shot at any moment—American snipers shot Nazis who climbed trees in U.S. uniforms. With all that going on, I knew I could die anytime."

"I wasn't trying to be a smartass. Sorry."

"Then don't make asshole comments, or you and I are done talking," Nathaniel warned in the voice of a man who'd faced death too many times.

The conversation ended there. Joshua realized he still didn't know how his grandfather made it home and then wound up on Tinian Island fighting the Japanese. Maybe, he hoped, on this visit Nathaniel would finally tell him.

CHAPTER 7

Day 1, St. Louis

As Joshua frantically typed the nursing home address into his phone, he took his eyes off the road. Suddenly, a horn blared. He jerked his head up to see a taxi barreling toward him. He slammed on the brakes—but it was too late. The screech of tires, the crunch of metal, the blinding flash of light—it all happened in an instant. The airbag exploded with the force of a shotgun blast a foot away, driving him backward into the seat, whipping his neck back and forth. His right arm burned as it smacked into his face. For a moment, he couldn't see through the smoke.

What had he done? Had he run a red light? Had he hurt anybody? The realization of his stupidity gnawed at him as he tried the driver's door, which wouldn't budge. He'd been so focused on reaching the nursing home, he'd committed the cardinal sin of messing with his phone while driving.

He stumbled out the passenger side, mind reeling. *What had he done?* Hyperventilating, fear overtook him. He forced deep breaths, trying to regain some control, but guilt and shame overwhelmed him.

Looking around, Joshua assessed the scene and was relieved he didn't see anyone lying in the street. As his rational mind kicked back in, he realized he'd run a red light and collided with a taxi. "Jesus, what a fucking idiot I am," he muttered, smacking himself on the forehead.

The cab driver, already irritated by the rude passengers he'd just dropped off, had seen Joshua's car coming. He swerved left, slammed the brakes, trying to avoid the crash—but it was too late. Glass showered over him.

"Shit! Goddamned idiot," the cabbie swore, checking the rearview mirror for blood. He spotted a few small cuts on his face and right arm, but oddly, his airbag hadn't deployed. Dark-skinned, with bushy black hair, thick eyebrows, a full black beard, hairy arms, and chest hair poking out from his Rolling Stones tee, he looked like he'd stepped off a Karachi street.

He jumped out and ran to the passenger side to survey the damage. Seeing the out-of-state Virginia plates, he shook his head. *Figures. Out-of-state, can't drive for shit.*

He spotted Joshua slumped against his red VW. Striding over, he shouted, "Why did you run the red light? Were you not paying attention?" He was pissed and ready to throw punches.

"I'm sorry," Joshua stammered. "The sun was in my eyes."

"Sun was in your eyes, my ass. You were on your fucking phone. What if I'd been a pedestrian? You could've killed me!" snapped the cabbie, picturing his wife pushing Junior in a stroller.

"I'm very sorry," Joshua repeated. "Are you all right?" He sized up the cab driver—young, around six feet, muscular, with a threatening air and a slight accent.

"Yeah, I'm okay," the cabbie grunted, starting to calm down. "But my cab isn't."

"Well, my car doesn't look too bad except the radiator's busted," Joshua observed. "Thank goodness. I think it'll still run. Want to pull into that parking lot and swap info?"

The cabbie almost snapped back but remembered the asshole fare he'd just dropped off. He didn't want to act the same way. "Yeah, let's do that," he agreed, pointing to the Jack in the Box lot. They disentangled the cars and drove over, Joshua's VW smoking from the broken radiator. As he parked, he wondered why the cabbie seemed threatening—but couldn't put his finger on it.

"Here's my info. Name's Joshua Meister. Here's my insurance card."

"My name's Michael Brown. I'll be filing a claim for damages and lost time. This is gonna suck."

Though he'd been using "Michael Brown from Pennsylvania" for years, it still sounded strange. His real name was Muqtar Ashadi, from Pakistan.

"I'm really sorry," Joshua said again. "I was trying to find the VA nursing home and wasn't paying enough attention."

"That's for sure," Muqtar muttered, eyeing the crunched side of his cab. "That's for sure."

"You want to call the police for a report? You're bleeding a little."

"No. Hell no," Muqtar shot back. "In this town, if nobody's hurt, the cops don't even show. And I sure as hell don't want to talk to them. But let me get a pic of your insurance and license—I'm gonna have to file a claim."

He decided not to mention he volunteered at the VA nursing home where his wife Julie worked as a nurse.

"Oh, okay," Joshua said, turning to inspect his VW. "Guess I'll be filing a claim too. Now that I really look at it—airbag's gone off, front end's smashed."

Muqtar nodded, then peered inside the VW at the limp, spent airbag. "Yeah, you'll need that fixed for sure. Did the airbag burn you?"

"It sure did—my neck and arm. Burned me pretty good," Joshua said, showing a red welt on his arm and turning his neck.

"That's gonna hurt later, man," Muqtar observed, mellowing out.

"It already does. Burning like hell."

"You should probably hit the ER, get it checked," advised Muqtar, recalling his nursing classes.

"Yeah, maybe. But I'll probably just grab some cream from a pharmacy."

Muqtar found himself feeling sorry for the out-of-towner. For a moment, he even thought about offering a ride. *Nah, too much.*

"Well, don't let it get infected, or you'll be real sorry," he cautioned, heading back to his crumpled cab.

"Thanks for the advice. I really am sorry. Glad no one's seriously hurt."

"Yeah. Me too. Drive safe," Muqtar replied, easing into his seat. *Could've been worse,* he thought. *Could've been dead.*

He slowly made his way to the garage, feeling the wind whistle through the shattered window.

On the way back, Muqtar radioed his boss. "Hey, Ralph. Had an accident."

"You're in luck, Brownie," Ralph said. "Cab 123 just freed up. You can drive that while yours is in the shop."

Brownie. Muqtar had wondered many times why Ralph called him that. Was it the color of his skin? His thick beard and eyebrows? Maybe. He decided to shave them and thin his brows.

His real name was Muqtar Ashadi. But in St. Louis, he was Michael Brown—an identity even his American wife didn't know wasn't real.

How'd you end up here? he often asked himself. The answer was always the same. *You did it to yourself, pendejo.* He chuckled at the word—he didn't fully understand it, but having heard the mechanics use it often, it somehow felt right.

CHAPTER 8

Muqtar Ashadi

In 2018, some seven years ago, Muqtar Ashadi came to the U.S. to study engineering, hoping to design infrastructure for Pakistan. But the American party scene derailed his plans, leading him to flunk out of NYU after less than a year and abandon his dreams. Now married to an American woman with a two-year-old son, Muqtar was studying nursing at a community college, yet the shame of his failure at NYU forever haunted him. Once a prodigy in his region, his departure for NYU had been a huge event, but now he was just a cab driver in St. Louis, evading the law. Muqtar couldn't forget the disappointment in his father's eyes during that final video chat. The prodigal son was gone.

"But son, you had everything going for you! You had a scholarship! You were the first person from this family to have the privilege of going to college! You were the first person in this entire region to go to college," his father shouted.

"You are no longer my son. Do not come back . . . ever." Those were the last words Muqtar ever heard his father speak. He remembered how his father slowly turned away from the camera, shoulders slumping, heart broken. Muqtar wanted so badly to reach through the screen, to hug him and promise everything would be all right.

He knew then that everything was lost. He had failed, breaking his father's heart. The shame of choosing alcohol and distractions over his dreams and his father's expectations haunted him, with no escape.

Muqtar's family, from the mountainous region of Peshawar bordering Afghanistan, had never allowed alcohol in their home. The youngest of fourteen children, he was the brightest. At eleven, Muqtar began going to an internet café, where he was allowed to use a computer in exchange for cleaning up. There he met Miss Rachel, an American teacher who gradually taught him English. They kept in touch long after, fueling his dream of studying in the U.S.—a dream he realized, then royally fucked up.

Muqtar's ability to solve math problems in his head at five amazed his teachers. His siblings teased him, saying he was so smart he was actually stupid, masquerading as the smart one. Being number eleven out of fourteen, and the seventh boy, his older brothers took great pleasure in playing tricks on him and holding him down to pour dirt in his mouth. "How well can you talk now, smart one?"

Muqtar would run to his father, Abdullah, for comfort, but none was ever forthcoming. "Toughen up, Muqtar. There are many bad and unfair experiences you will have in this world. Your brothers' mistreatment will only make you stronger and tougher." Not bad advice, really, because Muqtar learned how to fight back—dirty. By eighteen, he had kicked all their asses, and none of his brothers fucked with him anymore.

His pride swelled when the regional governor announced his scholarship to study engineering at NYU during his graduation party, with Alia, the girl he adored, standing by his side.

"How long will you be gone studying at the great American

university?" Alia asked, lifting her big dark eyes to meet his.

"Four years and a little more," Muqtar replied, his pulse quickening and another part of him stirring.

"Four years and a little more is a long time for a girl to wait," Alia teased. She was by all accounts a beautiful young woman. All the boys in their village of some 4,000 people went to her family's bakery in hopes of seeing her bend to fetch a loaf of bread. She was tall and slim for their village—almost 1.7 meters, barely 50 kilos. On big occasions like Muqtar's party, she wore a traditional shalwar kameez that couldn't hide her abundance up top.

"Well, yes, it's a long time, but I don't know what you mean by 'waiting,'" Muqtar teased back, knowing full well.

"Humph," Alia huffed, stomping on his toes. "Perhaps you are right. There is no point in waiting."

With that, she walked away, head held high, leaving Muqtar standing with his hands out toward where she'd disappeared into the crowd.

From that memory to this reality, thought Muqtar, wondering where Alia was and who the lucky man was who'd won her hand. It certainly wasn't him. *I wasn't the lucky one.* Then came his inner voice, chiding him, as it had many times before, images and voices from the past replaying in his mind.

"Muqtar, you want to go get a beer?" asked his dorm roommate Sammy.

"No thanks, man. I have to study for the math test next Tuesday."

"Next Tuesday?" Sammy scoffed. "Dude, it's Friday night. Next Tuesday may never come."

"I don't have any money either," Muqtar protested.

"Don't worry. Pitchers are only four bucks at University

Park."

That was how Muqtar's downfall began—four bucks at a time. As drinking time increased, study time dropped. Images now flickered from his memory bank, images he tried to forget. His religion forbade alcohol, and for the first two months at NYU, he held fast.

Yet he wanted to fit in with his new friends. One night, watching *The Invisible Man*, Muqtar took his first shot of tequila. His eyes watered, he coughed, throat ablaze. "Holy shit. That burns," he gasped.

His roommate handed him a beer. "Drink this. It'll put out the fire."

And that was how it began—a shot of tequila and a beer.

He recalled her sweet voice. "You must write me at least once a week," Alia had demanded, returning to him after the celebration had wound down. "And I will write you twice a week, to keep you updated on what's happening here."

"All right, Alia," Muqtar promised. "I'll write you faithfully."

"And you won't be tempted by the blonde American women, will you, Muqtar?" she teased, peering deep into his eyes.

"No, my love. No infidels for me," he promised again, laughing. Alia laughed too and grabbed both his hands.

"I can't wait for the day you get to really hold me, Muqtar. I mean *really* hold me," she breathed, emphasizing each word seductively.

He shifted his weight, hoping his black pants concealed his full excitement. "Me too," was all he could squeak out. "Me too."

Back to life, back to reality, he thought, shaking off the image of Alia reaching for him, inviting him to open her pasha and explore all her virtues.

"Mmm, Alia," he murmured, savoring the memory, wondering for the millionth time what it would have been like to make love to her. Alia never did open the pasha. However, at the end of that night, when no one was around, she took him behind a statue, knelt, and undid the string of his pants. *Oh Allah, you have blessed me,* he thought, shivering at the memory of that happy ending. Jerking himself back to the present—so to speak—Muqtar felt the sting of knowing Alia had surely given herself to another man by now.

Seven years out of the mountains, Muqtar had little to show—thirteen credit hours of engineering, seventeen hours of failure. His family, community, and homeland were distant memories, shattered by shame. He didn't even try to reach out to Alia after dropping out. He saw himself as worthless.

Jack Daniels, Coke, and energy drinks had ruined him. The alcohol gave him a buzz, the caffeine kept him awake, but the cycle left him drained. Engineering labs became his escape—a place to crash and hide from responsibility and from the privileged party lifestyle he couldn't keep up with.

No tutors for Muqtar—only caffeine. Then he met Allen, a chemistry major who also had a secret: he was a cook.

"What restaurant do you work at?" Muqtar asked after Allen said he cooked to make money. "Because I need cash too. Are they hiring?"

"No, Muqtard, you bozo. I don't work at a restaurant," sneered Allen.

"Oh, so you bake cookies or something and sell them?"

"You really are an idiot, Muqtard," sighed Allen, fishing in his jacket pocket. "Here. Try a little of this, then you'll know what kind of cook I am," he said, handing over a small bag of beige powder.

As Muqtar examined it, he asked, "Why do you call me

Muqtard when you know my name is Muqtar?"

"Because you're such a fucking retard, Muqtard."

Muqtar thought about the new nickname for a minute. "I don't really like that, Allen."

"Well, that's just too fucking bad. That's your name now," Allen emphasized.

"Fuck you, Allen."

"Fuck you, Muqtard."

Allen changed the subject. "Next time you're too tired to study, put a little of this up your nose. Wet your finger, dip it in, and snort it. Or roll a dollar bill, stick it in the bag, and snort while you inhale," he demonstrated. "This'll keep you sharp through the night."

"Thanks, man, I guess. I do have a hard time staying awake."

"No problem, Muqtard," Allen said, stressing the D again. "Let me know how your finals go. This stuff'll see you through."

"OK. Thanks again. I for sure need something. But fuck you again for the fucked-up nickname."

Allen just laughed—he'd gained a new customer.

Muqtar made it through his first semester finals. He limped across the finish line with three Cs, a D, thirteen barely passed hours, and two incompletes for labs he never finished.

"Whoo," he breathed, remembering how he'd survived on coffee, Red Bull, Jack and Coke, and that beige powder—methamphetamine, the most addictive drug of all.

Looking up at the sky, Muqtar muttered, "Why, Allah? Why did you let me down when I needed your strength and guidance?"

Yet even as he uttered the plea, he knew it wasn't Allah's fault. His inner voice told him so. He had been unfaithful. Once he'd prayed five times a day—then four, then only morning and night, then not at all.

Without prayer towers to call him, he struggled to stay faithful. His shame grew. The American lifestyle drained his will, replacing piety with alcohol and drugs. Over Christmas break, he learned to ski in the mountains, but it didn't compare to the failures he carried. He cheated on Alia and returned to campus to find another letter.

She wrote of love and longing, saying each letter from him was her only solace. Her words revealed her fear growing with his silence.

"Please, Muqtar, do not let some American woman steal you from me. Because you have written less and less over these months, the fear grows within me."

"Every night, when I finish at the bakery, I read all your letters again. I hold them to my chest in bed. Yet my soul hasn't been nourished with new words from you in so long. Doubt is creeping into my being."

"Do you still love me, Muqtar?"

"Are you going to come home and marry me, Muqtar?"

"Are you OK, Muqtar?"

"I love you, love you, love you."

"Please write soon. I am working at the bakery but have been offered a job in Lahore. I don't want to move without your blessing, without us having our life plan figured out."

"Please write SOON! I am starving here without your scribblings to feed me and inspire me."

"Missing you terribly and loving you totally,"
"Alia."

He remembered every word. The line about doubt creeping haunted him, knowing she feared what he had become. At school, he received a job offer as a research assistant, but the hours and pay didn't appeal. Why work and live straight when the fun was here with pretty party people? He shoved his piety and family's hopes to the back of his alcohol- and drug-addled mind.

Instead, he rented an apartment and dealt drugs for Allen, making easy money. His tough upbringing earned him a reputation—customers learned fast not to mess with him. He enjoyed the nightclub fame and never corrected anyone who assumed he was Arab.

Though raised conservative, he embraced the bad-ass persona, reveling in the money, women, and lifestyle. He never saved or sent money home. He ignored school, spent on clothes and a new Corvette, and partied on.

When customers came up short, only rarely did he have to get Medieval. He carried a bullwhip in his backpack and was good with it, leaving long red welts on anyone who crossed him. Word spread quickly: "Don't fuck with Muqtar. The Arab does not play."

CHAPTER 9

Muqtar's new high-flying lifestyle came to an end rather suddenly. One chilly, rainy morning, he drove to Allen's house to get the list of people to see and what to deliver. The holidays were coming soon, and Muqtar recalled how the previous year he'd gone skiing with his college friends over Christmas. They were gone now, except for the ones to whom he delivered drugs. No snow yet, though that would come soon enough. A pang of regret flooded him, twisting his stomach into knots.

Unwilling to honestly look at himself—and therefore to change—Muqtar reached for the half joint in his ashtray and lit it up. *Nothing like a good buzz early in the morning to take one's mind off the world*, he mused. As he neared Allen's house, his shame morphed into unease. Something felt off, though he had no reason to think so.

Inside, he hurried upstairs and found Allen in his study.

"What's going on with you today, Allen?" Muqtar asked. Allen's voice was strangely hoarse.

"Nothing much," Allen croaked, turning his chair to face him.

"What's wrong with your face, Allen?"

Allen stood and stepped closer. "What do you mean? There's nothing wrong with my face."

"Yes, there is. Your face is red and blotchy. Looks like you've been crying."

"Bullshit, man! Bullshit!" Allen retorted, looking away and reaching for his lockbox. "Now take these pills to Jack on 18th and Broadway, pick up five hundred from him. Then take this ounce of coke to Roy at his brownstone in Brooklyn."

"Do you want me to get any money from him?"

"From who?" Allen asked.

"From Roy, for the coke."

"No, he's coming by later," Allen replied, handing over two bags before sinking back into his chair.

"Cool," Muqtar said, turning to leave. But at the front door, a weird feeling stopped him.

"I'm going to get some coffee before I go," he shouted upstairs.

No response.

"I said, I'm getting a to-go cup of coffee, Allen."

Still nothing.

Muqtar then overheard Allen on the phone, talking fast in muffled tones. He crept up a couple stairs, stood by a rain-streaked window, and strained to hear. *What the fuck? Is Allen talking to the cops? Setting me up?* His blood ran cold. *He's describing my Corvette and what I'll be carrying.*

Realizing the betrayal, Muqtar dropped the dope into a pair of boots by the door, silently opened and closed it, and left. Fear gripped him as he drove. *Which way? Same route or another?* He checked the Corvette for any contraband, relieved to find none. His hands were clammy, heart racing, but by third gear he began to steady.

Approaching a red light, he gripped the wheel, eased off the gas, and hoped to time it. "Come on light . . . turn green." When it did, he inwardly cheered, punched the gas, and sped up—20,

30, 50. Then he backed off; no sense tempting cops.

Near his apartment, Muqtar let out a sigh of relief. *Not pulled over.* But a gnawing sense of doom made him circle around to the back parking lot—somewhere he never checked. Peeking around the corner, he saw two unfamiliar black SUVs. His pulse quickened. *Are those cop cars? Watching me? Or am I just paranoid*

"Stop being such a scared little pussy," he scolded himself.

"Oh yeah?" his inner voice spat. "What you heard Allen say wasn't a joke."

"Joke or not, I made it out of the neighborhood, no problem. So, the way I figure it, at worst, the cops didn't have their shit together, and I escaped."

"I wouldn't be so sure," the voice warned. "You aren't inside yet."

He tiptoed from the back lot to the front, climbed the five steps to his apartment, paused to look around, and unlocked the door.

Then all hell broke loose. The door of the apartment next to his exploded open with a deafening crash, and black-clad officers poured into the hall. Their heavy boots pounded the floor, riot shields gleamed under harsh lights, muzzles swept the corridor like searching eyes. They surrounded him and shouted, "Get on the ground, nigger!" as a dozen hands slammed his face into the concrete, grinding his cheek against the floor. Stupidly, he tried to stand.

"On the ground, motherfucker!" Whap! Whap!

"Now!" Whap!

"Spread your legs!"

"Put your hands behind your head!"

"Do you understand me, motherfucker?!"

They all seemed to scream at once. Whap! Whap! The police

batons cracked against his head and the backs of his legs, driving him to his knees.

Whap! Whap! Whap! Blows to his upper back and head flattened him face-first on the steps.

Then what seemed like a thousand hands probed everywhere—his pockets, jacket, armpits, up his crack.

"Where's the dope, punk?"

"Where are you hiding it?" demanded the cop in charge, squeezing the cuffs so tight on Muqtar's wrists they drew blood.

"Tell me where the fucking dope is, punk, and this goes easier for you," he shouted, jerking Muqtar's head up, flipping him over, and slamming it back on the concrete. Knee on his chest, he leaned close and screamed into his face.

"Listen, you goat-fucking Arab piece of shit. If you don't tell me where the dope is, you won't even make it to jail. Now where the fuck is it?" He yanked Muqtar's hair, lifting his head, then smashed it back down, again and again.

"I said where the fuck is the dope, you worthless piece of shit!" The cop pressed his nightstick to Muqtar's throat, cutting off air.

"I don't know anything about any dope," Muqtar choked. "I am a student here on scholarship. I am a Pakistani citizen. I want to—"

But he never finished asking for the Pakistani consulate. The cop smacked his forehead with the club so hard it knocked him out.

"Get the dope dog out here," barked the commanding officer. "We'll find the drugs if we have to tear every panel off his car."

The cops ripped apart Muqtar's Corvette but found nothing—no pills, no powder, not even weed. Lucky for him, the day before, he'd had it detailed, and when an employee found a baggie, Muqtar told him to keep it. A close call.

Otherwise, his luck was rotten. His college career was wrecked, business with Allen was finished. After hours handcuffed to a chair, the same cop who'd clubbed him returned and finally uncuffed him.

"You're free to go, sand nigger. But now I know who you are, and I'll be up your ass like fiberglass from now on. Do you get that?" He jerked Muqtar's head to face him.

"Yes, sir. I understand," Muqtar mumbled, rubbing his wrists as he left.

The next morning, groggy from a sleepless night, he checked his overflowing mailbox, sifting through junk and bills. He'd decided to return to junior college that fall, hoping to work his way back to NYU.

But things looked bleak. Most of his drug money was gone. Partying friends? Gone. The hot chicks who loved his hairy chest? Gone—no money or drugs, no love. Even the Corvette was trashed and soon to be gone. He tried to pump himself up as a survivor, remembering how he once beat up two men trying to rape him.

Clinging to hope, Muqtar vowed he'd redeem himself back home—until he spotted an official envelope bearing the Pakistani flag. His stomach dropped. The letter inside read:

> Dear Muqtar Ashadi:
> You failed your classes, and as a result you have been expelled from New York University. Therefore, your student visa has been revoked.
> You have ten (10) days to leave the United States and return to Pakistan. Failure to leave the United States and return to Pakistan now that your student

visa has been revoked is a crime and will render you
a criminal fugitive.

Please contact the Pakistani Embassy at 1414
Times Square Blvd., Suite 1100, New York City, New
York, 63415, telephone (212) 633-4114, to arrange for
your departure.

It was unsigned.

His dream of becoming an engineer in the U.S. lay shattered. Torn between staying illegally and risking deportation or returning to a life in the mountains, Muqtar chose to stay. He isolated himself from other Pakistanis, figuring he'd find a way.

Unable to enroll, he hoped to land a cash job and marry an American for a green card. With a New York driver's license, he planned to drive a cab—earn tips, meet women. *Not a bad plan,* he told himself. He burned the consulate letter and set his sights on Yellow Cab, then on Allen for answers.

"Hello, my name is Muqtar Ashadi. I am here to apply to be a cab driver for Yellow Cab."

The old man behind the desk looked up. "Applications are over there, by the fan. Yeah, right there. Fill it out, bring it back. Got a pen? OK."

He went back to dabbing white-out on what looked like a ledger, shaking and blowing on it, cursing, then writing on the dried crust.

Muqtar handed over his application, but the old man said it would take time to process. Desperate, Muqtar lied that he had four hungry children to feed that night. Unmoved, the man suggested the day labor hall on 41st and Main. Shoulders slumped, defeated, Muqtar turned to leave.

Then the man asked if he had a Social Security number.

Muqtar lied again, tried to downplay his accent, claimed to be American, but said he'd return with the number. With only forty-one dollars left, he realized he was no different than any other illegal immigrant—no job, no SSN, no future. Next step: collect from Allen. Maybe teach him a lesson.

Twenty minutes later, Muqtar emerged from the subway and cautiously approached Allen's house, scanning for police. The night air was cool, slightly damp from rain. Confident the coast was clear, he moved from shadow to shadow.

It was eerily quiet—too quiet. His heart sped up. Where was Allen? Probably thought Muqtar would be caught, convicted, deported. But he wasn't going down easy. Allen would learn the Arab does not play.

Muqtar saw lights on the first floor and wondered if the second-floor bathroom window was still unlocked.

"You never know, Muqtard. I might have to make a quick exit someday—out this window, down the drainpipe, gone," Allen once bragged.

Roger that, thought Muqtar. *Let's try it in reverse.* He grabbed the pipe, shimmied up. *God, this sucks. I'm fat. I'm out of shape.*

"Ugh," he groaned, scraping his shins, finally hauling himself onto the gravel roof. He climbed to the window using an old TV antenna, squeezed inside, and in the dark found his way to the office. Arms shaking, he found Allen's lockbox in the closet. Couldn't remember the combo—until he recalled the scrap of paper hidden in the lampshade. His fingers trembled as he retrieved it. There was the code.

Inside, he found cash, pills, drugs, and a manila envelope, all stuffed into a Taco Bell bag. On his way out, he remembered the dope he'd left in Allen's boots.

Just as he reached for the knob, a key scraped into the lock.

Oh shit. Trapped. Holding his breath, heart pounding, he bolted upstairs, taking two steps at a time, hoping his footsteps weren't heard.

He hid in the master closet, chest heaving, icy fear crushing him. Footsteps entered the bedroom—no way out now. Desperate, he felt around, grabbed a tennis racket—useless. Then his hands closed on cold steel: a ten-pound barbell. *Now we're talking.*

The light flipped on. Through a crack, he saw Allen. Rage surged.

He flung the door open, charged, barbell above his head. "Motherfucker, you're mine!"

Allen's eyes bulged, hands trembling, mouth agape, flitting from Muqtar's face to the barbell. He extended his palms, begging.

"Hey, man, calm down. It was a mistake. We're good, man, we're good."

"No, fuck no, we're not good, you motherfucker," Muqtar snarled, stepping closer.

Allen put his right hand behind his back. Thinking he was going for a gun, Muqtar swung. The barbell smashed Allen's forehead, spinning him, dropping him face-first. A gun slid from his waistband.

"Knew you had a gun, bitch. Now we're good," Muqtar said. Allen didn't move. Muqtar kicked him hard. Nothing. Then he slammed the barbell into the back of Allen's skull. A sick crack filled the room.

Satisfied, he wiped down everything he'd touched, replaced the barbell, stepped over Allen's body, and staged it as a robbery. He ripped a pocket, scattered cocaine, placed the gun by Allen's head, and unlocked the front door.

Proud of his work, heart finally slowing, he grabbed the drugs from the boots, wiped down the stairs, handrail, bathroom, office, and hallway, then climbed out the window. The Taco Bell bag spilled—he cursed, gathered everything, climbed back up, cleaned the window, and closed it. Scraped and hypervigilant, he checked the street. Finding no one, he shimmied down the pipe.

The cool night awaited him, his breath misting under streetlights. Unbeknownst to him, the envelope he took contained something far more valuable than money or pills: a key to his future in the U.S.

CHAPTER 10

Muqtar wanted to run like a madman, hauling ass out of Allen's neighborhood, but he forced himself to walk slowly, staying in the shadows and keeping a sharp lookout. When he finally reached his apartment, he checked the street and back parking lot before going inside, having hidden the Taco Bell bag in the bushes out back. There were no black SUVs, but *you never know where the pigs might be hiding, ready to break down the door and fuck with me again,* he thought.

After waiting about an hour, Muqtar felt safe enough to go outside, retrieve the bag, and bring the goodies in. He made sure the curtains were closed, then nervously poured everything onto his kitchen table.

- Three bundles of cash: $5,000 in each.
- A plastic bag with two ounces of cocaine.
- Three pill bottles—one with 30 Darvocets, another with 15 Tylenol with codeine, the last with 100 blues.
- Another plastic bag with an ounce of meth and a little bag holding maybe a quarter ounce of weed.
- A sealed 8½ × 11-inch manila envelope.

Muqtar counted his loot, relieved to have enough money to fix the Corvette. Still wary of who to sell the dope to, he set that aside to figure out later, too whipped from the night's events. Curiosity drew him to the envelope. Hoping for more cash, he opened it, only to find a newspaper clipping and a Social Security card for Michael Brown. *Huh.* Maybe the SSN could be the key to getting a real job. The envelope also contained a birth certificate for Michael Brown, born in 1999 in Pennsylvania. Elated, Muqtar started crafting a new story—imagining himself as the son of an American and a Pakistani woman.

> Stuart Brown went to the university to study with the professor for whom Karinne Syed worked. They met, fell in love, and the rest was history.

Whoa, big fella, his inside voice warned. *What happens if someone checks that Social Security number and finds out there are two Michael Browns with SSN 077-41-4100?* His soaring mood deflated, the wind dying in his mental sails.

Well, he mused, *better two of us with a real SSN than me with a number bought at a flea market. Still sucks, though.*

Then his eyes fell on another official-looking document. *What's this?* he thought, unfolding it.

> Death certificate. Michael Brown. August 7, 2002. Cause of death: drowning.

That sucks for the original Michael Brown, but it's fucking great for me, Muqtar exalted. There wouldn't be two Michael Browns with that SSN—just one, and it was him. He pumped his fists, thanked Allah, and nearly jumped for joy at his luck.

Finally, he picked up the newspaper clipping. The headline read: **Pennsylvania boy drowns while swimming in**

Lake Ottawa. He kept reading.

> Three-year-old Michael Brown drowned yesterday while swimming near Camp Castle in Ottaway National Forest. His brother, Allen, reported that Michael fell in, struck his head on a rock, and did not resurface. Divers located the boy, but attempts to revive him failed. Michael Brown's body will be returned to Pennsylvania, where funeral arrangements are pending.

Wow, thought Muqtar. Allen was there when his brother drowned. That must've sucked, watching his little brother go under and never come back. But why keep his brother's information all these years?

A reminder of a very sad past? Possibly.

Guilt over not saving his brother? Possibly.

Or a ready-made new identity if Allen ever got busted? *Bingo.*

Now fully embracing his new identity as Michael Brown, Muqtar felt a rush of warmth and determination. He got rid of the drugs, obtained a driver's license, moved to a new apartment in Queens, and sold the Corvette for nearly seventy grand. Though unsure of the future, he stuck to his plan—drive a cab while figuring things out.

Life became routine. The night before his new identity's twenty-first birthday, he celebrated at a pub, buying shots for a table of white girls. One seemed interested; they exchanged looks as they raised their glasses.

Muqtar lifted his, prompting his friend Arthur to ask if he was toasting himself. Muqtar explained that he'd bought tequila for the nearby table. Arthur teased him to go introduce himself—especially since it was almost his birthday. Though

shy and unsure how he'd be received, Muqtar approached anyway. His confidence wavered until the woman who'd been eyeing him turned and smiled. Relieved, he greeted her, and she
thanked him for the shot. He responded smoothly, asking what
brought them out.

"We just finished our last semester, so we're celebrating
graduation."

"Oh, that's great. I'm celebrating my birthday."

"Oh, really? Today's your birthday?"

"Well, no—actually tomorrow."

"July 11th? What year? Let me guess. 2000? No? 1998? No?
Help me out, girls."

They were laughing now, all taking guesses, with Muqtar
shaking his head at each one.

Looking directly at him, the fine one stuck out her hand.
"What's your name, birthday boy? I'm Julie Evans."

"My name's Michael Brown," Muqtar said, peering intently
at her to catch her reaction while gripping her hand firmly.

"Nice to meet you, Michael Brown," Julie replied, keeping
her hand in his and eyes locked on his.

"Nice to meet you, too." Inside, Muqtar was gushing, nearly trembling from the electric connection. The other women
chatted among themselves, feigning disinterest, so he focused
on Julie.

Not bad, he thought. Reddish-blonde hair, friendly smile, a
bit wide on the bottom but definitely worth tapping if the opportunity arose. It had been a long dry spell, and he was determined to reel this one in.

"What did you get your degree in, Julie Evans?"

"I'm a nurse now," she said proudly. "And I am going to spe-
cialize in geriatric care. You know, taking care of old folks."

"Cool. Old folks need love, too—I mean, they need care, too." Whoops. He'd let his own cat out of the bag. He hoped he hadn't blown it by sounding like the desperate, lonely loser he was.

"That's right," Julie said, scrutinizing him. "We all need care and love, no matter our age, don't we, Michael?"

He felt his face flush. Searching for a pivot, he blurted, "Are you from New York?" letting go of her hand.

"No, I'm from the Midwest. St. Louis. How about you?"

"I was born in Pennsylvania, came to New York for college, and stayed."

"That's interesting. What was your degree?"

A wave of heat flushed through him. *Tell the truth? Lie?* "Well, truth is, I partied too much my freshman year at NYU and got kicked out."

"Oh, that's too bad," Julie said sympathetically. "But it happens to a lot of people."

"Yeah, I suppose. But I'm still pretty ashamed of myself."

"Don't be," Julie said, taking his hand again and squeezing it. "A degree isn't everything."

"Thank you, Julie. That's one of the nicest things I've ever heard. Who knows? Maybe I'll go back someday."

"That's right, Michael. It's never too late." Julie glanced around. "Michael, do you know how to dance?"

"Uh, no. Uh, well, a little. Maybe—if you show me."

"Well, come on then," she said, rising. "Let's dance, birthday boy. Everybody deserves a gift on their birthday."

What started as a night with his friend ended with Muqtar at Julie's apartment, receiving a birthday gift he wouldn't soon forget. Over the next three months, they lived together in New York—Muqtar driving his cab, Julie working nights at Queens Hospital while waiting on her boards. Sometimes she visited her family in St. Louis, and Muqtar would pretend to go home too, keeping up appearances.

As Christmas neared, Julie said, "Michael, I know we've never really talked about it, but we need to discuss religion, raising a family, and our future."

"Oh, really?" Muqtar replied, clueless.

"Well, you know, a woman has to plan her life. There's only so much time," Julie said, voice trailing off.

"OK," was all he managed.

"OK, what?" Julie was miffed by his limp response, trying not to cry.

"OK, what do you want me to say?"

"Well, OK, don't say anything," was Julie's departing shot as she began to cry. "I'm going to bed. Goodnight!"

Muqtar did not respond. Rather, he looked out the window and thought wistfully of days gone by. Of the days when he had hoped to ask Alia to marry him and for her to have his children. That day was long gone; never to return.

He shook his head, returning to the present. Twenty-one, no degree, a murderer, living under a stolen identity. He couldn't go home—his family was better off thinking him dead. For all intents and purposes, Muqtar was dead, and Michael Brown was alive. America was still a good place, and though he and Julie occasionally got odd looks, most of the time, they had no problems.

Muqtar wrestled with the idea of having a child. Deceiving strangers was one thing; deceiving his own child felt morally wrong. He hadn't thought about morality in years, but now— with Julie talking family—he was conflicted. His thoughts pounded into a headache. He knew he needed to act. Julie, like Alia before, would eventually move on.

Then he remembered the morning of September 11, 2021. He woke in a good mood, only to see the news replaying 9/11. Julie stirred beside him.

"Wake up, Julie. You have to see this. They're showing the jets crash into the towers."

Julie turned, just as the second plane hit. "Oh my God! That was so awful. So many people."

Still stunned, Muqtar showered and dressed. "OK, Julie, I'm off to work. Call me when you get home, and we'll do dinner or something."

"All right, Michael. I'll call you later."

Just then, he caught the photos of the Saudi hijackers. *Man, they look just like me. Not good. Not good at all.* Americans would never forget.

All day, driving his cab, he worried Julie wouldn't want to be seen with him—his South Asian features often mistaken for Arab. Near midnight, her call finally came. Exhausted, she re-assured him she was fine. Julie asked if his family had been involved in 9/11. He clarified they were Pakistani, not Arab. After she confirmed she was starving, he offered to bring pizza. She eagerly agreed.

Julie was waiting, and Muqtar knew he'd found a good one. She accepted him as he was. He felt almost lucky: lucky to have avoided arrest, lucky to have an identity and a job, lucky to have found a good-hearted American woman—even if now she wanted marriage and kids.

CHAPTER 11

Life in New York was tough for Muqtar near the anniversary of 9/11, given his appearance. Some customers refused to get into his cab, and one even tried to have his permit revoked, calling him "a fucking Arab masquerading as an American."

Despite having all but eliminated his accent, the incident—and its fallout—shook him. Nothing ultimately came of the complaint, but it scared him enough to realize he needed to decide about Julie. With a nursing job opening for her in St. Louis and her longing to move home, Muqtar made up his mind to commit. He showed up at her apartment with pizza, ready to take the next step.

"Julie, do you remember talking to me about a future together and stuff?" Pretty clumsy opening.

Julie let out a sharp sigh, gripping the dish she was washing and dropping it into the sink with force. Her shoulders stiffened, her face twisted in a grimace, and she whirled around, her voice tightly controlled. "Of course."

"Uh, well, I've been thinking about us all day . . . and . . ."

Julie turned back to her dishes, clearly disgusted. "And what?"

"And I can't live without you in my life, so I want you to marry me. Will you marry me, Julie?"

As he spoke, Muqtar dropped to one knee and pulled out a

tiny diamond ring he'd bought earlier, reaching for Julie's left hand.

Julie started crying, her hand trembling as he slipped the ring on her finger.

Now it was his turn. "And . . . and?"

"Yes, yes, a thousand times yes, Michael. I will gladly be your wife." She threw herself into his arms, kissing and hugging him.

"Okay then. Let's tell your mom when we go there for Christmas."

Julie's dad, Sam Hawthorne, was not openly hostile when the couple arrived, but he looked Muqtar up and down, doing his best not to show his disgust at his daughter bringing home a fucking Arab. He nodded toward the living room for all of them to enter.

Julie had already told her family about "Michael's ethnic heritage." Nonetheless, her father was unhappy that his youngest had gotten involved with an Arab. Both Sam and his wife, Mary, had lived their entire lives in St. Louis, meeting in high school. They married in a Catholic church in 1990 and raised three kids—Julie being the youngest—in the same house they still occupied. The only time they'd been apart was when Sam was called to active duty from the Army reserves to fight in Iraq. He never talked about his time there. Like too many veterans, what he'd seen and done had warped and wounded him in ways he kept locked up inside.

Sam had landed a good job as a pipe fitter at a plant, which allowed Mary to stay home. But around the time Julie left for New York on her full nursing scholarship, the plant closed, and Sam had struggled ever since to find decent work.

"Hello, Mr. Hawthorne. Nice to meet you," Muqtar greeted, using near-perfect American English as he extended his hand.

"I didn't know you people shook hands," Sam replied, slowly offering his own.

Great, thought Muqtar. *Glad to see the racial bigotry sparked by 9/11 made it all the way to St. Louis, too.*

"Sir, I was born in Pennsylvania. I grew up shaking hands when meeting someone," he explained, smiling and gripping Sam's hand a little too tightly.

"Dad, don't judge Michael because of how he looks. He's as American as you and me," Julie cut in, grabbing Muqtar's left hand.

"That's right, Sam," added Mrs. Hawthorne. "Julie's told me all about how Michael grew up in Pennsylvania, how he went to high school there, and how he sadly lost his parents in a car accident with a drunk driver when he was eighteen and then found work in New York."

Thank God I did my homework, thought Muqtar. *My story checks out top to bottom.*

"I suppose," sighed Sam, resigned to the fact that his daughter had brought home an Arab. "I suppose." With that, he wandered off to the family room to watch football, leaving Julie, her mother, and Muqtar in the kitchen.

"Your sister and brother-in-law James will be over soon," Mrs. Hawthorne said brightly, trying to lift the mood. "They'll be glad to see you and meet Michael, too."

"Okay, Mom, that'll be great. What are you making for dinner?" Julie asked, lifting the lid on a pot, releasing a pleasant, steamy scent of boiling potatoes.

"Your favorite: pot roast."

"Oh yum. Michael, you're going to love Mom's cooking," Julie beamed.

"Well, if she taught you how to cook, I know it'll be amazing.

Everything you make is," said Muqtar, offering a compliment that pleased them both.

"You're going to fit in just fine here, Michael. Welcome to our family and to St. Louis," Mrs. Hawthorne said, squeezing his shoulder.

"Thank you—thank you very much," he replied warmly, remembering his own mother's cooking. He stepped outside to smoke, letting his thoughts drift back. *Would I ever eat my mother's food again? Would I ever see my homeland? What happened to my beloved Alia?* Too painful. *Let it go.*

Muqtar turned his mind to his new life with Julie, overwhelmed by the possibilities of marriage, children, and a home. Grateful for his new identity in St. Louis, he pushed away the darker memories and tried to justify the choices that led him here. When Julie called him in for dinner, life felt satisfyingly simple.

They settled into a small second-floor one-bedroom apartment with a view of downtown. Muqtar drove a cab and attended community college, while Julie thrived as a geriatric nurse. They were happy—though Muqtar was always watching over his shoulder, worried his past might one day catch up.

Over time, Julie's father softened, though still bitter about losing his job and how poorly vets were treated. Julie began helping her mother financially. Nearly two years in, they started planning for a house and a family.

"Michael, where do you want to get married?" Julie asked one evening.

"Well, here in St. Louis, I guess," he answered.

"No, silly. I mean do you want a church wedding, a courthouse wedding, a reception hall—where?"

"I don't care, Julie. Wherever you want is fine."

"Well, what church did you grow up in, Michael? Where did you go as a kid?"

Gulp. He'd never thought about that. *Had Allen ever mentioned going to church?* Not that Muqtar could recall. Just thinking about Allen made his lip curl. *That sorry motherfucker tried to fuck me—and ended up fucking himself.*

For years after what he called his "righteous revenge," he'd scanned the *New York Post* and *Times* for updates. At first, there were stories on the local channels, but after a few months, it was just another unsolved New York robbery-murder. Police said they had a suspect but never gave a description. For that, Muqtar quietly thanked Allah.

"Uh, well, Julie, truth is, since my mom and dad were of different faiths, we didn't go to church much—just a few times on Easter," he improvised.

"Oh, okay. Well, I want to wear a white dress and have a church wedding, then a reception. We've waited almost two years, and I've saved enough to do it how I want. Is that all right with you?" Julie's eyes searched his.

"Sure, Jules. I'm up for whatever you want. Just tell me where and when, and I'll be there," he assured her, relieved the topic of religion had moved on—at least for now.

Still, it hadn't left *his* mind. He thought of his brother Mohammed. It had been over five years since he'd left Pakistan. By now, surely Mohammed had completed his cleric studies and might even have his own mosque. Muqtar felt proud of his little brother—and sad he'd likely never hear Mohammed's call to prayer. Mohammed had always been the pure one, never missing prayers, often called on by the village to lead them. Even their father, Ali, leaned on him after Muqtar had shamed the family name.

CHAPTER 12

Julie and Muqtar married in a Presbyterian church on January 13, 2021, with a lively celebration that included tipsy antics from Mr. Hawthorne and Julie's sister dancing a bit too freely to "YMCA." That night, Julie revealed she had stopped taking birth control, startling Muqtar. After a moment of shock, he shrugged it off and embraced the news, thinking, *No balls, no babies.*

Nine months later, Michael Jr. was born. While Julie dreamed of family church outings and a Christmas baptism for Junior, Muqtar's thoughts often turned inward. He attended the christening and even some services, but his true focus was on carving out a future, with nursing school emerging as his next step.

He had met with church leaders as part of preparing to be married but couldn't relate to Christianity. He recognized the similarities in both religions—each having a prophet—but he'd never been a dedicated Muslim and wasn't about to become a dedicated Christian either. Beneath it all, Muqtar carried a heavy secret, knowing his past could never come out without shattering his carefully built new life.

"What about becoming a nurse?" Julie had read Muqtar's mind.

"You like chemistry and that sort of thing," she continued.

"I don't know," mused Muqtar. "I'm not sure I could pass the exams."

"Oh, sure you could. I did, remember?"

Muqtar definitely remembered the first night he and Julie had been together.

"Would I feel as exuberant about finishing as you did that night, Julie?"

"Probably so, yes. And you'd get the same satisfaction I did at the end of the evening too, if you ask properly," Julie teased, her voice dropping and a come-hither look lighting up her face.

"I'll think about that, Jules. That's a very tempting carrot you're placing at the end of the stick."

"You want to have a little bite of the carrot now, honey? Junior's asleep . . ." she tossed out coyly.

"How can I say no to that offer!" exclaimed Muqtar. He turned to his wife and spread her out, gently removing all her clothes until he arrived at the mother lode and dug deep, mining another evening's worth of gold.

That night, lying in bed as his bride slept soundly beside him, Muqtar seriously ruminated on her suggestion. With his background in the physical sciences and the solid pay nurses earned, it began to make sense. He decided to pursue it. Muqtar had already completed the prerequisites at community colleges in New York and St. Louis and figured he could finish in three years.

The next Monday, he researched the Missouri Board of Nursing's requirements and found only one hurdle: submitting fingerprints for his license. The thought of the government running his prints made him uneasy, but he pushed through the fear.

He reminded himself he was a new person now. If the worst happened—being caught for Allen's murder—he could always go back to Pakistan and find work as a nurse. He shoved the thought aside. With a *fuck it* mindset, Muqtar had his fingerprints taken, applied for his nursing license, and even went to get his photo for a U.S. passport. A few weeks later, he received a phone call from the financial aid department at St. Louis University, offering him assistance for nursing school.

Yes! Muqtar had been accepted.

Just minutes after celebrating, his cell phone rang again.

"Hello. Is this Michael Brown?"

"Yes."

"Mr. Brown," a dry male voice crackled, "we need you to come to the downtown police station. Do you know where it's located?"

Muqtar's knees went weak.

"Yes, I do, but why?"

"I don't know, sir. Be here before noon. When you arrive, ask for Detective Paul."

Now what? Has the ruse come to an end? Am I about to be locked up and deported, or sent back to New York, charged with murder, and then deported? Should I run? Should I tell Julie? These thoughts and a million more ran through his mind as he drove downtown.

"I'm here to see Detective Paul," Muqtar forced out to the police officer at the reception window.

"Have a seat over there after you write your name on this list," instructed the officer, pointing at a blank line on a long sheet attached to a clipboard.

Muqtar glanced at the headings: name, address, telephone number, purpose of visit. *Purpose of visit? What the hell do I put there?*

"Sir, I was called and asked to come talk to Detective Paul.

What should I put in this spot?" he asked, pointing.

"Well, why does Detective Paul want to see you?" the desk sergeant replied.

"I don't know."

"Then leave it blank, and I guess we'll all find out when Detective Paul comes to get you," the sergeant said sarcastically.

Get me? The wording made him uneasy. He eyed the front door, tempted to run, but before he could act, a man walked through an office door into the waiting area.

"Michael Brown?" Detective Paul called out, looking around. "Michael Brown?"

"Over here, sir," said Muqtar, standing up, trying to appear calm and collected despite his pounding heart.

"Come with me," the detective said, holding the office door open.

Oh God. I'm fucking done. Once I go through that door, I'm never coming out. I should never have applied to be a nurse. Being a cab driver was just fine. Now I'm fucked, and I'll never see my wife or son again.

"Have a seat, Mr. Brown," Detective Paul ordered once they reached a small office past a line of ringing telephones.

At least he didn't shut the door behind me, thought Muqtar as he sat.

"Were you at the corner of 14th Avenue and Dowling Street at about noon four days ago, Mr. Brown?"

Muqtar's mind began churning furiously. *Why does he want to know that?*

"Do you drive a cab for a living, Mr. Brown?"

"Yes, sir. I do," Muqtar admitted, relaxing slightly.

"We took your license plate number from an intersection camera, traced it back to the cab company, and from there to you."

Am I here for a traffic ticket? This is nuts.

"There was a robbery of a pawn shop there, and two people were shot. It looks like the criminals got into your cab," the detective continued.

Wow. Am I being treated as an accomplice? He glanced at the open door.

Sensing his nerves, Detective Paul added, "We're not looking for you. We're looking for those two men. First, I need you to describe them. Then tell me where you took them."

All the paranoid air rushed out of Muqtar's system. *Thank God. This isn't about me.*

"I remember two young Black guys I picked up when it was nearly dark on that corner."

"Where did you take them?"

"Uh, let's see," Muqtar said, stroking his chin. "I drove down 3rd Street to Bowden, turned right, then went about a mile to Highway 90." He gestured, mimicking the turns. "As I was about to get on the highway, they told me to stop and got out on the feeder."

"Which way did they go?"

"Well, I was facing north, getting ready to get on the highway. They exited on the driver's side, so they headed west, under the highway toward the projects."

"That figures," said Detective Paul, nodding, recalling how many times he'd responded to calls there. "Would you recognize them if you saw them again?"

"Huh. I don't know," Muqtar admitted. "They were just two young, dark-skinned Black men with close-cut hair, both about six feet tall, maybe 160 to 180 pounds each. Nothing else stood out."

Detective Paul stood and motioned for him to stand, too.

"Sorry I couldn't be of more help, Detective."

"No problem, Mr. Brown. I may bring you in for a lineup if we get that far."

"No problem. Here's my card—my cell's on the back if you need me to come in or, you know, need a cab," said Muqtar with a half-smile, handing it over.

Back in his cab, Muqtar slowly exhaled. *What a day. From thinking I was busted to learning I'd unknowingly been a getaway driver.* He resolved to pay more attention to his passengers. He called Julie to tell her about the incident, then continued his shift. The rest of the day was slow—only three fares—until he lined up outside the Westin, a usual airport hotspot. Two businessmen loaded into his cab.

"Where to, fellas?" he asked.

"The airport," one replied.

Muqtar eyed them in the rearview mirror. *I could recognize these two if I ever needed to.*

"What are you looking at?" snapped the man who had given the destination.

"Nothing, sir," Muqtar said quickly. "Just trying to remember if I'd picked either of you up before."

"Well, you certainly haven't," the man said, annoyed. "I'd remember an A-rab cab driver in St. Louis for sure," stretching out the A deliberately.

Muqtar was irritated but stayed silent. Twenty minutes later, they reached St. Louis International.

"What airline?"

"American."

He pulled up to the curb, glanced at the meter, and turned in his seat. "That'll be $27.50, gentlemen."

The rude passenger climbed out, retrieved his wallet, counted out a twenty, a five, and three ones, then threw them into the trunk as Muqtar lifted out the luggage.

"Keep the change, Arab," he spat.

For a moment, Muqtar thought about chasing after him, shoving the coins into his hand—or his face—but decided, as he often did, that drawing attention was the last thing he needed.

When he got home, Julie was already making dinner.

"Will you give Junior a bath after dinner, honey?" she called from the kitchen.

"Sure," Muqtar replied. "Just let me whip him at building Lego forts first."

"Go ahead and beat your one-year-old at fort building. Make yourself proud," Julie teased.

He sat down with the pile of Legos and played build-and-knock-down with Junior for nearly half an hour.

"Time to eat, little man," he said, standing up. "Let's wash our hands."

"OK, Daddy," Michael Junior squealed, running to the bathroom.

That night, Muqtar pondered the day—the police station, his nursing plans, his little family. He felt good about Junior's advanced speech, something the daycare staff often mentioned.

Hell, he thought, *my life didn't turn out the way I'd once pictured it—married to Alia, an engineer, respected by all—but it isn't so bad.* He chastised himself again for straying from the straight path but knew he couldn't blame Allah. Life could be a hell of a lot worse, he thought, before turning to cuddle with Julie and drifting off to sleep.

CHAPTER 13

Joshua Meister

Joshua waited for the wrecker to haul off his damaged VW, cursing himself for not pulling over to type the VA nursing home address into his navigation. As he looked again at the cab driver's business card, he replayed the man's accent and concluded he was likely from northern Pakistan. Despite his very sharp analytical skills, Joshua felt weak and unsure, self-pity rising as he reflected on his recent firing from the CIA and doubts about his future.

He realized he wouldn't make it to see his grandfather today. And as for Mei Lei? He'd probably get the door slammed in his face for being a failure. *Oh well,* he thought, trying to pull himself out of the slump. *I can't change the past.* As the wrecker headed toward the dealership, Joshua called his insurance agent. The agent informed him that the cab company had already filed a claim for the damage.

"Did the cab driver make a claim for injuries?"

"No. No, he sure didn't—only a claim to get the cab fixed. But he might start feeling bad in a day or two and make an injury claim," the agent explained.

"OK, good enough. Thanks for the info," Joshua said and hung up.

Joshua briefly thought again about the cab driver, Mr. Brown, and his Pakistani accent. He wondered if there was a large Pakistani community in St. Louis but quickly dismissed the thought. Just because Mr. Brown was Pakistani didn't mean he was part of a terrorist group, he reasoned. As soon as he thought that, he wondered where that racist notion had come from.

During his time at the CIA, he'd learned how Pakistan had allowed Osama Bin Laden to live there for years. Pakistan giving this mass murderer sanctuary pissed off many Americans, especially those at the Agency. Maybe that feeling had rubbed off on him, too. As he approached the dealership, he was relieved to see they were ready with his rental car paperwork, thanks to his full coverage. After filling out the forms, he took the keys from the young woman at the desk, distracted by her beautiful blue eyes and what lay beneath her red blazer as she gave him directions.

"When my car is repaired, do I bring the rental keys back to you, Miss?" queried Joshua hopefully.

"No. You can just leave them in the car, note the mileage and the amount of gas in the tank, then drop the keys and the form in the slot outside."

"Oh, OK," sighed a disappointed Joshua. Seeing her again in a week or so wouldn't have been all bad. He walked around the building, and a row of rental cars came into view. Joshua clicked the key, and a newish-looking red Volkswagen GTI's horn beeped. *How subtle. Perfect for an undercover spy like me.* Correction, he reminded himself, *former undercover spy.* Reality bites.

Before driving off, Joshua entered the Marriott's address into the nav system, vowing not to repeat his earlier mistake. As he drove, thoughts of Mei Lei overwhelmed him. He longed to reconnect with her but realized her family would never accept him, no matter what. *That love is lost.* He tried shifting focus to his grandfather, wondering if he still had his wits or if dementia had taken hold. Tomorrow would reveal the truth. At the hotel, Joshua quickly ate a hamburger, put away his clothes, and shut off the lights. As he lay down, he hoped his grandfather would remember him—after all, that was the reason for this trip—and then drifted off to a troubled sleep.

The next morning was crisp and fresh, about 45 degrees and sunny—a beautiful early spring day. Muqtar woke up, made Julie coffee, and put the cup on the night table by her side of the bed. Then he went into the little man's room.

"Get up, son. Let's go eat breakfast. Your meal this morning will be oatmeal with strawberries."

"Bananas too?" the little man requested, wiping his eyes.

"Okay, son. Your wish is my command," said Muqtar as he headed to the kitchen to find a banana. He could hear the shower running and knew Julie would soon appear in her nursing scrubs, empty coffee cup in hand.

"Do you want any breakfast today, dear?"

"No, thanks, honey. I don't have time. I'm on my way in early today because guess what—I've been promoted to be the head nurse of an entire wing."

"Whoo hoo! That is awesome, baby! I'm really proud of you! Maybe now you can get me in as a paid employee," Muqtar celebrated as he picked her up and spun her around.

"Thank you, honey. Now put me down. I'm pretty happy, too, and I'll check to see if I can get you hired for money instead of just being an unpaid intern."

Julie grabbed her purse and backpack and headed out. Muqtar turned back around to see Junior had eaten most of his oatmeal.

"Do you want anything else? A muffin or piece of toast?" he asked.

"No, Daddy."

"That is 'No, thank you, Daddy,'" he gently corrected.

"OK, Daddy. No, thank you," Junior repeated, emphasizing the last three words.

Muqtar decided to let the bit of petulance slide.

"OK, son. Go find your shoes, and I'll put your lunch in your backpack and meet you at the back door."

At the door, they spent a few minutes searching before finally finding the shoes. Once on, they climbed into the silver Honda SUV and headed to daycare. After drop-off, Muqtar went to the cab company's lot. He always smiled at the sign: *US Cabs— Ride With Us Anywhere In The US!*—ironic, since they only operated in St. Louis and the suburbs. Still, that was his world, and he was happy to drive anywhere in it. His smile faded when he saw his damaged cab. Despite the setback, he enjoyed the job, made decent money, and sometimes met interesting people, like the Muslim cleric he'd picked up yesterday visiting family from Pakistan.

"Do you miss your home?" the cleric inquired in Urdu.

"Excuse me, sir?" Muqtar guardedly replied in English.

"I hear an accent in your English, Mr. Brown," the cleric noted, studying the ID on the dash.

Muqtar's heart pounded, throat tightening. *Could this man have been sent to find me? Can he tell I'm a fraud? I don't like how he keeps looking at me. Yikes.*

"I was born and raised in Pennsylvania, sir. Maybe it's an

East Coast accent," he offered, hoping to throw him off.

The cleric smiled. "No, I think not, young man. I've traveled many places, including all over the U.S., and your accent is definitely not from here. Let me hear you speak some more, and I'll tell you where you learned English."

Before answering, Muqtar debated telling him his mother was from Pakistan. But then the cleric might ask her name, when she came, who her parents were, what mosque they attended . . .

ARRRGGGHHH!

His breath hitched, chest tight, a lump in his throat. What to say?

"I'm sorry, sir. I can't account for my strange accent—English is the only language I speak," Muqtar stammered, doing his best to control his raging emotions while trying to sound accent-free.

"Very well. You're obviously troubled by something in your past. You needn't be ashamed of being born a Muslim, even if you've renounced your family, country, and religion," the cleric said, staring intently through the rearview mirror.

"I can tell by your accent you were born in Pakistan, probably somewhere in the northern regions. That's why I spoke Urdu—I'm also from the mountains of northern Pakistan."

Great. The cleric had nailed him perfectly. *Of all people to come to St. Louis and climb into my cab . . . What are the odds? Fuck me.*

"Perhaps one day you'll want to reconcile with your past and stop living this life of denial," the cleric continued softly. "Allah welcomes all who come home, no matter when or why."

"Thank you, sir. I appreciate your kind words, but you're mistaken. I was born in Pennsylvania, raised a Christian, and have lived here all my life," insisted Muqtar, still wrestling to control his face and voice, lying to a holy man.

The cleric only shrugged and looked out the window.

"Nice weather this time of year in St. Louis, isn't it, Michael?" he observed, stretching out *Michael* deliberately.

"Yes, it is," Muqtar whispered, relieved they'd reached the house.

"We're here," he announced brightly.

"I see that, Michael," the cleric deadpanned, reaching for the door handle.

Muqtar jumped out, opened the trunk, and nearly bolted. He felt the cleric beside him, watching.

"The fare is $19.50, sir. Need help with your bags?"

"No, that isn't necessary, Michael. I've enjoyed our discussion today," said the cleric, his amused expression unreadable.

That makes one of us, thought Muqtar, squirming inside. As the cleric handed him a $20 and a $10, he took Muqtar's right hand in both of his.

"Life is only worth living if you live right by God. Bless you, my son."

The cleric walked toward the house. Muqtar looked down— tucked with the cash was the man's card.

Mohammed Rushi
Imam
77 S. 17th St.
Lahore, Pakistan
22 11 677 14 tel
Morushi@yahoo.com

Muqtar couldn't stop thinking about the Imam from his

hometown. The card, with its note offering help, made him uneasy. Did the cleric know about his past? Though tempted to toss it, he kept it as a reminder to stay cautious. Regret washed over him again—flunking out of NYU, killing Allen, wondering if the police still searched for him.

At the nursing home, he scanned the lobby, relieved to see no one suspicious. Then, out of nowhere, a man barreled around the corner, crashing into him. Fortunately, Muqtar was quick enough not to be bowled over. They locked eyes, faces inches apart—both recognizing each other from the wreck the day before. Muqtar shot Joshua an angry look.

"What the fuck, man?"

Joshua stepped back, ready to defend himself, but then Muqtar relaxed, put a hand on Joshua's shoulder, and laughed. "You weren't texting again, were you, man?"

"No, my dumb ass was trying to get to my grandfather's room on time," Joshua apologized, feeling stupid.

"No worries," Muqtar said, walking away.

Later, Julie texted—she had good news to share that night. Muqtar always picked up Junior at four. "Only an hour and a half before I hear something good. I sure could use it," he said to himself.

At the dispatcher's desk, the keys for cab 11 went up on the board.

"See you tomorrow, Brownie," the dispatcher said.

"Oh, by the way—the insurance adjuster came by. Guess how much the repair is gonna be?"

"I don't know. How much?"

"$5,300. Plus your $500 deductible."

"$5,300? What?"

"Yep. Unless you get it from that out-of-state guy who hit

you."

"Thanks for the great news. But hey, I did file with his insurance. And don't forget—tell Manuel to check the front brakes once my cab's fixed. They're squealing bad."

"That's not getting done by tomorrow, Brownie. What do you think this is—a real repair shop?" the dispatcher snorted.

"I don't know. One can always hope," Muqtar smiled.

One can always hope. The thought stuck with him as he drove to daycare. *There is hope for me,* he repeated, trying to believe it.

He parked, still bummed, and found the scrap of paper from Joshua—two times unlucky. He decided he'd call the next day to confirm the claim.

"Hello, son. How was your day?" he asked when Junior came running.

"Pretty good, Daddy, except I boo-booed," Junior said, pointing at his scraped forehead.

"Ouchie. That's quite a boo-boo," Muqtar said, pushing back Junior's curly hair, amazed how well the boy spoke.

Then Luz, Junior's caregiver, walked up.

"He was running on the playground and ran right into a pole," she explained.

"Is that what happened to you, son?"

"Yes," Junior nodded, arms stretched back. "I was running so fast I was almost flying, then I hit the pole."

"You have to watch where you're going," Muqtar cautioned. "Or you'll get more bumps."

"Yes, Daddy. But I was almost flying!"

"That's good. One day, you'll really learn to fly," dreamed

Muqtar. *Pilot someday? But then—do airlines do background checks? Would that be how my double life finally crumbles?* He shook it off. *I've been fingerprinted. I have a driver's license. I should be good. Should be.*

"Did you hit your head, too, Daddy?" Junior asked on the drive home.

"No, son. Why?"

"You look like you're in pain," Junior said, mimicking Muqtar's squinty look.

"No problem, son. I'm fine. You're pretty observant for not quite two. Soon we'll see what Mommy's cooked."

"Yum," Junior said. "Mommy cooks real good."

"Yum indeed, son. Yum indeed."

Julie's car was already there. *I hope she's had a good day. I could sure use her good news.*

"Hi, honey, we're home," he called as they walked in.

"Take your shoes off," Julie called. "Dinner'll be ready in twenty."

Junior raced off to build a Lego fort, and Muqtar went to greet Julie in the kitchen.

"How was nursing today?" he asked after kissing her.

"Full of hope and despair, as usual. And you?"

"Nothing worth repeating," he lied.

"You think you have an accent, honey?" Julie asked, stirring a pot.

"A little bit, baby," she went on. "Your mom must've had a strong accent when you were learning. That's why people from India or Pakistan speak with a British lilt—the Brits taught them."

"Is it that noticeable?"

"No, not at all. Are you uptight about it?"

"No, not really," he shrugged. "I just don't want to not fit in."

"No worries. Not in this house," Julie assured him.

He wasn't worried about home. It was the outside world—his accent, skin, beard. Even if he was fair for Pakistan, that only meant so much here. *Let's not go there,* he told himself.

"Did you have news for me, love?" he asked softly.

"Yes, I do!" Julie beamed. "You have an interview tomorrow with the head of nursing to be a paid assistant. Isn't that great?"

"I doubt it. She'll look at me, hear my accent, and say, 'Get out of here, sand nigger.'"

"What on earth's gotten into you?" Julie asked, appalled.

"You're in nursing school, getting all A's. Best of all, you have someone's recommendation—mine. You'll get it," Julie insisted, though her voice faltered. "Unless . . . you just want to drive cabs forever."

"You're right. I'm fit for the job. Ideally suited," he said, forcing positivity.

"That's the right attitude. Go in there tomorrow and kick its ass. Now go get your son, wash up, and let's eat!"

CHAPTER 14

Joshua woke up to a cold, cloudy day in St. Louis for early March 2024. He thought about his pending visit with his war hero grandfather and how World War II had started. *December 7th, a date which will live in infamy,* he recalled from President Roosevelt's speech. *What the hell were the Japanese thinking?*

His grandfather, Colonel Nathaniel Meister, had often sternly remarked, "The Japs knew of our industrial might, buying scrap steel and oil from us before the war. But when they invaded China, we cut off their supplies. So, they got pissed and decided to get even. Basically, they fucked with the bull and got the horns."

"What do you mean by that, Grampa?" Joshua remembered asking.

"We bombed the shit out of them; blew them off every island they occupied, all the way back across the Pacific. And we didn't stop there. We bombed the shit out of every major manufacturing center they had on their home islands and set up naval blockades surrounding the entire country. And as you know, we didn't stop there."

"So basically, Gramps, we were in a position to starve them out had we not decided to drop atomic bombs on Hiroshima and Nagasaki?"

"That's true, grandson, but we were in a mood to take revenge after Pearl Harbor. We wanted revenge, and the U.S. public was united behind getting it. In April 1945, the Germans had already been whipped, and the U.S. politicians feared that if we didn't end the war with Japan quickly, public sentiment would turn against them, and they'd get kicked out of office."

"So," Nathaniel continued, "when the Jewish scientists emigrated from Germany to the U.S., they brought with them the basic research on how to split the atom. When they got together with our scientists, two practical solutions on how to build a nuclear bomb that was deliverable came into being. The result was that two different bomb designs were used in building the A-bombs that were dropped on Hiroshima and Nagasaki."

"But that wasn't all we did to the Japs before they surrendered," he declared.

"What else did we do, Grampa?" Joshua inquired.

"I can't tell you the specifics, grandson. I'm sworn to secrecy. But I can tell you it didn't work out as planned."

Joshua puzzled over his grandfather's story, wondering if it was all just made up by an old soldier reliving his glory days. *Who knows?* he thought with a shrug.

Shaking off the thought, he headed out in search of coffee. After a moment's hesitation in the parking lot, he found his red VW GTI, noting it was a bit better than his own VW but not worth the money. *Money—he barely had enough to cover the $250 deductible on his wrecked car, let alone buy a new one.* No job, no prospects, and no real plan beyond visiting his grandfather before heading west to find his "destiny."

Joshua wondered where a jobless former CIA analyst with a knack for languages could go. He sighed, realizing he had no real prospects. He started the car, absentmindedly put on his seatbelt, and headed toward the VA, realizing only then what he forgot.

"Crap! I forgot to get some coffee!"

He punched "Starbucks" into the GPS and, after guzzling down a quick espresso, decided to explore St. Louis. Two hours later, he arrived at the J. Andrews Retirement Quarters, amused by the name "Happy Valley Retirement Home." It had peeling walls, flickering lights, and an unpleasant mix of smells. It wasn't terrible but far from "happy." As Joshua walked in, memories of his CIA firing resurfaced, reminding him that he sucked. *Maybe I was never suited for the agency,* he thought, *given that I didn't like killing.*

"Maggot, when you unholster that weapon, cock, aim, and fire. All in one motion—automatic. Like picking your nose or wiping your ass. I'm sure you got those down, don't you, homo?"

The drill sergeant brought to Langley to train the new recruits hadn't been very fond of Joshua or his pistol technique. Joshua preferred to unholster the weapon, rack the slide, aim, aim, aim, then fire. He was taught to fire only when ready, not before. His experience of wounding a deer when it twitched just as he fired was an experience he didn't want to repeat. Better to wait and be sure before firing—that was Joshua's rule.

"You dumb motherfucker! Were all the kids in your family retarded or just you? You take so much time aiming that by the time you get ready to shoot, your stupid ass will have been blown straight to hell. Which, by the way, you sissy bitch, is where you're going anyway and where you belong. Now do it again and do it right or I swear to God I will fucking shoot you myself!"

"Sir, yes, sir," Joshua offered meekly. So he resolved to shoot like Billy the Kid.

Snatching his Sig Sauer 9-millimeter out of the belt holster as fast as he could, Joshua chambered a round with his offhand without looking and began firing at the human silhouette some 25 feet away. The first round skipped off the ground about 10 feet in front of him, bounced up, and penetrated the target right in the groin. The second round hit the ceiling, ricocheted down, and hit the silhouette right between the eyes. The remaining seven were two chest shots, two lower torso hits, and three that went to places unknown.

Everyone on the firing line was watching. The drill sergeant cracked up laughing.

"Nice shooting, dipshit!" the sergeant screamed right in Joshua's ear. "You are fucking hopeless! Go back to typing, you pussy. You wouldn't qualify as a security guard at Walmart, you sorry puke! Get the fuck off my shooting range!"

"Sir, no, sir!" Joshua insisted respectfully, not willing to be denied. "I have one more chance to qualify."

Sergeant Wilson glared at Joshua, veins bulging from his forehead and temples. "Go ahead, you worthless sack of shit! You have seven seconds to drop the motherfucker, hitting the kill zone at least five times. You got that, bitch?" Wilson yelled.

"Sir, yes, sir. I understand," Joshua murmured.

"Then hurry the fuck up and be thinking about what fucking library you're going to work at next!"

Joshua hesitated, staring at the target, summoning his courage.

Pow! Pow! Pow! Pow!

Gunfire erupted in rapid succession from behind and to his left. Instinctively, Joshua dove to the right, hitting the ground at the first shot as he yanked out his gun. At the second shot, he rolled right and chambered a round. By the third, he aimed—ready to shoot the drill sergeant before the fourth round.

The sergeant cracked up laughing again. "Not bad reactions for a faggot. Why didn't you shoot me?"

"Sir, well, sir, you aren't my target at this time," Joshua responded defiantly.

"OK," grumped the sergeant. "Get your bitch ass up and see if you can hit the fucking target five times in the time allowed, which I doubt. Now, bitch!"

Joshua was furious and filled with self-doubt, wondering if he should just teach French. He steadied himself, preparing for more gunfire. When the curtain dropped, he drew, racked the slide, and fired nine shots in six seconds. Though he felt good about the timing, he had no clue where the bullets went. As the target reeled in, feelings of failure and desolation washed over him, his mind returning to his family's military legacy. *I want my mom.*

"Well, you lucky cocksucker," Sergeant Wilson bellowed. "Five fucking kill shots and all nine on target." The sergeant shook his head, looking away—Joshua swore he was smiling.

"All your bitch ass needed was a little motivation," the sergeant cackled. "You aren't the first piece of shit I've shown how to shoot," he declared proudly. "But it'll be your last fucking day on earth if you ever hesitate. Do you understand that, you dick-licking bastard?"

Feeling a whole lot better, Joshua replied evenly, "Sergeant, yes, sergeant." By now he was drenched in sweat and needed to pee. *Sorry-ass weak bladder.* He turned to leave.

"I didn't say you could leave the firing line yet, you fucking worm!" the sergeant shouted.

Joshua faced him, wondering about the punishment. The sergeant grinned, close enough for Joshua to smell coffee and tobacco. "You don't deserve it, but here's your certificate," he sneered, crushing Joshua's hand in a brutal handshake.

Now filled with pride and feeling cocky, Joshua shot back, "Sergeant, thank you, sergeant. I hope to see you in the field someday."

"I fucking well don't," the sergeant shouted. "The sight of your worthless ass sickens me."

So much for mellowing. "Now get the fuck off my shooting range so some real men can come in."

Joshua almost gave a military salute, then the finger, but thought better of both. He retreated respectfully, eyes on the sergeant, waiting for more grief, but the man ignored him.

Phew! Lucky to get out alive, much less as the top shooter of 60—pretty amazing for an amateur. *Maybe I did have my fore-bears' genes after all.* That thought made Joshua feel pretty good, and he slept very well that night.

As Joshua approached the front desk, his chest tightened, heart hammering in quick, unsteady beats. Seeing his only living relative was a big deal—the one person he truly cared about. Otherwise, he was alone, adrift.

No job, no plans beyond the West Coast. His small victory on the firing line didn't comfort him much. *Strange, sad life,* he thought, trying to size up the nurse at the desk CIA-style—no luck.

"Hello, Nurse Julie Brown," greeted Joshua, reading her name tag. "I'm Joshua Meister, here to see Colonel Nathaniel

Meister."

"Well, that's nice, Mr. Meister, but this isn't my station," Julie informed him. "Nurse Wyandotte will be here in a moment to assist you. Please sign the logbook and sit over there," she directed, pointing to a row of plastic chairs.

"Thank you, Nurse Brown," Joshua said, feeling stupid for announcing himself so boldly. He wrote his name, then sat.

When Nurse Wyandotte appeared, he quickly realized she was the one. Approaching her, he again introduced himself, though awkwardly. Nurse Wyandotte, mid-20s, hair in a knot, decent figure, seemed normal, and he failed to size her up like a good analyst.

She barely looked up. "Hello and no . . . How can I help you, sir?"

A bit embarrassed, Joshua hurried: "Yes, ma'am. I'm Joshua Meister, here to visit Colonel Nathaniel Meister."

"Is he expecting you?" she asked, glancing at her watch.

"Uh, no, not really," he stammered. "I'm his grandson from D.C., thought I'd just pop in."

Oh, God. What a dumbass. Why did I say that? Two stupid comments in a row.

"Just popped in, huh?" Nurse Wyandotte repeated, smiling slightly and studying his face.

"If you'll have a seat over there," she said, pointing back, "I'll check with the Colonel. What's your name again?" She pulled out a pen.

"Joshua Meister, ma'am. The Colonel is my grandfather," he repeated, trying to sound convincing.

She wrote it down, checked the log, then disappeared. Five minutes later, she returned smiling.

"The Colonel is in good spirits and looking forward to seeing his grandson. Follow me."

As they walked, she reminded him it was everyone's duty to care for veterans, that the VA served nearly 40 million American vets.

"So," she concluded with a smile, "be sure to thank your grandfather for his service. Men like him are why we're free today."

"I'll do that, Nurse Wyandotte. Gladly," Joshua said. As she unlocked the door to Room 106, he took the chance to check her out from behind—in two ways. *I'm so clever with my word play,* he thought, praising himself. From behind and her behind—and Miss Wyandotte had a nice one.

Ah, well. Maybe later.

CHAPTER 15

Colonel Nathaniel Meister, whom Joshua called Grampa because *grandfather* always sounded too formal—and was too hard to say when he was a little kid—was standing on the far side of his room, looking out the window. Joshua saw the old man leaning on the windowsill, slightly bent over, looking toward the west. Quite tall for a man of his generation, more than six feet, Nathaniel still cut a good silhouette.

Colonel Meister didn't hear Joshua enter the room; age and the roar of airplane engines during World War II had damaged his hearing. Joshua slowly walked across the room so as not to startle the war hero. Nathaniel stood bolt upright by the window ledge, gaze fixed far away. He didn't hear the slight creaking of the wooden floor as Joshua crossed or the window rattling from the wind. Many years of deafening bomb blasts and machine-gun fire had taken his hearing. Now his world was silent where sound once lived. Joshua looked back at Nurse Wyandotte as the door closed, then called out loudly.

"Grampa, it's me, your grandson, Joshua Meister."

Nathaniel turned from the window and saw Joshua standing nearby. His face lit up with a big smile.

"Joshua! How good of you to pop in to see me," Nathaniel said with a twinkle in his eye, obviously having some fun with what Nurse Wyandotte had told him about Joshua's *pop in* visit.

"Yes, Grampa, that's correct. I drove halfway across the country to pop in to see you," Joshua laughed, face turning red.

"It is great to see ya. Come here and give me a hug."

Joshua stepped up and they embraced tightly, holding on for a long moment. When they finally parted, they reminisced about the past and caught up on the present, savoring their time together. Nathaniel forgot his aches, loneliness, and guilt, while Joshua let go of the weight of being fired, a lost love, and an uncertain future.

Seeing his grandfather, cigarette in hand, stirred a bittersweet ache in Joshua. He longed for the days when his grandfather would pull into the driveway in a shiny convertible, inviting him along for a ride. Now he felt a pang of sadness and shame, knowing those moments were gone—and he couldn't return the favor.

"Hey, old man."

"Hey, kid."

"Whatcha doing?"

"Smoking a cigarette. What are you doing?"

"I'm driving to California and thought I'd stop by here and say hi."

"Your life must be pretty slow if the best thing you can come up with to do is drive to California and swing through St. Louis on the way."

"That's a real nice thing to say, Grampa."

"Yeah, well, maybe so. But things are really slow around here, and I'm losing my mind, so I'm feeling a little bitter."

"That isn't my fault, Grampa. If you don't want me to stay, I'll take off."

"No, I don't want you to go. I'm sorry for being rude."

"No problem, Grampa. I just caught you at a bad time."

"Most times are bad times for me these days, grandson."

"Well, you seem OK to me right now."

"I am OK right now, but I could slip off into the netherworld at any moment."

"That sucks, Grampa."

"Sure does, grandson. Now why the hell are you here?" he repeated, giving Joshua the look of a man who'd heard his bullshit before.

"I'm on my way to California."

"Aren't you supposed to be working in Washington, D.C.?"

"I was, Grampa," Joshua admitted, looking down at his shoes, "but I got fired."

"How come? Couldn't get your happy ass out of bed on time?"

God, my life is like an open book, thought Joshua. *Everybody, including my grandfather, knows I'm a worthless slacker.*

"Yes, sir. That's right. My ex-boss was a military prick who didn't do shit and couldn't figure out shit—except how to get to work on time to cover his worthless ass. Fucking Colonel Klink."

As Joshua said that, he felt like spitting on an imaginary image of his prick former boss.

Nathaniel was quiet for a moment.

"In my time, most of those military guys, especially the big brass, were better at covering shit up and burying it than figuring shit out and dealing with it."

Nathaniel flicked his ciggy ashes into an ashtray and turned to face Joshua directly.

"The government has sent a few guys around here to check on me lately. I think they must be spiking my food or something, because it was after they came by that I started feeling so loopy."

"What? That doesn't make sense, Grampa. You served our

country for fifty years and you're a war hero. What could they possibly want with you?" Joshua asked indignantly.

"I have no clue, sonny," the Colonel said, shaking his head. "Well, actually, I do know—and I promised I'd never tell. But I've decided I'm going to tell you," he finished, looking Joshua straight in the eye.

Gosh, Joshua thought. *Grampa's either going crazy or senile or something.* But he was looking with a steady gaze, and Joshua wasn't getting a weird vibe. *What could Grampa be wanting to tell me?*

"I'm listening."

No response.

"I've missed you, old man."

"I've missed you too, grandson. I was thinking about you earlier after I got your letter saying you were coming. It has to have been nearly five years since we last saw each other."

"That's right, Grampa; at Dad's funeral. Then before that, I saw you in D.C. when the Army brought you in to give you a medal—meritorious conduct, or some such thing," Joshua teased, knowing full well his grandfather had been given the Medal of Honor.

"Meritorious conduct, my ass!" huffed Nathaniel. "How about getting a medal for getting shot down, shot at, captured, bayonetted, escaping a Nazi prison camp, then going back to the camp to free a bunch of guys?"

"I know, Grampa. I'm just teasing. Everyone in our family is super proud that the government finally recognized how brave you were to go back and free those men after you'd already escaped. The question I've always had," Joshua said as he pulled out a desk chair and sat while his grandfather sat on the edge of the bed, "is why did you do it?"

"Why did I do it? Why did I do it?" Nathaniel interrogated himself, a faraway look crossing his face. "Well, I did it because it was the right thing to do."

"OK," agreed Joshua, deciding to probe a bit. "What was right about it?"

"Are you really that fucking stupid, grandson, to ask a question like that? Are you really?" Nathaniel snapped in a disgusted tone.

"If you'd joined the Air Force like I told you instead of going to work for the fucking CIA, you'd know what it means to have brothers. Not brothers as in came from the same mom, but brothers you'd give your life for; that you'd fought with, ate with, lived and died with. Brave sons of bitches, every one of those bastards I went back and got."

By the time Nathaniel finished, his jaw was clenched and his nostrils flared, his face darkening to a furious shade of crimson red. He was pissed.

"Sorry, Grampa. I wasn't questioning what you did—just trying to find out more of what motivated you," Joshua apologized.

"I knew that each and every one of those men would've done the exact same thing for me that I did for them, and that's what made it the right thing to do," Nathaniel said emphatically, remembering each of those faces he freed, along with the many who'd died along the way.

"Can I ask you more questions about the war, Grampa?" Joshua quietly ventured.

"Sure. Go ahead. Just don't ask any more dumbass questions," Nathaniel warned.

"I'll do my best. OK, Grampa, you'd been through all that combat in Germany, been shot down, captured, and escaped," Joshua recounted. "What made you decide to go fight the Japanese?"

Nathaniel, eyeing Joshua warily, still pissed, eased up.

"Decide to go? Oh hell no, I didn't decide shit. I was an experienced bombardier—had dropped bombs from all the bombers we had, including the B-29 Superfortress, the one shot out from under me over Germany. After I made it back to the States, I was asked where I wanted to go for some R&R," Nathaniel recalled, settling into his story.

"It just so happened that B-29s were being ferried to the Solomon Islands and the Philippines to fight the Japs by way of Hawaii. My commanding officer told us my crew and I would fly one from Washington state, where they were built, to Hawaii. Drop ourselves off for a vacation and let another crew fly it on to wherever it needed to go," he explained.

Joshua was fascinated—he'd never heard this part.

"So we get to Honolulu, land the plane, and go into town to have some fun. But damned if some Navy shore patrol guys didn't show up and hustle us back to base," Nathaniel lamented. "Shit, we'd only been there an hour or two, but the party was over."

Not wanting to seem more of a dumbass, Joshua hesitated, then asked, "What do you mean, 'the party was over'?"

"What I mean is," Nathaniel raised his voice, "those fuckers stateside tricked us. Thought we'd land in Hawaii and vacation. But the Navy guys showed us our orders—they said we were to leave at 0500 the next morning and fly to the Mariana Islands. I was so pissed," he finished, shaking his head.

"But," Nathaniel added with a sigh, "orders are orders. That's how I ended up fighting the fucking Japs, too. But I'll say, after what those sneaky bastards did at Pearl Harbor, I didn't mind dropping bombs on them. Payback, you know."

"I understand. How many missions did you fly in the Pacific, Grampa?"

"Eleven, plus one special one right at the end."

"What? What do you mean, one special one?"

Nathaniel looked directly at Joshua, eyes piercing.

"I was sworn to secrecy about that one, grandson. Sworn to secrecy by General MacArthur himself."

"Oh, Grampa," Joshua said sympathetically. "I understand. I took an oath myself when I joined the CIA."

"I'm not talking about some bullshit oath to keep secret how many US citizens' phone records you looked at illegally," Nathaniel snapped.

"Sorry, Grampa," Joshua said, looking away, slightly pissed at the insult. "I wasn't trying to offend you."

"You didn't offend me, grandson. It's just that . . . I've kept a terrible secret for nearly eighty years . . . a terrible secret," Nathaniel's voice trailed off. He turned to the window, shaking, making sounds like he was crying. Joshua had never seen him cry—not even when his wife died.

Joshua walked over, put his hand on Nathaniel's shoulder. "Is there anything I can do to help?" he asked softly.

"No, no, there isn't, grandson," Nathaniel said firmly. "Nothing anyone can do to fix what I did at the end of the war."

Joshua frowned, puzzled. Watching the strongest man he'd ever known sob like a child left him feeling helpless and adrift. *What could Grampa's secret possibly be?*

He sat on the bed to wait. Minutes later, Nathaniel turned, lit a cigarette, and sat too. Taking Joshua's hands, he cleared his throat.

"I was the bombardier of the B-29 that, on 12 August 1945, dropped a hydrogen bomb on Tokyo. Not atomic bombs like Hiroshima or Nagasaki. A hydrogen bomb," he said, clearly enunciating *hydrogen*.

"But it didn't go off!" Nathaniel exclaimed. "And I believe it still sits at the bottom of Tokyo Bay all these years later."

Holy shit. Joshua was stunned. The U.S. dropped a hydrogen bomb meant to wipe out Tokyo three days before Japan formally surrendered? And it might still be there?

CHAPTER 16

Joshua struggled to process what he'd just heard. A hydrogen bomb, dropped on Tokyo three days before the Japanese surrendered—and still lying at the bottom of Tokyo Bay? He opened his mouth, but nothing came out. His head spun with confusion and amazement.

"Grampa, how do you know the bomb is still sitting on the bottom of Tokyo Bay?" Joshua finally managed.

"Well, have you ever heard of one being pulled out of Tokyo Bay, grandson?" Nathaniel replied with a sly look.

"No, I surely haven't, Grampa. But on the other hand, I never heard we dropped a hydrogen bomb on Tokyo until five minutes ago either," Joshua pointed out.

"Good point, grandson. Good point," Nathaniel sighed. "The reason I know it's still there is because the co-pilot of that B-29 is still alive. We used to stay in touch. After the war, he went to work for the CIA, and from time to time he'd say to me, 'Our baby still hasn't been born,' and stuff like that. I knew exactly what he meant."

"When's the last time you heard from him, Grampa?"

"Probably about five years ago, just after they moved me in here," Nathaniel recalled. "He called and asked me the coordinates of where the bomb hit the ground in Tokyo . . ."

Nathaniel's voice trailed off again as he looked away, a haunted expression clouding his face.

Joshua sat there stunned, silent for several minutes. Eventually he found his voice.

"Why'd he ask where the bomb hit the ground when you just said it hit the water?"

Nathaniel whipped around to face Joshua. "Because I lied about where it hit. Yes. Like I was there looking through my bombsight right now—I know exactly where it hit."

"So, if you flew over Tokyo Bay or looked at a map, could you put an X where it hit?" Joshua pressed, leaning forward, eyes narrowed.

"Better than that, grandson. I've got the exact coordinates burned into my brain, and I wrote them down too. And even better," Nathaniel went on with a sly grin, "as I said a minute ago, when the brass asked for the coordinates afterward, I gave them the wrong ones on purpose."

At that, Nathaniel started chuckling, clearly amused by his decades-old deception.

"Why'd you lead them astray, Grampa?" Joshua asked, thoroughly confused.

"Most of those assholes were scum from the start, that's why, Joshua. The pilot was a Major named Morrissey—a real pretty boy, son of somebody famous. All excited to take over the mission from the Captain who normally flew the aircraft. Morrissey kept bragging on the way to Tokyo, saying this mission would make him a hero, that he'd get the Medal of Honor. Payback is a bitch. Shit like that."

"What happened to him, Grampa?" Joshua followed up.

"Well, he was damned disappointed when that bomb didn't go off, I'll tell you that. All his bullshit bravado sank right down to the bottom of Tokyo Bay," Nathaniel finished, almost gleeful, a note of sarcastic satisfaction in his voice.

"In fact, even though protocol was to drop the weapon, arm it on the way down, and get the hell out before it exploded, douchebag Morrissey flew around and around for probably forty minutes trying to make it go off. Getting us shot at the whole time before finally turning for home."

"So why didn't you tell him where it hit?" Joshua pushed gently.

"Because I didn't like or trust the cocksucker, that's why," Nathaniel said flatly. "And for years, anytime those CIA assholes came to whatever base I was assigned, I gave them the wrong coordinates too."

Joshua was still puzzled. "OK, Grampa, but I don't get it. If people from our own government wanted you to tell them where the hydrogen bomb was, why wouldn't you tell them?"

"Because they'd have fucking killed me too—like they did to nearly everyone else on that flight, that's why," Nathaniel justified.

"How many guys were in the crew that day, Grampa?"

"Not a full crew—we only had one bomb to drop. Let's see . . . there was the pilot, Major Morrissey, co-pilot Abe Winter, navigator Joe Angleton, me, and the two guys working the winches, John Schneider and James Andrews."

"And you said they're all gone now, didn't you?"

"Yep, sure did. Those three—Angleton, Schneider, Andrews—died right after the war. But the fucking pilot, co-pilot, and me did not. And you know why those two weren't killed, grandson?" Nathaniel peered hard at Joshua.

"Because . . . they know where the bomb is too?" Joshua guessed carefully.

"No, hell no, Joshua. I thought you were supposed to be fucking smart. I'm the only motherfucker on the planet who knows where that goddamned bomb is," Nathaniel shouted. "You got that?"

Joshua hung his head, ashamed. "Uh, yes sir, I do. Is it because they're war heroes?"

"No, you stupid motherfucker!" Nathaniel roared again. "It's because the government thinks that cocksucker Morrissey or somebody like him might be able to weasel it out of me someday. Now do you get it? Jesus," he muttered, turning away to the window again.

"Sorry, Grampa. I'm still trying to put all this together," Joshua said quietly.

Speaking over his shoulder now, Nathaniel went on. "Sorry, grandson, I got carried away. They didn't kill Abe because he came from a very prominent Jewish family in New York with lots of political connections."

But still pissed at Joshua's slow understanding, Nathaniel turned back, voice sharp again.

"Look, we dropped an atomic bomb on Hiroshima on August 6, 1945—nicknamed Little Boy. You got that?"

"Yes, Grampa."

"On August 9, we dropped a second atomic bomb on Nagasaki. That one was called Fat Man. Did they teach you that at your fancy university?" he asked, sarcasm dripping.

"Yes, Grampa," Joshua answered meekly.

"On August 15, the Japs formally surrendered."

"I know that too," Joshua offered.

"Well, what you don't fucking know is that our military geniuses didn't want the Emperor of Japan to live. They were afraid he'd start some holy war once we occupied Japan. So to get rid of him, the military made a plan to drop a hydrogen bomb on the Emperor's Palace. It was named Payback."

"A hydrogen bomb, Grampa?"

"Yes indeed. A hydrogen bomb. The first of its kind."

"Excuse me, Grampa," Joshua interrupted, fearing another barrage of expletives, "but we didn't develop the hydrogen bomb until the early 1950s."

"Well, no shit, Sherlock. That's what we're supposed to believe. But, according to the bomb rigger Al Beattie, Payback had all the good shit in it—just like a modern H-bomb. That's why it's so fucking valuable. The U.S. didn't want, and doesn't want today, anyone to find it but us," Nathaniel disclosed.

"A lot of sorry motherfuckers in the world, including our so-called allies, would love to see how that bomb is put together," he continued. "And a lot more would love to get their hands on it because there's enough plutonium inside to blow up a bunch of shit. Now do you understand?"

"Yes, I do understand now," Joshua said, the full impact finally taking shape in his mind. "So what day was this mission?"

"12 August 1945 at 0200 Pacific time is when we took off. Dropped the bomb at 1215."

Joshua leaned in, eyes narrowed, every word drawing him closer to the truth. "Where did it hit?"

"That's the secret now, isn't it, boy? That's the secret. You know more about where it hit than anyone else in the world other than me," Nathaniel replied, grinning impishly. "But it, for sure, didn't come down where I told the brass it did. And guess what?"

"What?"

"You're going to go find it."

Joshua's mouth opened but no words came out. He nearly fell backward from the shock. Eyebrows knitted together, eyes blinking, trying to process it all. A tense silence filled the room.

Nathaniel, seemingly oblivious to Joshua's stunned state, sat on the bed, swung his legs up on the mattress, and ordered, "Leave me now, Joshua. I'm tired. Be here tomorrow at 0800 sharp, Joshua. I'll tell you more then. Chow is at 0700. I'll be waiting here after that."

"One more question, Grampa, please," Joshua croaked.

"OK. What?"

"Why again was the bomb called Payback?"

"Because it was to pay those scurrilous bastards back for Pearl Harbor."

Joshua nodded, understanding. As he looked around, he thought he saw a shadow slip under the door.

"Jesus, I'm getting paranoid too, seeing shadows and shit," Joshua muttered. With that, he turned, opened the door, and stepped out.

He scanned the hallway up and down but saw no one. He could barely focus as he walked, mind racing. Stunned, excited, and a little scared at the prospect of learning more about this hydrogen bomb mission, Joshua wondered, *Have I already heard more than I wanted to hear?*

Now on to the real question, he thought. *Is Grampa crazy—or did all of this actually happen?* His mind flipped back and forth, wavering between the two possibilities.

CHAPTER 17

After Joshua left the nursing home, Muqtar started thinking about what Joshua had told him about his grandfather, Colonel Nathaniel in Room 106. He couldn't recall anything the Colonel had ever said that was particularly peculiar or odd, just the occasional old-guy outbursts about the sad state of America, or how the U.S. doesn't fight wars to win anymore, only to feed the war machine, and so on.

After he and Joshua parted ways, Muqtar bumped into his wife in the hallway.

"Hey, Julie, have you heard or noticed anything unusual about Colonel Nathaniel in Room 106?"

"Noticed anything unusual? Anything like what?" Julie responded.

"Anything about past events, war stories, stuff like that," Muqtar pressed.

Julie paused, thinking for a few seconds. "No, nothing comes to mind. Why?"

"Well, do you remember seeing the guy who came in here earlier today to visit Colonel Nathaniel?"

"I do remember that guy—a good-looking guy at that," Julie said, winking.

"The guy who came by earlier is his grandson, Joshua," she went on, speaking slowly as she recalled the encounter. "I met him today at the front. Seemed like a nice enough guy, but nothing remarkable," she added. "Why do you ask?"

"I don't know why," puzzled Muqtar. "And what were you do-ing noticing that he was a good-looking guy anyway?"

Julie laughed. "Nothing. Nothing, dear. Did you notice some-thing odd?"

"Yes. The Colonel was shouting a couple of times while he and his grandson were visiting in his room. What he was shout-ing sounded like a war story or something." Muqtar's voice fad-ed as he tried to recall more.

Julie was still thinking. "I've seen a lot of these old war vets re-live their experiences—sometimes as if they're in battle right then. But no, nothing unusual about Colonel Meister's behavior crosses my mind. Sorry, honey."

Confused by what he'd overheard between Joshua and the Colonel, Muqtar decided to confront Colonel Meister directly. He knocked and introduced himself, but the Colonel snapped at him to go away. As Muqtar walked off, he heard the Colonel speaking again. Bold enough to listen, he pressed his ear to the door. What he heard was astonishing: the Colonel was going through a pre-flight checklist, giving both the commands and responses himself.

"Fuel level outer tank starboard side."

"Full, check."

"Fuel tank outer tank port side."

"Full, check."

"Bomb doors operational."

"Bomb doors operational, check."

Strange, thought Muqtar.

Then Nathaniel continued.

"What the fuck do you mean I dropped the bomb too early?"

"Yes, you did, you stupid motherfucker."

"You're the stupid motherfucker, Morrissey. You didn't arm the motherfucker like you were supposed to."

"Meister, you stupid motherfucker. You're going to be court-martialed because you deliberately dropped the bomb too early."

"Fuck you, Morrissey. No, I didn't."

Muqtar stood there nervously, scanning the hallway to see if anyone noticed him eavesdropping. Finally, he muttered, "Fuck it. I'm out of here," and walked away, shaking his head. I need to get to the bottom of this mystery, he thought. What bomb was dropped too early? With how his grandson was gushing earlier, I'm sure there's more to this than an old vet just replaying a wartime story.

Meanwhile, inside, Nathaniel stopped and shook his head, realizing he'd been talking out loud about the day he dropped a hydrogen bomb on Tokyo. God, I must be losing it, he chastised himself. Blabbering about what happened on that flight, holding the biggest secret of all time—reckless and stupid.

Despite his doubts, Nathaniel's memory of that final mission from Tinian Island remained crystal clear.

The Mission

"What time do we leave in the a.m., Major?" Nathaniel asked at the preflight briefing.

"0200."

"What's our target, Major?"

"Classified until in the air, Nate," was the reply.

Nathaniel glanced around the briefing room—a simple

thatched-roof hut with a dirt floor and mismatched tables and chairs all facing a large chalkboard. Normally, the board listed flight assignments, targets, schedules, but today it was blank. The only men present were the six crew members of *Tiger Droppings*, a name sarcastically coined by their pilot, Major James Morrissey.

Morrissey was a hardened veteran, known for ditching his shot-up bomber in the ocean during a Germany mission and surviving thanks to a French fishing boat and an American Navy vessel. Though he'd been awarded a Silver Star, Morrissey bragged about it as if he'd single-handedly won the war.

"Anything else we need to know, Major?" Nathaniel tried, hoping to catch a clue about this strange briefing.

"No, nothing," barked Morrissey. "Just don't get shit-faced tonight on that palm tree hooch you've been concocting, Nate. I want all you motherfuckers on top of your game tomorrow morning. I'll tell you this: tomorrow morning's mission is the most important mission of World War II. So be ready."

Major Morrissey dismissed the group, leaving Nathaniel confused by his claim that this was the *most important mission of WWII*. He doubted Morrissey's ego-driven words, but who knew. Later that night, an enlisted man knocked on Nathaniel's door at 0100, reminding him of the time. Despite many harrowing missions in enemy territory, Nathaniel felt a strange sense of fear, cursing himself for it.

What the hell is wrong with me? he wondered, disgusted. Am I losing my nerve? My appetite for war? Nothing can happen to me that hasn't already been done. He wasn't afraid of being captured—he thought the Japanese were amateurs at torture compared to the Nazis. Still, the unease lingered. Dying? Sharks if we ditch? Who knows. Doesn't matter anyway—I have no choice but to get on that plane. With a shrug, he stood and headed out the door.

The early morning of 12 August 1945 was clear and moon-lit. The sky stretched forever, a crisp full moon casting a silver glow that threw sharp-edged shadows on the ground. On the runway sat the waiting B-29. Nearby, a truck arrived carrying a large metal box, escorted by armed soldiers in jeeps and two civilian-filled Plymouths.

Walking toward the flight line, Nathaniel watched the procession. *What the hell kind of bomb load is this?* he wondered, eyeing the box. Better check it out. As he approached, soldiers in the jeeps noticed.

"Halt and identify yourself!" Nathaniel heard. The moonlight glinted off the barrels of several machine guns pointed straight at him. He stopped, showed his dog tags, and said, "Lieutenant Nathaniel Meister, U.S. Army Air Force. I'm the bombardier who's going to drop whatever the fucking thing is in that box."

"Yes, sir. Sorry, sir. Taking precautions, sir. Top secret mission, sir," reported one soldier as they lowered their weapons and moved aside.

Nathaniel walked around the big box, now being disassembled by the non-uniformed men. Once a side was removed, he peered in—there was the biggest bomb he'd ever seen. Though he couldn't see its full shape, it had to be at least six feet wide and ten or twelve feet long. Not really round or shaped like a typical 500- or 1,000-pounder; more like a cylinder with two poles sticking out each end.

"That doesn't look very aerodynamic," Nathaniel remarked to no one in particular. The civilians kept working, ignoring him. So he moved to the bomb bay doors of the B-29 to see how this monster was going to fit.

He noticed the bay had been reconfigured—racks replaced by a strange mounting rig with four poles meant to cradle the bomb. As he stood contemplating it, a civilian approached.

"Are you the bombardier?"

Nathaniel turned. "Why, yes, I am. Who are you?"

"I'm the man who designed and built the bomb bay mechanism for this weapon," the civilian replied flatly.

"Oh, OK. Anything I need to know in particular?"

"Yes. From the time you hit the switch to release the weapon, there'll be a two-second delay before it actually drops," the civilian explained, gesturing upward.

"Shit, really? Now I've gotta calculate and factor in a two-second delay so it hits where it's supposed to?"

"Yes, Lieutenant. But really, this drop doesn't have to be pinpoint perfect," the man added cryptically.

That puzzled Nathaniel. If precision wasn't critical, why him—one of the best bombardiers around? The civilian continued, saying the bomb was more than just a weapon; it was designed for *revenge*. Payback. When Nathaniel pressed for details, the man confirmed it was to avenge Pearl Harbor. As he walked away, he tossed over his shoulder, "After today, your life will be completely changed."

Jesus Christ. What does that even mean—*life completely changed?* Nathaniel thought angrily. I don't want change. I want normal. A house, a wife, four kids, a job—is that too much to ask?

Pissed by the prospect of change he didn't want, he briefly considered faking sick or disappearing before takeoff but dismissed it. Orders were orders. For a moment, he touched that cold, scared place inside. *Maybe this is the day I die.* With that grim thought, he began suiting up.

The airfield was eerily quiet. No crews loading bombs or fuel—just a company of Marines with machine guns guarding the B-29. Peculiar, Nathaniel thought, given how the lead-up had been anything but normal.

Hoping for answers, he checked the command hut—empty. The civilians' barracks were deserted too, beds made, no sign anyone had ever been there. Back at the flight line, he was again stopped by Marines.

"Who are you, sir, and your connection to this aircraft?"

"Lieutenant Nathaniel Meister. Bombardier. Here's my ID."

"Yes, sir. Proceed," they replied, saluting and stepping aside.

Nathaniel climbed aboard. He noticed Morrissey deep in conversation with a civilian. Tired of sleuthing, he moved to the bomb bay. Two forklifts lifted the bomb into place. The same civilian with the dual control boxes adjusted thick chains from ceiling-mounted winches, hooking them to the bomb's poles. Once hoisted, the aircraft groaned under the weight.

"Payback time," the civilian muttered, admiring his work. He reminded Nathaniel about the two-second delay but offered no details on the actual target. Annoyed, Nathaniel hoped Morrissey would shed light.

Then he overheard Morrissey.

"Listen, Major, you don't have orders to drop the weapon yet. You'll approach the target, radio mission command with your position. If, and only if, you're given permission, do you proceed," the civilian emphasized.

"Got it. Establish position, radio in, confirm authority, then bombs away."

"Right—except don't assume you'll get permission. Understood?"

"Yes, Mr. Ridgeway. Wait for permission. If granted, drop the bomb. If denied, return to base."

"Correct. Good luck. You may make history today."

The civilian walked off. Morrissey climbed in.

"Ready to go?" Nathaniel asked, taking his bombardier seat.

Morrissey turned, eyes wild. "We're gonna win the war today, Meister. No shit. It's payback time. When we drop this mother-fucker on that nip Emperor's Palace and blow his ass to hell, the war's over. We'll be the biggest fucking heroes of the war."

"Oh, really," Nathaniel sneered. "I fucking doubt that."

"Doubt it if you want, dipshit," Morrissey shot back. "When this bomb goes off, you'll see."

Then he snapped, "Just make sure you dial in that two-second delay. Got it?"

"Yes, Major. I know my fucking job," Nathaniel growled.

The crew took their positions. Engines roared to life. As they climbed, Nathaniel noticed *Payback* painted on the bomb. Now he understood the mission. Morrissey radioed, "Mission: Cherry Blossom; Target: Tokyo." Then shouted, "Here we come, you yellow pieces of shit. Payback time! Kill the emperor! Bombs away!" Nathaniel thought, *Payback . . . for Pearl Harbor. Got it.*

As the bomber rose to 29,000 feet over a starry sea, Nathaniel's mind churned. This was their sixth Tokyo run in ten days, but this bomb felt different—heavier, with a gravity all its own. His unease deepened. Checking his watch, he waited for Morrissey's voice.

"Commence bombing run."

Nathaniel flipped on the bombsight. Ocean, ships. He felt oddly calm. Duty or conscience? He wrestled inside. Then Morrissey's voice again.

"Open bomb bay doors."

Wind howled. Any second now. His conscience screamed:

Drop it now. Don't kill the emperor. Millions don't deserve to die. NOW!

As Tokyo Bay came into view, turbulence rocked the plane. Nathaniel's finger hit the button.

He watched the bomb fall, splash, and sink. He quickly scribbled the true coordinates on a matchbook, tucked it into his pocket. Morrissey's shrieking came through his headset.

"You stupid motherfucker! What the fuck is wrong with you?!"

Nathaniel stayed silent. Morrissey ran back, screaming with a map. "Show me where it hit. Show me or I'll have you arrested for treason!"

Calm, Nathaniel pointed to dry land far from the bay. Morrissey rushed back to compute. Nathaniel hid a smile—he'd protected Tokyo from utter destruction.

As flak peppered the sky, Morrissey ranted, accusing Nathaniel of treason, vowing prison or worse. Nathaniel coolly retorted that if Morrissey had done *his* job, the bomb would've gone off. Morrissey snarled, turned back to the controls, and ordered radio silence.

Nathaniel exhaled. He had just saved millions—though at what cost to himself, he didn't yet know.

CHAPTER 18

The sun was out in full force when the B-29 smoothly landed on Tinian, just as pretty much everyone on the base was out. Nathaniel looked out a window and saw soldiers and ground crewmen everywhere, watching the aircraft as she taxied to the command center. He couldn't see all of their faces, but the ones he did catch were shaking their heads, spitting on the ground, or flipping the bird at its occupants.

Nathaniel waited for the rest of the crew to disembark before he climbed down. As he stepped off the ladder facing the aircraft, the air was thick and heavy with hostility, hot and humid in the early afternoon sun. A few gave him sympathetic looks, but most sent angry, dark expressions his way. The word had already spread: Nathaniel had purposely dropped the bomb too early.

This might be the last time I see anything as a free man, he thought, a chill running through him.

To his left, Morrissey was animatedly talking to the base commander. To his right, the four civilians who had supervised the bomb loading were already approaching. The rest of the crew had scattered.

What do I say? Nathaniel wondered. He resolved to stick to his story, knowing it wouldn't be long before someone asked him to explain.

"Nathaniel, we want you to tell us what happened over Tokyo," commanded the youngest of them, a tall, slim man.

"Tim, is it?" Nathaniel asked, eyeing the name on his ID tag.

"Yes," nodded Tim. "Tim Hennessy. Tell us what happened," he said, now joined by the other three, all crowding around Nathaniel.

"Is it permissible for me to talk to you civilians before I go through flight debriefing?" Nathaniel tried.

"We're not just civilians," Tim snapped back. "We're soldiers, just like you, plucked out of active duty to oversee the development and deployment of the weapon you just dropped—unsuccessfully, I take it."

He paused, eyes narrowing. "The four of us are engineers by training, and just so you know, we all served in active combat before being put on this team."

"What team is that?" Nathaniel wanted to know.

"The H-bomb team, Nathaniel. We were selected to take the most powerful bomb the U.S. has ever built and figure out how to fit it into a B-29 and how to trigger it without destroying the plane that dropped it."

Tim stepped closer, sending daggers with his eyes. Slowly, emphatically, and with contempt, he added, "We did our job. Why didn't you do yours?"

"I don't know what to tell you, Tim," Nathaniel stuttered apologetically. "I was told the target was the Japanese Emperor's Palace. We were flying on a direct path to the palace when we hit some turbulence that made me hit the button, and down she went," he muttered, hands dropping in a motion that traced the bomb's path.

"So why didn't the bomb go off anyway?" demanded one of the other men, voice sharp.

"I don't know. I don't have a fucking clue," Nathaniel stammered. "The Major said it was because he had to send a signal to the bomb, and by me dropping the big mother too early, he wasn't able to send it," Nathaniel explained with a helpless shrug.

"Wait a minute," Tim said, holding up a hand. He and the others stepped away, huddling for a quick, whispered conference. A few minutes later, they came back.

In a lighter tone, Tim asked, "Can you show me the device the Major told you would send a signal to the bomb, Nathaniel?"

"Sure. If he left it on the plane, sure."

Nathaniel climbed aboard, rummaged around, and found the device—something like a phone. He handed it to Tim after stepping back onto the tarmac. Morrissey was nowhere in sight. Tim flicked a switch that lit up a red bulb and asked if Nathaniel had ever seen that red light during the flight.

"All I knew was about the two-second delay," Nathaniel replied. When pressed for details, he described the bombing run: 15 miles from Tokyo at 29,000 feet, bomb bay doors open, accidentally hit the release button when the turbulence hit. The bomb dropped two seconds later.

"How long did it fall before it hit the ground?" Tim moved in, practically nose-to-nose.

"Let me think." Nathaniel looked skyward, replaying it. "The plane lurched, I hit the button, the Major started screaming. I looked away, then tracked it. My best guess—40 to 45 seconds from release to impact."

"OK. Now recall as best you can, Lieutenant, what was Major Morrissey doing during this forty-second period?" Tim enunciated each word.

"Oh, I don't fucking know for sure," Nathaniel addressed all four. "He was just screaming at me, so after a while I looked back through the bombsight and ignored him. I don't know what he did."

"Did you ever hear him say 'system armed, signal sent?'" another man prompted.

"Nope. He never said anything like that."

"Did he say 'signal sent, system armed?'" Tim corrected.

"Nope. Nothing like that. The Major just kept cussing at me, calling me a traitor, saying I'd be court-martialed and hung, that I dropped it early on purpose. Shit like that."

"When you looked at the Major for those few seconds, did he have *this* in his hand?" Tim asked, holding up the device.

"No," Nathaniel said, thinking. "Now that I really think on it, he never picked that up until after the bomb hit the ground—when we turned around trying to retrace our route. That was more than five minutes later."

"He never took it out of the bag until after the bomb hit?" Tim repeated incredulously, shaking the device.

"That's right," Nathaniel confirmed. "Never until then."

"Did you ever see the red light like this?" another asked, flicking it on.

"No. Never until just now."

"Do you know where the bomb hit the ground, Lieutenant?" the same man wanted to know.

"Yes. The approximate latitude is 35 degrees, 32 minutes, 28 seconds, and the longitude is 139 degrees, 42 minutes, 29 seconds. Both approximate—I was distracted by the Major screaming at me."

Tim gave him a nod. "May I ask you something else?"

"Sure," Nathaniel said.

"What difference did it make when you dropped it? The

Major said it'd wipe out everything within ten square miles. Wouldn't that have still hit the palace even dropped early?"

"That's true," Tim conceded. "Had it gone off when dropped—even prematurely—the majority of Tokyo, including the Emperor's Palace, would've been obliterated." Then he added, with a grim look, "But the Major's failure to send the signal meant the bomb never armed. So there was no payback."

"Well, the Major told me he only had two seconds to send it and it was my fault for not giving him enough time."

"No, that's not true," Tim shot back. He held up a finger. "Major Morrissey should've had this in hand on final approach," then two fingers, "turned off the safety, which lights the red bulb," then tapped the side of the device. "Fifteen seconds after drop, he was to press this to arm the bomb. Five seconds later, press again to detonate. That would've created a sight bigger than anything Hiroshima or Nagasaki saw."

"But he didn't, and it didn't," Nathaniel sighed, oddly relieved.

"Correct," Tim agreed. "He didn't and it didn't."

"So what's to stop us from flying back over Tokyo and pressing the button now?" Nathaniel asked, thinking positively.

"That won't work," Tim said, his voice hollow. "The bomb's designed to go off in the air. If it's less than 3,000 feet above sea level when armed, it fails. Built-in fail-safe to prevent accidental ground triggers."

"Well, shit. So much for that idea."

"Yeah. Shit indeed. All we can hope now is the Japs surrender before they find it, figure it out, and drop it on us. That'd really fucking suck."

"Tim—why do I keep hearing the word *Payback* about this bomb?"

Tim stepped in close, eye locked on eye. "Because that's the code name we gave her. Payback for Pearl Harbor. Many of us lost family there."

The four walked off. Nathaniel spotted Morrissey coming with two armed guards. *Here comes the storm,* he thought.

"Soldiers, arrest that man!" Morrissey yelled.

The guards flanked Nathaniel, marched him toward the mess hall. Morrissey kept ranting about treason. They led Nathaniel into a makeshift cell—Seabees still hammering rebar and wood into bars. For a fleeting second he thought of escaping, but where would he run on an island? Even if he could steal a B-29, where would he go?

Resigned, he sat in the half-built cell. Footsteps approached. The door swung open. Three men entered, Morrissey among them.

"Attention! Brigadier General David Paul is present!" a soldier barked.

Nathaniel jumped up and saluted. The general was huge—at least 6'4", thinning brown hair cut tight, long face, giant hands, moved like a big cat in total control. Large and in charge, no question.

"At ease," ordered the General. "At ease, Lieutenant."

Nathaniel stood at ease, not feeling it one damn bit. The general slowly circled him.

"You don't look like a traitor, son. Are you a traitor?" the General boomed, stopping inches from Nathaniel's face.

"Well, answer me, boy. Are you a fucking traitor to the United States of America?"

"Sir, no, sir!" Nathaniel shouted.

"Are not *what,* son? Answer me—your life literally depends on it."

"Sir, General sir, I am not a fucking traitor to the United States of America, sir!" Nathaniel yelled, every word crisp, eyes locked forward.

"Major Morrissey says you're the worst traitor in U.S. Army history," General Paul said, casting a glance at Morrissey.

"Sir, I'm not a traitor. Major Morrissey is wrong. The bomb didn't go off because he didn't arm it."

The General drilled him with question after question. Nathaniel explained the turbulence, how his thumb accidentally hit the button. Morrissey tried to hedge, admitting they hit "minor turbulence," not enough to cause a slip. Nathaniel countered: the Major had failed to arm the bomb. Had he done so, Tokyo would be gone.

General Paul wheeled on Morrissey. "Did you send the signal to arm the weapon?"

Morrissey stammered, finally squeaked out, "No, sir."

"Why the fuck not?" the General demanded.

"Because I fucked up, sir. I was so pissed at Meister I forgot to arm it."

"So you thought he fucked up, and in your rage you fucked up worse. That it?"

"Yes, sir."

Paul pinned him with a glare. "And when you tried to retrace the route to arm it then, what happened?"

Morrissey admitted they were driven off by flak. Nathaniel added that once the bomb dropped below 3,000 feet, it couldn't be armed by design. The General spun back on Morrissey, forcing him to admit he'd known that all along.

Finally, after grilling them both, the General barked, "Soldier, release Lieutenant Meister. Major, I'll deal with you later. No court martial. Not today. Not ever."

He gave them both a steely look. "This gets reported up the chain to who needs to know—and no one else. You will never speak of this again. Do you understand my orders?"

"Sir, yes, sir!" both shouted, saluting.

The General marched out. Nathaniel sighed, feeling the crushing weight of a court martial lift. Dead tired from more than twenty hours awake, he staggered to the barracks and collapsed.

CHAPTER 19

Nathaniel never forgot the events of that day, nor where the bomb lay in Tokyo Bay. Two days after his talk with Daniel—the engineer who had overseen the Payback project—Japan surrendered. Nathaniel was assigned to a small team tasked with finding the bomb, but despite over a year of searching, they never came close. Nathaniel kept quiet, knowing the entire time they were miles off from the real location.

In the years that followed, his superiors questioned him repeatedly about the mission. In 1947, Major Morrissey joined the CIA, while Nathaniel was promoted and served tours in various global hotspots. By 1952, the United States finally detonated the first *official* H-bomb, a hundred times more powerful than the A-bomb, just as Daniel had once promised. Nathaniel thought Daniel would have been proud to see that day.

The 12 August 1945 mission was buried deep. Japan had already sent its surrender message before the B-29 even left Tinian—though word hadn't reached them yet on the island, or maybe it had and someone decided to ignore it. Either way, it was as if the mission never happened, scrubbed from the record books like a ghost flight.

After the war, Nathaniel stayed close with most of his old crew—except Morrissey, whom he outright despised. Oddly, of the six men on the last mission, only Nathaniel, Morrissey, and

Abe Winter were still alive. The others died under suspicious circumstances: a hunting accident, a sudden heart attack, a car crash on a clear, dry road. Nathaniel couldn't help thinking that if he'd dropped the bomb at the right time, maybe they'd all have been hailed as heroes—and maybe they'd all still be alive.

Now retired in St. Louis, Nathaniel carried the weight of their deaths like stones in his chest. He longed to share the truth with someone, maybe his grandson Joshua—who'd recently left the CIA himself. Nathaniel had always kept up with Joshua, hoping that one day, the boy would be the one to find the bomb and finally set the story straight. As he drifted off into a deep sleep, he wrestled with whether to reveal everything to Joshua when he arrived.

Meanwhile, Joshua was 20 minutes into a drive that ended at a bar. Military time: 2150. He picked out a small table in the corner, from where he could see the front door. It was the perfect vantage, and he felt a quiet pride at using his "spy skills" to scope it out.

"Hello, Mo," purred a voice over his left shoulder—a soft, sultry sound that startled the shit out of him.

He tried to mask his shock. It was Betsy. Somehow, she'd snuck up behind him after he'd spent all that time picking out the perfect spot.

"Did I scare you?"

"Uh, no. Well—yeah, kinda," Joshua admitted, sheepish. "How'd you get behind me?"

"I came in the back door, Mo. Over there." She pointed to his right, flashing a mischievous grin.

Great. Once again, his razor-sharp spy instincts had failed him. He scanned to his right. Sure enough—there was the back door, half-hidden by beer cases. Well, sort of hidden. He noted the dim exit sign above it. Not exactly concealed, but enough to console himself.

"Sure enough. There's the back door, all right," he muttered.

He then noticed Betsy had changed out of her scrubs. *Good catch, eagle-eye.* "Oh, I see you changed your clothes."

"Yep. Sure did. You're very observant," she teased.

Red crept up his neck. Before his embarrassment could climb higher, he asked if she wanted a drink.

"Sure. Miller Lite."

"Alrighty," he said, off to handle his mission. When he returned, he took a closer look—Betsy looked *way* better in jeans and a pink top than she did in her nurse's uniform. Pretty hot, actually.

"You look better now than you did today at the nursing home," he blurted, shoving his whole foot straight down his throat.

"Thanks," Betsy replied dryly. Not worth a dirty look. "It is good to finally be off work. I've worked nine days straight, but now I've got the next two off."

Things are looking up, Joshua thought.

"So what do you do for fun around here in St. Louis?"

"I own a Harley I like to ride when the weather's nice. Usually take it out to my family's property."

Joshua's face must've twitched, because Betsy pounced. "What, Mo? You don't think women should own Harleys?"

Careful here, boy, he warned himself. *One wrong word and there'll be no info gathering—and definitely no getting lucky tonight.*

"No, it's just—I figured with you being a nurse, probably seeing lots of motorcycle accident cases, you'd shy away from them."

Nice recovery, Mo. Sort of.

Betsy shrugged, recalling her ER days. Said she'd seen plenty of mangled bodies, but it didn't stop her need to ride. Joshua imagined her on a Harley, then got sidetracked wondering about tattoos.

"Got any Harley tattoos?" he tried.

"Maybe I do," she purred, leaning close, "but you'll never see them."

Realizing he'd stepped in it again, he apologized. "Look, I'm actually here visiting my grandfather. I can be kind of a smartass, but I can be nice too."

"And I have a confession to make, Betsy."

"Oh really, Mo. Do I look like a priest?"

"No, not so much," Joshua chuckled.

"Well, what then, sinner? What would you like to confess?" she said, taking his hands, eyes locked on his.

"Uh . . . uh," he stammered.

"Out with it, sinner," she insisted, squeezing his hands.

"OK, fuck it. I lied about my nickname being Mo."

"No shit. Really. I knew you were lying the way you first said it."

"Knowing that, why'd you come meet me anyway?"

"Who cares about a dumb nickname? I figured I'd give you a chance to come clean. If you did, that was good. If not—well, that'd say a lot too."

"Oh Jesus, I feel like a schmuck," Joshua admitted.

"You should feel like a schmuck, Mo—whatever your name actually is."

"It's LT. My dad called me that—short for 'little tyke.' I thought I was being clever. Sorry."

"Let me see your driver's license. What makes you think you've gotta be secret squirrel when you're just visiting an old folks' home? Not exactly classified intel there."

"You'd be surprised, Betsy," he tried, still half-joking.

She wasn't impressed. "Look, Joshua, I looked you up. I know you worked for the CIA. But if you want to get along with me, drop the spy bullshit you pulled at the front desk."

Joshua let out a long breath. "OK, Betsy, you're right." He made a theatrical twirl, like tossing off a cape. "There—no more cloak of secrecy. I'm just plain old Joshua."

She laughed. "Now we're getting somewhere."

Over the next hour, they relaxed. Betsy told Joshua that his grandfather had spoken of him often. "The Colonel said you never shut up as a kid. Maybe it's your habit to engage your mouth while leaving your brain in neutral."

"Probably so," Joshua laughed, starting to tire of getting roasted. He switched subjects. "You ever do shots?"

"Sure."

"What do you like?"

"Well, tequila makes my clothes fall off, as the song goes."

"Tequila it is."

Joshua woke up with a splitting headache and other parts equally sore after way too much tequila and way too much fun. Sunlight drilled right into his skull. He sat up, squinted, smelled his own breath, and decided it could ignite if struck by a match. He stumbled to the bathroom—bloodshot eyes and a pounding head greeting him in the mirror—then staggered to the living room so as not to wake Betsy.

She was face-down, snoring lightly, sheets twisted around her. That Harley must work wonders; she had some serious muscles. Despite the hangover, Joshua felt oddly refreshed. Time to get serious about his grandfather's mystery. Why had the FBI come around? Had Nathaniel told them about the H-bomb?

Joshua heard the shower and smelled coffee. Despite the tequila haze, he replayed last night—he hadn't uncovered any secrets, but Betsy's body had been responsive enough to count for something.

"Good morning," Betsy greeted, in a pink bathrobe with her hair up. "Did you sleep good?"

"Like a rock."

"I guess so. You barely moved all night—after you fell asleep."

"How about you?"

"Great. Want some coffee?"

"Yes. Coffee might save me."

She smiled. "Do you remember how many shots of tequila you had?"

"Oh my gosh. No. More than ten, maybe? How many did you have?"

"You had eight. That was enough for me to decide to bring you home. Do you know where your car is?"

"Uh . . . back at the bar?"

"No. Try again."

"Right outside?"

"Nope. You made me follow you as you drove back to the nursing home. Then we came here."

"Was I driving OK?"

"Not too bad. I wasn't exactly sober myself."

"Why did I want to take it there?"

She laughed. "You said your grandfather might need it 'to go to the store.'"

"He hasn't driven in years."

"Maybe you thought he'd need it to flee before more government men came," Betsy teased.

"Wait—you told me yesterday no one visited except me."

"That's what I said before I knew who you were. Last night I told you about the FBI, remember?"

"Hmmm. Yes, you did," Joshua lied. "Remind me again."

She recounted two men showing up about four weeks ago, asking questions about Nathaniel. "They didn't seem dangerous—but threatening? Sure. Anyone who can mess with my nursing license is threatening."

"They show ID?"

"Not at first. But one left a business card. It said FBI."

"What did they want to know?"

"What your grandfather talked about. Who visited. Who he hung out with. I didn't tell them about his war stories. Something made me keep that to myself."

"War stories?"

She told him about the special mission over Tokyo, the modified plane, the five practice flights, the H-bomb that didn't go off.

Joshua's mouth dropped open. His brain seized up. Should he laugh it off or warn Betsy to never speak of it again?

"That's too weird. The Japanese surrendered on August 15."

"Yeah. The mission was on August 12."

"What did my grandfather say happened to the bomb?"

"He said it didn't go off. And he knows where it landed."

"But no one ever found it?"

"Not according to him."

"Do you believe him?"

Betsy looked at him and whispered, "No. But maybe that's

why the feds came."

Joshua felt his stomach knot. Who else had Nathaniel told? Why was he telling Betsy? And was the FBI visit connected? *God damn it. This makes my mission a lot riskier,* he thought. And he was right.

He decided he'd call Stuart Leven at Justice—a brilliant but socially awkward old friend who owed him. Maybe Stuart could verify the mission. But first he needed to visit Nathaniel again. And keep Betsy calm.

"Hey, Bets—did those agents seem like they'd come back?"

"Nope. They came, asked questions, talked to your grandfather for about twenty minutes, then left. He ran them off, yelling the whole way."

"Are you sure they were FBI?"

"I can smell a cop a mile off. Black suits, black SUV, little antenna. And one handed me a card that said FBI."

"OK. Fair enough." He grinned. "Hey, is it OK if I shower here?"

"You asked me that last night too. I told you then I don't work today. And," she added with a sly smile, "I don't need any more tequila."

Too early to see Grampa anyway, Joshua thought. He stood, fully rising in every sense. "After you, ma cherie Betsy."

A little later, sweat-drenched and satisfied, Joshua lay in her bed, hangover gone. He heard the shower, smelled the humidity, and thought of joining her—but was too spent. Betsy was an unlikely but surprisingly valuable source. His old roommate used to say life was about connections, and apparently Joshua's were often with women—just like 007.

He couldn't help but grin, then remind himself: he still had to figure out how to keep the FBI from his grandfather. After a quick shower, he planned to visit Nathaniel—but not before seeing if Betsy was still cool.

He cracked the bathroom door. "Hoo," Betsy squealed. "You scared me!"

"Sorry. But turnabout's fair play."

She laughed. "I'm just not used to having someone here. Ready to shower?"

"Yes, but all my stuff's in the car at the nursing home."

"No, genius. You put your suitcase in my car last night."

Sheer unconscious genius, Joshua told himself. "I knew that. Testing you."

"Right. Where is it then?"

"In your living room?" he tried.

"Nice try. You left it in my car."

They both laughed. He grabbed it, showered, then offered breakfast. Betsy suggested a spot for tacos. He agreed, but worried about being seen at the home.

"Any way to get to my grandfather's room unnoticed?"

"Yeah. Through the laundry room. And there are no cameras—place is too old and cheap."

Joshua checked his watch: 0730. Not enough time for tacos *and* to be on time.

"Oh, Bets—maybe best you don't tell anyone else what my grandfather told you."

"My lips are sealed," she promised, miming a lock.

CHAPTER 20

Adrenaline coursed through Joshua's veins as fear and excitement dominated his being. He couldn't shake the thought of how different the world would be if his grandfather, the bombardier, hadn't dropped the first hydrogen bomb on Japan before it was armed, causing it to splash harmlessly into Tokyo Bay rather than exploding over the Imperial Palace and decimating Tokyo.

Joshua now feared the secret of the bomb had been revealed too many times, increasing the likelihood of someone else finding it. He hoped the story was either a veteran's fantasy or that the bomb had been discovered long ago.

He could see the logic behind the U.S. dropping a hydrogen bomb on Japan—those sneak-attack motherfuckers. But the idea of searching Tokyo Bay for a buried bomb that well could be a fantasy didn't sound appealing.

Despite his doubts, Joshua trusted his grandfather's story. As he sat in Betsy's kitchen at her antique wooden table, his hands explored the grain of the surface, his brow furrowed as he contemplated what he knew and what he didn't. He gripped the edges tightly as his grandfather's confession lingered in his consciousness, improbable but unwavering.

He exhaled slowly, then gave a small nod; his skepticism melted into quiet belief. Nathaniel wasn't the type to fabricate something so important. Joshua concluded that because his grampa had never lied to him before, he wasn't lying now. And with his CIA experience, Joshua understood how morally challenging decisions had to be made in pursuit of national security—or in compliance with one's conscience, ultimately.

Head now clear, and looking at his watch, Joshua saw he still had time to head to the nursing home, his plan for the day coming into focus.

Joshua called out to Betsy, who was drying her hair. "Hey, Bets, sorry, but I am going to have to take off. No time for breakfast. I have to be back at the nursing home at 0800, and I cannot be late."

He heard the hair dryer shut off. "Did you say you were leaving, Joshua?"

He went to the bathroom door. "Yes. No time for breakfast tacos. I have to be back at the nursing home by 0800 sharp or my grandfather will shoot me."

"Oh, okay. Well, you know you don't necessarily have to go to a restaurant to eat a taco," invited Betsy as she opened the bathroom door wearing nothing but a towel.

"Oh, you tasty temptress, you, Miss Betsy. If only I had time . . ."

"Yes. Too bad. So, no tacos, eh? If only you had time indeed."

"Shit. Can I get a rain check until tonight?"

"Sure. Why not? I got called to go into work today anyway, so I'll see you there."

"Excellent! Bye for now." And with that Joshua hauled ass out the door as his Uber arrived, and on to the nursing home, where he stowed his suitcase in his rental car.

There was a different nurse at the front desk that morning. Joshua signed the guest book, looked at his watch, and was relieved to see he was right on time. He had thought about sneaking in through the back entrance but decided to keep that option open for another occasion.

Once in the hallway that could be seen from the lobby area, Joshua counted doors on the left: one, two, three—Room 106; his grandfather's room.

Joshua knocked on the door.

Knock, knock, knock.

Knock, knock, knock.

The stranger always knocks twice, so some author said.

"Who the hell is it?" Joshua's grandfather shouted.

"It's your grandson," Joshua whispered.

"Who? Go the hell away, whoever you are," Nathaniel barked, not remembering that he and Joshua had arranged for him to come back at 0800.

"Grampa, it's me, Joshua," he whispered a bit louder, not knowing why he was whispering.

He knocked again, the sounds echoing down the empty hallway. Joshua waited, shifting his weight from one foot to the other, but no sounds emanated from the room.

Joshua felt paranoid but couldn't pinpoint why. His eyes darted from left to right in the dimly lit hallway, his fingers twitching at his sides. Every shadow seemed to move, every distant sound too sharp, too deliberate. Joshua swallowed hard, his pulse quickening, but no clear threat revealed itself—just the gnawing sense that something was off.

He was there to learn about his grandfather's WWII experiences and the mystery of the hydrogen bomb, but no thoughts eased the bad feeling. Finally, hearing noise inside the room, he tried to slip his driver's license past the striker, but it didn't work, making him even more anxious.

"Grampa, it's me, Joshua. Let me in," he urgently whispered.

Nothing. More fear crept in. He looked around and saw the gap underneath the door and slid his ID there. His grandfather's voice came from inside: "What's this? Oh, it's you! I thought you'd be here at 0800, but it's 0759. On time. Well done."

The door opened, and Joshua quickly entered, relieved, locking it behind him. Glancing at what had been his grandfather's aviator's watch, he saw it was 0759—relieved to avoid a lecture on punctuality.

Nathaniel noted, "Right on time, grandson. Let's talk."

Joshua sat on the bed as Nathaniel probed, "Why are you sneaking around? And why are you late? Just say who you are, and I would've let you in." Nathaniel forgot he had just praised Joshua for being on time.

"I did, Grampa, and I was here at 0759 sharp, but let's forget about that for now. Grampa, I want to talk quietly about who has come to see you lately," primed Joshua.

"Why talk quietly, boy? What's somebody going to do to me, put me in a home?" he chuckled.

"That's funny. But what isn't funny is that I was told two creepy-looking FBI dudes came to see you a couple of weeks ago, and the walls have ears," Joshua whispered, shifting his eyes toward the lobby.

"Oh, yeah. Those two FBI assholes. I thought you were them pounding on my door, which is why I was telling you to go the hell away. I believe they were the same two jerk-offs who came by about a year ago," Nathaniel recounted.

"What did they want with an old broken-down fossil like you, Grampa?" Joshua teased with a grin.

Nathaniel's sharp look was enough of a reminder that Joshua's flippant remark wasn't as funny as he thought.

"I may be old and broken down, boy, but I remember some

things that some very important people wish I would forget—or take to the grave with me."

"Does what you remember have anything to do with why the Feds came to see you?" Joshua pressed.

"Most definitely." The Colonel paused, then said surreptitiously, "I am the only one who knows where the bomb landed."

"What bomb are you talking about, Grampa? You dropped lots of bombs," Joshua prodded, wrinkling his forehead, trying to elicit more of the same story his grandfather had told him the day before.

"Can't tell you, boy. I was sworn to secrecy by the U.S. Army Air Corps," Nathaniel stated with conviction as he looked away, having forgotten he had already told Joshua the story.

"Well, can you tell me if your secret has anything to do with why the suits keep coming to see you?" Joshua insisted.

"Yep. Those boys want to transfer me out of here to a special old folks' home—just for war heroes, they told me," Nathaniel recalled.

"I've never heard of any place like that, Grampa. I'd be suspicious of anything the government offered."

"You aren't as dumb as you look, boy. Just kidding. But anyway, you're right. I am suspicious. That's why I'm still here and why I won't talk to those fellas again," Nathaniel declared.

Still wanting to know more about the bomb, hoping to verify the story if told twice, Joshua brought it up for the third time.

"So, Grampa, I used to work for the government. Your secret is safe with me."

"Yeah, right, boy," Nathaniel scoffed. "You can't even keep a job, much less a secret."

Ouch. That one hurt.

"Fine. Suit yourself. Go to your grave with your whoop-de-do secret," Joshua snapped.

All was quiet for a few moments as both sat with their thoughts. Then, trying to restart the conversation, Joshua said, hoping to prime the pump one last time, "Why are some FBI clowns so interested in talking to you now?"

"I don't know for sure, but I may have opened my mouth to one of the nurses about my secret past," Nathaniel confessed.

"What secret past, Grampa?" Joshua pressed, knowing full well that Nathaniel had already told at least one nurse—Betsy.

"I can't tell you. It's a secret."

"Well, if you already blabbed it to the nurses, then it can't be much of a secret," Joshua countered. "And by the way, Grampa, you blabbed the whole story to me yesterday."

Nathaniel was taken aback by Joshua's rudeness and disrespect, and was pissed that he couldn't remember what he and Joshua had talked about the day before. Many seconds ticked by. "I don't know if I blabbed my secret to you or not, smart ass. You asked me why the government assholes came, and that is the only reason I can think of."

"Look, Grampa. Those guys will probably be back any minute, and no doubt they'll run me out of here, so if you have something to say to me, say it now," demanded Joshua as he tried the "I'm the superior" tone technique that had not worked at all with Nurse Betsy the day before.

Nathaniel turned and faced the window, brow furrowed, intently staring at the trees as the wind tossed the branches about, thoughts of the past drifting back and forth like smoke. Then he cleared his throat, turned back to Joshua, and revealed, "Look, grandson. It turns out that now I am the only one left out of my flight crew who is still alive. Every other man on that B-29 kept the secret of our last mission to his grave, including Abe Winter, who is probably dead, too."

"How do you know they kept whatever it is a secret? You didn't stay in touch with all of them, did you?" Joshua pressed, still acting coy.

"You can really be a pain in the ass, Joshua. The reason I know they all kept their mouths shut is because if the secret got out, it would be big news all over the world."

"Oh, really?" Joshua was really egging his grandfather on now.

"Yes, really. Goddamn it. And second of all, half the men died within a year or two after the war ended."

"You were involved in something that important—that it would be huge news even today, nearly eighty years after the war?"

"Goddamn right it would. Bigger than anything, and more important to national security now than ever before; more important than anything you ever did."

"Okay, Grampa," Joshua said, ignoring the stab. "So what happens if the government assholes bust through that door now and whisk you away to never be heard from again? Then what happens to national security and to your secret?"

Nathaniel paused and continued to stare out the window, looking way back in time—silent. His shoulders fell, and he sighed a huge sigh. Joshua could tell the memory hurt.

With his back still to Joshua, Nathaniel reached down and rummaged through his nightstand, pulling out a tattered matchbook and an old piece of paper. After reading something inside the cover, he sighed deeply, then turned to Joshua and divulged, "I dropped a hydrogen bomb on Japan."

Joshua involuntarily took a step back, his mouth dropped open as he absorbed the words, realizing Nathaniel was repeating the story he had shared the day before.

"You dropped a hydrogen bomb on Japan? Hiroshima or Nagasaki?"

"Neither, boy. That's why it's such a big secret. We dropped it on Tokyo to take out the emperor and the military commanders who were planning how to defend their country against our invasion."

"Sure. Okay, Grampa. I know quite a bit about Japan, and there's no history of us dropping an H-bomb on Tokyo."

"No shit, Sherlock. That's why it's such a big secret! I dropped an H-bomb, but it never went off."

"So, the H-bomb you dropped was a dud, huh? Are you sure you're not making this shit up? The bombs went off just fine when we dropped them on Hiroshima and Nagasaki."

"Yeah, well again, smart ass, they were pure atomic bombs. The one we dropped used experimental technology. It was the world's first hydrogen bomb, and it was a hundred times more powerful than the one we dropped on Hiroshima. And no, the H-bomb was not a dud."

Joshua was still very skeptical. Had his grandfather lost it? Was he delusional? Pretty elaborate delusion, he must say.

"So if the bomb was not a dud and it didn't explode, then where is the bomb now?" Joshua demanded.

"I watched it hit Tokyo Bay through my bombardier's scope, so my guess is that it got buried in the muck at the bottom of the bay."

"Did the military go and retrieve it after Japan surrendered?"

"No, not as far as I know—although they could have kept that a secret, too. But the reason I don't think they did is because they never knew the actual coordinates of where the bomb landed. And because the government pinheads are bugging me about it still."

"Maybe," Joshua mused. "But maybe they don't want some old fart talking a bunch of crap to get people stirred up for nothing."

"I thought about that too, Joshua. But if I did say something to one of the nurses, it couldn't have been much. Not near enough to have two suits show up now."

"I suppose that's true, Grampa. At a minimum, if what you say is true, it would be embarrassing and possibly dangerous."

"If what I say is true?" Nathaniel retorted indignantly. "If what I say is true? Fuck that. I bet through the Freedom of Information Act you can find that a B-29 left Tinian Island at 0200 on 12 August 1945. If you find the crew list, you'll find my name on it. Why do you think I was sent to the Marianas when everybody else who served in the European theater was sent back home?"

"I don't know, Grampa. I don't know," Joshua answered softly. His mind was having a hard time digesting this now confirmed revelation.

A mix of doubt, anger, and awe filled Joshua's mind as his grandfather repeated the same story from the day before. But before he could respond, the door burst open, revealing two government agents behind Betsy, who was holding the master key.

"Whoa! Who are you to bust into a private room?" Joshua demanded, spinning around quickly to stand in front of the intruders.

"We didn't bust in. We're the FBI," announced the agent in front. "We asked the nurse to let us in after hearing what sounded like a struggle."

Joshua glared at Betsy, but she avoided his gaze and walked away. "I have to get back to work," she muttered.

"No. You stay here," the agent ordered.

Joshua snapped, "There's no struggle here. Who are you to concern yourselves with my grandfather?"

"I'm Special Agent Bushong, and this is Special Agent Miller," the man stated, showing their FBI badges.

"Who are you?" Bushong demanded.

"I am Colonel Meister's grandson," Joshua countered, declining to be more specific.

"Oh, yeah. We know who you are," confirmed Bushong, the agent in front with the military buzz cut as he stepped completely into the room. "You're Joshua Meister, the CIA spud who got fired for incompetence and insubordination," he spat out contemptuously.

Ignoring the sting but feeling heat rise in his face, Joshua insisted, "Now what do you want with my grandfather?"

"That's classified," Bushong snapped.

Miller, stepping in, added, "You remember national security, right? That was part of your job before you were terminated."

Sarcastically, Joshua retorted, "What importance could a ninety-nine-year-old man have for national security?"

Bushong stepped forward, yelling, "You don't get it, Meister. You never did. The world doesn't revolve around your little Chinese whore. The U.S. is safe now because it sheds fleas like you!"

"Safe for what, asshole?" Joshua shouted back, not backing down but wondering in the back of his mind how they knew about Mei Lei. "Safer for people to be put in jail or disappear? Safer for dicks like you to come and harass a military hero?" Joshua proclaimed, backing up now right in front of his grandfather.

"Military hero, my ass. He failed to complete the mission he was assigned to," Bushong growled.

Interesting admission, douchebag, thought Joshua.

"Have you ever been in combat, assholes?" Nathaniel asked sarcastically as he peered over Joshua's shoulder. "Or are you two the types of cowards that sneak around at night tapping the telephones of American citizens without a warrant?"

Bushong glared at Nathaniel, and in a very controlled cadence uttered, "Overseas intercepts are legal, Colonel. It is legal for us to do whatever we have to do to protect the United States from those who would destroy our country from within or without."

Joshua was sure Bushong had spoken those same words a thousand times before.

"Who is there to protect the citizens of our country from assholes like you who tear apart our nation from the inside?" Nathaniel shot back.

"We are at war now, Colonel, both on and off the actual military battlefield. And I don't have to justify what I do to protect you, your worthless grandson, and all the rest of our citizens," Bushong stated in a calm, steely voice.

"Now get your things together. You're going to a much better place," Bushong ordered.

"I am not going anywhere with you assholes," Nathaniel responded defiantly, sitting down on his bed.

"Yes, you are, and here is the paperwork to back it up," Bushong commanded as Miller whipped out some documents and threw them at Joshua, hitting him in the chest.

"Let me see those," Joshua said as he bent down to pick up the papers.

"The paperwork isn't for you, dipshit. It's for the nursing home," Bushong declared authoritatively.

What can I do to stop these assholes? Joshua wondered, still highly pissed at the remark about Mei Lei.

Seeing the look on Joshua's face, Bushong scoffed and added, "By the way, you aren't the only one who speaks Chinese. I spent two years in Hong Kong."

God, will I ever learn to hide my expressions? Joshua thought as he kicked himself internally.

"Now get your things together!" Bushong shouted at Nathaniel.

"No!" Nathaniel cried out defiantly. "Not no, but hell no!"

"Nurse!" Bushong called out as he opened the door to the room. "Nurse, come here and bring the syringe," he commanded.

A few seconds later, Nurse Betsy stepped forward with a needle and a bottle filled with yellow liquid.

"The Colonel is behaving irrationally and requires medication before transport."

Joshua was confused and disappointed. How could Betsy have reacted so quickly if she hadn't known what was coming? He glared at her, feeling betrayed, but she only looked at her hands.

"Nurse, give the Colonel the injection to calm him," Bushong ordered, pointing at Nathaniel.

"The only one agitated is you, Agent Bushong, and my grandfather is not going anywhere with you," Joshua shot back, sizing up the situation.

Bushong snapped, "You're out of line. I don't need a court order to move a citizen with critical information to a secure location!" He jabbed his finger at Joshua's chest.

Bushong turned from Joshua to Betsy and bellowed, "Give the old man the needle and then call the St. Louis PD. This man is interfering with an FBI special agent's performance of his duties, and I want him arrested. Now!"

Betsy looked at Joshua plaintively, but before she could speak, Nathaniel interjected in a sad, resigned tone.

"No need for any of that. I will come with you."

Joshua spun around and faced Nathaniel.

"No, Grampa. You don't have to go. They can't make you. You have rights. You're a citizen. You're a hero," Joshua implored.

"Not anymore," Nathaniel croaked out as the light began to fade from his eyes. "Not anymore."

With that, Nathaniel turned to his closet and began gathering some papers and the few items he kept in there.

"Leave the room now, squid," Bushong demanded. "You are interfering with a special agent in the performance of his duties. Nurse, give the Colonel the shot anyway; we don't need the old cocksucker creating any more of a scene."

"Fuck off, Bushong. What duties are those, asshole? Personal valet service?" Joshua retorted sarcastically.

Nathaniel moved to the nightstand and put a pack of matches and a pack of cigarettes in his shirt pocket. He handed Joshua another pack of matches and a fresh pack of smokes.

Nathaniel looked Joshua straight in the face with an unwavering gaze of pride and honor. Joshua was choking up at the realization that he would never see his grandfather again, but he fought back the tears—these assholes would not see him cry. Then Nathaniel handed Joshua his Colt 1911 and five medal boxes, including a blue one that contained his Medal of Honor.

After handing them over, Nathaniel looked down, sighed, and shook his head. Joshua took the unloaded gun, tucked it into his waistband, and glared contemptuously at the FBI agents watching him. He reverently held onto the Medal of Honor, knowing the bravery his grandfather had displayed to earn it, refusing to let the ass clowns see it.

Joshua closed the blue box, gathered the other boxes, and moved past the agents to the doorway where Nurse Betsy stood with the syringe. He turned and silently watched his grandfather pack, again choking back tears, knowing deep down he would never see him again.

"Where are you taking him?" Joshua asked quietly.

"Where he will be safe, maggot," was Bushong's terse reply. "Give him the shot, nurse. The old man looks tense."

Nathaniel stuck out his old skinny arm, and Betsy gave him the shot. Then she slipped away.

"How will I contact him?" Joshua asked.

"Send a letter to the FBI, and we'll see that it gets to him," Bushong replied condescendingly.

"What if I want to talk to him on the telephone?" Joshua demanded.

With an annoyed look, Bushong countered, "Once your grandfather gets situated, he will contact you."

"Grampa, do you have my cell number?"

"No, I don't. But I'm sure I won't be calling," Nathaniel replied weakly.

"Well, let me give it to you anyway," Joshua offered. "You might change your mind."

"Look, dweeb. If your grandfather wants to call you, we will find you. We have your telephone number, and we know all about you," Bushong said with disdain.

That comment reminded Joshua of the Chinese whore remark, and he felt himself getting even more pissed. His jaw tightened, his skin prickled with heat, and his hands balled up into fists. The adrenaline surged and his face turned beet red.

The image of Mei Lei's face flashed through his mind, and defending her honor contorted his face with anger and humiliation for not having the power to do anything about it at that moment.

"Bushong, this isn't over. The next time I see you, we'll see who the whore is," Joshua declared, ready to fight and wishing the .45 was loaded.

Bushong grinned. "If I ever run into you again, faggot, you'll be pissing your pants before I'm done with you."

Nathaniel looked at Joshua with love and sadness as the medicine took effect. Without acknowledging the FBI agents, he quietly stated, "I am ready to go."

Feeling betrayed by Nurse Betsy, Joshua turned outward toward the hallway, his eyes filled with tears. Bushong sneered, "When you're done crying, pussy, get out of the way."

Joshua, wobbling on the edge between fighting or not while on the brink of losing his last family member, wished the agents hadn't witnessed his vulnerable moment.

"Love you, Grampa," Joshua said, looking down as he hugged the old man.

"Love you too, grandson," Nathaniel replied, gripping Joshua's shoulders for what was likely the last time.

"See you in hell, bitch," Bushong flung at Joshua over his shoulder as the three men walked down the hall.

Joshua wanted to lash out, but he couldn't. When they were out of sight, a ragged sob escaped him. Tears burned tracks down his face; he was seething with rage that overwhelmed him as he pounded his fists on the wall—lost and alone. His shoulders slumped and his legs grew weak, his gaze fixed on the floor, empty. The sadness and despair dominated his entire being. What had started as an adventure had turned into a nightmare.

Joshua was grateful for the time he had with his grandfather before the Feds took him, but his thoughts quickly turned to Nurse Betsy, filling him with even more anger. How could she betray him after he'd treated her well? But then he realized—he barely knew her, and her job was on the line. Joshua wondered if she'd ratted out his grandfather to the Feds.

One thing was certain: someone owed him an explanation. Joshua walked toward the back door where his grandfather and the other vets used to gather.

Joshua opened the pack of cigarettes his grandfather had given him, extracted one, and thought, *How am I going to spark this fag?* He pulled out the matches and noticed they were quite tattered and that inside the cover there was handwriting. What was written there was not a girl's phone number or a combination to a safe. Joshua's grandfather had written the following:

12 August 1945
35° 36' 1.012" N
139° 52' 0.512" E

Joshua's hands shook uncontrollably as he fumbled with the pack. The world felt blurry, out of focus, out of control. He had never felt like such an emotional mess. He made himself breathe slowly and deeply, trying to regain some control. After a few minutes, he was finally able to hold a match steadily enough to light a cigarette. He inhaled deeply as he tucked the matches and cigarettes into his shirt pocket, holding back the strong desire to cough as the acrid smoke filled his lungs.

Joshua stood there and reflected on past conversations with his father and grandfather about WWII, the arms race, and various wars, including Vietnam, Korea, and Iraq. His family had served in every war since the Revolutionary War, but Vietnam had revealed the ugly truth about the real reasons behind wars—hidden political agendas and ulterior motives.

Joshua's philosophical mental meanderings were interrupted by a familiar female voice.

"I didn't know you smoked."

Turning around, Joshua bitterly snapped, "I didn't know you were a rat."

Betsy's eyes filled with tears, a look of guilt and sorrow covering her face. She couldn't bear to see his pain, knowing she had partially caused it. She reached out her right hand to touch Joshua's chest and murmured, "I had no choice. My job was on the line."

"Is that why you called the Feds to come grab my grandfather from the nursing home?" accused Joshua, pushing her hand away.

"No, it's not like that. It didn't happen like that at all," Betsy responded in a panicked tone, lifting her open hands toward him beseechingly. "They called here," she continued. "They asked if the Colonel had any regular visitors and stuff like that."

"So you just volunteered that Grampa was running his mouth about World War II, not even asking why they wanted to know if he had any recent visitors," Joshua lashed out as he threw the half-burned cigarette onto the concrete and crushed it with his shoe. "Is that it, Betsy?"

"No, it didn't happen like that at all," Betsy explained, moving toward him and touching his arms, wanting him to hold her, seeking some reassurance from him.

Joshua was not in a reassuring mood and refused to let her close. Her touch made him flinch. He stepped back, a rigid wall. His jaw was tight, his gaze distant.

"What was I to do?" Betsy wanted to make everything right. "I didn't know you then, and we get questions all the time about residents here. And I for sure didn't know they were coming today," she justified, folding and unfolding her fingers nervously.

"Really?" Joshua responded angrily. "How often do you get phone calls from the FBI wanting information about World War II heroes who reside here?"

"Well, never," Betsy admitted meekly.

Looking for approval or forgiveness or something, Betsy continued, "But I do have some good news to share with you, Joshua."

Not able to conceive of anything good she could possibly have to say, and exceedingly disgusted, he retorted, "What good news could you possibly fucking have for me, Bets?"

"The injection I gave to your grandfather," Betsy explained, "will make it appear that your grandfather is having a heart attack, and they will either have to take him to a hospital or bring him back here to be seen by one of our doctors."

"No shit, Betsy? Really?" Joshua wasn't at all sure he believed her.

"No shit, Sherlock; really," purred Betsy, proud of her spy effort. "Just wait a few more minutes."

About that time, they heard a big commotion in the reception area and an alarm went off.

Betsy smiled at Joshua and pronounced, "That is the alarm for the M.D. who is on site to get to a phone and call the front desk to find out what the emergency is."

"See what I told you, Joshua," Betsy proudly proclaimed. "They're back!"

Betsy and Joshua watched as the two government agents

dragged Nathaniel into the emergency room, unconscious and limp. They threw him onto the table, emptied his suitcase, and began searching through his belongings until the doctor arrived and ordered them out.

Joshua grabbed Betsy, worried. "Are you sure he'll be okay? He looks dead."

"He'll be fine in an hour," she reassured him, placing her hand on his.

Joshua didn't pull away this time as he thought about what he'd do for Betsy if his grandfather pulled through. They watched as the FBI agents argued with the doctor, then left. Betsy went to the room and returned with good news: "He'll be back to normal by this afternoon."

"Are you sure? Are you sure there won't be any permanent side effects from the shot?" Joshua had to know, still very worried about his grandfather but emotionally starting to come back to earth.

"I'm sure, Joshua. I talked to our staff doctor, then I personally checked his pulse, oxygen saturation rate, and listened to his heart. For an old guy, he is good!" reported Betsy.

Joshua breathed a sigh of relief and could breathe again. Now, more than ever, he needed to get to the bottom of the mystery—especially since the FBI was too interested and would be back to snatch his grandfather.

"Okay, Bets, I am out of here for now. Will you be here when my grandfather comes back around?"

"Maybe. I only have to work until noon today. But I am pretty sure he will be awake and moving around by then. In fact, I will stick around until I am sure that he is okay. Okay?"

"That would be very much appreciated, Betsy. Thanks a bunch. See you tonight, okay?"

"That's a deal, Mo."
"See you at the bar?"
"Perfect."
"YOU owe me."
"No. YOU owe me."

CHAPTER 21

Joshua sat in the rental car, reflecting on the events of the day. The sun was high, and the day had warmed. He felt really bad seeing his war-hero grandfather treated like that. Poor man. Joshua had peeked into the recovery room prior to leaving the facility and saw his grandfather lying there, not moving, mouth wide open. One of his skinny arms lay across his chest and the other hung off the metal table. Joshua waited until he could see the rhythmic movements of breath going in and out before he was reassured that Nathaniel was alive.

A different nurse was in the room, talking to the veteran in a sing-song voice, condescendingly patting his hand as if Nathaniel were a child. A knot tightened in Joshua's stomach. He remembered stories his grandfather used to tell, tales of bravery and sacrifice, now a stark contrast to this quiet indignity. Joshua's gaze drifted to the faded Medal of Honor photograph on the wall—his grandfather, younger, stronger, a rifle held high. *Victory.*

The word echoed hollowly in his mind. He thought of the newsreel footage, the mushroom cloud, the hushed whispers about the sheer number of lives lost. *Victory . . . at what cost?* The question lingered, heavy and unsettling, and he started to think about how WWII really ended.

Physically exhausted and mentally whipped, Joshua started the car and drove to Jack in the Box. The food didn't matter much—what mattered was making a plan with his grandfather, knowing the FBI pricks would return. He decided to return to the nursing home the next morning at 0800.

Desperately needing rest, he collapsed onto the bed without bothering with the sheets. After setting an alarm, he woke up to Jimi Hendrix playing "Foxy Lady" at 2000. A fitting song for who he was about to see. He had time to grab more fast food and haul ass to the bar. Parking a couple of blocks away, he walked quickly, looking left and right, feeling paranoid. *What if those FBI pricks decided to come and grab him to squeeze him for what he knew?* He shuddered at the thought.

At the bar, he ordered a beer while waiting for Betsy. A grin spread across his face as he recalled the fun from the night before, his spirits now lifted, wondering what tonight might bring.

Just then a sweet voice purred in his ear.

"Are you free tonight, big boy?"

Startled for the second time by the voice from behind, even though he recognized it as Betsy's, Joshua spun around in his seat, smiled, stood up, pulled out her chair, and recovered: "Fancy seeing you here. Have we met before?"

"Yes, of course we have, silly boy . . . and I scared you that time too!" Betsy laughed.

"Yes," Joshua sighed. "You got me again."

"I have good news for you, spy boy," Betsy announced slyly.

Joshua looked around a bit nervously, trying to discern if anyone had heard her statement.

"Shh, Goose! This could be dangerous," Joshua whispered with real emphasis.

"I'm sorry, Joshua," apologized Betsy, looking down at the floor. But then she quickly looked up, her face brightening. "But

I do have what could be really good news."

"Oh, really? What is that, Betsy?" he inquired, lightening up in look and tone. "And oh, by the way, people have gotten shot for sneaking up on me."

"Oh right, spy master. You don't even have a gun."

"Yes, I do, but I don't have any bullets. But if I did, you would be in real trouble."

"Right. I'm so scared. Anyway, I waited until about 1 o'clock before I left. Your grandfather had been to lunch and was already back in his room doing fine."

"Sweeet. Very sweet," Joshua emphasized as he leaned over to give Betsy a gentle kiss.

Now holding her face in his hands, Joshua spoke ever so sweetly to Betsy: "Sounds like another tequila night to me, baby."

Betsy shivered a little and gushed, "I can hardly wait for my clothes to fall off again."

Although Joshua felt that the remainder of the evening after the bar was a lot of fun, he was mostly preoccupied with thoughts of what would come of the information he had—what clues and secrets the matches held, what tomorrow would bring—still wondering if any of this shit was really true.

After their marathon lovemaking session had concluded, Betsy looked up at Joshua, seeking approval. "Is everything okay now? Have I made up for earlier?"

"Yes, Betsy, I am drained dry. Have I taken good care of you?" Joshua wanted to know, giving her a fond look as he warmly caressed her arm.

"Oh yes!" she emphasized.

"You made everything okay again by your bravery today, Bets."

"Anything you want me to do now, I will," assured a now purring Betsy.

It was hard—literally—not to go for it again upon hearing Betsy's comment, but Joshua had to think. However, another part of Joshua overruled thinking. *Time for that later.*

As he lay there, spent and satisfied, blood still coursing through his body at an elevated rate, Joshua recalled the previous day and the eerie encounter with the orderly—the nurse's aide he'd run into twice, once by car and once in person. On the second occasion, they had stared at each other, both sensing something was off, but neither spoke. *Had he heard his grandfather going on about 12 August too? Jesus. Who else?*

Joshua berated himself for forgetting his training and surroundings, and for blabbing to the aide. He felt like a failure: he couldn't keep his cool, couldn't anticipate the government's interference, let his emotions show, and had failed at the CIA.

He felt sorry for himself, especially remembering how little he knew his father, although he didn't know from where that thought came. But then, a smile crept across his face at the thought of Betsy—at least she had proven to be a friend, and a whole lot of fun too.

Coming out of his contemplations for a minute, Joshua looked at Betsy and asked, "Did any of those assholes even tell you why they were interested in my grandfather?"

"Hmmm," Betsy contemplated, holding her finger to her chin. "I will have to think about what they said because they did not say anything to me directly."

"All I can remember is," Betsy recalled, looking at Joshua, "they showed up about two weeks ago. And then you showed up yesterday," she finished brightly.

"And then . . ."

"And then you convinced me to sleep with you, Mo."

"I convinced you, Bets?"

"Yes, you did," Betsy retorted in a petulant, perturbed tone.

Joshua let Betsy off the hook. "And I am really glad you let me convince you. And speaking of which, are you in a convincible mood now?"

"Again?"

"Yes."

"Maybe."

"Well, what do I have to do to convince you?"

"You know where to start, spy boy, so get busy!"

Before anything had happened that day, Muqtar was excited and nervous about his interview to be brought on board as a paid full-time employee, but his mind kept drifting back to what Joshua had said about his grandfather, Colonel Nathaniel, and the mutterings he had overheard. Muqtar couldn't recall anything specific or unusual from Nathaniel's outbursts, just complaints about America's wars and corporate greed.

Arriving early for his interview, Muqtar ran into his wife, Julie, and posed the question: "Have you heard anything about Colonel Nathaniel in Room 106?"

"Anything like what?" she wanted to know.

"War stories or anything strange," Muqtar explained.

Julie thought for a moment. "Well, one day he left the door open and was sitting on his bed with his hands out in front of him, like he was holding something."

Julie went on. "I remember thinking he was looking down as if he was looking into a microscope. Why?"

"I don't know really. Just something about him tells me he has a secret from World War II."

"Well, Michael, you do remember that two FBI guys came to see the Colonel about two weeks ago."

"Oh, that's right. I do remember that," recalled Muqtar, laughing at the memory of the old Colonel shouting obscenities at the FBI agents as he chased them down the hallway.

Julie noticed that Muqtar was now staring off into space, so she demanded, "Aren't you supposed to be preparing for your interview?"

"Yes, honey. Why?"

"Why? Because you look like you are imagining traveling in space, not explaining why you want to work here, that's why," she scolded.

Coming back to earth following his wife's reproach, Muqtar looked at his watch. "Well, wish me luck, babe. I am off to the interview."

"Good luck, honey. I know you will do great."

The interview did go well. The head nurse had lots of nice things to say about Julie and her promotion, as well as complimenting him on his work skills.

"Mr. Brown, I can honestly say that I wish we had more people around here who were as diligent about doing their job as you have been while working as an unpaid orderly. I am pleased to offer you a full-time position."

"Thank you, Mrs. Weatherby. I will do my best to live up to my wife's high standards."

"I'm sure you will."

Muqtar was feeling real good; almost everything was right with the world.

Then a nurse flung open the door and shouted, "Mrs. Weatherby, come quick. There is a big ruckus going on upstairs at Colonel Meister's room and you need to come."

"Should I call the police?" Mrs. Weatherby wanted to know.

"No," replied the unidentified nurse. "The ones causing the ruckus are the police—the FBI."

Mrs. Weatherby rushed out, saying, "We'll see you tomorrow at 0600, Michael." Muqtar considered following her but decided against it, not wanting to get involved with the police or FBI.

Confused and curious, Muqtar figured his wife might know more. He decided to wait for the FBI to leave before heading home. About twenty minutes later, he left through the back exit and walked to his car, still wondering about the Colonel.

As he drove around to the front of the nursing home, a black Tahoe sped in, almost hitting him. "Shit, watch out!" Muqtar yelled, veering out of the way. He watched, captivated by the scene, as two men dragged the unconscious Colonel inside. Muqtar figured they were the FBI, so he stayed out of it.

He hoped the Colonel was okay. Later that afternoon, he returned to the nursing home, hoping to talk to the Colonel before dinner. Muqtar called his wife, who had worked the early shift, made an excuse about being late to pick up the kid, and headed up to Room 106. He knocked but heard no response. After a second knock, still nothing. Worried the old man was passed out, Muqtar knocked again.

KNOCK! KNOCK! KNOCK!

Muqtar put his ear to the door and could hear some movement inside.

"Who is it?" demanded the Colonel in a gruff growl.

"It is me, Colonel. Michael Brown," he announced.

"What do you want?" was the response.

"Nothing really, sir. I just came by to check on you," confessed Muqtar.

Muqtar was a bit surprised when the door opened.

"Well, come on in then, Michael," welcomed Nathaniel.

Muqtar was even more surprised at the warm invitation. *Maybe getting hassled by the Feds mellowed out the old man,* he surmised.

The Colonel continued to speak. "I need your help doing something."

"Okay, Colonel. What do you need?"

"Do you know what a Google map is, Michael?"

"Yes, sir. I sure do."

"Well, okay then. Can you print me a Google map?"

"Yes, of course. What do you want a Google map of, sir?"

"I want a Google map of Tokyo, including Tokyo Bay, with latitude and longitudinal markings on the edges. Can that be done, Michael?"

Muqtar thought about the request for a minute and then declared, "Yes, indeed. I can do that. In fact, I can go and print one right now and bring it back to your room, if you like."

The Colonel smiled. "That would be great, Michael. I would appreciate that very much."

Muqtar left to print a Google map of Tokyo Bay, his mind filled with questions. Why did the Colonel need it? What did it have to do with the FBI's attempted kidnapping?

Returning with the map, he knocked on the door but again no response. He knocked louder—still nothing. He checked the doorknob and found the door to be unlocked. He opened the door and entered to find the Colonel staring out the window.

"Colonel, it's me, Michael. I have the map," Muqtar announced.

"Thank you," Nathaniel answered, turning and extending

his hand.

Muqtar handed him the map. The Colonel sat on the bed, tracing the edges with his fingers, pausing now and then as if recalling something. His fingers stopped at a spot in the middle of Tokyo Bay.

"Humph," the Colonel declared. Muqtar couldn't really hear what the Colonel then whispered to himself, but he swore the Colonel surreptitiously uttered, "X marks the spot."

Looking up at Muqtar, then toward the door, Nathaniel simply stated, "Thank you. You can go now."

Muqtar left the room, trying to recall where the Colonel's fingers had met on the map. Outside, he traced the spot on a second map he had made, wondering what could be in Tokyo Bay.

He puzzled over it as he hurried down the hallway, not wanting anyone to ask what he was doing there, while thinking it might be a World War II secret or a bomb site. *But why would anyone care about a bomb submerged in Tokyo Bay for nearly eighty years?* There was nothing unique in the area, but he couldn't shake his desire to know the Colonel's secret.

Determined to uncover the truth, Muqtar resolved to investigate further. But for now, the mystery would have to wait.

CHAPTER 22

The next morning, while Betsy showered, Joshua pulled the old matchbook from his pocket, musing over the mysteries its coordinates might reveal. He felt increasingly certain of the veracity of his grandfather's tale: a World War II hydrogen bomb was dropped in Tokyo Bay and was still hidden there. Laughing at his own thoughts of grand secrets and conspiracies, Joshua resolved to stay patient and let events unfold.

Betsy emerged from the bathroom wrapped in a towel, her hair damp. "Are you going to take a shower?" she wanted to know.

"Sure am," Joshua replied, glancing her way. That glance caught a shot of her bare leg, reaching all the way up to the gates of heaven.

"In a minute," Joshua pronounced, motioning for her to come over to him.

"Are you going to get me all sweaty again?"

"Most definitely," Joshua assured her. An hour later, having made good on his promise, it was time for Betsy to go to work and time for him to get back to the nursing home to see how the mystery quest was going to manifest.

Joshua kissed Betsy as they walked to her car and made a request: "Betsy, please try to find the paperwork on my grandfather and see if it shows who ratted him out to the Feds—and make me a copy if you can."

"Sure will," she agreed. Betsy then took his hand in hers and asked wistfully, "When are you going to leave town?"

"Pretty soon, baby. I'll know my plan better once my grandfather and I meet up today. I need to get some money together for the trip to Japan to figure out what is there—or not there. I am going to go, but I'll be back. It's not like I'm going over there to stay," Joshua told her.

Betsy was sad, he could tell. Joshua wanted to lift her spirits.

"Betsy, have you ever been to Japan?"

"Huh? Japan? No. Joshua, I've never even been to New York or LA," Betsy admitted. "Why do you ask?"

"As I said, I have a feeling my path is going to lead me to Tokyo soon, and I thought you might want to go with me," Joshua offered, sort of sincerely.

"I doubt that very much, Joshua. You have a quest to follow, and I am only a stopping point along the way," she commented bravely, not wanting to sound sad—but Betsy felt the truth of what she said.

Joshua and Betsy both knew her surmise was correct, that he would soon be gone, most likely for good. If not on this trip, then eventually. But they were both determined not to let the remainder of their time together, however much that might be, turn into a bummer.

"All right, baby. I'll see you back here after work," Joshua stated enthusiastically. "In fact, why don't you make us a reservation at the best restaurant in St. Louis, wherever you want to go, no matter the cost. I'm buying."

"OK. I thought you said you were broke? Well, anyway, I'll see if I can get off early, and we'll go to this great steakhouse I've heard about but never been to." Betsy seemed quite perked up at this thought. "Meet me back here no later than six. I'll make reservations for seven. OK?"

"Yep, that sounds good," Joshua acknowledged, now feeling as though the world—at least the world of Betsy and Joshua—was somehow made right by this dinner date. He wrestled briefly with thoughts that maybe he had used Betsy for her body, her place, and her information. That was probably all true, he conceded, but then again, she had benefited too. That thought made him smile, which led him to think about what would likely happen that night, and that thought made other parts of his body smile too.

"Maybe I can help ease your pain a little after we have dinner," Betsy proposed as she squeezed Joshua's arm and looked up at him with her flirty eyes.

That comment evoked a positive, involuntary response in Joshua.

"Sure. That sounds good. What time did you say you get off?"

"I leave work at 6, but as to getting off, we'll have to see, won't we?"

They both laughed.

After a final squeeze of his arm, she stepped into her car, leaving Joshua to wrestle with his thoughts. Fixating on the matchbook, he became certain the numbers inside were coordinates. Determined to uncover his grandfather's mystery bomb named *Payback,* his resolve to go to Tokyo deepened. A quick nap cleared his mind before he entered the coordinates into Google Maps, pinpointing a spot in Tokyo Bay—proof of the hydrogen bomb's resting place.

Yet, as his focus sharpened, his thoughts drifted to Mei Lei, her business aspirations, and their poignant goodbye in Ann Arbor, the ache of her absence still lingering. *"Joshua, you have given me much joy and happiness over the last 18 months while we* have been friends."

As he opened his mouth to speak, Mei Lei pressed her finger to his lips to quiet him and continued.

"Our lives, having come together for this short time, must now separate forever," Mei Lei stated calmly. *"For I must return to my world, to my family and its customs, and you must go forward with your plans to become a spy."*

Mei Lei tenderly cupped Joshua's face, gazing deeply into his eyes. *"I've never known love like this before,"* she confessed. *"You've filled me with warmth and peace. I'll carry this love with me to Hong Kong, cherishing it forever."*

Tears streamed down Joshua's face in spite of his best effort to hold them back as he met Mei Lei's warm, loving gaze with his own tear-streaked look. He had tried everything to convince her to stay—to build a life together in New York, maybe even at the UN—but it was futile. She belonged to a prosperous, proud family in Hong Kong, and Joshua had nothing to offer but dreams and a love that burned deeply for her.

Blinking back the tears, he confirmed once more, "So, Mei Lei, are you saying we'll never communicate again once you're back in Hong Kong?" He already knew her answer: she couldn't let him be a part of her life going forward, no matter how much it hurt both of them.

"Joshua, you know how awkward that would be for me to have to explain to my mother that I had a relationship with an American. We have talked about it many times, have we not?" Mei Lei said sweetly.

"Yes, my dear. I know your mother would not want you to be with an American. I know . . ." Joshua's voice trailed off in futility, knowing there was no hope of changing her mind.

"Right, Joshua, that would not be acceptable in my world,

not now, not ever," Mei Lei reminded him again for the nth time. "So please forward my mail and my grades to me and that will be the end of it, the end of us."

True enough. Chinese society had been closed to outsiders for thousands of years, and that was not going to change merely because Joshua so desperately wanted it to. In the '70s China finally opened up to the West, and the society *should* open up too, he would argue.

"In 2019, China's economy is roaring, doing business everywhere, and you could be the bellwether of societal change, Mei Lei," Joshua would say.

Joshua knew Mei Lei's refusal to stay stemmed from her family's deep-seated traditions; the Ho family upheld the belief that Chinese people should only marry within their own. Their relationship had always sparked debates between them, from cultural divides to history's darkest moments. Joshua defended the U.S.'s use of atomic bombs to end World War II, while Mei Lei mourned the immense suffering on all sides, her compassion extending even to those who had wronged her own people.

She often argued that the loudest voices advocating war drowned out those of peace, whether in Japan during Pearl Harbor or the U.S. in Iraq and Afghanistan. Mei Lei's idealism, deeply rooted in kindness and peace, clashed with Joshua's skepticism. When he pressed her on China's own transgressions, like Tiananmen Square or Uyghur oppression, she deflected, wary of the risks such discussions posed.

Joshua's thoughts drifted to their late-night college debates, where his love for her made every conversation electric, even if they never fully bridged their differences. The memory pulled him back to the present. If a hydrogen bomb still lay in Tokyo Bay, he couldn't trust anyone—not the U.S. government or global powers—to handle it responsibly. He had to find it first, and he had to do it alone.

Determined, Joshua decided to contact Stuart, an old CIA officemate who he again recalled owed him a favor. Stuart, a brilliant linguist with a knack for accents, had once been caught by Joshua mid-romp with an office assistant—a secret Joshua had kept. The memory of Stuart, pants down and caught mid-stroke red-handed, made Joshua chuckle.

Stuart turned and saw Joshua looking at him. Joshua quickly shut the door and strolled to his office to absorb what had just happened. He couldn't help himself but laugh—and laugh he did. A lot. About thirty or forty minutes later, Stuart skulked into the office, looking embarrassed but satisfied.

"Well, Stuart, did you give her your best shot?" Joshua demanded.

Stuart started giggling like a fool, his face turning red.

"I sure did. I banged the hell out of her," Stuart announced proudly, then nervously added, "Are you going to rat me out?"

"No, Stuart," Joshua reassured him. "Your secret is safe with me. Just next time, get a room!"

Still smiling at the memory, Joshua knew he could count on Stuart's help in uncovering what the FBI wanted with his grandfather.

CHAPTER 23

Nathaniel woke up disoriented, unsure of the day, but the thought of his grandson visiting again brought him clarity and excitement. A smile tugged at his lips. What day was it? Tuesday? Wednesday? His eyes fluttered open as he greeted the soft light of a new spring morning. The fog lifted. He pushed himself up, the aches forgotten. Today was a good day. After more than seventy-five years, he was ready to reveal the secret he had guarded since 12 August 1945—a secret he had feared could ruin his life, career, and family if revealed.

He remembered the covert mission: a bomb dropped after Japan had already told the Americans they were going to surrender; a mission launched without cameras, backup aircraft, or spotters. The mission's secrecy and questionable authorization haunted him, leaving him unsure if President Truman even knew about it. Despite multiple debriefings, including three rounds of truth serum, Nathaniel had never disclosed the bomb's true location, citing turbulence and distractions as the reason. He believed it rested undisturbed in Tokyo Bay, buried in soft muck, hidden from the world.

On his way to the nursing home, Joshua called his insurance

company, who confirmed that repairs to the cab were under-way. He again thought it odd to have run into Mr. Brown both in the car and then again at the nursing home, and wondered if he'd see him again to apologize once more for the accident.

As Joshua weaved through morning traffic, he realized he was running late. He was supposed to meet his grandfather at 8:00 a.m., but with the time now at 7:45, he knew he'd be late and felt frustrated with himself—but he for sure wasn't going to speed. He hoped his grandfather wouldn't be too angry and thought showing him his old watch might help. The 23-jewel Gruen watch, given to key crew members who flew B-29s in World War II, had been passed down to his father and then to him. The watch still kept perfect time after a repair by a watch-maker in Marshall, Michigan.

"Goddamnit!" Nathaniel exploded. Here it was, nearly 0810, and Joshua wasn't there yet. Didn't that child realize that time was important, that deadlines were important? That time spent was never recovered? Shit! Motherfucker! Nathaniel's thoughts grew darker as he sat back down on his bed to wait. He then began to worry. Did the FBI snatch Joshua?

"I fucking hate waiting," Nathaniel spewed out loud.

About that time—0811, to be exact—Nathaniel heard a knock at his door.

"Who's there?" he wanted to know.

"It's me, your grandson Joshua. Running late, Grampa."

"What fucking time is it?" interrogated Nathaniel through the door, relieved that Joshua had arrived, but still pissed.

"Uh, let's see," apologized Joshua as he pulled up his shirt sleeve to check the time, knowing full well that he was very late. He considered lying about what time it was but thought it best not to combine being late with a lie.

"The time is 0811, sir," reported Joshua courteously and respectfully, with just a touch of pleading in his voice.

Nathaniel arose from the bed and walked to the door. Without saying a word, he opened it, saw Joshua standing there, then turned away to walk to the window, disgusted.

"What time did we agree that you would meet me here today, grandson?"

"Uh, 0800, sir."

"0800 what?"

"0800 sharp, Grampa."

Pirouetting slowly, Nathaniel demanded, "Why are you late? I was worried!"

Joshua confessed, "No good reason. I'm sorry." He hoped his grandfather would be understanding and let the tardiness go enough to tell him the whole story.

"Sit down," Nathaniel ordered. "I'll tell you everything. As you know, the surprise attack on Pearl Harbor in 1941 galvanized American support for the war.

"Although I didn't know it at the time, there were zealots in the military who wanted to bomb the Japanese back to the Stone Age, to pay them back for their scurrilous act no matter the cost or outcome. Now, the U.S. didn't have the atomic bomb ready to drop on Germany when it was defeated in April 1945."

"However, the A-bomb was plenty ready to drop on the Japanese in August 1945. Logistically, Japan was different than Germany for two reasons. First, we and our allies were already crawling up Hitler's backside and closing in on Berlin in early 1945. So it was only a matter of time before we crushed the remains of the Nazi machine."

"Second, the Japanese islands, especially the main island of Japan, were well fortified and well defended. The Japanese had already demonstrated a willingness to sacrifice their men in suicide missions—a practice they would have certainly continued had we invaded Japan."

"So, history-wise, the decision was made to drop an atomic bomb on Hiroshima in hopes that they would surrender, thus preventing a lot of Allied Force bloodshed. We got the attention of the Japanese with Hiroshima, but they did not wave the white flag—too much jingoistic pride, I guess."

"Regardless, we dropped the second A-bomb on Nagasaki three days later, which the brass was sure would get the job done. And it did. Six days after the second A-bomb was dropped, the Japanese unconditionally surrendered. But that wasn't good enough for many members of the military and probably wasn't good enough for many politicians either. However, I don't know that for a fact. What I did find out later was that the day after Nagasaki, the Japanese government sent word through an attaché that they were going to surrender."

"Anyway, I was sent to the Mariana Islands in early May 1945 to serve as a bombardier on a B-29 Superfortress. I thought the assignment was very rude, after all I had been through in Europe. Because for me, the war was over. However, no one gave a shit about what my experience had been in Europe nor what I wanted. They just wanted me to get my ass to the Pacific front as ordered, so that's where I went."

Nathaniel continued: "When I got there, I was assigned to a specially rigged B-29. They called those special models 'silversides' or some such thing. The point is there were three of these silversides at the base on Tinian Island. You've heard of two of them: *Enola Gay* and *Boxcar*."

"Our airplane was called *Tiger Droppings*. Don't you think that was a pretty good name?" Nathaniel paused, looking at Joshua.

"I sure do," replied Joshua, who actually liked the name.

"She was a fine airplane, and for weeks we'd get up at two or three in the morning, take off toward Japan, drop a dummy bomb over the mainland, and return to base."

"Along comes early August, and three huge crates were delivered to the airbase while several military transports dropped off a horde of civilian guys. The civilians weren't like worker bees; they were college-educated guys who had a reason to be there. Guards were posted where the civilians were housed, and strict orders were given to stay the fuck away from them."

"Which we did, except when the dummy bombs were loaded. They were so damned heavy it practically took an army to load them. Once, in fact, a dummy bomb was loaded on the afternoon before an early morning mission. The combination of heat and weight during the day caused two tires to burst, so they didn't try that anymore."

"I got to talking with the civilian guys during the dry runs and was told that our three airplanes were going to end the war. I, of course, thought that was all hype and bullshit, having been pumped full of it prior to too many missions before."

"Looking back on it, when the *Enola Gay* took off on August 6th, the whole base was abuzz with anticipation. Three or four or five other aircraft accompanied her on the mission. When all of them returned to base unscathed, it was a big letdown. We thought the mission had failed, but we really didn't know because everything was still super hush-hush."

"Three days later, *Boxcar* takes off with a whole entourage of escort planes and again a whole lot of anticipation and excitement was felt throughout the base. She also returned unharmed, and by now, the rest of us had no idea what the fuck was happening. Those of us assigned to *Tiger Droppings* were curious but uninformed. We figured we were up next, but for what, we did not know."

Nathaniel paused to light a cigarette.

"Grampa, isn't your room non-smoking only?"

"Yeah. So?" scoffed Nathaniel indignantly. "Nobody gives me shit about anything I do anymore. They just want me to die and for my secret to die with me."

"I understand," Joshua said knowingly, hoping Nathaniel would get to the point.

"About August 10th, or maybe early August 11th—the days and nights blurred together back then—we were summoned to the command tent and told we were going on a live mission to bomb the Tokyo area on 12 August. We all kind of looked at each other because Tokyo didn't have any remaining manufacturing capacity. We had already bombed the shit out of it," Nathaniel remembered.

"So, OK. We all thought, what's the purpose of this mission? To drop propaganda leaflets? To show force? What? Supposedly the Japanese were already whipped from the effects of the two missions a few days before, although we didn't know exactly how. What were we going to do to add to the mix?"

"No one knew. We just had our orders. I wasn't satisfied with that, having been fucked around by the military before, so I talked with one of the civilians later—a guy named Daniel—and found out our bomb was different. It was a hydrogen bomb, an H-bomb, the very first one, and it was at least a hundred times more powerful than the other two, which were atomic bombs."

"Grampa," interrupted Joshua, who had researched the history of the atomic bomb the evening before, "we didn't create the H-bomb until 1952."

"So says you, grandson, and so thinks the rest of the world.

But the world is wrong and so are you. We dropped an H-bomb on Tokyo, but it didn't go off. An H-bomb—not a puny A-bomb."

"So why didn't it go off, Grampa? Was it a dud? Technical failure? What?" Joshua pressed.

Nathaniel looked sharply at Joshua, crushed his cigarette on the floor with exaggerated force, took a deep breath, turned toward the window—and began to cry; shaking and crying.

What? Joshua had never seen his grandfather cry. He had never seen him shed a tear of happiness, sadness, or regret, and here he was, crying for the third time in as many days. Joshua waited silently, unsure how to respond.

After a couple of minutes, Nathaniel sighed and croaked, "I've been waiting to let that out for more than seventy-five years."

"Let what out?" Joshua gently prompted.

"Let out my feelings about the mission of 12 August 1945."

Joshua was a bit surprised and confused by this but decided to wait for his grandfather to explain further.

"Once we got in the air, the pilot, Major Morrissey—who was a class-A prick—told us our mission was to drop the H-bomb on the Emperor's Palace to take him out and destroy everything within ten square miles of the target," Nathaniel continued. "The mission was called *Cherry Blossom*," he added.

"But as we flew along, I began to feel very uneasy about taking out the Emperor. I just didn't feel it was the right thing to do. You see, I knew the Japanese people believed the Emperor was a god, and I didn't think taking him out would hasten the end of the war, first of all. And it seemed like the equivalent—more or less—of killing the Pope. Both were symbols of peace, not war."

"So as we flew along, I concocted a plan to jettison the bomb early if the opportunity came. I wanted it to look like an honest error, not deliberate disobedience of an order. Fortunately, after the bomb bay doors opened, we hit some air turbulence, so I hit the switch and let 'er go."

"I get that, Grampa," Joshua said. "So you dropped it early. Why didn't it go off?"

"That's the almost funny part, grandson," Nathaniel said, managing a faint smile at the memory. "In the furor that ensued after I dropped the bomb, Major Morrissey failed to send the radio signal to arm it. Once it fell below three thousand feet, there was a failsafe mechanism linked to an altimeter that prevented it from being armed. So, it didn't explode."

"Major Morrissey was too pissed and preoccupied, screaming threats about me being court-martialed, to do his job. That prick did try, however, to get me sent to Leavenworth or even hung for treason. But when I explained what happened—and of course, I told the bigwigs about the major's fuck-up—they shit-canned the whole inquiry."

"The only thing they asked me about—and kept asking me for years and years—was where the bomb had hit the ground. But I never told them," Nathaniel finished, almost gleeful. "I figured my secret was a good life insurance policy, and by the looks of it, I was right," he concluded, smiling as he looked around the room.

"All right, Grampa. I understand now," Joshua nodded. Well, mostly.

Coming back to the present, Joshua asked, "Is the bomb still buried in the bay?"

"That, I don't know, grandson. If it was found, it never made the newspaper. That I know for sure, because I've looked for news of it ever since and never heard a peep nor seen a headline."

"So why tell me about it now, Grampa?"

"Why? Because the world would be a better place if it were found by the right person, that's why," Nathaniel proclaimed. "And you are the right person for the job. In fact, you're the only person for the job."

Joshua was flattered. "So you want me to go to Japan and recover the bomb? Why pick me for this, Grampa?"

"Yes, yes I do. And why? Because you have all the physical tools, the mental makeup, and the fortitude to see the mission through to the end. You also speak Japanese and Chinese and all the other '-ese,' grandson, so you can get along," Nathaniel said emphatically, having clearly thought through who he'd entrust with this task.

Without pausing, Joshua said, "Yes, Grampa. I'll do it. You can trust me one hundred percent."

"Excellent! Excellent! I knew I could count on you."

Then, reaching into his pocket, Nathaniel produced a wrinkled, yellowed piece of paper and handed it to Joshua as if it were the crown jewels.

Joshua accepted the gift and slowly opened the paper. Inside were written the same coordinates—35° 36' 1.012" N and 139° 52' 0.512" E—as on the tattered pack of matches. *Grampa must be slipping,* Joshua thought. *He's forgotten what he told me yesterday and what he divulged to Nurse Betsy. To be fair, he was accosted and drugged.*

Nathaniel spoke. "For almost eighty years, I kept the pack of matches where I'd written down the coordinates, but I guess those FBI bastards either stole them from me or they fell out of my pocket. But somehow I remembered them well enough to write them down for you today," he finished proudly.

"Thank you, Grampa," Joshua said, pulling the match pack

from his pocket.

"Well, I'll be goddamned. Where did you find those?"

"You slipped them to me when the FBI cocksuckers were about to haul you off."

"Well, so I did, I guess," Nathaniel said, not recalling the exchange as he took the matches from Joshua's hand and looked at them.

Joshua was stunned by the incredible secret he now held—a key piece of World War II history, verified through his grandfather's memory and the matches. He realized the danger he could face if he uncovered and revealed the bombing plan his grandfather had foiled. Should he contact the Japanese authorities, his old CIA boss, or keep the secret to himself? As he pondered these options, Nathaniel interrupted.

"Grandson, you're probably wondering what you should do next. I've wondered that for almost eighty years, not knowing which way to turn. Keep the secret? Reveal the secret? Search for the bomb myself? All had their pluses and minuses. Yet for me, to reveal the actual whereabouts of the bomb after lying about it for so long would—or could—subject me and probably you too to criminal charges, or a knife in the back, or worse."

"So I created a trap for myself. A trap from which there was, and still is, no escaping. But you, grandson," Nathaniel said proudly, raising his bony, weathered hand to Joshua's shoulder, "you and only you can do the right thing by finding the bomb and disposing of it safely. I've worried for all these years that something could set it off, and Lord, what an explosion—what damage that would cause."

Joshua met his grandfather's serious gaze. "Let me get this straight, Grampa. You want me to find a hydrogen bomb and dispose of it safely? Is that right?"

Nathaniel nodded. "Most assuredly. Yes, grandson. That is exactly what I want you to do. Find the bomb and dispose of it safely," he repeated. Then he added, "And do not tell a soul in their government or ours what you've done."

"Why not tell someone connected to the government, Grampa?"

"Because politicians can't be trusted. If you reveal the whereabouts of the bomb to a government official, I am certain you'll be killed, or locked in a looney tunes hospital—I'm not sure what. But in my heart, I know absolutely that you, personally, would be the loser in the end. Exposing deep, dark secrets like this could create big international political problems for the U.S. The revelation would definitely result in you being sacrificed and crushed in the process."

The thought of Joshua being tortured or killed filled Nathaniel's eyes with tears again, and his head fell forward.

"I get your point, Grampa. And I agree—the U.S. government might try something. But wouldn't the Japanese be grateful to know?"

"Maybe or maybe not. There are plenty of Japanese who still hate the U.S. for dropping the A-bombs. Resurrecting old feelings combined with knowing the actual target was the Emperor's Palace could stir a lot of present-day anger in powerful people—and some crazy ones. Revealing the secret to any government folks carries too much risk. Besides, the Japanese don't possess any nuclear weapons. This H-bomb would be a perfect template for their scientists to reverse engineer, letting them join the nuclear fraternity."

Lifting his head and looking straight at Joshua, Nathaniel concluded, "I don't want that responsibility and neither do you. It's best to find it, retrieve it, and safely dispose of it . . . discreetly."

Joshua nodded. "Alright then. That's what I'll do. Find it, retrieve it, and dispose of it safely," he repeated, making the phrase his mantra. But how? *How the fuck am I supposed to do this?* he wondered. *I have no money, I don't actually speak Japanese, and I have no connections there. Nothing.*

A cascade of sarcastic scenarios filled his mind. *Excuse me, sir? I'm on a bomb quest. Do you mind if I dig up Tokyo Bay for a 10,000-pound bomb? It'll only take a minute.* Or: *"Excuse me, sir? I need to rent a backhoe and a huge dump truck so I can dig up and haul off a ginormous bomb left over from World War II that didn't explode."* But no; that second thought wasn't right, because the bomb was buried in muck somewhere at the bottom of Tokyo Bay. *"Excuse me, sir? Can I enlist the help of a crew with a barge and crane to help me extricate a 10,000-pound bomb off the bottom of Tokyo Bay?"*

Uh, no. That wouldn't work either, Joshua thought, amused by his proposed scenarios. The option of being open wasn't worth further consideration; the primary requirement was to keep this assignment extremely low-profile—as in discreet, discreet. Crap. What to do? No other options came to mind that wouldn't draw attention to the task at hand.

"Well, Grampa," Joshua said, feeling defeated for not coming up with any viable plan, "I can't figure out how to pull this off without attracting undue attention"—emphasizing "undue."

"I don't have any money to get the equipment for the excavation, and I have no idea what all I'll even need. I sure don't know how to keep it secret, either. And I don't have any way to transport the bomb once I dig it up to get it to a safe location."

"Money, you say? Money is a problem, grandson?"

"Well, of course it is, Grampa. I'm pretty much broke and unemployed."

"Don't worry about money, Joshua. I have plenty to finance the project."

This news shocked Joshua. As far as he knew, no one in his family had any money to speak of—certainly not enough to fund an ocean-based excavation operation.

"That certainly solves the first problem. Since you're telling me your secrets, Grampa, do you mind telling me how you got that money? It couldn't have been from your military pay," scoffed Joshua, thinking of how lousy his own pay had been at the CIA.

"I don't mind telling you at all, grandson. My civilian buddy Daniel told me to buy IBM stock when it was first offered back in '53, and I did. The last I checked," Nathaniel went on, walking over to open his small safe, "I owned a little more than $2.5 million worth of IBM stock. Here. Read this," he said, handing Joshua a statement he had fished out.

Sure enough, Joshua saw the figure: $2.623 million. At which point, he blurted out, "Then why the fuck are you living here?" as he looked around the cramped ten-by-twenty-foot room.

"That's an easy one to answer, grandson. I gave my life to this country, serving in the military, and now it's their turn to take care of me. I never wanted to be a rich man—just a soldier," Nathaniel continued. "It just turned out I made a lucky investment that now can be put to good use!" He grinned. "And just so you know, you're going to inherit the money when I die."

I'll say, Joshua thought. I'll put that money to one hell of a good use, indeed—now and in the future.

"OK, Grampa. The money problem is solved. Now do you have any thoughts on how to extricate this 10,000-pound behemoth from however deep it lies—or lays, however you're supposed to say that—in Tokyo Bay?"

"Sure do, grandson. That's the best part." Nathaniel was prepared, reaching again for something that turned out to be another scrap of paper and a Google map of Tokyo Bay.

"Where did you get this, Grampa? I didn't know you were proficient on computers."

"I'm not, grandson. I got the male nurse's aide to help me."

"A nurse's aide? Wasn't that a little risky, Grampa? Which one? The aide might put two and two together, right?" Joshua pressed, feeling paranoid.

"No fucking way," Nathaniel retorted. "I didn't fucking tell him why I wanted the map, just that I wanted it. And it was the Arab-looking one."

"Shit. So you asked the Arab-looking male nurse to print out the map, Grampa? Do you remember his name?" Joshua was nearly panicking now, afraid of who his grandfather had unknowingly pulled into this.

"Yes, I do. His name tag said 'Brown, M.' He's a nurse's aide. Rather swarthy looking, but a nice enough young man, and he had no trouble helping me."

That's an unreal coincidence, Joshua thought, practically shitting his pants. The same guy I crashed into with my car—then ran into in the hallway here—is the one who printed the map of Tokyo Bay. God, what next? Joshua turned his attention back to the map.

"What are these markings on the edge, Grampa?"

"Those are the latitude and longitude lines, grandson. And here's the best part. You won't have to dig up anything at all, because like I told you before, the bomb didn't hit dry land. It hit the water—right here, right in the middle of Tokyo Bay."

Nathaniel picked up a pencil and drew an X on the map. "This is where she lies, if she's still there, resting in sixty feet of water according to the map."

Joshua didn't know what to say. Originally, he'd pictured a land operation—digging a big hole and pulling out a bomb. He'd forgotten his grandfather mentioned it was at the bottom of Tokyo Bay, and in "only" sixty feet of water at that. Now it changed from using a backhoe to needing a dredging operation, a barge-mounted crane to pull it up, and then a second barge to place it on. He shrugged. Either way, he was certain he'd be found out before he could finish. Whether by land or by sea, the task looked formidable. No—actually impossible.

"What do you think will happen to me if I get caught doing this?"

Nathaniel thought for a second. "Depends at what point in the process you are. You'd probably be turned over to the American consulate either way, but it's very unlikely you'd ever see the inside of a Japanese jail cell."

"OK, then let's assume I'm caught while hoisting the bomb off the bottom of the bay. In other words, caught red-handed. Do I tell the Japanese what I'm trying to extricate?"

Nathaniel mulled this over. Finally, he said, "If you're caught, you're caught. Don't say a word other than to ask to be turned over to the Americans. Then the Japanese and American governments will work it out."

"Assuming that's how it goes, what does our government do to me?"

"They'd probably grill you like a tuna fish, grandson. And you'd be smart to rat me out so I could face the heat."

"Let's take it to the extreme, then, Grampa. I get caught, I get grilled, I rat you out. What happens to you?"

Nathaniel hesitated. "They'd probably grill me, too, then kill me by faking a heart attack. Very unlikely I'd be charged with anything—and very, very unlikely I'd survive the experience."

"And me?"

"Probably they'd brand you a traitor, put you on the no-fly list, tap your phone, monitor your computer for the rest of your life. Stuff like that. You'd never get a government job—most likely never get a job with a major corporation either, as you'd be secretly blackballed. For sure, you'd never be charged with a crime, because if they did, the trial would draw too much attention." Nathaniel paused, then added, "Of course you might suffer a fatal heart attack, too."

"That sucks, Grampa. That scenario sucks for both of us. Sucks mightily."

"Sure does. But do you have a better idea? I've been thinking about this for almost eighty years, and I haven't come up with a better plan. However, I'm open to suggestions."

Joshua considered the options. "As I see it, the options are: One, leave the bomb where it is and risk a catastrophic explosion if another Fukushima-like event happens, or if it just decides to go off. Two, tell the American government and let them deal with it. That'd be hugely embarrassing and very likely get both of us killed. Three, tell the Japanese government. Same embarrassment for the U.S., gives Japan an H-bomb template, and also likely gets us killed. Four, get to Japan, mount an excavation project, retrieve the bomb, and dispose of it carefully—while keeping it all secret."

"That sounds about right, grandson," Nathaniel agreed brightly. "Which option do you pick?"

"Option four, of course, Grampa. It's the only way. It's my quest. It's my bomb quest!" Joshua declared, hoping his conviction would settle into his gut as firmly as it sounded.

Joshua struggled to find more brave words, but an awkward—no, contemplative—silence fell. Both men stared out the window, searching for some way to convey confidence that this plan could actually work, but no words came to either of them.

The truth was the chances of pulling off such an audacious plan were close to nil—or, as Joshua's friend from Texas used to say, "The chances of winning are slim to none, and slim just rode out."

Joshua cleared his throat, hoping that would jumpstart some words, but none came.

After a couple of minutes, Nathaniel asked, "You do speak Japanese, don't you, grandson?"

Joshua turned to look at him. "Uh, no, Grampa. I speak very little Japanese, but I do speak Mandarin Chinese and Cantonese."

"Well, shoot, grandson, that's one small hurdle you can easily jump over. You have the ability to learn any language in a snap," Nathaniel announced confidently, snapping his fingers.

That's true, Joshua thought. Once I master a few basic Japanese phrases, I'll be able to understand the Japanese police when they arrest me. Some bonus that is.

Nathaniel began to look uncertain. What once seemed a simple task—finding the bomb—now felt impossible, especially in Tokyo's rigidly organized society. "Maybe we should forget it, grandson," he conceded, suggesting they leave the bomb undisturbed. But Joshua, drawn to the X on the map, felt his sense of adventure swell, proud his grandfather had chosen him despite the fears whispering in the back of his mind. Nathaniel handed him the old paper, and Joshua held it up to the light, reading the typed message.

Mission: Cherry Blossom.

Joshua felt a surge of excitement. His fate was set; he was

about to embark on a mission to find a World War II hydrogen bomb. No plans for killing anyone—just a quest to recover the bomb itself. Like an Indiana Jones adventure, but actually real, with a heavy, buried bomb as the prize. His enthusiasm waned slightly at the thought of the muck he'd have to navigate. Still, he knew what he had to do—this was his mission, his destiny.

"Nope, Grampa. I'm going," Joshua declared decisively. "I'm going to get to Japan and find the bomb. That's first. I've even figured out how I'm going to find it."

"Oh yeah? How's that, grandson?" Nathaniel asked, emerging from his cloud of worry.

"I'm going to take a fish finder with me and locate it that way."

"What's a fish finder?"

"It's an underwater device that uses sonar to find fish. It sends signals back to the boat that show schools of fish."

"Will that work to find a bomb buried in the mud?"

"I hope so. If not, I'll look along the ocean floor. Hopefully, it won't be totally submerged. But with a GPS, I can enter the latitude and longitude you gave me and get right on top of where the bomb went in."

Joshua's mind was racing now. "That gives me another idea. I'll take a metal detector and scuba gear, too. Then I'll dive at the spot and search the bottom. Even buried, I bet a metal detector will pick up something as big as our bomb."

"Scuba dive, eh?" Nathaniel mused. "That would be a discreet way to find out if the bomb's still down there, that's for sure." He turned to Joshua. "I like it. Now we have a plan," Nathaniel said, leaning back, taking a deep breath, and looking around the room. "I can finally relax a little bit, knowing that after carrying this load for eighty years, the final chapter of my life's book is about to close. Man, I need a smoke."

"I wouldn't necessarily say that, Grampa," Joshua cautioned, ignoring his grampa's need to spark a fag. "But at least we have an initial plan that'll show whether or not we've got something to go on."

"You're right, of course, grandson," Nathaniel affirmed. "I'm getting ahead of myself—but goddamn, this is one hell of a start!"

Nathaniel stood, went over to Joshua, and rubbed his head for luck. "Do you remember when you were little and you'd sit on my lap and I'd rub your head like this?" he asked, still rubbing.

"Yes, Grampa, I sure do," Joshua answered, twisting away. "I also remember those rubs would turn into noogies every time," he laughed.

Nathaniel laughed too, remembering how he'd follow the head rubs with a series of knuckle raps on his grandson's gourd. "Ah, those are some pretty good memories, huh, grandson? I'm pretty sure pounding on your head helped turn you into the fine young man—that is, brave and fine young man—that you are now. Now give me back my ciggies."

Joshua handed him the pack but kept the matches, then looked away. That was the nicest compliment his grandfather had ever given him. The words made him tear up just enough that he didn't want Nathaniel to see him crying and ruin the image of his grandson being brave.

"Well, alrighty then, Grampa. I should go and start figuring out the logistics of how I'm going to pull off this stunt."

"OK, grandson," Nathaniel agreed. "I'm tired. Come back at 1200 hours sharp and take me to lunch. We'll need to go to the stockbroker's office to add your name to the account so you can access it and fund the adventure—or quest, as you put it."

Joshua checked his antique watch and nodded. "OK. I'll be back at 1200 sharp, and we'll do that."

"1200 sharp or 1200 something, eh?"

"1200 sharp," Joshua shot back, suppressing the urge to flip his grampa the bird.

With that, Joshua stood, and so did Nathaniel. Without thinking, Joshua stepped toward his grandfather, looked him straight in the eye, and gave him another big hug.

Nathaniel returned it, then pulled back and stared into his grandson's eyes. "Joshua, you make me proud by your belief in me and by your willingness to undertake this crazy scheme. No matter what happens from here on out, you're the best."

Nathaniel hugged Joshua again, burying his head into his grandson's chest so Joshua wouldn't see his tears.

CHAPTER 24

Muqtar woke to the voice of his wife singing as she came into the bedroom. Her voice filled the room with happy sounds as she danced to her own rhythm.

"What song is that, Julie? I have never heard it before."

"That, my love, is 'Country Roads' by John Denver," Julie explained. "A classic tune sung by your future contestant-on-The-Voice wife."

Muqtar rolled over and put a pillow over his head, faking misery because of having to listen to his wife's singing.

"Please, God, spare me any further renditions of 'Country Roads' or the like. My ears can't take it."

Julie ran to the bed and jumped onto her husband's back.

"There!" she declared, grinding her elbow into Muqtar's ribs. "This should teach you to criticize my singing."

"Now you have fallen into my trap, woman," commanded Muqtar, turning over to grab and pull her closer to him. "Now I shall have my way with you."

"I don't think so, Mister," she said, rejecting his advances as she pushed herself up off Muqtar. "There is a child to feed and work to be done, and unless you have won the lottery, I must attend to both."

"All right, my dear, you are right. No time for fun. Chores and child must be dealt with, so onward and upward," was Muqtar's voice of resignation as he threw off the covers, swung his feet onto the floor, and stood up.

Muqtar, after his morning shower, sat down to watch the news, eventually landing on Al-Jazeera. A segment about drone strikes and collateral damage caught his attention, especially images of destroyed buildings in South Asia, including one in a mountainous region that looked eerily familiar—his home village in Pakistan. The building hit was next to his former girl-friend Alia's family bakery; maybe the family home.

Realizing the missile likely killed everyone nearby, Muqtar sank to his knees, overcome with guilt. His reckless choices, including abandoning his education and resorting to drugs, made him feel responsible for everything. Muqtar was certain Alia was killed from the force of the bomb blast—and maybe his family was too. The damage was too extensive and too close to have spared her. Muqtar felt sick to his stomach.

Consumed by remorse, Muqtar couldn't shake the dark cloud. Thoughts of his son with Julie only deepened his guilt, as he felt that Alia should have been the mother. In his depths of self-loathing, Muqtar considered reaching out to see who was killed, hoping Alia had survived, but feared exposing himself. After five years of silence, he knew any communication could lead to unwanted scrutiny.

Still determined to find out, Muqtar hatched a plan to contact the Pakistani Embassy, pretending to be a family member to inquire about the victims of the attack. It was risky, but he believed it might provide the answers he desperately sought about Alia's fate.

Muqtar decided to ask Google how to contact the embassy, so he rose to his feet and walked over to his desk, the place where he kept his schoolbooks and his computer. A short time later, the Google search provided him the answer.

Pakistan Embassy

St. Louis, Missouri

Telephone number: 303-761-4152

Muqtar, feeling ashamed of his life choices, prepared to call the Pakistani Embassy, pretending to be a relative of Alia Khan. He rehearsed his lines in Urdu, slipped back into his native tongue, trying to convince himself that he could handle the call. As the phone rang, his anxiety grew, and when someone finally answered, he responded in Urdu, introducing himself as Ishmael Abdul Khan, Alia's brother, asking about the victims of the recent drone strike in his village.

The embassy worker connected him to the consular officer handling such inquiries. While waiting, Muqtar's anxiety intensified, paranoid thoughts flooding his mind. He feared the call might be traced back to him, wondering if the U.S. government or the Pakistani government was monitoring the line. He regretted not using a burner phone to protect his identity. His self-criticism was interrupted when a male voice finally spoke.

"Hello. This is Ahmed Sameer. How can I help you?"

Muqtar drummed up his courage and responded in Urdu again.

"Hello. My name is Ishmael Abdul Khan. I am the brother of Alia Khan, and I want to know about the recent drone missile strike that hit my home village in Pashmina."

"Hello, Ishmael. It doesn't sound like you have spoken Urdu in quite some time," replied Mr. Sameer in English. "Let me check for you on the recent missile strikes in your region."

Then the phone was silent for a couple of minutes, with just the sounds of someone typing coming through the phone.

"When did you say the strike occurred?"

"Three days ago, according to what I saw on Al-Jazeera," replied Muqtar in English, having given up on communicating in Urdu.

"Let's see. Three days ago in the Pashmina region," said Mr. Sameer, pausing between comments. "Oh, yes, here it is. Yes, eleven people were killed in a building near the downtown square by a missile strike at 0700 on March 22, 2025. Terrible thing," concluded Mr. Sameer.

"Do you have any of the names of the victims?" Muqtar blurted out, with his heart about to burst from his chest.

"No, no, I don't. There is nothing on the news release that discloses the names of the people killed by the missile strike. I'm sorry," apologized Mr. Sameer. "But let me check somewhere else. Hold a moment, please."

"Oh. OK. Thanks," a dejected Muqtar sadly stated as his heart fell to the floor.

"I don't see anything else, Mr. Khan. If you would like to leave me your telephone number, sir, I would be glad to call you back when the names of the victims are released," Mr. Sameer offered.

"No, no. That's OK. I will wait until one of my family members gets to a phone and calls me," was Muqtar's quick response.

Just what he did not need: for the Pakistani Embassy to call him back while he was having dinner with Julie and Junior.

"Well, OK, then. Sorry I couldn't be of more help to you, sir," a chipper-sounding Mr. Sameer finished with. "But you might want to practice your Urdu a bit before they call," he chided pleasantly.

"Yes, sir. Thank you for your time." *And fuck you for that last comment,* thought Muqtar, who had enough bad feelings already.

Muqtar was unsure of what to do next to find out who had died in the drone strike, but he soon decided that Al-Jazeera might have the information he needed. He planned to buy a burner phone after work to contact them. Muqtar hurried to work, taking illegal shortcuts to arrive on time, but his heart was heavy with the thought that the missile strike had killed Alia, his first love.

At work, Muqtar focused on his duties, but he noticed something was different with Colonel Meister. Ever since his grandson's visit, the Colonel had become more obsessed with his World War II past, especially about a Google map he had asked Muqtar to help create. The Colonel was unusually secretive and insistent that Muqtar keep the existence of the map quiet. While Muqtar enjoyed working with the veterans, he couldn't shake the feeling that something about the Colonel's behavior was off since his grandson arrived.

During the conversation that accompanied the creation of the map, Muqtar came to find out that the Colonel had served as a bombardier in World War II and had fought on both the European and Japanese fronts. Thinking about the Colonel, Muqtar caught up with Julie while she was placing pills in Dixie cups and questioned her.

"Hey, good morning, honey. How's it going?"

"Fine, baby, just making sure everyone is getting what they need, as usual," Julie answered while looking down at her tray where sat several small cups she had filled with various colored pills and capsules.

"Good enough, honey. You are the most organized person here. Without you, I'm sure the entire operation would grind to a screeching halt," complimented Muqtar.

"Oh, right, Michael. The success of this entire nursing home depends on me," laughed Julie.

"Honey, have you noticed anything different about Colonel Meister in Room 106 lately?" inquired Muqtar.

"No, nothing that different other than the FBI debacle yesterday," recalled Julie, thinking back on her recent interactions with the Colonel. "Why do you ask?"

"Well, he got pretty excited because his grandson had come to see him. It was unlike any type of reaction I had seen from him before," explained Muqtar. "He asked me to help him get a Google map of Tokyo, which was different for him to ask me for anything. And then he wanted the map to contain latitude and longitude lines on it."

"Did you help him out, Michael? He is such a nice man."

"Yes, I sure did, although it took quite a while to create what he wanted. But what was a bit peculiar was the Colonel's insistence that I keep it all a secret, that I was not to tell anyone about our project, as the Colonel put it."

Julie wrinkled her forehead again, trying to recall if she had noticed anything of the sort.

"Well, that's strange," she murmured, still trying to remember anything odd about her recent interactions with the Colonel. "But his meds are the same. They haven't changed. And his state of health, both physically and mentally, is stable. That is, except for the big circus that occurred yesterday when the FBI came and tried to take the Colonel with them."

"Yeah, honey, what the hell was that about?"

"I don't know. The same two agents came to see the Colonel about two weeks ago and he cussed them out and they left. So when they came back yesterday, they had papers to move him out of here. However," confided Julie, looking around to make sure no one else was listening, "one of the other nurses gave the Colonel a knock-out drug, so when he passed out they had to bring him back here to be seen by our resident doctor. That was pretty funny, I'll say." Julie smiled at the memory.

Muqtar smiled too, amused by his wife's rendition of events.

"I guess there is nothing to make of it then," was Muqtar's dismissive comment as he turned to walk away.

"Hold on, Michael," Julie ordered, grabbing his arm. "Talk about acting strangely: what happened to you? You look like you have just seen a ghost."

"I kind of think I did," he sort of confessed, leaving out the revelation of the missile strike. "When I went by the Colonel's room, I heard him go through this entire checklist of what sounded to me like preflight commands."

"Oh, really?" quizzed Julie. "What did he say?"

"Stuff like, *check the bomb bay doors* and *check the bombsight*—stuff like that," explained Muqtar.

"That is very peculiar," commented Julie, "but not completely unusual."

"Why do you say that, baby?" he wanted to know.

"Well, now that I think about it, some of the veterans regress back into war mode and sometimes say and do some very odd things. I remember a couple of times when residents have barricaded the doors," recalled Julie, "making us have to take the hinges off the doors to get in."

"Have you ever heard of or seen Colonel Nathaniel behave like that?" pressed Muqtar, anxious to know.

"No, I can't say that I have specifically seen or heard Colonel Nathaniel act out from his war days, but if anybody would have the memories to do so, it would be Colonel Nathaniel."

"Why's that, baby?"

"Because he is a real war hero, Michael; a Medal of Honor recipient. From what I was told when he first came here," recounted Julie, "Colonel Nathaniel got shot down over Germany, was captured and tortured but somehow managed to escape. If I remember rightly, once the Colonel escaped he came back and helped several other soldiers escape, killing 10 or 12 Nazis in the process. After several days, the Colonel made his way to the Americans fighting in France, avoiding the Germans. That must have been fun. However, what is ironic about the Colonel's experience is once the Germans surrendered, the Army put him on a plane and sent him to the Pacific front."

"Is that true, honey? The U.S. Army did not give him a reprieve from fighting after what he went through?"

"Nope. What I was told was that the Colonel didn't even get a seven-day leave. The Army debriefed him and sent him on to the Pacific to join the 7th Army Air Force. Apparently, Colonel Nathaniel was known as the best bombardier in the Army, known for his accurate, pinpoint bombing technique."

"That skill certainly would have been useful if the airplane was only going to drop one bomb, wouldn't it?" mused Muqtar.

"What do you mean by that?" Julie wanted to know, with a puzzled look on her face.

"Just that I thought I heard Colonel Nathaniel say 'one bomb for one god,' and 'Kill the emperor; Bomb's away!' obviously meaning that the target was the Emperor of Japan. He was the one god," related Muqtar with an excited tone in his voice.

"One bomb, one god," repeated Muqtar as the phrase quickly became his mantra. "I'm going to have to do some Googling on that topic when we get home from work tonight, honey. I have to check this out more thoroughly! But for now, however, I have meds to deliver."

Muqtar looked at his watch and saw that it was 7:55 a.m. The Colonel, like most of the military men who lived there, had a schedule—a schedule for everything, including when they went to breakfast in the mess hall, as many of them called the cafeteria.

Colonel Meister's daily routine had not changed. Each morning at 0700, he would slowly walk, ramrod straight, to the mess hall with military precision, and the rest of the men in the nursing home followed a similar routine. Muqtar, who had learned to deliver the morning meds on a strict time schedule, realized he had started his rounds early but had forgotten the pills. Returning to the pharmacy, he grabbed the cart and began his rounds, knocking on doors a bit after the designated times. Because his timing was off that day, his late deliveries were not well received by the veterans, which added to his frustration, as guilty thoughts about his past and Alia dominated his consciousness.

After completing his rounds, Muqtar reported to Julie about the residents who hadn't answered their doors. He then headed to Colonel Meister's room, hoping to learn more about the map's significance.

As he approached Colonel Meister's room, Muqtar was again reminded and amused by the fact that some of the men were very particular about the number, the type, and the spacing of door knocks. The Colonel was not one of those guys. In fact, he was one of the most flexible vets in the nursing home. One time, when he was almost five minutes late getting to the Colonel's room on his morning meds round, Muqtar was ready with an apology for the Colonel when he opened his door.

"Sorry, Colonel, for being late, but Major Adams opened his door and then passed out, so I had to wait until a nurse came to take over."

"Nothing to worry about, son. I'm sure my body will adapt to the five-minute delay of receiving its medicine," accepted Nathaniel, smiling. "After all I have been through in my life, I am just grateful to have a solid roof over my head, three squares a day, a cot, and feeling no fear when someone comes to the door."

"If you don't mind me asking, sir, why would someone coming to your door cause you to feel fear?"

"I don't mind you asking, son, as I am not ashamed at this point in life to admit that I was scared shitless at one point when I heard any noise at all."

"Why is that, Colonel?"

"I was shot down over France in World War II, was shot at while coming down in my parachute, and although I obviously survived that, I did get captured by the Nazis."

Muqtar was a bit shocked by that news. He had never met anyone who had been a prisoner of war before, especially one from World War II.

"Well, how did you escape, Colonel, or did your escape?"

"Yes, I sure did get away from those evil bastards, and in the process of escaping, I was able to kill at least a dozen of them," recalled Nathaniel, with fire in his eyes.

"Oh," remarked Muqtar.

"Yes, and once I escaped, I spent about a week making my way to and across France, hiding and listening, trying to avoid running into the fucking Nazis. That is where my awareness of and fear of noises came from."

Muqtar was taken aback. Colonel Meister was a legitimate badass in his day. That was definitely clear to Muqtar. This recollection, combined with his recent conversations with the Colonel, made Muqtar want to know more about the man's life, and in particular why the Colonel wanted a map of Tokyo Bay. Given his mood, Muqtar thought today was a great day to use his free time to go visit the Colonel.

As Muqtar proceeded down the hallway to Colonel Meister's room, he heard the Colonel shout: "Payback Time! Target Tokyo! Kill the Emperor! Bomb's away!"

That was the second time Muqtar had heard the Colonel shout that out. He hesitated for a second, hoping to hear more, but no further sounds came through the door. Three quick knocks on the door and he heard Nathaniel coming to open it. The Colonel was his favorite, for sure, and Muqtar couldn't help but smile a little as the war hero came to open the door.

"Oh, good morning, son. What brings you by?" cheerily asked Nathaniel, looking at his watch.

"Oh, nothing, Colonel, nothing special. Just thought you might have some more war stories to share."

"Well, come on in then," welcomed Nathaniel, gesturing for Muqtar to enter the room and sit down. He walked in and sat down on the desk chair that faced the window, and the Colonel sat down next to him in the recliner.

"What would you like to hear about today, son?"

"Uh, well, is it true that you flew bombing missions over both Germany and Japan, Colonel?"

"Why, yes. That is true, son. But I was the bombardier, not the pilot. However, I did have the privilege of dropping bombs on both sets of those bastards," responded Nathaniel in a satisfied tone.

"Privilege, sir?" a confused Muqtar replied, not following the Colonel's use of the word.

"I'm being a smartass, son. Flying those bombers and dropping those bombs was no privilege; it was an order. In my day, you followed orders no matter what, when, or how. And if you didn't, the consequences were that a lot of your fellow soldiers could suffer or die, or the brass would throw your ass in the hoosegow."

"The hoos cow, sir? What is that?" Muqtar needed clarification, again confused.

Nathaniel started laughing. "The hoos cow. The hoos cow? Hell, I thought everyone knew what that word meant. It's 'hoosegow,' and it means jail," as he emphasized the word jail.

"Jail, you know, the place you go that has bars and guards and all sorts of not-fun shit to ruin your day," teased Nathaniel.

"Oh, OK. I got it. I just had never heard that word before, Colonel." But he had been to jail. Yikes at that memory!

Nathaniel looked right at Muqtar and stated: "You're not from around here, are you, son?"

"Uh, that's correct, sir. I am from Pennsylvania."

Nathaniel peered intently into Muqtar's eyes, very closely taking in his skin color, facial features, hair, and eyes.

"Pennsylvania, huh?" repeated Nathaniel slowly. "You may have grown up in Pennsylvania, but I doubt you were born there."

"That's true," agreed Muqtar. "I did grow up in Pennsylvania, but I was not born there. I was born in Pakistan and was adopted out of an orphanage by an American couple from Philadelphia."

Nathaniel nodded. "That makes sense to me. You were lucky enough to come to the U.S. after being unlucky enough to lose your parents. How old were you when you were adopted?"

"Only 3 months, I was told. I don't remember anything other than being brought up in Pennsylvania."

"Did you ever go back to Pakistan to check out your roots or to see if you had other family members still living there?"

That question stung Muqtar, but he could definitely respond honestly.

"No, I have not been back to Pakistan since I left. I might go back someday, but no time soon."

"I understand," countered Nathaniel, sympathetically. "Some doors once closed are best to remain shut. But what brought you out here to St. Louis of all places?"

Muqtar thought about what to say for a moment and then replied: "I had nothing going on back East. I did not like school, and I knew my parents were disappointed when I dropped out, so I loaded my things into my car and headed west when my wife, Julie, came out here."

He felt another pang of guilt as he recalled how much anguish his parents must have felt when he was kicked out of NYU.

Nathaniel had one more question.

"Did your U.S. parents ever tell you what name you were born with in Pakistan? Surely it was not 'Michael Brown,'" asserted Nathaniel.

"Nope, they never did. I always thought I was a baby with no name, that my parents had died or abandoned me before they gave me a name."

"Hmmm," considered Nathaniel, feeling a bit sorry for Muqtar not having parents and not even a name. But being positive, he remarked: "No worries. You have a name now and a wife, and I think you told me you have a son."

"That's right, Colonel," affirmed Muqtar, brightening up considerably at the thought of his wife and son. "I am blessed to be living here in the U.S. with a great wife and little boy with no fear of a drone missile strike taking them out."

As soon as that last comment slipped out of his mouth, Muqtar felt like he had betrayed himself and left himself open for more questions about drone missile attacks.

Sure enough, Nathaniel picked up on the comment.

"What about missile strikes, son?"

Trying to steer the conversation away from a subject way too close to home, Muqtar lied: "Nothing really, Colonel. I saw something on the news about a drone missile attack in a remote village in Pakistan, and it stuck in my mind."

Nathaniel reflected on this exchange for a minute or so before responding.

"Those drone missile strikes done remotely from a building in Georgia to a target 4,000 miles away—there is something fundamentally wrong with that, I believe," Nathaniel opined as he turned to face Muqtar.

"You see, when you are flying into enemy territory and there are enemy aircraft trying to shoot you down, you get all pumped up with adrenaline and want to kill the enemy because they are trying to kill you," Nathaniel said.

"However," Nathaniel observed, "when you are sitting in an air-conditioned room with your good buddies talking in the background about going to a sports bar after work, there is no way you can feel the same emotions when you touch off a missile that you feel when you hit the bomb release button in a B-25 or a B-29 and watch them explode when they hit the ground."

Nathaniel's thoughts of modern warfare versus his war experiences took him back to his last experience in World War II—the time when he could not and did not follow orders. He turned and looked away from Muqtar, gazing out the window, watching the wind blow the new leaves emerging on the branches, lost in his thoughts of war and orders and a lifelong-kept secret. A secret Nathaniel had finally been able to unload on someone: his grandson.

"Are you OK, Colonel?" was Muqtar's concerned question.

"Yes, I sure am," asserted Nathaniel, gathering his thoughts. "What else do you want to talk about?"

"OK. Do you remember the Google map you had me create for you the other day, Colonel? The one with the latitudinal and longitudinal lines on it?"

"Yes, I remember. Why?"

"Last night, I did some more searching and came up with a color map of the area you had me look at before, that is Tokyo Bay. But this time the map has little identifiers on it that depict various landmarks in the area like Disneyworld Tokyo, the shipyards and such. It also shows the various depths of the Bay. Up here on land is the Japanese Emperor's Palace that you were looking for on the black-and-white map I gave you," stated Muqtar, pointing at the palace on the color map he had created the night before.

"What do you think," Muqtar proudly asked, handing the map to the Colonel.

Nathaniel reached for the glasses he always kept on the small table beside the easy chair, put them on, and began to study the color map very intently. Then he looked away as if trying to recall something.

After a minute, the Colonel looked back and carefully and very religiously moved his fingers on the map; one hand going down from the top, the other going left to right, stopping somewhere below the middle of Tokyo Bay.

"That is the spot. That is where it hit and that is where it lays," Nathaniel whispered to himself softly, seemingly oblivious to Muqtar's presence right next to him as he tapped the map.

"That is what spot, Colonel?" spoke Muqtar.

Nathaniel snapped back to reality at that question and laid the map on the nightstand. "Nothing, Michael, nothing really," he replied dismissively.

"Really, Colonel?" pressed Muqtar. "You had me create this map with the lines on it for nothing?" he continued, reaching over to put his finger on the map somewhere near where Nathaniel had traced the intersecting point.

Nathaniel abruptly turned aside, snatched up the map, and placed it upside down on the nightstand.

"Just an old memory for an old warhorse, Michael. Nothing more."

But Muqtar would not let it go.

"Is the spot on the map where your fingers met, is it a spot where a ship went down during the war?" insisted Muqtar somewhat ignorantly, given that the U.S. had no ships in Tokyo

Bay until after the Japanese had surrendered.

"No, not that. Nothing like that, Michael," answered Nathaniel, still trying to soft-pedal the subject, hoping it would go away. "Just a mental exercise I was doing to see if I could still do some simple visualization."

"Oh, OK, Colonel." Still not content with the answers he had been given, Muqtar took a different tact.

"Didn't you drop a lot of bombs on Japan once you had been transferred to the Pacific front?"

Nathaniel felt like he had been found out now. After all these years of keeping his secret, he had outed himself. He began to chastise himself for his stupidity in asking Michael to create the map and for tracing the bomb's location while he was in the room. Now that door was open. Shit!

"No, not too many, really. Only about a half a dozen runs right near the end of the war is all."

"Why did the government send you over there then? From what little I recall from World War II history, toward the end of the war the U.S. had massive amounts of men and machinery on the Pacific front. What made you so special, Colonel?" pointed out Muqtar in a kidding tone.

"Nothing, Michael, nothing at all," Nathaniel's jaw tightened, his eyes narrowing as he cut Michael off, his voice sharp and unyielding. "Enough," he announced, the finality in his tone leaving no room for further discussion.

Muqtar knew the conversation was over, but he was most intrigued to find out what the Colonel was not revealing, because surely he would not have had him create the map of Tokyo Bay for no reason, would he? Was it just an old vet's fantasy or something more? And if it was something more, what more could it be? Muqtar was indeed intrigued.

"Alright, Colonel," apologized Muqtar, getting up to leave. "I enjoyed our conversation. Thanks. I will be back this afternoon when I do my second medicine dispersal rounds."

"Okay, Michael," stated Nathaniel, not looking up. "If you see any more FBI guys here, please tell them I died or moved out or something," commented Nathaniel as he lifted his head with a smile on his face.

"Dealing with those guys must have been a hell of a scare, too, huh, Colonel?"

"Yeah, as I said when we started talking, I like it here because I feel safe here. Well, at least I did until very recently," finished Nathaniel, alluding to the two FBI goons who tried to hijack him.

"You bet, Colonel. If any more FBI guys come around looking for you, I will tell them you died in your sleep," was Muqtar's response as he turned and opened the door to leave the room.

Nathaniel sat lost in thought, berating himself for revealing too much about the secret he'd kept for so long. Nathaniel stared blankly at the floor, his hands resting loosely in his lap. His gaze seemed distant, unfocused, as though the world around him had faded, leaving him alone with his thoughts.

He worried that Michael, the nurse's aide, might be a secret agent sent to uncover the bomb's location. His mind ran through the possibilities, but he reminded himself that only Joshua actually knew about the third bomb and the mission. No one else knew the specifics, just that there was a point on a map in Tokyo Bay. Trying to calm himself, Nathaniel wrote down the coordinates on the back of the map and placed it in the drawer of his nightstand, and sat back in his chair, feeling a little better.

Meanwhile, Muqtar, having finished his rounds, was confronted by his wife in the hallway near the Colonel's room. He was caught off guard and scrambling for an explanation.

"Michael, what are you doing here?" Julie demanded.

"Me? Oh, nothing, honey. I'm good."

"No, you're not. I have never seen you look like this, Michael. What is bothering you today?"

Busted, Muqtar realized. "Nothing, honey. Nothing at all," he lied, hoping to quickly divert the subject from what was troubling him down to the depths of his soul, while feeling relieved that Julie had not pressed the point of why he was in the Colonel's room. "I just got pissed off when I talked to the insurance company about the guy who hit me the other day."

"Oh, yeah? What pissed you off about that, dear?"

"They told me they would not give me a free rental car while my cab was getting fixed is what made me mad, baby," responded Muqtar, partially telling her the truth.

Seeking to make her husband feel better, Julie consoled him by saying: "That's not a problem for us, honey. We will continue to get along without a rental car. No big deal. And besides," Julie added, "you can quit the cab-driving job now since you have been hired to work here full-time."

"You're right, honey. I shouldn't have let those insurance a-holes get to me. But I had such a good plan to use the rental car to be an Uber driver. However, like you said, we can live without the cab-driving money because I have a real job now," agreed Muqtar, smiling. He was relieved that he had a decent explanation for how he appeared, in spite of the fact that he was lying because there was another cab for him to use. Not that the explanation changed how he felt, because Julie's comment took him right back to where he had started the day: wracked with guilt and anger.

Muqtar trudged down the hallway, weighed down by sadness and despair, struggling to focus on anything other than the troubling thoughts of what had happened back home. To distract himself, he fixated on the mystery of what might be in Tokyo Bay. That evening, he scoured the internet but found no record of a World War II plot to bomb the Japanese emperor. He discovered that the U.S. used carpet bombing over Japan, but the atomic bombings of August 6th and 9th were the last of the war.

Muqtar wondered if Colonel Nathaniel was delusional or if there was a third bomb, a practice flight, or something hidden in history. What did he mean by "that is where it lays"? With no answers, the mystery continued to occupy his thoughts, even though he tried to dismiss it as a senile old man's tale.

CHAPTER 25

Muqtar obsessively pondered the significance of the intersecting lines on the Google map, wondering if they marked where the Colonel's plane was shot down or where a hidden treasure lay. He considered sneaking into the Colonel's room for clues, recalling his past success breaking into Allen's house. However, he realized the risks—being caught could cost both him and Julie their jobs and potentially expose his true identity.

Despite the danger, Muqtar couldn't shake the allure of solving the mystery. He knew the residents at the nursing home followed strict schedules, though the Colonel's had recently been disrupted by his grandson and the FBI's presence. Muqtar's own duties left him little free time, and obtaining a key to the Colonel's room was the next hurdle to overcome.

Muqtar's fixation with breaking into the Colonel's room distracted him from the tragedy of his village being bombed. He again recalled sneaking into Allen's house years ago, a memory that stirred the same illicit thrill he felt when he took a life and adopted a new identity. Feeling driven to uncover the Colonel's secret, Muqtar devised a plan, similar to his past heists.

Muqtar realized his first task was to get a key to the Colonel's room. His stare lingered on the locked door, then he turned, heading for the front desk, his mind set on getting the key.

After considering his options, he recalled that the maintenance guy had a set of keys he often left on his workbench while he took breaks. Despite the small window of opportunity, Muqtar couldn't resist the pull to sneak into the Colonel's room and solve the mystery, feeling a rush akin to his past criminal activities.

Muqtar's plan was simple: during the Colonel's fifty-minute lunch, he would grab the maintenance man's keys, sneak into the Colonel's room, search for the secret, and return the keys unnoticed. He considered using his wife's keys, but she always kept hers in her front pocket, and again, if caught—both would be fired, and his true identity could be exposed. The maintenance man's key idea was the safest option.

At 11:30 a.m., he began his preparations, delivering meds while waiting for his opportunity. By 11:40, he was ready, too excited to eat. As he passed the front desk, he saw someone who resembled the Colonel's grandson, sparking more suspicion as he continued plotting his heist.

Before he could sneak away, the guy in the waiting area looked up, recognized Muqtar, and spoke.

"Hey, excuse me. I know you a little bit. I'm Joshua," the man said as he extended his hand. "I ran into you the other day in my car and again the day before yesterday in the hallway."

"Oh, yes. How could I forget you?" replied Muqtar, shaking Joshua's hand. "My cab should be fixed by the weekend."

"That's good. I received a call from my insurance company and gave a statement taking the blame for the wreck. So there shouldn't be a problem as far as my insurance paying the cost of all the repairs—no deductible for you to have to pay."

Muqtar nodded. "Well, accidents do happen, and I'm glad there won't be a deductible to pay. No one was hurt, just some bent metal and broken plastic," he replied in a conciliatory tone.

Then, feeling emboldened, Muqtar asked, "What brings you here today?"

"Oh, I'm here to pick up my grandfather, Colonel Nathaniel Meister, and take him to lunch. He's a stickler for being on time, having been in the military practically his entire life," Joshua said, smiling at the thought.

"My grandfather told me to be here by 11:50, no later, so here I am," Joshua continued as he spread his arms and turned his palms up.

"You're right about that, Joshua," agreed Muqtar. "Your grandfather—and most of the men in here—are very punctual, and they expect the same punctuality from everyone who interacts with them, including me," he emphasized.

Looking at his watch, Muqtar announced, "Time to go. More rounds to complete, and I better be on time. That's the rule around here."

"Sure is," Joshua agreed, extending his hand again. "I'm leaving after lunch today, but it was good to run into you again, although not literally," he added with a laugh. His laughter pulled Muqtar out of his head for a moment, and he laughed too as he shook Joshua's hand.

"It was good to see you again, too," said Muqtar, emphasizing the word *see*. "Maybe we'll run into each other again somewhere—but not on the road."

"Maybe," Joshua replied. Both men laughed as Muqtar turned away and Joshua sat back down.

Muqtar's plan was on track. With the Colonel heading to lunch, the risks of being caught were low. At 11:44, Muqtar positioned himself where he could see the Colonel's room. At 11:45, the Colonel left on schedule, and Muqtar moved quickly.

He went to the basement to look for Jesse, the maintenance

man. At 11:59, Jesse took his lunch break. Muqtar seized the opportunity, slipping into the maintenance room and grabbing the keys from Jesse's desk. Mission step one complete.

Fuck, Muqtar silently exclaimed to himself. *Now what? Which one of these motherfuckers among fifty keys is the master key to the residents' rooms? Goddamn it,* he cursed again to himself. *I'll never be able to sort this out in time. Motherfucker. There goes my plan. Shit.* He kept cursing as he rifled through key after key. *C'mon, bitch, show yourself,* urged Muqtar.

Finally! There it was—not a master key after all, but a key with a small piece of paper taped to it that read *Room 106. Fucking cool.* Now whether to try taking the key off the ring or taking the whole wad was his next dilemma. *Fuck it. Take the whole wad,* his inside voice told him. Muqtar stashed the entire ring of keys into his pants pocket and hauled ass.

Once out of the maintenance area, he managed to breathe a bit and think. He walked briskly up the stairs, past the reception area, and started down the hall to the Colonel's room.

Oh shit, swore Muqtar silently as he saw his wife emerge from one of the rooms. She looked as startled as he did by their unexpected encounter.

"Hi, honey," greeted Julie. "What are you doing here?"

"Oh, nothing," lied Muqtar. "Just checking to see if Major Thomas in Room 110 took his eleven o'clock meds."

"Really, Michael?" Julie questioned. "I've never known that to be one of your duties."

"That's true, honey. It isn't one of my usual functions around here, but I just had a feeling I should check on Major Thomas today."

Julie was not satisfied. She kept on. "Did you note your concerns in the morning report?"

"No, I did not, honey. It wasn't really a concern, just a thought," he demurred, downplaying the significance of his lie.

"Kind of like your intuition was telling you something. Is that what you're following up on, babe?" Julie wanted to know.

"Yeah, kind of like that, honey," answered Muqtar, now beginning to sweat as he held his left leg back to hide the bulge of keys in his pocket.

"Do you want me to go with you?"

"No, that won't be necessary, honey."

"All right then. I'm going to see the head administrator at noon."

With that, Julie turned to walk away, calling over her shoulder, "Don't forget to eat what I packed for you this morning."

"Okay, honey. I won't," Muqtar called after her. *Shit. That was too close. And time is my enemy,* he thought as he made his way to Room 106, shaking his head at this second untimely, unscheduled meeting with his wife.

Muqtar unlocked the door and slipped into the room. Inside, he found no immediate clues. Dejected by his lack of success, he began to search the room in earnest, starting with the nightstand but finding nothing helpful. The Google map of Tokyo Bay, tucked in the drawer, offered no obvious markings or hints. He laid it on top. He rummaged through the upper drawer, hands shaking with impatience, then yanked open the lower drawer, scattering papers and trinkets across the bottom. The map fluttered to the floor, landing face down. Nothing. He let out a sharp breath, angst mounting with each empty search.

His anxiety grew. When he looked again at the map, he noticed numbers written on the back—a potential clue. *What is this series of numbers?* wondered Muqtar. Two sets, written in ink, smudged but still mostly legible.

35 degrees 36' 1.012" N
139 degrees 52' 0.512" E

Muqtar studied the numbers but couldn't figure out their meaning—perhaps a code, a combination, or an address. He quickly jotted them down on a pharmacy list, then carefully returned everything to its original place in the drawers. After ensuring the room was back in order, he exited without being seen. With adrenaline still coursing through his veins and on hyper alert, he locked the door and prayed he wouldn't run into Julie again. As he walked, his mind raced, trying to calm itself, now focused on figuring out the mystery of the numbers.

He reached the stairwell and stopped to listen. No sounds came from the maintenance area where Jesse worked. Relieved by the quiet, he pounded down the stairs. Muqtar made his way to Jesse's workbench, dropped the keys where he had found them, and left.

Muqtar exhaled as he reached the main floor. Back to work; prying completed. But a bigger mystery lingered: the numbers from the Google map. He couldn't recall them exactly and didn't want to pull out the paper to look. Pushing his cart to the pharmacy, he had no choice but to pull out his checklist with the numbers written on it, yet no solution to the puzzle came to mind. He decided to focus on work for now, hoping the answer would surface later, whether consciously or not. Muqtar tried to put his finger on why he was so fascinated by this mystery but couldn't quite grasp it. Somewhere deep inside he felt he had a quest to embark upon, and maybe the Colonel's story had something to do with it. For what reason he would charge off in search of something was a conundrum. Little did he know he would soon find out why.

Joshua was a bit puzzled as he waited out front for his grand-father, wondering why he had encountered the nurse's aide Mi-chael so many times. He had been trained to be mindful—and even suspicious—of coincidences, and running into the same stranger three times was a definite peculiarity. The car wreck could be written off as just an unfortunate incident, okay. Liter-ally running into the guy at the nursing home was strange, and seeing him there again was downright peculiar; a coincidence as it were.

The CIA had taught him that there are no coincidences. Ev-erything has a reason behind it. So again, okay, what was the reason for their paths colliding and now being intertwined? How was their relationship going to play out? Joshua stood there with his forehead scrunched up, scratching his head as he looked out the front door at the surrounding landscape for clues, contemplating.

About then, his grandfather showed up. Actually, right at the agreed-upon time of 11:45, Nathaniel arrived.

"Hello, grandson. Glad to see you made it here on time. You know I fucking hate tardiness."

"Yes, Grampa. I surely do know that, which is why I arrived here twenty minutes early. I didn't want a repeat of being late, so I gave myself extra travel time, just in case."

"That's good planning, Joshua, and it is always good to have a plan."

Glancing around to see if anyone was looking, Nathaniel whispered surreptitiously, eyes glinting with excitement. "And boy, do we have a plan to make."

Joshua followed his grandfather's eyes and once again saw the same nurse's aide, this time pushing a cart down the hallway.

"Grampa, do you see that guy pushing the cart?" Joshua pointed, gesturing toward the aide.

"Sure do. That is Michael. He's a good guy. In fact, he's the guy who printed the Google map I showed you yesterday."

A cold knot twisted in Joshua's stomach as his mind raced. He replayed his grandfather's words, trying to catch any slip-up he might have made in the presence of the aide. Joshua's heart pounded, the thought of the aide knowing too much sending a rush of panic through him.

Because he felt alarmed that his grandfather might have accidentally revealed his secret to the aide, Joshua demanded, "What? You didn't tell him anything about our plan, did you, Grampa?"

"Fuck, no. I didn't tell him or anybody else other than you a goddamned thing about our 'plan,'" Nathaniel remarked in an annoyed tone, making quote marks with his hands.

"OK, OK, Grampa. I'm just nervous and more than a little bit paranoid. You understand that, don't you?" Joshua quietly asked, looking for approval.

"You better be both, grandson," asserted Nathaniel, now over being pissed at Joshua for asking such a ridiculous question. "Because if you aren't, you'll probably end up dead or worse . . ."

"Shit. Give me a minute, grandson. I forgot something in the room." When Nathaniel returned, they began walking to the car. Little did Colonel Meister know that had he returned to his room two minutes earlier, Muqtar would have been inside. Muqtar was lucky again.

Upon their arrival at the car, Nathaniel stopped and reached into his shirt pocket for his cigarettes.

"Hold on a minute, Joshua. I'm going to have a cigarette before we go." With that, he pulled a pack of matches from his pocket and extracted a ciggy from the pack.

"OK, Grampa. No problem. The weather is nice today," observed Joshua as he surveyed the scene and thought about sharing a smoke with his grampa.

"Not much to look at, is there?" remarked Nathaniel, looking at the building. He struck a match and lit a Camel. As Nathaniel inhaled the smoke, Joshua kept checking out everything.

"No, not really. It isn't like looking at mountains or ocean, that's for sure. But I've seen worse."

Nathaniel nodded in agreement. "That's for sure," he said, thinking back to the Nazi jail from which he had escaped.

Now finished, Nathaniel threw the cigarette down and stepped on the butt. "Let's go." And off they went.

Nathaniel did not have a particular restaurant in mind, so Joshua asked Siri for suggestions, and they chose a place that reputedly had the best hamburger in St. Louis. As they rode along, Nathaniel spoke.

"Do you know why I wrote the coordinates of where the bomb hit the water on the old pack of matches I gave you yesterday?" Nathaniel rhetorically asked.

"Do you mean why you didn't rewrite the coordinates onto a piece of paper or something, Grampa?" replied a slightly confused Joshua.

"Yes, that's right. Why did I keep the information on a pack of matches?"

"Uh, because they reminded you of old times and you wanted to preserve the memory. Is that why, Grampa?"

Nathaniel was a bit surprised by the answer because it did make sense, but that wasn't the reason.

"No, grandson, that wasn't why, although the matches do take me back to that fateful day, that's for sure. No, that isn't why," Nathaniel continued. "I wrote the coordinates on a pack of matches because I felt like if anyone caught wind of my secret and were about to search me, I could light the whole pack at once and destroy the evidence," Nathaniel bragged, smiling at his genius. "I'll show you," he said, taking the old pack from Joshua.

"See how only a couple of matches have been used from this pack, grandson?" Nathaniel offered, holding them closer so Joshua could see.

"Well, sure enough, Grampa," Joshua confirmed, looking over at the matches, not having a clue what his grandfather's point was while still sort of trying to watch where he was driving. "That's pretty clever. A lot better than getting the data points tattooed on your forearm. Those would have been pretty hard to get rid of should you have needed to do so, huh, Grampa?"

Nathaniel looked over at Joshua, not very amused by his grandson's attempt at humor.

"This is serious shit, Joshua. Quit fucking around."

Joshua stayed quiet as the two continued to ride along.

"Do you think the matches in the original pack still even light after all these years, Grampa?"

Nathaniel had not thought of that potential contingency—that the matches might be difficult to light—but he had to admit it was a distinct possibility.

"Well, to tell you the truth, I don't know, but when we get to the restaurant, let's torch one and we'll sure as fuck find out."

Turning into the restaurant parking lot, Joshua picked a spot toward the rear and backed in. They exited the car, whereupon Nathaniel opened the pack, removed one of the matches, closed the cover, and struck it. Nothing.

He scratched the match again. Nothing.

Nathaniel turned the match over and struck the lighting surface. Nothing, nothing, nothing.

Nathaniel threw the offending match to the ground and ripped out another one.

"You better light, you sorry motherfucker," Nathaniel demanded, scowling at the match in front of his face.

Joshua watched Nathaniel's theatrical moment as if watching a magician about to pull a rabbit out of a hat but kept quiet, knowing if he spoke he'd be the target of another curse-filled tongue-lashing.

One strike: nothing.

Second strike: a tiny whiff of smoke but no fire.

Nathaniel, worked up, threw down match #2 and ripped out another, pressing his finger on the head while striking it. It sparked and flared, burning Nathaniel's finger, but he held it up proudly for Joshua to see. Joshua considered clapping but refrained, watching as the match burned down. Nathaniel quickly dropped it before it reached his fingers.

"How 'bout that? I knew I could still light a match," Nathaniel proclaimed. "Hell, it's only been eighty-five fucking years since I lit my first cigarette."

"You're right about that," agreed Joshua, knowing better than to disagree. "These World War II matches have plenty of life left in them. Probably will still be good in another eighty years."

Nathaniel gave Joshua a sour look, not amused by his grandson's sarcasm.

"Come on, Joshua. Let's go eat," Nathaniel said, having folded the match cover back into the matchbook, mission accomplished. "I'm hungry."

As they were eating lunch, Joshua began wondering how he was going to pull off the discovery and salvaging of a 10,000-pound bomb.

"Any thoughts, Grampa, on how I should go about actually accomplishing this mission?"

Nathaniel cocked his head back, raised his right hand, and began stroking his freshly shaved chin as he considered the options.

"Well, let's see. First, you have to get to Japan. Do you have a valid passport?"

"Yes, Grampa. I do."

"Do you have it with you?"

"Yes, Grampa. As a matter of fact, I do."

"OK, good." Nathaniel dropped his head down and rubbed his hands together, thinking of what kind of effort would be required to do the job.

"Once you get there, you'll have to get out in the harbor and locate the bomb. And you mentioned that you know how to scuba dive, right?"

"Yes, Grampa. I am a certified open-water diver," affirmed Joshua, having already thought past the first two steps brought up by his grandfather.

Joshua interrupted his grandfather's thinking. "Grampa, I'm pretty sure I can find the bomb in the water if it's there. My biggest problem is how to lift the bomb off the seabed and onto something once I locate it. Any thoughts on that?"

Nathaniel shook his head. He had no idea how that aspect of the plan could be accomplished. Searching for something to say that would advance the plan, Nathaniel offered, "You're going to need some help once you get there, that's for sure."

Joshua wanted to say, *no shit, Sherlock,* but decided to keep that comment to himself. Rather, he agreed, "Right, Grampa. But I don't know any Japanese people. Do you?"

"No, I sure don't, grandson. Not a soul."

Now they were both stumped. Finding the bomb was one thing; retrieving the huge mother was another subject altogether, they both realized.

"Don't you know somebody from your college days who's Japanese, Joshua?" probed Nathaniel.

"No, not a soul," was Joshua's response, echoing his grandfather's previous comment. "The only Asian person I know is a Chinese girl I dated in college, Mei Lei Ho, and Hong Kong is a long way from Tokyo."

Believing that this connection was the only thread upon which the success of the plan so tenuously hung, Nathaniel lobbed some more questions at Joshua.

"When's the last time you talked to her? How did the relationship end? Does she hate you now?" Nathaniel shot off in rapid succession.

"I called her early this morning, and before that about five years ago, when she completed her graduate degree and went home. And not badly, and yes, I think so," responded Joshua in the order in which the questions were asked.

"Well, perhaps you can reach out to her again and see if she has connections in Japan," suggested Nathaniel, ignoring the last part of the answer.

Joshua shook his head side to side as Nathaniel posed the question.

"No, that for sure won't work, Grampa, because the Japanese

are still widely hated by the Chinese for the way the Japanese treated the Chinese before and during World War II. More importantly, Mei Lei was not happy that I called her today because when she left Michigan several years ago, she specifically told me never to contact her again."

"Oh, okay. What did you do to piss her off? Show up for dinner late?" Nathaniel gigged as he searched his thoughts for another option.

Joshua ignored the remark. "Grampa, I think we're putting the cart before the horse. Let's get me to Japan first and see if the bomb still lies at the bottom of Tokyo Bay. If it's there, then we'll concoct a plan to retrieve it. If the bomb is no longer there, then no harm done and we can put this piece of history to bed forever."

"Agreed," nodded Nathaniel. "First things first. Now let's eat and get on over to the stockbroker and put you on the account."

With that, no more words were said between the two as they finished eating, each lost in their own thoughts of the past, present, and future.

CHAPTER 26

Joshua's lips raised into a small smile as he mulled over the details. The first part was falling into place exactly as he'd hoped, the confidence in his chest growing with each passing moment.

After dropping his grandfather at the retirement home, he returned to his hotel and ordered scuba gear and other supplies from Amazon, shipping them to the Tokyo Hilton. He then booked a flight from St. Louis to Tokyo, with a twenty-two-hour travel time. Despite plans to have dinner with Betsy before his departure, Joshua was too preoccupied with returning the rental car, picking up his repaired VW, and getting back to the retirement home before heading to the airport. Dinner seemed unlikely.

Betsy had agreed to meet Joshua in the parking lot behind the nursing home.

"Now why are you going to Japan all of a sudden, Joshua?" Betsy wondered as she sat down in Joshua's rental car. "Are you going there to see your Japanese girlfriend?"

Joshua had been thinking about what to tell her for a while and was a bit surprised at her question.

"Oh no, no, nothing like that. I am going to Japan because my grandfather thinks he left something over there after World War II that he wants me to find."

"Something to find. What is it? A watch, a war buddy, a child, your former girlfriend?" insisted Betsy, remembering the early morning call he had made from her apartment to the mysterious Mei Lei.

Joshua, not wanting to lie to Betsy again and realizing that he was a lousy liar anyway, articulated the plan. "I am going to look for a bomb that my grandfather believes is still there, which could hurt a lot of people if it were to explode. And no, not to hook up with a former girlfriend."

Betsy was silent for a moment, feeling somewhat despondent that Joshua was leaving—and who knew if he would ever return. As she considered what she knew, Betsy didn't think all of the pieces fit together. "Well, I know the Colonel was a bombardier in World War II, and I know that he was awarded the Medal of Honor. But for the life of me I cannot figure out what bomb left over from World War II could be that dangerous."

"I can't tell you more than what I just did, Bets. A lot of people would like to know what my grandfather knows, including the FBI," claimed Joshua.

Betsy nodded her head, recalling the events of yesterday. She shrugged her shoulders. "Well, okay then. When will you be back?"

"If all goes as planned, I will be back in about a week, or maybe less." Joshua took Betsy's chin in his hands to assure her. "You are part of my life now, Betsy. I will be back, and you and I will get our chance."

"Chance for what, Joshua? Chance for what?" Betsy repeated.

"I don't know, Betsy. I haven't figured that out either. But I feel good about us. Don't you?" Joshua replied, putting the onus back on her.

Betsy moved backward, allowing Joshua's hands to fall away from her chin, and looked up at him. "Yes. That is what scares me."

Joshua was now very nervous and uncomfortable at how deep the conversation had become.

"Trust me, Betsy. You know I am not lying because you would know it, as I am such a shitty liar. But I will be back soon, and we will see where things go. Is that okay?"

"I guess it will have to be," Betsy sighed, resigned to see what would happen. "So, no time for dinner, I presume?"

"Sorry, Betsy, I have some time but not enough to do a steak dinner justice."

"I figured," Betsy replied in the same resigned tone.

Joshua reached down to kiss Betsy, and the electricity was very intense when their lips met. What had started out as a one-night fling was now a whole lot more to both of them.

Joshua hesitated, his fingers caressing the soft skin of her face, wanting to hold on for just a moment longer. Slowly, he let her pull back, his lips lingering in the space between them, unwilling to break the connection but knowing he had to.

They were in the parking lot at her job, after all. He admitted to himself that he was feeling unbalanced—good about Betsy but rather disconsolate because of the way the conversation had gone with Mei Lei.

Joshua couldn't understand Mei Lei's cold response. They hadn't spoken in over five years, and he hadn't tried to reach out before, so her frosty tone caught him off guard. Maybe she was involved with someone else or had buried her feelings for him, but it seemed clear she didn't want contact. He wasn't trying to rekindle anything, but her abruptness still stung. Despite his confusion and hurt, he decided to put her out of his mind.

Joshua felt sadness leaving his grandfather and regret for leaving Betsy behind, but the lingering sting from his conversation with Mei Lei was hard to shake. From distant and elusive to deeply in love, then back to aloof—he wondered what had changed. Time, distance, and family, he guessed. Though he still loved Mei Lei, it was clear she had shut away those feelings. He rethought the earlier conversation.

"Hello, Mei Lei. This is Joshua."

A long pause, then in English, Mei Lei spoke.

"Who is this?"

"This is Joshua, Joshua Meister. Your long-lost friend from college," he encouragingly replied in Chinese, glad that while the words were forming in his mouth he substituted *friend* for *lover.*

Another long pause.

"What do you want?" Mei Lei demanded.

"Do you remember me?" Joshua inquired, now unsure of himself.

"Yes," was the terse response. "What do you want?" Mei Lei demanded again.

"Well, uh, well, I am coming to Tokyo soon," Joshua stammered.

No reply. A long silence ensued.

"Mei Lei, are you still there?"

"Yes."

"Well, I was thinking that since I am coming to Japan we could get together," Joshua gushed out, unable to control himself.

"No, that would not be possible," was Mei Lei's stern response. "For the very reasons I told you I would never see you again when we parted ways after college."

"I understand that, Mei Lei, I do, but I may need your help in Tokyo."

"No, Joshua. No."

"Look, Mei Lei," begged Joshua. "I am not coming to Tokyo just to see you, to try to rekindle a romance. I am coming on a government mission," he lied, "of great importance to the safety and well-being of the Japanese people," Joshua concluded truthfully.

Another interminable pause ensued as Mei Lei considered what Joshua said.

"If you are coming to Tokyo on a government mission, I am sure the government will provide you with all the assistance you will need."

Thinking as fast as he could, Joshua kept on. "Look, Mei Lei. I am not kidding when I tell you the purpose of my coming to Tokyo is of enormous importance to the Japanese people, for their safety and security."

Mei Lei quickly shot back. "Then why are they sending you, of all people, on a mission of such great importance, and why isn't your government taking care of all the details?"

"Because I am fluent in Japanese, is the first answer," Joshua lied again, coming up off the mat self-confidence-wise. "And because the matter is so confidential there can be no overt support to limit the possibility that the mission details will be leaked to the wrong people," he finished in a flurry.

"The CIA picked you for this mission," Mei Lei scoffed. "Of all the people the CIA has, you were picked to handle a mission of such tremendous importance." Mei Lei was mocking him now.

Joshua's jaw tightened and his eyes narrowed as he fought to control his emotions, determined to convincingly convey the message. He lifted his right hand to his forehead and ran his fingers back through his hair. Joshua looked over at Betsy, who hadn't a clue what Joshua was saying as he was speaking in Chinese. But the pissed-off look on his face must have given away how poorly the conversation was going.

"Have I ever lied to you, Mei Lei?" Joshua offered, then added hastily, "about anything important?"

"You lied to me about what time you would pick me up; you lied about your mother's background; you lied about your grades. Yes, Joshua, you lied to me about a lot of things. I am not sure you know the difference between a lie and the truth," Mei Lei spat out as she clicked off a few of his foibles. "And most importantly, you lied when you promised that you would not contact me once I returned home. And oh, by the way, I live in Hong Kong, not Tokyo!" At this point, Mei Lei was nearly shouting in Joshua's ear.

"OK, Mei Lei, calm down. I am sorry I broke the last promise I made you, especially so. But I promise you my purpose in breaking the no-contact rule is not for social reasons but for reasons of Japanese national security," Joshua urged.

"What reasons?"

"Uh, I can't tell you over the phone, but I will tell you once I get to Japan," Joshua promised.

"I must go now. Goodbye, Joshua."

"Goodbye, Mei Lei. Talk to you soon."

No response; only the silence of a dial tone.

Turning to Betsy, Joshua sighed, repeatedly clapped his hand against his forehead, and began shaking his head.

"That didn't go well, did it?" Betsy surmised.

"No, not too well at all," was Joshua's quiet reply.

Joshua stared up at the sky, remembering the conversation,

and said to himself, *Now what,* he wondered. *Now what?* What other options do I have? None came to mind.

Betsy's question brought him back to the present. "When are you going to Japan?"

"My flight to San Francisco leaves at about ten o'clock tonight."

Joshua answered but was distracted, still thinking about the morning's phone call. Back to the present, Joshua wondered if he should even go to Japan. Was this whole thing just a farce, a comedy in which he was the main buffoon? Or was there really a need—an urgent need—for him to act, to find out if there was a bomb buried somewhere in Tokyo Bay with its casing possibly deteriorating. Perhaps, Joshua thought, his best bet would be to turn over what he knew to the FBI or CIA and let the pros handle it. After all, Joshua was discouraged because he couldn't keep a girlfriend and not even keep a job working for the CIA, much less orchestrate the location, discovery, and extraction of a 100-kiloton hydrogen bomb.

The last thought felt like a betrayal, a cowardly act not worthy of his family's patriotic heritage. To not travel to Japan would be to turn his back on two hundred years of his family's service to his country—and not the least of the consequences would be Joshua betraying his grandfather. Joshua's relatives emigrated from Germany to the French-owned area now known as Louisiana in 1750; five brothers arrived with steel-making skills.

They established a business making metal hoops for wooden barrels and also began casting rifle barrels. One of the brothers became adept at building wooden rifle stocks, and their now assembled flintlocks were in high demand because they rarely misfired and were deadly accurate. One of the rifles found its way to Boston, and a man named George Washington, upon seeing the excellent craftsmanship, commissioned the Meister brothers to build him a .50-caliber. When the revolution came, two of the brothers were summoned to Washington to show others how to build their rifles, and many a British soldier was on the receiving end of their bullets.

One of the flintlocks sat on the family mantle above the flags of the two brothers who died in combat in Vietnam. For generations, the Meisters had displayed courage under fire and calm, steely determination in achieving their objectives, both on and off the battlefield.

Joshua knew he could not trust those in power. He had seen too much during the short time he worked for the CIA. Those bastards would either eliminate him and everyone who knew about the bomb or at least discredit him and his grandfather, ruining their lives should Joshua go public with the information. He had learned his lesson from the Joe Wilson–Valerie Plame matter.

So, no, there would be no seeking help from the government on this mission. Yet, going it alone, without the help of a contact in Tokyo, was the thought that stumped Joshua. He had never undertaken a task solo, much less ever conceived of trying to find and dig up a hydrogen bomb that weighed 10,000 pounds, whose casing was, in all likelihood, damaged.

Gosh, Joshua mused. *What would I do if I did find the bomb and did somehow manage to bring it to the surface? Put it on the back of a flatbed truck and parade it through the streets of Tokyo?* That, Joshua resolved, he would have to figure out later. His first mission to Tokyo would include two goals: first, to somehow verify the existence of the bomb; and second, if there, to figure out how to safely extract it. Joshua once again decided to leave the question of what to do with the bomb once it was recovered for a later date.

Joshua realized he had drifted away from Betsy, and therefore, feeling a bit embarrassed for having become so lost in thought, turned to her and asked, "Excuse me. What was your question?"

Betsy raised an eyebrow, her lips pressed into a tight line as she glanced at him, a flicker of irritation crossing her face, and repeated, "When are you going to Japan? And you already answered me. Jesus."

In actuality, Joshua had not forgotten the question. And he knew he had answered it, but he felt inconsiderate for having faded away for a moment, and by asking her to repeat the question, he hoped to appear less so. The ploy didn't work.

"Sorry, Bets. Yes, I am still going to go, in spite of my former friend's cold response to my inquiry for help," Joshua glumly concluded.

Joshua's inner voice spoke up. *Maybe Mei Lei will change her mind by the time I get there.* He knew better than to say that out loud, as Betsy's intuition was already on full alert.

"Do you have a passport and all that?"

"Yes, I do. You have my telephone number, and oh, while I'm at it, here is my email address that I hope to check every day while I am in Tokyo, so you can contact me by email, too."

"OK," Betsy acknowledged, picking up the piece of paper where Joshua had written down the information and placing it in her purse.

"Well, Bets, what shall we do after you finish work today?" Joshua inquired with a mischievous gleam in his eye.

She shifted in her seat.

"Well, it will be too late to go out, but I will be hungry. What would you like to do? That was what I was trying to get at when you were ignoring me earlier."

"Sorry about that. How about we order a pizza and drink a couple of beers?"

"Sounds good. I think there are at least a couple more shots of tequila left in the bottle, too."

"Excellent. Maybe there's another shot or two to be had later, as well."

"If you behave, Joshua. You're going to be gone for a while."

"I will do as I am told, Bets."

Joshua was looking forward to licking the salt with Betsy squeezing the lime.

Betsy hopped out, turned, and walked into the nursing home, leaving Joshua alone with his thoughts. He shrugged, sighed to shake off the negativity, and drove to the dealership to drop off the rental car and pick up his repaired VW. He barely checked the repairs before heading back to the nursing home.

At the front desk of the nursing home, Joshua waited for Nathaniel's room to be called, occasionally glancing up, hoping to see Betsy, but she didn't appear. Instead, he noticed the same male nurse's aide, Michael, who this time gave him an angry, defiant look. Joshua was concerned, thinking it might be due to insurance issues, but before he could speak to him, Michael disappeared down the hallway.

How odd, thought Joshua. The thought was soon dismissed when he recognized his grandfather's shape as he walked down the hall.

"Good afternoon, Grampa," greeted Joshua as he rose to his feet. Joshua shook Nathaniel's hand, and the two walked toward the front door.

"Where are you going, Colonel?" requested the woman at the front desk.

Swiveling his head to the left, Nathaniel countered, "Nowhere, Mary. Just saying goodbye to my grandson, then I will be right back."

"Oh, OK. Just checking. It is my job, you know," was nurse Mary's reply as the last sound of what she said faded away while the door closed behind them.

"Goddamn, she is annoying," Nathaniel complained. "So fucking nosy. I might leave this place a couple of times a month, and every time I do I hear the same shit."

"Well, it is her job to make sure none of you old fuckers wander off and get lost, isn't it?" retorted Joshua, immediately feeling bad for being rude to his grandfather.

"I suppose it is," admitted Nathaniel in a voice that sounded resigned to his fate as an old fucker in his declining years.

Back to what was happening, Nathaniel wanted to know, "Did you get everything ordered that you need for the first part of the mission?"

Joshua tingled with excitement.

"I sure did. All of my equipment and everything should be waiting for me at my hotel when I arrive in Japan."

"Excellent," affirmed Nathaniel, equally excited.

"Did you have any problem using the credit card?"

"Nope. Not a bit. I have my own PIN code, so everything is looking good."

"Well, alright then," Nathaniel expressed, standing back a second to get a good, complete view of his grandson.

"You are the man for the job. The only one who can do the job. I'm proud of you for taking this on. I'm proud that you are my grandson," emphasized Nathaniel, practically beaming.

"Thanks, Grampa. Thanks a lot! I will do the job. Nothing can stop me," assured Joshua, as much assuring himself as he was assuring his grandfather.

Joshua reached out to hug his grandfather, who hugged him back, and then both of them looked down, feeling uncomfortable at their display of emotion. Joshua was pretty sure his grandfather looked away so that Joshua would not see the tears in his grandfather's eyes. Joshua pretended not to notice because he had teared up, too.

"See ya, Grampa. See you in about a week or so."

"OK. See ya, Joshua! Keep your wits about you."

"I will, and I will call you every morning at 10:00 a.m., St. Louis time, to let you know how it is going. OK?"

"OK," confirmed Nathaniel as he turned around and headed back up the stairs to the front door. Joshua watched him walk away and disappear through the door, hoping he would look back one more time, but Nathaniel did not.

Joshua sighed as he watched his grandfather limp slightly as he climbed the stairs, worried about what might happen to him while he was gone. As he drove to Betsy's apartment, he again wondered what he had gotten himself into. At worst, he'd satisfy his grandfather's curiosity and find nothing; at best, he'd uncover a hydrogen bomb. The thought of finding the bomb was formidable, both in scale and significance. The enormity of the task brought him back to focus—he was about to leave for Japan, and his bomb quest was about to begin in earnest.

CHAPTER 27

Nothing much of consequence occurred during Muqtar's day at work, just the usual handing out of pills and checking on the vets. His thoughts kept drifting to the mystery of the numbers the Colonel had written down. After finishing his shift, he picked up his son, Michael Jr., whose excited chatter distracted him from the conundrum. When Julie arrived home an hour later, she was pleased to find that Muqtar had started dinner and Junior was building Lego forts at the table.

"Well done, honey! I'm impressed," complimented Julie.

"Thank you, baby. I am on a roll today, that's for sure," confirmed Muqtar, thinking about his successful caper at the nursing home.

Julie took over dinner, and Muqtar retreated to the study. He pulled up Google Maps, enabling the longitude/latitude function, and returned to Tokyo Bay, trying to recall the numbers he had written down. Julie had found the paper earlier and placed it with other papers on top of the refrigerator. Later, Muqtar retrieved the list and went outside for his evening smoke.

Tapping his cigarette pack, he glanced at the numbers, observing how shaky his handwriting was from the nervousness of the Colonel's room burglary. He smiled at the memory, then his thoughts drifted to his childhood in Pakistan—narrow, deteriorating streets filled with potholes, vendors, and a mix of vehicles. He remembered the revolution promising prosperity, but for Muqtar and his thirteen siblings, it brought only hardship: two died of disease, one was jailed, and only Muqtar made it to the U.S. on an academic scholarship. His younger brother Mohammed was the bright light of the family.

Then his thoughts turned to the fun days back in New York, Muqtar thought nostalgically. Lots of girls in America with their short skirts, blonde hair, and flirty ways. Decadent sluts that were the spawn of a rotting, corrupt society was the official pronouncement of American culture by the oh-so-pious Muslim elite. That recollection and assessment made him smile, too.

Muqtar looked back at the scrawled handwriting that he was going to enter into the computer in a few minutes. Just then, his wife came outside to join him. He showed her the checklist.

"What do these numbers mean, Julie?"

"What numbers?"

"The numbers here on the checklist," Muqtar indicated, handing the paper to her.

"Oh, that," Julie laughed. "The handwriting looks like it was done by one of the old men at the nursing home."

"Okay, okay, smarty-pants, give me that back," Muqtar insisted as he reached for the paper. "But you don't know what they mean either?"

"I'm not sure, really. I think these numbers are a combination to a lock or something."

"No, they can't be that," considered Muqtar. "I copied these numbers from some numbers that I saw in Colonel Meister's room. I think they may represent geographical coordinates."

"Well, I don't know," answered Julie. "He was in the Army Air Corps during World War II. I know that because I've seen his medals. And what were you doing in the Colonel's room anyway?"

Muqtar almost choked. "Uh, uh, this morning after my rounds, he asked me to come into his room to talk," he stammered, thinking as fast as he could.

"That is unusual for him to ask anyone to come into his room," commented Julie, not sure her husband was being forthright.

"Yeah, I thought it was, too," offered Muqtar, making shit up on the fly. "I guess maybe his experience with the FBI guys yesterday changed him."

"That could be it. Come on in now. It is time to eat."

"Okay, honey. I will be right there."

He let out a breath he hadn't realized he'd been holding. The tension in his shoulders eased, and he unclenched his jaw. He gave her a genuine smile, the first in hours.

Relieved his wife wasn't suspicious, Muqtar returned to his thoughts. Could the numbers be a secret code from the Colonel's WWII days? Maybe they point to where a secret bomb was dropped? He dismissed the idea, thinking if that had happened someone would have found it by now. Still, he decided to check to see if the numbers had any link to the war with Japan, and the Colonel was a bombardier.

After smoking another cigarette, Muqtar figured further research wouldn't hurt. Back in his office after dinner, he entered the numbers into the computer and asked AI what they represented. Sure enough, AI concluded they were a location in Tokyo Bay. But what bomb was the Colonel looking for there? Muqtar knew the Colonel had been a B-29 bombardier during the war, but he needed more information on Nathaniel's role. At least the numbers now corresponded to a point in Japan.

The thought of gathering intel reminded him of the missile strike on his village in Pakistan, and he became enraged again.

He blamed America for possibly killing his former fiancée, an innocent woman whose life had been cut short by a "smart bomb"—which Muqtar felt was far from smart. And what potentially happened to his family too?

The depth of his anger surprised him. He was really, really furious, and the desire for revenge lit a flame inside him. His stomach hurt, and beads of angry sweat formed on his forehead. Muqtar knew he had to find a way to make those who bombed his village pay for their sins, to pay for their arrogance, to pay in blood for the blood they caused the villagers to bleed. Praise God! Death to the infidels! Allahu Akbar!

Muqtar's mind mulled over various thoughts of how to extract revenge against the United States, his outrage over the drone strike on his village in Pakistan fueling his mindset. He needed to find out what happened to his first love without revealing his identity. He couldn't trust anyone in the U.S. or back home to tell him, so he decided to contact Al-Jazeera to uncover the truth.

As he pondered where "home" really was—his village in Pakistan, New York, Pennsylvania, or St. Louis—he realized he was a "nowhere man." Shaking off those thoughts, he focused on the bomb mystery, hoping he would find more clues.

After turning over all of the possibilities that came to mind, Muqtar went to the bedroom and slipped into bed. There, he kissed his wife goodnight and tried to sleep, but his mind kept churning and burning. The idea that his adopted homeland could kill innocent people over where a supposed terrorist cell was located was hard to grasp. What kind of threat to or attack on the U.S. could have come from so far away?

Muqtar recalled his initial excitement upon arriving in the U.S., seeing it as the land of opportunity. However, he now bitterly regretted his own missed chance and felt a growing resentment toward the U.S. for its unjust drone strike on his village. For the first time, he felt a deep separation from the country he had once admired. His once good feelings had now transformed into a desire for revenge—a desire that was consuming him. He was going to make the U.S. pay for its transgression, regardless of whether who ended up paying was innocent or guilty.

He struggled with the conflict between his love for his wife and child and his desire for vengeance, but Muqtar was determined to strike back. He knew he had to focus on uncovering the mystery of the bomb, and he knew somehow the coordinates the Colonel had provided contained the answer. As he lay in bed, Muqtar suppressed his feelings, determined to act as a good husband while silently plotting his next move.

"Wait a minute," Muqtar spoke as he jumped off the bed, startling Julie.

"What is it, honey?" Julie murmured sleepily.

"Nothing, baby. I just had a thought and I wanted to write it down before I forgot."

"Oh, okay," Julie replied, rolling back over.

Muqtar made his way to the office and fired up the laptop. Once in, he went back to the Google map and again looked at the point of intersection. Then he expanded the view to look at the Mariana Islands. Sure enough, the point on the map corresponded with the route an American bomber would take to fly to the Emperor's palace.

Hell, yes, thought Muqtar. The bomb the Colonel was talking about must have been meant to be dropped on the Emperor's palace; that's why he said, *"Kill the emperor."* For sure, the Colonel had kept the secret about the bomb since the war for a reason, so the answer to the mystery of the bomb must be somehow still very important.

Muqtar was now satisfied with his sleuthing and fell asleep with a smile on his face. Before he completely fell asleep, Muqtar set a new goal in his mind: to find out exactly what was so special about the bomb at the bottom of Tokyo Bay.

CHAPTER 28

Joshua anxiously watched the time, sitting outside Betsy's apartment, hoping Betsy would leave work early so they could enjoy some moments together before his evening flight. As her car approached, coming at him out of the setting sun, he felt a mix of excitement and guilt over his crude thoughts, reminding himself that what he truly wanted was to connect with her deeply—especially if this might be their last chance.

Betsy could tell what was on Joshua's mind when he came into view, standing outside of his car.

"I know what you want, Mr. Horny."

Joshua's face turned red for the umpteenth time. What a shitty spy I am; probably better to have been fired than give away U.S. secrets by my face that tells all.

"Oh yeah. You might be right, Betsy. However, you look pretty ready to go yourself."

"True enough, spy boy. Who knows when you will return or if you will ever return, huh?"

"Oh no, Betsy, I am definitely coming back. This trip is just a rendezvous to see if the bomb is still laying on the bottom of Tokyo Bay. You aren't getting rid of me that easy, little girl," commanded Joshua, pulling Betsy close to him. "And who knows, when I figure it all out, I might just get a job in St. Louis and stay here."

"That's what I wanted to hear, big boy," rejoined Betsy, not quite believing him but reaching up to give Joshua a warm, inviting kiss anyway.

Spontaneously, Joshua reached his arms around Betsy, scooped her up, and carried her to the front door of her apartment. They fumbled with her keys until the door finally opened. Then, without any hesitation, they became entangled—first on the floor, then on the couch, and ended up on Betsy's bed exhausted.

"That ought to hold you a week or so," Betsy announced proudly.

"You are right about that, Bets. It will take a week for Big J to recover. Then I will be back for more, a lot more. So be ready, girlfriend. Big J will be back in town."

With that, the two untangled themselves from each other. No time left to eat. Joshua exited the apartment and headed toward the airport.

Day 3 in Japan

After a restless night in Tokyo, torn between thoughts of Mei Lei and Betsy, Joshua woke energized despite the time zone disorientation and the looming challenges that lay ahead. Determined to tackle the day—bomb hunt included—he had a hearty breakfast at the hotel and managed to secure a to-go sandwich and an iced tea, despite the cultural and language barriers between him and the polite Japanese staff. Armed with provisions and optimism, Joshua set off in an Uber, hoping the day would lead him to a five-ton metal tube resting at the bay's bottom.

Mr. Hosaki was standing next to the boat as Joshua approached.

"Good morning, Mr. Joshua," greeted Mr. Hosaki pleasantly, bowing slightly.

"Good morning, Mr. Hosaki-san," returned Joshua, bowing more deeply.

"Your boat is ready to take you anywhere you wish today, Mr. Joshua," was Mr. Hosaki's next gracious comment. "And," while looking to the east, "the weather looks splendid, so you will have calm waters, too, for scouting out movie locations and for diving if you so desire."

Yikes. Busted and thoroughly red-faced. "Thank you, Mr. Hosaki-san, for your courtesies. I may be out looking around for most of the day today."

"The day is yours, Mr. Joshua. What kind of movie are you researching, and why look for locations in Tokyo Bay? Hardly anyone dives in the bay. Is that part of the movie plan?" rapid-fired Mr. Hosaki.

Thinking as fast as he could, Joshua came up with: "The movie is being financed by some wealthy Japanese, and part of it is to be filmed underwater, and Tokyo Bay is as good a place to film underwater as anywhere else."

Satisfied with the answer, Mr. Hosaki cautioned: "Do what you wish; just avoid the large container ships and do not tarry about near the sub-sea tunnel," warned Mr. Hosaki. "The authorities keep a close eye on that area."

"Thank you again, Mr. Hosaki-san. I will abide by the rules and steer clear of both."

"Oh, and by the way, Mr. Joshua, your scuba gear is right where you left it. And I took the liberty to get you a fresh air tank."

Oh shit. Joshua felt a wave of panic pass through him and paranoia overtake him. I have been found out and, worse than that, I didn't think about needing an air tank. What should I say? What a fucking moron I am. Does Mr. Hosaki know what I am really doing? Why is he being so nosy? God damn it.

A million thoughts raced through his mind; the foremost of which was that no one can be trusted. Was my explanation good enough on how the movie shoot and diving fit together? Joshua could not think of how to link the two together any better, so he decided to keep his mouth shut and not say anything other than "Thank you very much." Oh well, he concluded glumly; sadly not my first self-caused security breach.

With that, Joshua stepped onto the boat and prepared to cast off.

"I have already warmed the engine for you this morning, so you should have no problems. And by the way, if you need to get the tank refilled again, the dive shop is four doors down," reported Mr. Hosaki, pointing to the west.

Joshua, face flushed, silently bowed to Mr. Hosaki, caught the bowline, coiled it neatly, and took control of the boat. Easing out of the marina below the 8 km/hr limit, he admired the calm bay and sunny weather. Using Siri to recall yesterday's destination, Joshua adjusted his course to avoid revealing where he was really going.

Once past the slow zone, he accelerated to 40 km/hr, skirting the industrial coast near an amusement park—his cue to veer sharply south toward his hopeful discovery. Excitement built as he approached, his thoughts traveling way ahead with anticipation and a little bit of trepidation. Glancing at the GPS and then at the disappearing marina behind, Joshua grinned, 95 percent ready for whatever lay ahead.

Still, Joshua thought, if Mr. Hosaki had a good pair of binoculars, he could find Joshua and track his movements and location. Nothing I can do about that now, concluded Joshua, setting aside that consideration for the moment as he was 100 percent focused on finding the bomb. Nothing could deter him from the mission at hand—at least nothing that was apparent to Joshua as he throttled back the engine.

Joshua switched on the fish-finder. Damn it. He had forgotten to buy a fishing pole to give himself cover. Oh well. He would get one for tomorrow. Gosh, Joshua wondered, do people even fish in Tokyo Bay, or is it too polluted to eat the fish that live here? Certainly, Joshua concluded, someone must fish here because the boat was equipped with a fish-finder. Duh. Note to self: return fish-finder to U.S. as the boat has one.

Three hundred feet, two hundred, one hundred—slow, stop. Joshua studied the fish-finder and his phone. He was directly over the coordinates, but the screen showed nothing—just a sloping bay floor sixty feet below. No bomb, no outlines, nothing. Frustrated and dejected, he wondered if this was a futile, expensive wild goose chase.

Then he remembered: the bomb wouldn't have dropped straight down. Traveling at 250 mph heading northwest on impact, it would not have suddenly stopped. Reinvigorated, Joshua adjusted his plan, crisscrossing the bay in a northwest pattern heading away from the point of impact. Eyes fixed on a shoreline landmark and the fish-finder, he moved slowly, hoping—and even praying—for a breakthrough.

About sixty or seventy yards from ground zero, Joshua thought he saw something on the screen. He steered the boat in the direction of what he thought was an anomaly on the sea floor, not just the bay bottom. His heart was pounding now as he circled the area he was seeing on the screen. What he saw was not normal; not normal at all. What Joshua was looking at was a shape coming up off the bottom of the bay, not at all well defined, but a shape nonetheless.

The fish-finder had revealed an unusual shape, clearly not part of the natural ocean floor. Joshua repositioned the boat thirty yards southeast, dropped anchor, and prepared to dive. Donning his wetsuit and scuba gear, he felt a mix of excitement and nerves. Scanning the horizon for any onlookers, he saw none and plunged into the cold, murky water.

At ten feet, visibility worsened, so he activated his flashlight and descended further, holding the anchor line for guidance. By sixty feet, he realized he'd forgotten the metal detector—darn it—but he pressed on, feeling his way ahead cautiously. At sixty-five feet, he touched the soft ocean floor but struggled to orient himself, unable to locate the anomaly found on the fish-finder.

Well, fuck it, thought Joshua. I will just creepy-crawl along the bottom heading northwest, zigzagging, going further and further out using my dive compass until I find what I'm looking for. Joshua looked at his dive watch. Lots of air left.

Using his dive compass, Joshua methodically searched, moving in a zigzag pattern—left and right, left and right, moving northwest a little bit at a time. After twenty minutes of this tedious effort, his hand brushed something solid. Shining his light, he saw metal—rounded and large. Excited, he felt along the edges, realizing most of the object was buried beneath the muck. Joshua shined his light and rubbed the protruding edge. Sure enough, what he saw was metal and big, and when Joshua was able to see through the cloud of silt he had kicked up, he could clearly see the letters *PAY* stenciled on the exposed edge.

Oh my God! Joshua had found the bomb.

Joshua's heart galloped as he weighed his options. With enough air left, he decided to investigate further, feeling along the exposed edge of the object. Swimming carefully to avoid stirring up silt, he swam into a pole protruding from the edge of the object—painful but important. His grandfather's description of the bomb was accurate. Excellent.

Holding the pole and floating above the rounded edge where it met the ocean floor, he paused, staring down. Was this a miracle or a nightmare? Life would've been simpler if he hadn't found the bomb, but he was committed now. His English grandmother's saying, *"In for a penny, in for a pound,"* echoed in his mind—its meaning now crystal clear.

Joshua faced a dilemma: leave the bomb undisturbed and keep his discovery a secret, or undertake the Herculean task of extracting, lifting, and safely disposing of it. The flashlight revealed more details—a cylindrical tube with a rounded end, about six feet in diameter, mostly buried, with two poles protruding upward roughly six feet apart. It matched his grandfather's description: ten feet long, six feet wide, and weighing around 10,000 pounds.

The enormity of the task hit him. Without connections or fluency in Japanese, pulling off a covert salvage operation seemed impossible. Oxygen running low, Joshua ascended, vowing to find a way. Determined and excited, he resolved to retrieve the bomb, no matter what.

Back on the boat, Joshua repositioned fifty feet northwest of where he believed the bomb lay. He looked at the GPS coordinates on his phone and confirmed they were the same as what his grandfather had written down eighty years earlier: 35° 36' 1.012" N and 139° 52' 0.512" E.

Satisfied, he headed back to the marina, eager to share the discovery with his grandfather.

Later, pacing in his hotel room, he anticipated the call home. The bomb's location made it retrievable, and its casing appeared intact—no major damage or rust. *Any minute now,* he thought, his pulse quickening. He could barely contain his excitement. What if . . . ? The possibilities swirled in his mind.

But every time his thoughts turned to the task of the excavation project, Joshua would sigh a huge sigh. *How the fuck was he going to do the job? No, not do. How the hell was he even going to start the job? Christ almighty.* The obstacles seemed insurmountable, and the odds of success very low.

Thank goodness, now was the time to call home: 10:00 a.m. in St. Louis. Joshua's mind rested a bit as he dialed his grandfather's phone number. Hopefully, between his grandfather and himself, they would come up with a workable plan. Failing that, at least they would come up with some sort of a plan.

"Hello."

"Hello, Grampa. It's me, Joshua, calling from Japan."

"Hello. I was expecting your call earlier," griped Nathaniel.

"Come on, Grampa. It is only 10:04 your time," pleaded Joshua.

"Right. 10:04. You were supposed to call at ten hundred sharp." Joshua did not know what to say to that, so an awkward silence ensued. Part of him wanted to say, *Fuck you. Come and dig up your own bomb, old man.* But maybe the old man was sending him a coded message.

In fact, he was. Muqtar was in Nathaniel's room at the time the phone rang, dispensing the Colonel's meds, and Nathaniel did not want to let the nurse's aide know who he was talking to nor what he was talking about. Sensing something was amiss, Joshua said, "OK. I will call at twelve hundred hours sharp."

"OK. Goodbye," was the reply, and then silence as the phone line went dead.

Muqtar was intrigued by the brief conversation and the Colonel's instruction to call back at twelve hundred hours. Determined to be nearby, he finished his rounds, ensuring the elderly patients took their medications. With thirteen minutes to spare before noon, Muqtar devised a plan to be near Room 106. At 11:57, he grabbed a bottle of aspirin, unscrewed the lid, and spilled the pills in front of the Colonel's door. He knelt to pick them up as the clock struck noon, and the Colonel's phone rang right on cue.

"Hello, Joshua. Is that you?" Muqtar heard the Colonel say.

"Yes, Grampa. It is me. Twelve hundred hours exactly."

"Right you are, Joshua. Perfect timing. I couldn't talk earlier because there was an orderly in the room."

"Oh, OK, Grampa. I figured something was up. Which orderly was it?"

"The dark-skinned one named Michael. And yes, with him being in here I did not want to take any chances of him overhearing our conversation."

"I completely get that, Grampa, and I have news for you."

Silence . . . silence. Nathaniel's heart was pounding like crazy, so much so that he could not talk. Finally, he croaked out, "What news?"

"I found the bomb, Grampa! I found the bomb!"

"Holy shit, Joshua! You found the fucking bomb!" exclaimed Nathaniel, practically shouting.

"I sure did, Grampa. About fifty yards northwest from the coordinates you gave me. I found it and in only about sixty-five feet of water."

"Wow, that's incredible that after all these many years, you have found the hydrogen bomb we were going to drop on the Emperor's Palace." Nathaniel was incredibly relieved by the revelation.

"Yep, sure did," Joshua proudly proclaimed. "I dove down at the exact spot you gave me and worked my way northwest from there, figuring that was the direction you were flying when you cut it loose."

"That is correct. Well, how is the fucking thing, anyway? Is it as big as I remember? About six feet in diameter and ten feet long?"

"I can't really tell how long it is because most of it is buried in the muck on the ocean floor. But it is, for sure, six feet in diameter. I measured it with my hands. And it says on the bulged-out end *Payback*."

"Fucking A, grandson. That is outstanding news. Outstanding. Payback indeed. Now all we have to do is figure out how to get the big, heavy bastard up and out of there," contemplated Nathaniel, feeling so excited a shiver ran up and down his spine. He couldn't stand it.

"Right, Grampa. That's the next step and a big step, it is," reflected Joshua. "And I am at a loss as to how to do it. Do you have any ideas, Grampa?"

Nathaniel looked out the window, mouth agape, as he began stroking his chin and neck.

"Let's see, let me think about this. First, we have to get the prize off the bottom. I saw a documentary where they ran cables underneath a WWII submarine and were able to float it up."

"Yeah, that sounds good, Grampa, but how in the world are we going to be able to mount any kind of a salvage operation without drawing attention? And that is assuming we can find a salvage company willing to take on the job in the first place."

"Well, hell, Joshua, maybe we should just forget the whole thing," conceded Nathaniel. "I feel good enough, I guess, that you found the prize to begin with."

"Yeah, maybe, Grampa, but the potential for the prize to go off or for someone else to find it and use it for nefarious purposes concerns me greatly," rejoined Joshua, using his grandfather's term to describe the bomb.

"Very true, Joshua, very true. We don't want the world's first-of-its-kind hydrogen bomb to fall into the wrong hands, that's for sure."

"All right, Grampa. I'm going to go to bed now, and when I wake up I'm going to look on the internet for companies that do ocean salvage operations. Maybe we will get lucky and I will find someone to take on the task who will also keep their mouth shut."

"Yes, do that, Joshua. That is the next step and I have more than two million dollars to fund the effort and to keep some mouths shut, as you put it."

"OK, Grampa. I'm going to bed now, and I will call you again tomorrow to let you know what I find out. But basically I think we have to continue to push forward."

"Agreed. OK, Joshua. Goodbye."

Nathaniel hung up the phone not knowing that a computer began recording the conversation after the third time the word *bomb* was used, and furthermore, that right outside his door, a man with his own motivations was avidly listening; absorbing every word that was said.

"Holy shit," Muqtar repeated to himself. The Colonel dropped a hydrogen bomb that landed in Tokyo Bay during World War II that did not go off for some reason. Now his grandson is over there trying to come up with a plan to dredge the bomb up from the bottom of the bay. Incredible. If he hadn't heard the conversation himself, Muqtar never would have believed what was said.

The next thought that came into Muqtar's head was an evil one; a thought of righteous vengeance to pay back the U.S. for the deaths of many, many innocent people. Specifically, to pay back the U.S. for killing people like Aila and his family in Pakistan, who died for no reason; anonymous pawns in a worldwide power game.

With this knowledge Muqtar began to believe that he could change the game. All he had to do was get his hands on a bomb; a weapon of mass destruction, his very own WMD. Fortuitously, one was available, sitting in Tokyo Bay for the taking. He just had to figure out a way to get the bomb before the Colonel's grandson did. That is the hard part. *That is the hard part,* Muqtar repeated to himself. Where could he turn to get help in this endeavor? Who would have the resources to pull this off? Who would be burning with the desire for revenge like he was?

Thinking back to one of his days as a cab driver, Muqtar remembered a man, an Imam who spoke to him in Urdu, and through the recollection he hatched a plan. He decided to look for the Imam's card. If Muqtar found the card, maybe the Imam would be willing to help; to connect him with other Pakistanis similarly pissed off with the indiscriminate slaughter of innocents living in Pakistani villages blown up by drone missile attacks; pissed off enough to want to engage in a mission to obtain a hydrogen bomb and even up the score. *That will take a very special person,* thought Muqtar. He prayed to Allah for the first time in five years that such a man existed and that he, Muqtar

Ashadi, was that man.

Having picked up his son and now at home, Muqtar went through the motions of his usual routine, caring for his son and fixing dinner. Watching his boy play, he felt a fierce love and a duty to protect his family. But this love conflicted with his anger toward the Americans and his desire for revenge, especially after the death of his people in Pakistan.

Torn between harming the U.S. and protecting his American family, Muqtar chose to focus solely on retrieving the bomb from Tokyo Bay, pushing aside the emotional toll that his potential actions would create. The challenge of securing the bomb became his sole priority; his quest.

Muqtar hurried to his desk to see if he could find the Imam's business card, and while sifting through the papers, he heard the garage door open. Julie was home, and that always put a smile on his face and put his mind at ease. He returned to his search as his wife pulled into the garage. Junior jumped up and ran to the garage door that led into the kitchen to surprise Mom like he always did. About that time, Muqtar found the business card he was looking for and put the card in his wallet.

"Surprise, Momma!" exclaimed Junior as he came around a corner and hugged her. Julie flashed a big smile and acted as though she was surprised, as she always did, and she hugged him back. Muqtar, having walked into the kitchen, looked over and smiled, too.

"What's for dinner, honey?" asked Julie.

"My world-famous smothered chicken," replied Muqtar.

"Yummy," chorused mother and son in unison. Muqtar sat at the dinner table quietly, the warmth of his home surrounding him, the soft hum of daily life in the background. His mind wandered to the past, and a heavy weight settled in his chest. The thought of revenge felt like a storm brewing, threatening to rip apart everything he held dear. Muqtar reflected that life at home was good, and he knew pursuing revenge would destroy this peace and change everything. Shaking off these thoughts, he focused on the present, ready to enjoy the evening with his family—dinner, playtime, baths, maybe a little fun with Julie, and bedtime.

CHAPTER 29

Joshua wrestled with his options after finding the bomb: abandon the project, inform the CIA, or continue his original plan to retrieve it without being detected. He put off the final decision, as he hadn't even found a salvage company yet, but planned to revisit the bomb's location the next day. He was troubled by the potential consequences of informing the CIA. Would they reward him or see him as a liability? His past experience with the agency, witnessing many who were sacrificed to keep secrets, made him wary of what the CIA might do. The fear of what the CIA would consider as merely collateral damage weighed heavily on him. *Fuck that.* Joshua did not want to be the next man to be sacrificed for the cause. What cause was that anyway? Oh, yes: the safety of and preservation of the United States. Joshua concluded that from the government's perspective, sacrificing him would not cause a ripple in the fabric of keeping America safe; especially since he was a former employee of the CIA, not a current one. But because he had worked for the CIA he still had security clearance, and perhaps he could research a way to let the agency know without giving himself away. *Hmmm.* Joshua reaffirmed his decision not to directly inform the U.S. government at this time and focused on his next steps. The following day, he planned to use a metal detector to measure the bomb's exact length, remembering his grandfather's description of it as ten feet long. Joshua was determined to somehow handle the retrieval himself. Feeling strong about his decision, Joshua quickly fell asleep, jet-lagged and exhausted.

Day 4 in Japan

Joshua woke up refreshed and ready to tackle the challenge of retrieving the bomb. After a big American-style breakfast and again ensuring that no one was paying attention to him, he headed back to the marina. He decided against contacting Betsy, focusing instead on the logistics of his mission.

His first task was refilling his scuba tank. After exchanging pleasantries with Mr. Hosaki, Joshua came away from the conversation feeling that Mr. Hosaki had asked too many questions, was too inquisitive. *Shit. Is Mr. Hosaki a CIA plant? What is his deal?* Joshua wished his powers of perception were sharper. He doubted he could discern who was friend or foe. *Oh well, onward!*

Joshua walked to the nearby dive shop and while there, he swapped his tank for a full one, and when he gestured for a second, the employee provided it without issue. Joshua paid and left, feeling good about how smoothly the morning had begun.

Joshua lugged the two 40-pound tanks back to the boat, out of breath and arms aching but ready to press on. When he arrived at the location, Joshua set the anchor 100 feet west of the bomb's location to avoid detection and to create the appearance of movement. He peered off into the distance wishing he had brought binoculars, scanning the horizon for anyone looking at him. No other boats were anywhere nearby. *Man, someone had to be looking at him.* He looked onshore again, looking for the glint of binoculars or the reflection of a rifle scope but saw none. Mollified, he suited up, gathered up his gear, including the flashlight, second air tank, metal detector, and shovel, and dove in.

The descent and swim took longer than expected due to all of the equipment, eating into his air supply. Once at the bomb, Joshua carefully examined it, noting two metal stanchions with holes cut into them—one on each end of the exposed end of the bomb.

Now on the bottom next to the bomb, Joshua dug at the muck around the second stanchion, noting its thick, rectangular steel shape and its three-inch hole cut into the top. An idea struck him: if there were four intact stanchions with holes in them maybe they could be used to hoist the bomb up and out. Not a bad idea.

He dug for a while, but progress was slow as the muck kept refilling the hole. Checking his dive watch, he realized he was running out of time. As the silt clouded his view, he switched tanks and used the metal detector, confirming the length and width of the bomb, which was reassuring that the dimensions provided by his grandfather were correct. His dive watch showed he was almost out of air, and ascending to the surface would take extra time because he had been sixty-five feet deep for nearly ninety minutes.

Now satisfied, Joshua dropped the metal detector and the shovel next to the prize, grabbed the empty air tank and up he went, swimming at an angle toward the boat. Divers are supposed to stop at twenty feet below the surface to allow one's body to adjust before surfacing. Not this time because at thirty feet down, the air stopped. Joshua was trained on what to do when you run out of air so he did not panic. He thought about dropping everything he was carrying but he was a confident swimmer, so he slowly exhaled and calmly kicked his way to the surface.

Once aboard, he breathed a sigh of relief as his death would have put a kink in the recovery plans. Joshua smiled at his strange sense of humor. However, he was stumped as to what to do next as he scanned the horizon 360 degrees looking for anybody who might be looking at him. Nobody. Good. Back to the project, he didn't have any equipment to suck the dirt away; the only equipment he had was a shovel and his digging with it didn't work.

The soft ocean floor kept collapsing, and after all of his effort only two feet of the second pole was exposed. *Shoot.* Joshua decided to approach the next digging attempt at a twenty-degree angle to avoid this. However, he was discouraged realizing that digging with a hand shovel would not cut it ultimately anyway.

Joshua went back to the dive shop and exchanged his tanks for two new ones and returned to the location; again scouring the horizon for anyone looking at him as he dropped anchor in a slightly different spot. Back on bottom, Joshua found a nine-foot pipe. He thought it might help locate the stanchions located at the buried end of the bomb by poking it in the general area. With nothing else to try, he used the pipe to probe around the buried end of the bomb, hoping to find the poles. The pipe slid in easily, and Joshua felt hopeful that it was near the bomb's edge where the third and fourth poles were likely located.

Clank. He felt the pipe hit something solid. *What was that?* Had Joshua hit the side of the bomb or had he found the stanchion? Joshua wiggled the pipe back and forth. *Clank. Nothing.*

Clank. Nothing.

Crap. I missed the spot where the pole should be welded to the bomb's edge, realized Joshua. Not one to give up, Joshua pulled the pipe back out and started the process over again and again and again and again, moving an inch or so at a time, expanding the search area as best he could in all directions. Fortunately, the muck was already disturbed and as a result, Joshua couldn't see shit. Then he felt something different.

What he felt wasn't the smooth curving side of the cylinder; Joshua's fingers dug into the muck and they brushed against the edge of the cylinder, pausing as they encountered something unusual—a square hard edge, smooth yet distinct. He ran his hand along it, going up and down, feeling its length under his touch, knowing it had to be somehow attached.

Joshua was thrilled to discover this was a third pole attached to the bomb, realizing he now had three poles with holes at their ends to hoist it. The plan was coming together. However, seeing his dive watch, he realized he was running out of time again. Despite needing to surface, he couldn't resist one more try. He dove into the muck, and after straining, his hand felt the other pole. *Yay!* With virtually no time left, he hurriedly swam upward, leaving his gear behind, preparing for an emergency ascent and as he reached twenty feet—his air was gone.

Not again. What a weird and frightening sensation that was. No air and no warning; just no air when Joshua tried to breathe in. He remembered the rules of diving and forced himself to continue his controlled ascent while breathing out a little bit at a time. Lungs bursting, Joshua finally made his way to the surface and gasped for air. That was too fucking close. But he had made his way to the top and now he had a plan. Joshua felt most satisfied with his discovery of the intact stanchions and could hardly wait to tell the news to his grandfather.

Joshua returned to the marina, eyes constantly darting back and forth looking for bogies. A dark cloud of foreboding invaded his senses partially killing the buzz of excitement he was feeling at what he had discovered. Nonetheless, his chest swelled with pride at his accomplishment; his feelings of being a worthless loser no more. He was thrilled to have found the bomb, confident in his plan to lift it using the poles attached to each end. However, he was also scared: worried about being discovered, failing the mission, and the lingering fear that someone was searching for either him or the bomb—something he didn't know to prepare for. After completing his mental assessment, he shrugged off his fear and with a satisfied swagger he lugged the empty air tanks to the dive shop, bemused by how heavy they were, even without air.

Now there was nothing else to do but return to the hotel and wait. So, he did. The hours slowly passed as Joshua waited impatiently for midnight, the time when he was to call his grandfather. Finally, his watch showed exactly 23:55 and Joshua dialed the number. Then Joshua hung up the phone. Something told him to call from the telephone in his room rather than from his cell phone. He didn't question his intuition as he sat on the bed and reached for the hotel phone. As usual, there was a significant wait time once the dialing was completed for the satellites to make the connection.

Then finally: "Hello, Colonel Nathaniel Meister here."

"Hello, Grampa. It's me, Joshua."

"Hello, Joshua. I see you called right on time this morning but I don't recognize the number. You must finally be getting trained on the importance of being on time."

"Not so much, Grampa. Not in my own life, anyway. I just

know how important it is to you."

"You're right, grandson. As you know, being on time is and has always been important to me. And if you were smart, it would be important to you, too. Wasn't your failure to get to work on time the reason why you were fired from the CIA?"

"Yes, Grampa, we have been over that too many times," recalled Joshua, highly perturbed by the question; more than a bit pissed to be reminded of this again. "Failure to be at my desk by 0800 was the reason, actually the excuse, why I was fired from the CIA but that is not why I fucking called," he shouted. As soon as those words came out of Joshua's mouth, he regretted saying them, sort of.

Another awkward silence followed this exchange. Joshua shaking his head from side to side, pissed because he had such good news to share, yet his grandfather wanted to focus on what fucking time it was. So, Joshua said nothing for a couple of minutes.

"You still there?" offered Nathaniel rather timidly.

"Yes, I am still here," answered Joshua quietly.

"Do you have any news to tell me?"

"I sure do. I just didn't know if you wanted to offer me any more opinions on the virtue and value of being on time or hear my fucking news," conveyed Joshua, who couldn't help himself from speaking loudly with considerably more than a hint of pissed off-ed-ness in his voice. After all, Joshua thought indignantly, *I am the one whose ass would be in the frying pan if anyone were to come and investigate what I am doing diving in Tokyo Bay.*

Nathaniel realized he had stepped way over the line as he listened to Joshua's response.

"Sorry, grandson. I just get so wound up waiting on your call that I get ahead of myself," Nathaniel apologized.

"No problem, Grampa. This project is quite nerve-wracking because I am constantly looking around to see if anyone is watching me; to see if anyone has caught on to what I am doing. The reason why you didn't recognize the telephone number is because I called you using the hotel telephone. But I mean really, Grampa, on the upside, if you think about my situation, who else can say they have been unceremoniously fired by the CIA, then two weeks later be scuba-diving in Tokyo Bay looking for and finding a secret lost World War II hydrogen bomb?"

Nathaniel was relieved that Joshua's tone had lightened up. "No one else, grandson, only you. Congratulations!" Then he paused for a second. "So, what's new?"

"Well, OK. Grampa, do you remember how you described that the big mother had four poles or stanchions, two attached at each end and the poles had holes cut in them and that the bomb was suspended from them in the aircraft?"

"Why, yes. I sure do remember that," recalled Nathaniel. "There were two on each end positioned 180 degrees apart."

"Exactly, Grampa. Well, I found two of the poles sticking out of the muck when I dove today and then I stuck a metal pipe into the muck on the other side and found one there too; still attached."

Nathaniel was somewhat puzzled by the significance of this find.

"What does that mean? How does that help us?"

"That's the coolest part, Grampa. I'm going to attach balloons to the holes in the poles, inflate them with air from a scuba tank and see if I can float the big bitch up off the bottom that way." Joshua was ecstatic as he described his plan, stretching his hands out to simulate a balloon getting blown up, getting more pumped up as he went along.

Nathaniel absorbed this idea for a moment.

"Grandson, that is just fucking outstanding," Nathaniel exclaimed. "Outstanding and brilliant. We can use the fact that the bomb won't weigh 10,000 pounds underwater, thus allowing the air in the balloons to pick it up and float it." Nathaniel felt a chill go up and down his spine. The plan was actually coming together; way better than Nathaniel had ever really thought the plan would.

Shaking his head, Nathaniel wondered: "Do you have any balloons and rope to try out your idea?"

"No, I sure don't, Grampa. I'm going to use weather balloons and heavy-duty lifting straps for the effort, and I don't have any here, that's for sure. I'm going to check out websites in the morning to figure out how people float up the ancient shipwrecks and so forth like you talked about with the submarine. Then I'm going to see where I can buy the equipment."

"Good thinking, grandson. I suggest you look around for a salvage company while you are over there."

"Gosh, Grampa. I have been thinking about that, too. Assuming we can lift it up off the bottom, getting it to the surface and loaded onto a barge or something is another story altogether, wouldn't you agree?"

"Yes. And I guess buying a salvage ship is out of the question, huh, grandson?"

"Most likely, yes, it is way too expensive to buy a salvage ship, Grampa. We're going to have to rent a salvage ship and a crew that will keep their respective mouths shut."

Nathaniel considered this reality, grimaced and said: "That has always been the sticking point, hasn't it, Joshua? I always believed that you would find it once we got this mission underway, but I did not—still haven't—figured out how we're going to discreetly get the prize the hell out of there."

"Me neither, Grampa. I'm going to do my homework to-morrow morning and see if Amazon or the like sells this kind of stuff. Some company or companies surely have to sell the equipment because there are ocean floor salvage operations all over the world. Shoot, Grampa, every time there is a major hur-ricane, boats sink and have to be floated up."

"That's true, grandson. But not trying to be negative, boats are meant to float."

"Right, Grampa. I was just using boats as an example. I'm sure from time to time containers fall in the ocean, too. I feel confident that I will find a salvage company. It is just the dis-creetness required that is the issue."

"Agreed. So, your plan is to check out equipment availability and salvage operations tomorrow?"

"Yes, it sure is. My plan is to take the next step and the next step after that until we get it handled or get stymied." Or caught, Joshua thought to himself.

"Good enough," nodded Nathaniel on the other end of the line. "Call me tomorrow morning at 1000 sharp and let me know if you have had any luck."

"OK, Grampa, talk to you tomorrow."

"OK. Good luck."

Nathaniel and Joshua didn't realize that their conversation was again being recorded after using the word *bomb* for the third time. Muqtar, again stationed in the hallway, overheard their exchange, and the CIA's algorithm on their supercom-puter had already flagged the words *bomb, hydrogen bomb,* and *CIA,* thus triggering the second recording of their conversation. Joshua had switched phones, so the recording only picked up the latter parts of their conversation. Fortunately, the content wasn't heavily suspicious, so no red flag was raised, and no immediate action was taken, but both recordings made their way to the desk of a CIA analyst. The algorithm set up an automatic intercept on their phone numbers to automatically record all future calls.

A CIA identity trace revealed that one of the speakers was former CIA employee Joshua Meister. The other was classified as an unknown male. The CIA computer did this by scanning all known voices in its system and of course, Joshua's voice was there. The locations of each were also identified by the CIA system because it is able to triangulate the pings and establish locations thereby; St. Louis for the unknown male and Tokyo, Japan, for ex-CIA analyst Meister.

A CIA analyst, Alex Lozano, listened to the two intercepted calls and, though it didn't seem like an immediate threat, he created a file and noted the call pattern, expecting another around 11:00 a.m. the next day. Meanwhile, Muqtar, stunned by the revelation that the Colonel's grandson had found and was going to attempt to retrieve the hydrogen bomb dropped at the end of WWII, was torn. He was both impressed and excited by the mission's significance but faced a dilemma: continue building a peaceful life with his American family or return to his roots and seek vengeance. He couldn't decide.

Meanwhile in Tokyo, Joshua woke up in the middle of the night in a cold sweat. Visions of his past employment and the government's powers of surveillance were dancing through his head. He realized that he and his grandfather had played fast and loose with the words they were using on the telephone, which had to be why his intuition had guided him to use the hotel phone earlier.

Joshua cursed himself for being so careless, realizing that

discussing hydrogen bombs over the phone could attract un-wanted attention. He feared that he and his grandfather could disappear, just like others had for far less. Though he vowed not to speak in a way that could alert authorities again, a nagging feeling of impending danger kept him up all night. Joshua de-cided to call his grandfather. It was about 0700 in St. Louis, just before time for breakfast at the home. Joshua knew his grand-father would be awake. Joshua called at 0655 to be sure the call was connected by 0700 hours sharp.

"Hello," was Nathaniel's brusque greeting.

"Hello, Grampa. I have nothing new to say. I am coming home today and I will see you tomorrow. Goodbye."

Joshua hung up, leaving Nathaniel mystified.

Coming home today? Nothing new to say? What the hell? The more Nathaniel thought about the very brief conversation the more worried he became. Nathaniel grew very suspicious after the brief phone call was cut short, wondering if the line was compromised or if Joshua had backed out. He decided to wait until he saw his grandson in person to address his concerns.

Meanwhile, Muqtar, who overheard "hello," was equally baf-fled. He had spent the night contemplating his next move but knew he couldn't involve the American authorities without ex-posing his past.

Muqtar fished out the business card of the Imam. He parked the med cart in its normal spot and went outside to smoke a cigarette just like he normally did every day. Muqtar called the number and after a couple of rings:

"Hello," greeted the voice in English.

"Hello," Muqtar greeted in English also, relieved that he didn't have to fight through how to adequately converse in Urdu. "Is this Imam Rushi? This is Michael Brown. I believe I gave you a ride once in my cab when you were visiting St. Louis."

"Oh, hello, Michael Brown. Yes, this is Mohammed Rushi. I remember you. Nice to hear from you. What is the reason for your call?" demanded the voice, getting right to the point.

"You were right about me when we met, Imam. I am from a small village in northern Pakistan," Muqtar confessed. "I was hoping you could help me find out what exactly happened in my village when it was hit by an American drone strike about a week ago."

"Hmmm. OK. What makes you think I would know what happened to your village?"

Muqtar hesitated. "Nothing, actually. I was just hoping you would know since you are familiar with my region."

"That is true, I am from your region; a village about fifteen km from your home is where I grew up. Funny that you called at this moment, because I am traveling home in just a few days."

Muqtar was quite encouraged by this news.

"Is there any chance, sir, that you could go to my village and find out what happened, who was killed, who was hurt and so forth?"

The voice on the other end of the phone hesitated.

"I suppose so. I have to go through your village to get to mine. Who is it that you want me to look up, because I doubt there are very many people named Brown in that part of Pakistan."

"Oh, that. My original name is Muqtar Ashadi. I changed my name when I came to the U.S."

Declining to ask Muqtar why he changed his name, the voice wanted to know: "Who do you want me to look up?"

Muqtar rattled off several family members' names and emphasized the name of his girlfriend, Alia, the person he wanted to check on the most.

"OK. I will do it," affirmed the voice. "I will call you in two days at 6:00 a.m. St. Louis time. Be sure to answer your phone."

"Thank you, sir. Thank you so very much. I will be waiting for your call," responded Muqtar most appreciatively.

Muqtar's heart took off, a surge of energy lifting him, but his palms were damp with anxiety sweat. His mind flicked between excitement and uncertainty, the thrill of the moment battling the tightening in his chest as he awaited news that could either confirm his family's safety or reveal tragedy. By reopening the door to his past, he knew consequences were inevitable.

CHAPTER 30

Day 5 in Japan

The next morning, Joshua informed Mr. Hosaki of a sudden change in plans, explaining he had to return to the U.S. immediately. Grateful for Mr. Hosaki's help, he asked to store his scuba gear there until his return, promising to be back in under three weeks. After a polite bow, and with no further questions from Mr. Hosaki that morning, Joshua left for the airport, his growing paranoia making him glance over his shoulder at every turn.

Throughout the trip to the airport, the sense of being watched gnawed at him. At security and at the gate, he scrutinized his surroundings but noticed nothing suspicious although his pulse rate increased until he cleared the check-in. Once aboard the plane, exhaustion overtook him, and he fell into a deep sleep.

Waking as the plane landed in Los Angeles, Joshua felt surprisingly rested and secure. Clearing Customs without issue, he headed straight to his domestic gate for the flight to St. Louis. With the bomb's location confirmed and extraction plans loosely formed, he took stock of his situation. No government agents appeared, and no one seemed to be tracking him. His examining the situation exercise did not take away the feeling of unease, however.

Debating whether to call his grandfather or visit him un-announced, Joshua opted for the latter, wary of the unsettling feeling that someone might be eavesdropping on his calls. Too bad for Joshua and his thoughts about telephones because just then his phone rang. It was his grandfather calling. Despite his misgivings, Joshua answered the call.

"Hello."

"Hello. Joshua, is that you?"

Resisting the slight temptation to say *Yes, motherfucker, who did you think it was after you dialed my number,* Joshua stated: "Yes, Grampa, it is me."

"OK, good. Did you say you are coming back here today?"

"Yes, Grampa, I did, and I am in L.A. about to board a flight to St. Louis."

"Oh, OK. How much money did you spend in Japan?"

"Gosh, Grampa, I don't know; probably five or six thousand including the equipment."

"Did you bring the equipment home with you, grandson?"

"No, I sure didn't. I left everything in Japan for when I go back."

"That's good to hear that you are planning to go back. You got off the phone so fast with me that I thought something had gone wrong."

"No, nothing went wrong, per se, Grampa. I was just nervous about talking on the phone long-distance."

Nathaniel paused for a moment.

"I get it, Joshua. You became worried that someone might be listening to us talking about the bomb while you were in Japan, right?" Nathaniel inquired.

Joshua winced at hearing the word *bomb* and could almost hear the giant listening apparatus of the U.S. government turn its huge ears toward their conversation, stimulated by the use of the word *bomb*.

"Grampa, I think it is best that we never say that word again because someone who might be listening would not understand the joke."

"Oh, shit, you're right, Joshua. Better to be safe than sorry," admitted Nathaniel ruefully, whipping himself for his stupidity.

"No problem, Grampa. I will be back in St. Louis around three this afternoon and I will come see you after I retrieve my suitcase."

"Good. That sounds good, grandson. I look forward to seeing you this afternoon."

"OK, Grampa. See you soon."

It was too late. Joshua was right—the algorithm, already on alert from previous flagged conversations, began recording as soon as the voices started. The recording landed on analyst Alex Lozano's screen, and he clicked to listen. When he heard the word *bomb* in context, his curiosity spiked. This time the computer located Joshua in Los Angeles and the unnamed male was still in St. Louis. Alex knew that accessing domestic telephone calls by the CIA was a no-no but talking about hydrogen bombs was a bigger no-no in his opinion, so Alex clicked a box for the computer to continue to record the two men's conversations no matter where they were.

Confirming the identities of Joshua Meister and his grandfather, Nathaniel Meister, Alex dug deeper. Nathaniel's record revealed a stellar career: a retired Air Force colonel, WWII hero, Medal of Honor recipient, and one of the few to fight on both fronts. Joshua, meanwhile, had a complete CIA file—gifted, a Mensa member, fluent in six languages, and inquisitive. Terminated for tardiness?

Alex raised an eyebrow. Fired by General Sanders, a notorious hard-liner with a long history of driving out valuable personnel. That tracked. But what mischief could Joshua and his grandfather be up to now? Was the mention of a bomb genuine, or a clever ruse to mislead potential eavesdroppers for some reason?

Clearly, they did not want to be overheard and clearly the Colonel referenced "the bomb." *What bomb? Where? How strange.* Alex ran their credit card statements and searched through their bank accounts. He saw the purchases of the airline tickets, the scuba equipment, the metal detector and the rental of a boat and a hotel room in Tokyo.

Why would Joshua rent a boat at Tokyo Bay? Were the two of them looking to blow up something in the harbor? Maybe plant a bomb in the underground tunnel that crosses Tokyo Bay? Alex called up a satellite view of Tokyo Bay and focused on the path of the tunnel. Nothing in particular stood out, but at the mouth of the tunnel were two patrol boats.

Alex reasoned that the patrol boats closely monitored the tunnel, investigating any boat that approached. He began narrowing down potential targets in Tokyo Bay: a traffic tunnel, an amusement park, a container port, and an oil terminal.

Bingo—the oil terminal. If Alex was right, it made sense. The terminal handled crude oil transfers and also housed a natural gas plant where liquefied natural gas, highly flammable and pressurized, was unloaded.

If his analysis were true, Col. Nathaniel Meister and ex-CIA analyst Joshua Meister were plotting to blow up the terminal. But why Tokyo? Blowing up an oil or gas facility in the U.S. would be easier. And the logistical challenges—acquiring materials, building a bomb, gaining access—were significant. Alex leaned back, deep in thought. Something didn't add up.

He decided to send an email to Joshua's former boss to see if the General would shed some light on the subject. In the email, Alex quoted the bit from the first conversation where the word *bomb* was mentioned and also wrote out the entirety of the third intercepted conversation. Less than an hour later, his phone rang.

"Lozano?"

"Yes."

"This is General Sanders, CIA."

"Yes."

"I received your email."

"Yes."

"What the fuck do you think those assholes are up to?"

Knowing which two assholes the general was referring to made it easy to respond.

"Unknown, General. The supercomputer is running the algorithms as we speak. All of their personal data, people they know, places they have been are being crunched."

"Fuck all that, Lozano," growled the general harshly. "The U.S. government is paying you to analyze, so what's your analysis?"

"Nothing definite, sir. I am inclined to think they are plotting to blow up the liquid natural gas unloading terminal in Tokyo Bay. The terminal is the most logical target," Alex speculated.

"So they might be planning to blow up Tokyo Bay, huh?" mused the general.

"Not all of Tokyo Bay, sir. But my calculation shows that if they or anyone could successfully blow up a ship full of compressed liquid natural gas or the terminal itself, Tokyo Bay would be shut down for about three months for the clean-up.

Plus, Japan relies on natural gas to run the country," Alex added.

"Does either one of them own any stock in Nissan or Toyota or in any shipping lines?"

"No, sir. Neither one does." A pretty clever observation from the old windbag, thought Alex. He continued. "Colonel Nathaniel has about two and a half million worth of IBM stock. He sold about $50,000 of IBM stock a few days ago and opened a checking account with the proceeds. Colonel Meister put Joshua Meister's name on the account and Joshua Meister went to Japan that day."

Anticipating the general's next question, Alex continued: "Joshua bought scuba equipment, a metal detector, a foldable shovel, and an underwater flashlight that he had shipped to the downtown Hilton in Tokyo. Joshua Meister also rented a boat for a week when he arrived in Tokyo."

"Has anyone talked to the place where Joshua rented the boat?"

"The owner of the boat rental place is on the list for our operatives to talk to, and we are also downloading photos from the satellite that may show where the boat traveled in the bay."

"Did Meister make any other phone calls that we know about or did the Colonel call anyone else?"

"No. Neither one called anyone else during the five days Joshua was in Tokyo." Alex looked at his screen as something was coming across.

"General, the satellite photos are coming in now. I am sending them to you. There are twenty in total as the only satellite looking at Tokyo Bay makes a pass every six hours."

"OK, Lozano. I see the photos but I don't see shit. What do you see?"

"If you look at the upper left corner of photo 2, you can see what has to be the rental boat in the bay with what looks like the anchor down. Same thing in photo 6, except the boat is about 100 yards to the northwest."

"How close is the boat to the natural gas terminal?"

"Let me measure that for you, sir. It is about 1,000 meters from the natural gas terminal."

"Goddamn it," exploded the general. "I never liked that oh-so-smart graduate from the University of Michigan who could speak fifty fucking languages. I fired that piece of shit because he could never get to work on time." The general took a raspy breath and turned his attention back to Alex.

"Are there any pipelines between where the boat is anchored and the natural gas facility?"

"No, sir. None at all," confirmed Alex, again impressed that the general wasn't as stupid as he had been described as being. "The natural gas lines are nowhere near the site where the boat was anchored. In fact, there is nothing of significance within 1,000 meters of where the boat is."

"Nothing at all?" queried the general.

"Nothing at all."

"Then what the fuck is that clever cocksucker up to?"

"Unknown at this point, sir."

"OK. Do you know where Joshua is going when he returns to the U.S.?"

"Yes, sir. He has already arrived back in St. Louis where his grandfather lives at the retired military officers' nursing home."

"OK. Contact the FBI field office in St. Louis and tell them you are going down there."

"When do you want me to leave, sir?"

"Right away, Lozano. Right away. If that fucking loser Meister has something up his sleeve, I want to know what it is before he does anything nefarious."

"Yes, sir. Right away, sir."

Alex promptly made arrangements to travel to St. Louis, feeling a touch of pride at being prepared to answer the crusty old general's questions. After twenty years with the CIA, this would be only his third field assignment—and his first as the lead. But for some unknown reason he decided to hold off on contacting the FBI.

After collecting his luggage, Joshua drove through the airport parking lot, scanning for signs of surveillance. He looked around to see if anyone was eyeing him, stopped and climbed under his car to see if there was a tracking device attached to the underside and checked his rearview mirror once he started to move again to see if anyone was following him, but everything seemed clear. Good enough. He headed to the nursing home to check on his grandfather.

Arriving at the nursing home, he noticed no black Tahoes in the lot, offering him some relief. After having the receptionist call his grandfather, they met at the front desk and left without speaking much.

Once in the VW, Joshua shone with pride, "The mission to Tokyo Bay was a complete success. The bomb's exposed end reads 'PAYBACK' in big letters."

"That's what I thought and that's what I wanted to hear," Nathaniel replied, smiling a big smile while slapping Joshua repeatedly on the shoulder. "So, what is bothering you?"

"I don't know, Grampa. I don't know for sure. I just have a

creepy feeling that hit me while we were talking on the phone."

"What prompted the creepy feeling, grandson?"

"Not sure, Grampa. I can't really put my finger on it, but when we last said the word *bomb,* my intuition antennas went on full alert and have stayed that way ever since."

"I'm the dumb ass that said the word *bomb,*" Nathaniel recalled ruefully. "Do you think someone was listening in on our conversation, Joshua?"

"I do, Grampa. I do. I just don't know what they actually heard, which is why I cut off the phone call and came home."

"Did you notice anything strange or out of place on your flight or at Customs or anything?"

"Nope. Nothing. Have you noticed anything odd going on around here?"

Nathaniel shrugged his shoulders nonverbally saying *no* before quickly changing the subject. "So, tell me, grandson. How are we going to get the bomb up off the bottom of the bay?"

Joshua was excited to discuss the prospective plan.

"Do you remember describing the bomb to me and how it was built with stanchions or poles at each corner with holes cut in them?"

"Yes, I sure do. That is how the big mother was suspended in the modified bomb bay; hanging from hooks that attached to those holes."

"OK. Well, one of the poles was fully exposed and not damaged. The second pole on the same end was partly buried but also intact. I found both of those during my first dive," Joshua recounted. "On my second dive, I found a piece of metal pipe on the ocean floor. I jammed the pipe over and over into the silt on the end that was buried until I felt the distinct shape of something metal sticking out of the cylinder. I figured what I hit was one of the poles on the other side, so I stuck my whole body in the hole and sure enough, I felt the third pole and it was still attached. Because of how soft the ocean floor is and because the bomb hit the bottom of the bay with the poles sticking up, I have no reason to think that the fourth lifting pole that is buried in the mud is damaged either." Joshua announced, his entire being tingling with excitement.

Nathaniel was processing this information as Joshua was speaking, trying to recollect what he had seen seventy-five-plus years ago. He did remember the four poles with the holes and the yellow lifting straps that had hooks attached to the holes.

"That's great news, Joshua. Now what?"

"Now what is that I am going to research how they salvage boats and containers up off the ocean floor using weather balloons or the equivalent, then go back for Round 2," Joshua finished triumphantly.

Nathaniel thought this plan over carefully, then agreed: "I think your idea will work, grandson. I really do. You just have to figure out how much lifting capacity you will need to pick up 10,000 pounds and buy enough balloons or whatever to pick up the big bitch."

"Absolutely right, Grampa. You have it right. And here's the best part. Are you ready for this?" Joshua posed, eyes gleaming.

"I don't know if I am or not, grandson. Hit me."

"Once I free up the big bitch, I am going to get her floating just above the ocean floor. If I can't find a company to lift the bomb up and onto a barge then I'm going to attach a rope to the poles and to the back of a boat and tow the motherfucker out of Tokyo Bay underwater myself and no one will be the wiser."

Nathaniel was impressed.

"That is outstanding, Joshua! Just outstanding! What a great idea. Float the prize out of there like a submarine sixty feet underwater."

Nathaniel thought for a second and continued, "How are you going to get it onto something, like onto a barge, once you get it out of Tokyo Bay?"

Joshua looked down for a second. "I haven't gotten that far, grandfather. I'm still working on that. I may just have to drag it as far out into the ocean as I can and then drop it, I guess."

Nathaniel considered the idea for a minute. "How much do you think it would cost to get a tugboat to pull the bomb out of the harbor?"

"Too much, Grampa. And it would be too obvious," Joshua believed. "If we can't mount a proper salvage operation, then our next best bet is to rent a big fishing boat, one with two 300-horsepower engines. Then I will tow the bomb out to deep water and let it go down to the bottom of the ocean. Somewhere where no one will ever find it and where it will hopefully never cause any problems, even if someday it does blow up somehow."

Nathaniel took in all of the news, each bit filling in another piece of the puzzle, a big smile lifting up the corners of his mouth as he breathed out a long exhale of satisfaction. He thought about how deep the ocean was off the coast of the main island of Japan and how far out to sea Joshua would have to tow the bomb to sink it in deep waters. He reflected on all of what he had been told. "You know, I never thought of what I would do with the bomb if I ever found it. I just never allowed myself to think that far ahead. Now that it has been found, I'm kind of at a loss as to what to do next. But in reality, what you have proposed is a pretty damned good idea. Float it up, tow it way out and drop it at sea all sounds real good to me. But maybe you can snoop around and find a salvage company that will do it on the QT."

Joshua nodded his head as his grandfather spoke.

"I have had a lot of time to think about how to do this without being detected while at the same time accomplishing the goal. My first effort when I get back to Tokyo is to see if I can find a salvage company. If that doesn't work out, my alternative plan seems to be the most logical and most likely to succeed," explained Joshua, trying to feel as confident as he sounded.

Nathaniel smiled. "How much do you think it will cost to buy the lifting straps, the underwater balloons or whatever they are called and whatever else you are going to need?"

"Not that much, actually. My preliminary research shows the total cost to be about $10,000 max," Joshua reported. "The problem is that with today's technology, if the government has somehow intercepted our telephone calls, they will have already accessed every aspect of our lives. It wouldn't surprise me at all if they are looking at us as we speak, that they know I have been to Japan and they know what I bought, where I stayed and know about the boat I rented. Knowing how sneaky those bastards are we have to be extremely careful with what we say from now on."

"You're absolutely right, grandson," sighed Nathaniel, nodding in agreement. "If they check on you, they will check on me, too, and somewhere buried there might be an obscure reference to the last bombing mission of World War II. That would not be good."

"When you say that would not be good, is there something else to the story that I don't know?"

"I'm not sure, Joshua, but I did hear that after the war, during the U.S. occupation of Japan, after we didn't find it that the Navy mounted a salvage operation to find and remove the mines in the harbor and that they may have looked for the bomb, too."

"That makes sense, Grampa, but obviously, they didn't find the motherfucker, did they?" Joshua remarked laughing.

"No, they sure didn't," rejoined Nathaniel, laughing, too. "But their failure to find the bomb might have had something to do with the fact that the coordinates they were given were more than a little off the mark," reported Nathaniel gleefully, showing all of his teeth in a smile, almost giggling thinking about G.I.s digging up half of Tokyo.

The two men chuckled, their faces lighting up as they exchanged a look of shared amusement. They had a good laugh because of the trick Nathaniel had pulled on the government; one that even today would get him killed. Then as Joshua thought about the situation some more, he asked, "Why didn't you tell them the right coordinates at the time, Grampa?"

"You don't know, Joshua? I didn't tell you? Well, shit. The reason was that I was afraid the Army assholes who concocted the plan would kill me once they found the bomb. That turned out to be true. Just after I was shipped home, I was walking down a sidewalk in Chicago. This car came along, and I heard it accelerating real fast. I turned around to see who it was and why they were gunning the motor and I'll be goddamned if the car wasn't coming right up over the curb to hit me."

"Wow, Grampa! You never told me about that."

"No, I never did, but it scared the shit out of me and made me wonder what was going on. So anyway, I jumped toward a set of tables that were set up outside the restaurant where I was standing and the car went over a parking meter, hit one of the tables, then veered back onto the road, missing me."

Nathaniel took a minute to catch his breath as he recalled

the event.

"One of the chairs the car hit came flying at me and cut me right here." Nathaniel stated, showing Joshua a three-inch-long scar on his neck.

Nathaniel continued. "What was strange was the way many of the crewmembers on the flight died in unusual ways over the next two years. All of them died except the asshole major who I may have told you went on to work at the CIA, the Jewish co-pilot and me."

Joshua thought about this revelation for a minute.

"Do you have any idea why you weren't killed after the first failed attempt? Why they didn't come after you again?"

"Not really sure, but I think maybe it was because I didn't ever mention the mission to anyone ever, even after the odd events that killed my buddies." Nathaniel stroked his chin remembering his buddies as he spoke. "Probably what really saved me was they may have thought I would eventually tell where the bomb hit and also because I stayed in the military. Around the same time, they gave me a wad of medals and made me a full bird colonel. So, I might have been too prominent a war hero to kill. But really, I don't know why I wasn't killed."

"Speaking for myself, Grampa, I am happy they never succeeded," Joshua announced, feeling proud of the old guy as he looked at his grandfather and smiled. "And I am proud that amongst the wad of medals they gave you was the last one, the Medal of Honor for what you did when you escaped from the Nazi prison."

"I guess so, grandson. I guess so," humbly spoke Nathaniel, shrugging off the compliment.

"I just hope I haven't reignited the government's desire to kill me and now to want to kill you, too," Nathaniel declared as he hung his head low. "My guess is that those fuckers that were here the other day will be back sooner than later and that will probably be the end of me."

"I sure as fuck hope not, Grampa," Joshua hoped. "It's too late to stop our mission quest. We owe it to your dead crewmembers, to the Japanese people who live near Tokyo Bay and to you and me to finish the job. And once we succeed, they won't have a reason to off you anymore."

"You're right, Joshua. You're absolutely right," agreed Nathaniel resolutely, lifting his chin back up. "We have a mission, a quest as you put it and we have to do our best to complete it. And as for me, if I go to my grave tomorrow, I will be happy knowing that you believed me and found the bomb. Oh, when are you going back to Tokyo?"

"I am leaving again early tomorrow morning, Grampa."

By this time, they had made their way back to the nursing home.

"OK, Grampa. Keep your eyes and ears open for anything unusual. You never know who might be watching or listening. Oh and here is a new phone to use when we talk. I wrote my new number on the back of it."

"Very clever grandson and agreed. I will keep a sharp eye . . . and you do, too."

"I will. Love you, Grampa. Oh, by the way, let's refer to the bomb from now on as the 'treasure.' That way we may throw them off if they are listening if they think we are treasure hunting," reasoned Joshua.

Nathaniel hesitated. He hadn't expressed any feelings of love nor felt any really since his wife had died in 1990, but what was said next came from his heart:

"I love you, too, grandson. Good luck treasure hunting!" With that, the two men hugged; both having thoughts in the backs of their minds that they might never see each other again.

As Joshua cruised away from the nursing home, he called Betsy knowing that she would likely still be at work while also knowing that she would want to hear from him. Frankly, Joshua said to himself, *I want to talk to Betsy and see her, too, before I return to the land of the rising sun.*

"Hello, stranger. Are you enjoying Tokyo and the little Asian women?" Betsy tossed that gig in, not having forgotten the phone call he made to a female in Hong Kong.

"Why, no, Betsy, I am not," stammered Joshua, somewhat taken aback by her comment. Women were the furthest thing from his mind.

"Oh, okay. What's up? I am still at work."

"Oh, nothing really. I am back from Japan for a day and wanted to see you tonight."

"You're back from Japan!" Betsy exclaimed. "You bet I do. Shall we meet at the blues bar and start from where we left off?"

"Absolutely. I will see you there around say nine-ish?"

"Better yet, why don't you meet me at my apartment at about seven and we can get reacquainted before we go out," Betsy offered coyly, having rethought what she wanted.

"I am definitely up for that, Bets. See you at seven with bells on."

"Okay, see ya."

"See ya then."

After hanging up, Joshua recalled learning the phrase *with bells on* from his English grandmother, who often used quirky expressions. She was a British beauty queen from a titled English family. Beatrice Mary Dewhurst, "Bette," married his grandfather on his father's side after World War II and was promptly disowned for it. She had grown up with maids, butlers, and a chauffeur and did not know how to cook or wash clothes. A funny story Grandfather Meister would sometimes tell was that Bette ironed his socks when they were first married. The two sweethearts were married six weeks after they met and were together for fifty years before he died.

Thinking about Grandma Bette made him wonder if she'd be proud of him now. He decided she would, as he was doing what he believed was right under the circumstances. Feeling content with his choices, he drove off to grab some fast food, knowing he'd need the energy for the hours ahead. *Alrighty then!*

CHAPTER 31

Alex Lozano arrived in St. Louis and sat in the parking lot of the nursing home, reviewing his notes. He had assigned himself the mission and was visibly sweating because he wasn't supposed to work domestically. Breathing in deeply and then holding his breath was Alex's method of calming his nerves but it wasn't working. He was way out of bounds and he knew it because CIA agents are not supposed to engage in activities in the U.S. The gray area was the mission came about because of recorded overseas conversations. In Alex's mind that beginning point was sort of a justification.

When Joshua and his grandfather pulled up, Alex nearly jumped out of his skin as he immediately recognized them from the photos he had downloaded. He slumped down in the driver's seat to avoid being seen.

After Nathaniel exited the car, Joshua sped off, and Alex waited a couple of minutes before heading inside. He had an appointment with the head administrator, Daphne Flores, and he arrived right on time. At the front desk, he showed the fake documents he had created, and the nurse directed him to a seat.

As Alex sat down, he noticed a nurse's aide, Michael Brown, pass by pushing a pill cart, and when Alex looked at him he quickly looked away. Alex thought that was odd, which in turn gave rise to Alex having a suspicion about him. Alex made a mental note to learn more about the aide.

"Hello, Mr. Lozano. My name is Daphne Flores. I am the head administrator here," she announced as she entered the lobby, extending her hand. Alex shook her hand and introduced himself as well.

Once in her office, Alex told her that he was there to perform an audit because there had been problems reported regarding the supply chain.

"That is quite odd, Mr. Lozano. In the past year we have not reported any shortages or losses in our inventory that I know of," Nurse Flores reported as she wrinkled her forehead.

"You are right about that, Miss Flores," was Alex's prepared response. "This is more of a control study with your facility being singled out as one that has 100 percent compliance with the applicable standards," continued Alex, making up the lie on the fly.

That comment made Nurse Flores perk up. "That is nice to hear, Mr. Lozano. What can we do to help in the audit?"

"The first thing I will need is a desk, a computer and a chair, with the computer log-in so I can check the facility's orders against the received inventory," requested Alex. "Along with that, I will need a list of all of the employees and access to their personnel files."

"Sure thing, Mr. Lozano. You may sit at the desk in the empty office next door," Nurse Flores offered, gesturing to her right. "I will get a temporary computer password for you and the personnel files are in the cabinet just outside my door to the right."

"Thank you very much, Miss Flores. You have been very helpful. I will be back in the morning to begin my work," stated Alex as he rose from his chair to leave.

"OK, very good, sir. See you in the morning."

As Alex walked back to the reception area, he took in the surroundings but found nothing noteworthy—except for the absence of the orderly he had seen earlier. His mind was focused on two questions: what were Colonel Nathaniel and his grandson planning, and where was the orderly?

Alex was working outside the normal parameters that apply to CIA agents. While he was within the boundaries when listening to telephone conversations from overseas, he was prohibited from working in the United States and he knew it. By all rights, Alex should have contacted the local FBI office to tell them he was coming but he did not.

Alex believed that if he cracked the Meister case he would receive the promotion he had long been awaiting. He believed he had been passed over many times because he was Mexican and because he spoke English with a slight accent and maybe because he was only five feet seven inches tall. English was his second language. Alex was the fifth of six children born to Jose and Esmeralda Lozano and was the first and only one to graduate from college.

His parents had emigrated from Guadalajara and worked hard to build a life for themselves in Texas. They instilled the virtue of hard work in all of their children and were proud when Alex landed his job at the CIA. His brothers would tease him about being James Bond but he was the prodigal son. Soon after he joined the CIA Alex was able to fast-track his parents' application to become American citizens and he earned many brownie points for that effort.

His only downfall was that he had not married and produced any grandchildren.

"Oh, Alex, ¿qué pasa con tú? ¿No le gusta las mujeres?" Mrs. Lozano would ask.

"Yes, Mom, I like women but I don't have time to get serious. My job takes all of my time and energy."

"No, mijo. Su vida es más importante de su trabajo."

"I know, Mom, but . . . well . . . some day, Mom, some day."

The next morning, Alex arrived early to observe the staff, including Michael Brown and his wife, Julie, who both came in for the morning shift. Once inside, Alex carefully studied Michael and pulled his personnel file. Michael Brown, married with a son, on the surface seemed unremarkable, but Alex couldn't shake the feeling that something was off. After running his profile through the CIA's systems, Alex wondered if his suspicions were driven by unconscious racial bias, but he justified it as part of his job to remain vigilant against potential threats.

Alex next reviewed Colonel Nathaniel Meister's file, finding nothing alarming. At ninety-nine years old, Nathaniel was a decorated WWII hero, rewarded for escaping his Nazi captors after being shot down during his twenty-seventh mission. What stood out to Alex was Nathaniel's redeployment to the Japanese front after Germany's surrender, which was unusual. Most soldiers who fought in Europe were sent home, but not Nathaniel, who was regarded as the best precision bombardier in the Army Air Force, earning every medal, including the Medal of Honor.

Despite Nathaniel's impeccable record, Alex remained puzzled by his later deployment to the Mariana Islands and the additional B-29 missions over Japan. After thoroughly reviewing his service record, Alex found nothing of concern.

Turning again to Michael Brown, the nurse's aide, Alex was surprised to find no record of him existing prior to 2019, raising his suspicions about the man.

Alex suspected Michael Brown was of Pakistani or Indian descent. When he uploaded Brown's photo into the CIA system, it confirmed he was a first-generation Pakistani from a mountainous region near Afghanistan, a known hotspot for terrorist activity. Several drone strikes had recently targeted villages in the area.

This discovery sent chills down Alex's spine. What kind of conspiracy was he uncovering? The Colonel, a former CIA agent, and a Pakistani man using a fake name—were they all involved in a plot to bomb Tokyo or even the U.S.? The combination of individuals seemed too strange to ignore.

Alex decided to interview Michael Brown—the so-called Michael Brown—first.

"Nurse Flores, would it be possible for me to speak with some of the staff today?"

"Why, certainly, Mr. Lozano. Do you want me to bring them in here?"

"No, I think it would be better if I just wandered around to get a feel for the way the home operates and ask questions of whomever I run across."

"Sure. OK. That would be fine. You may speak with whomever you like."

With permission granted, Alex set out to find Michael Brown, starting with the pharmacy, where the pill cart would likely be.

Meanwhile, Muqtar had barely slept, the strange man's suspicious look the day before replaying in his mind. He spent the evening savoring moments with his wife and son, knowing they might be his last moments with them for a long time, perhaps forever. He took selfies with his family, kissed his son goodbye, and left $25,000 for them before heading to work at the nursing home. There, he followed his usual routine, checking the doctors' orders and preparing the pills, all while feeling the weight of what he might soon have to do; that is to bolt.

About three-quarters of the way through his morning rounds, Muqtar heard an unfamiliar voice behind him.

"Good morning. Are you Michael Brown?"

Muqtar whirled around knowing it would be the man he saw in the lobby yesterday. Sure enough, it was him. Muqtar checked to see if the man had a gun or handcuffs and saw neither, so that was a small bit of relief.

"Yes, I am Michael Brown," Muqtar replied as he extended his hand, moist with fear.

"What can I do for you?" trying to sound nonchalant as his heart jumped up, pounding like a trip hammer.

"Oh, nothing really," was Alex's casual reply while shaking Muqtar's hand. "I just want to ask you a few questions. Is that OK? By the way, I am Alex Lozano. Nice to meet you."

"Nice to meet you, too. Sure, ask away," was Muqtar's attempt at a bold answer.

"How long have you been working here?"

"About a year and a half now."

"Where did you get your nurse's training?"

"I am in nursing school now. My wife is the head nurse at this facility."

"Oh. What is her name?"

"Her name is Julie Brown."

"Do you and your wife have any children?"

"Yes, we do. We have a one-and-a-half-year-old son, Michael Brown, Jr. Do you mind if I ask you a question, sir?"

"No, not at all," Alex replied.

"What are you doing here?"

"I am doing an audit on the supply chain, looking for ways to make the veterans' world better," Alex lied, looking directly into Muqtar's eyes.

Muqtar knew damned good and well that Mr. Lozano was lying, and he also knew damned good and well that Mr. Lozano knew he was lying, too. *Now what,* Muqtar thought.

"Where are you from originally, Mr. Brown?" queried Alex.

"I'm from Pennsylvania. I moved from there to New York after high school and have lived out here for a couple of years, as I said a minute ago. Why do you ask," was Muqtar's retort, now getting annoyed and scared at the persistent questioning.

"Just curious. I try to put faces with places. It is a hobby of mine and your face does not look like someone who was born in Pennsylvania."

Muqtar said nothing, but inside he was beginning to boil; the fear now gone. *Who the fuck was this insipid prick anyway? If he has a warrant, fucking arrest me or get the fuck out of my face,* Muqtar thought.

"OK. And your point is, sir?" demanded Muqtar in a most pointed way.

"Oh, nothing, nothing really. It's just that your features give you the appearance of someone from the northern region of Pakistan near the border with Afghanistan."

Muqtar said nothing as hearing this comment turned his anger to fear. He froze. Mr. Lozano had nailed him perfectly. *Wow. What next?*

"Were your birth parents from that part of Pakistan, Mr. Brown?"

"I don't know. I was adopted as an infant and grew up in Pennsylvania."

Alex knew he had pushed his conversation with Muqtar about as far as the conversation could go.

"Thank you very much for your time, Mr. Brown. It was a pleasure talking to you."

Muqtar, who had been drinking a Coke when Alex approached him, took a final swig, threw the bottle in the trash and turned to walk away.

"The pleasure was all mine, sir. Let me know if there is anything else I can do to help with the audit, Mr. Lozano," was Muqtar's sarcastic parting comment.

"Oh, shoot. There is one more question that I have for you, Mr. Brown. What is your relationship with Colonel Nathaniel Meister?"

Muqtar thought very carefully about what he was going to say before answering. "Colonel Meister asked me to show him how to look stuff up on the computer. So, I did. Is there anything wrong with that, sir?" Muqtar shot back in a pissed-off tone.

"No, no. Nothing wrong with that. And again, thank you for your time."

Muqtar stayed silent. After he left, Alex carefully retrieved the Coke bottle, ensuring not to smudge Michael Brown's fingerprints. He placed it in a manila envelope and intended to call the local FBI to have them check it for prints.

Muqtar's head was pounding and he felt sick to his stomach. He clung tightly to the pill cart handle with both hands. Muqtar was afraid if he let go he would fall to the ground; his legs had turned to mush. His entire being was consumed by a cold fear, torn between fleeing or staying. As he continued his rounds, his love for his family clashed with his fear of being caught. The decision was made for him when he saw Alex in the parking lot, handing a manila envelope to two men in suits in an all-black Chevrolet Tahoe.

Shit! That is the Coke bottle I threw away. The bottle has my fingerprints all over it, realized Muqtar. *I am so fucked now,* he lamented. *I have to go now before they run my fingerprints and trace them back to Muqtar Ashadi, criminal fugitive, illegal alien and murderer, to boot. Wait a minute; my original fingerprints were never taken but if the feds dig far enough, they might connect me to an unsolved murder in New York.*

The fear-induced brain fog dissipated and what he had to do became crystal clear. Muqtar had to leave the country now before whoever this Alex prick was put two and two together. He was glad he had left money for his wife. Muqtar's mission was now to escape before anyone noticed he was gone.

Alex, feeling confident, knew the FBI would soon identify the fingerprints on the Coke bottle, and he was convinced that Michael Brown was a Pakistani with ties to a region known for its militant activity. He had been very sly with the FBI when he turned over the Coke bottle, bullshitting them that the person's fingerprints belonged to an international terrorist who had undergone plastic surgery to avoid being recognized and captured.

Alex was walking a fine line counting on the FBI to not launch their own investigation into what a CIA agent was doing operating in the U.S. He felt that checking the fingerprints was worth the risk. Alex was ready to investigate the next person on his list—Colonel Meister—sure that the elderly man would be easily manipulated into revealing something.

Alex knocked on Nathaniel's door.

"Yes? Who is it?" inquired the voice behind the door.

"It's me, Alex Lozano."

"I don't know any Alex Lozano."

"No, you don't know me yet, sir. But I am with the United States government and I have a matter of extreme importance to discuss with you," was Alex's ploy to get Nathaniel to open the door.

"Mister, I don't know you and I don't care who you are with. I am ninety-nine years old and I have no desire to be involved with anyone or anything that has to do with the U.S. government other than for the VA to send me my retirement money every month and that is it," was Nathaniel's retort.

"No reason to be like that, Colonel. This will only take a few minutes."

"Go away," commanded Nathaniel.

"I will not go away," insisted Alex. "You may be in possession of information vital to the national security of these United States and I'm not leaving until we talk face-to-face."

With that, Alex heard the door unlock, and when the door opened, there the two men stood face-to-face.

"Say what you have to say and then leave," demanded Nathaniel.

"It isn't what I have to say, Colonel. It is what you have to say that is of critical importance to our national security," explained Alex.

Nathaniel stood in the doorway waiting, looking down at Alex but not speaking a word.

Alex began again. "Colonel, it has come to my attention that you have a nephew named Joshua Meister who formerly worked for the U.S. government."

Nathaniel stood there, still silent.

So, Alex turned his comment into a question.

"Do you have a nephew named Joshua Meister who formerly worked for the U.S. government?"

"No," was Nathaniel's one-word response.

The answer surprised Alex. "Have you seen him lately?"

"Seen who?"

"Your nephew, Joshua Meister."

"I don't have a nephew named Joshua Meister."

Alex looked at his notes, then spoke again. "I apologize. Do you have a grandson named Joshua Meister?"

"Yes."

Fucking smart ass, Alex thought. "Has Joshua Meister recently traveled overseas?"

"Why don't you ask him?"

"Because I am asking you, Colonel." Agent Lozano then slowly and emphatically asked the question again. "Has your grandson Joshua Meister recently traveled overseas to Japan?"

"Yes."

"Was he in Tokyo last week?"

"Yes."

"What was he doing there?"

Silence.

"Was he there to plant a bomb?"

"No."

"Was he there to blow up something?"

"No."

"Maybe I should go there and find out for myself."

"Maybe you should."

Both men could see that Alex's line of questioning was not going anywhere, so Alex decided to try a different tact.

"Look, Colonel. I realize that this conversation may be unpleasant for you, but I have to know what your grandson is up to in order to protect America and preserve world peace." Alex had abandoned his authoritative tone and had moved on to appealing to the Colonel's sense of patriotism.

Nathaniel, who did not like the questions and did not like the short man, decided to change his tact, too. The Colonel cleared his throat.

"Mr. Lozano, my grandson is a fine young man and a shining example of what is right in this country. He is bright, articulate and motivated to achieve. Joshua did go to Japan, but as a tourist only, not as some kind of terrorist planning on blowing up Japan with a bomb," Nathaniel made clear.

"I'm sure what brings you here, sir, to ask me these fucked-up questions," Nathaniel continued, "is some telephone conversation intercept that made its way to your desk. Am I right?"

Alex was surprised to hear that. "You are right, Colonel. How did you know that?"

"Don't forget, son, that I worked for the United States government for more than fifty years. There is a hell of a lot that I watched develop over the years as far as eavesdropping is concerned. I think everybody knows that the computers listen to and analyze every telephone conversation there is. My bet is when Joshua and I were talking about the two bombs that we dropped on Japan to end World War II that somehow those parts of our conversation triggered some kind of download that made its way to you. Am I right again, Mr. Lozano?"

Alex was very impressed with the old man's acumen and admitted again.

"You are right, Colonel, certain keywords stimulate the computer to record overseas conversations. And yes, your using the word 'bomb' repeatedly did catch the attention of the computer algorithm. But frankly, Colonel, the recorded portions of your conversations did not involve references to the World War II bombings of Hiroshima and Nagasaki."

"So says you, Mr. Lozano. So says you. The last I knew, the U.S. government was not allowed to record conversations of U.S. citizens calling to or from the United States, isn't that right, sir?"

"No, that is not correct, Colonel; not since Congress passed President Bush's Patriot Act. The government can record whoever it wants wherever it wants as long as there is a connection with what is said and America's national security interests."

"That is real nice," Nathaniel spat out. "Anyway, after the Japanese surrendered, I spent three months explaining to the brass what happened on that last mission over Tokyo, and I will be goddamned if I am going to explain shit to anybody ever again," Nathaniel proclaimed. "And people wonder why this country is going down the tubes," he added derisively.

"And people are going to wonder why you are hiding something important to our country's security, too, aren't they, Colonel? Do I need to go to Japan myself to find out?" threatened Alex.

As he began to shut the door, Nathaniel offered up his final comment.

"It is a sad day in hell when some pipsqueak like you has the audacity to question the patriotism of someone like me."

Alex put his hand on the door to stop it from closing.

"Is that right, Colonel? Is that right? Well then, why don't you explain to me your relationship with the Pakistani nurse's aide who spends so much time with you?" Alex knew by the Colonel's reaction that he had hit a good point.

Nathaniel had not expected that comment as he pulled his chin in and absorbed Alex's words. "What the fuck are you saying now? What Pakistani nurse?"

"Nurse's aide, Colonel. The male nurse's aide who dispenses the meds who calls himself Michael Brown. The word is that you and he are close and that he has helped you use the computer. Why is that, Colonel? What is that about?" challenged a fired-up Alex.

"I don't have a clue what you are talking about, Mr. Lozano, and this conversation is over."

"It's over when I say it's over."

"Oh yeah. Then get over this," Nathaniel shouted as he stepped forward, pushed Alex in the chest, knocking him across the hallway and into the wall.

Nathaniel slammed the door shut and locked it. Alex gathered himself, looked around to be sure no one was looking and quickly walked away, muttering to himself, "I'll show him."

Nathaniel reflected on the conversation and began to have the feeling that the walls were closing in on him. First the FBI drugs me then this asshole shows up from some unknown agency. Joshua had better find the bomb fast or some government spook will find out about it and fuck up their plan.

Alex realized that somehow Michael Brown might have overheard their entire conversation and also realized that the Colonel knew much more than he had revealed. Alex was particularly puzzled by the Colonel's mention of having to explain his last mission to Tokyo to the upper brass. He made a note to thoroughly review Nathaniel's service records. Meanwhile, Alex decided to track down Joshua, suspecting that Nathaniel's confrontation would prompt him to call his grandson, which he did immediately after shutting the door.

"Joshua, some asshole from a government agency just showed up at my room and accused you, me and some Pakistani nurse's aide of conspiring together to blow up something in Tokyo."

This comment threw Joshua for a loop. He had not expected such a direct contact so soon.

"What is this asshole's name, Grampa?"

"I don't really remember. I was so pissed off at the fucking guy for coming to my room without even asking to make an appointment with me that I didn't quite catch his name. . . . Lozano or something."

"Anything else, Grampa?"

"Yeah, he said we were in cahoots with the nurse's helper Michael Brown to blow up some shit."

"Man, we both know this guy, Michael Brown. He is the nurse's aide who I crashed into the first day I came to St. Louis."

"Yes, he is. He works here as a nurse's aide and he is the one who helped me download a Google map of Tokyo Bay that had latitudes and longitudes on it."

"Shit. I remember that. I literally ran into him twice the first day I arrived here. What does Brown know about us?" questioned Joshua.

"Nothing," affirmed Nathaniel. "Well, I should say he could only know a little bit of the details if he stood outside my door and heard me talking to you."

Joshua considered the scenario for a moment.

"Any chance the aide saw on the map where the lines crossed?"

"Not likely, but he may have an approximate idea of where the lines cross because he was in my room when I first looked at the map."

"Oh, shit again, Grampa. I was afraid we might have tipped off the computer trackers with our last conversation from Tokyo, but I didn't think they would have jumped on us this fast. And now who knows what the nurse's aide or Lozano have in mind."

"And it was my dumb ass using the word *bomb* that tipped them off," bemoaned Nathaniel, looking down at his feet.

"Yeah, maybe, Grampa. They're paying attention to us just as easily could have been me being on their radar and under surveillance since I left the CIA on bad terms," commented Joshua, trying to make his grandfather feel better.

"But anyway, Grampa, we have to figure out what to do next," Joshua said as he considered their options. "I think we find the nurse's aide and ask him some questions of our own. What do you think?"

"Sure, that sounds good. Let's find that fucker and shake his tree," replied Nathaniel, brightening up.

Both men agreed to meet at the pharmacy in twenty minutes, the time it would take Joshua to drive back to the nursing home.

Once back at the nursing home, Joshua scoped out the parking lot to see if there were any unfamiliar vehicles there. Of course, looking around was a useless exercise, because Joshua had no idea what cars were normally there, but looking around made him feel better that he was following CIA protocol.

Not noticing anything that looked out of place, Joshua stepped out of his car and walked briskly through the parking lot, up the stairs and into the building. Joshua didn't stop at the front desk; rather he marched straight toward his grandfather's room.

Joshua rounded a corner and for the third time ran right into Muqtar or rather stopped just before they collided. Nurse's aide Brown appeared to be in a hurry himself.

"Oh, sorry," Joshua apologized, excusing himself. "Hey I'd like to talk to you." He shouted. The nurse's aide shot him a dirty look but said nothing. Rather, he put his head down and headed off toward the front door. Joshua felt the negative vibe and thought about following Brown but felt that seeing his grandfather first was more important.

Once having arrived at the room, Joshua gathered himself together and knocked on the door.

"Who is it?" inquired Nathaniel in a gruff-sounding voice.

"It's me, Grampa. Joshua."

The door swung open and Joshua observed that his grandfather's face was still beet red from his earlier confrontation with Agent Lozano.

"Are you all right, Grampa?"

"Yeah, I'm fine. That little dipshit from the government didn't bother me a bit. He had to be from the CIA because he knew about our overseas telephone conversations."

"OK, you're probably right and your face is beet red."

Nathaniel looked in the mirror. "So it is. I guess maybe that cocksucker did get me riled up a little bit, talking national security and all that patriotic bullshit."

"Did he say anything that might have been a clue as to why he is here?"

"No, not really," recalled Nathaniel, reflecting. "But I sure let something slip out," he confessed.

"What did you say, Grampa?"

"I told the motherfucker to fuck off because I was interrogated for three months after the war ended about my last flight mission and I wasn't going to talk about it anymore."

"Oh, shit, Grampa. That could be bad for us if he connects the dots," lamented Joshua. "Do you know, Grampa, whether or not the post-war investigation was classified?"

"No, I don't know one way or the other, grandson. My impression was that the Army destroyed all of the records pertaining to the third bomb, but they might have kept some somewhere."

"I would bet the CIA guy follows up on the lead, Grampa,

so we have to move fast. Did he or you say anything else that is important?"

Nathaniel pressed his fingers to his temples, his brow furrowing in frustration. His mind swirled, but no matter how hard he tried to focus, the particulars of the conversation had slipped away, clouded by the anger that still simmered in him.

"No, nothing comes to mind, except he said he wanted to talk to you, too, and that he had already spoken to the Mexican nurse's aide who he thinks is in it with us."

"Grampa, the nurse's aide is not a Mexican. He is either Indian or Pakistani," corrected Joshua.

"What the fuck ever. Mexican, hooligan, I don't give a fuck," was Nathaniel's retort, more pissed now than ever.

"Sorry, Grampa. I don't mean to get you worked up. Just that now we have to move quickly while time is still a little bit on our side. Let's sit down and talk about what I have in mind, OK?"

"OK. Let's get our plan together. Oh shit, I forgot that the little weasel said he might go to Japan himself."

"Oh shit."

For the next fifteen minutes, Joshua outlined his next steps and considered how to handle a potential confrontation with Lozano, though he didn't even know what the agent looked like. He was returning to Japan that night to source supplies—ropes, balloons, hooks, a shovel—and hoped for a stroke of luck. He knew that towing the bomb to sea would create bubbles, and he hadn't decided whether to attempt it during the day or at night, weighing the pros and cons of each. Nathaniel nodded in approval.

"I like your plan, Joshua. First of all, it may actually work. Second of all, you may be able to do it without attracting undue attention. But if something fucks up," warned Nathaniel, "just get out of there as best you can and we will abandon the project."

"Agreed, Grampa, and duly noted. I was thinking about leaving tomorrow but I have been checking the flights and if I leave now, I can make it to L.A. in time to catch the overnight flight to Tokyo."

Nathaniel nodded his head again in agreement.

"Well, then, you better get going before that little pipsqueak Lozano or Lozaro or whoever gets ahold of you and grills you, too."

"I thought of that, Grampa. From the sounds of what he tried, I agree with you that Lozano is a CIA agent. What is strange about that is the CIA is not supposed to work in the USA, only out of the country. The FBI is supposed to handle all of the domestic problems. However, having worked for them, I know they regularly go outside the legal boundaries if it suits them. Anyway, I'm going to go down the back stairwell and out the back of the building, then circle around to the parking lot to avoid a confrontation. Do you think there is any point in the two of us tracking down the nurse's aide now?"

Nathaniel pondered for a moment. "No. Not really. And if we did, we might run into the CIA squid who no doubt would want to try to grill you, too."

"Agreed, grandfather. I know how they work. Okay, I am going to leave out the back way. I will call you in two days at the regular time with news about the progress of the mission. Don't let anyone know you have this phone, okay?"

"Okay. Sounds good. Use this phone. Two days; regular time. Good luck, grandson."

"Thanks, Grampa. See ya."

"See ya when you return."

Joshua sneaked out the back to avoid the CIA agent, praying for safe travels as he drove to the airport, his mind racing with worry and anticipation. He remembered he had to tell Betsy his plans had changed—no time to meet at the bar.

Alex searched the nursing home but couldn't find Joshua or the aide. After checking the front desk and parking lot, the thought dawned on him as the red drained from his cheeks that Joshua had sneaked out and was likely on his way to the airport with the aide. Alex balled up his hands into fists and pounded the wall. "Sorry motherfuckers. You haven't fooled me. You'll see," he vowed.

Alex had learned nothing from his interview with the Colonel, except for a comment about a three-month investigation into his last bombing mission. Alex decided to go back to the nursing home the next morning just in case Brown or Meister showed up and afterwards to return to Washington to figure out the significance of the Colonel's final mission.

On his way to the hotel, Alex alerted the local FBI to track Michael Brown's movements and the results of his fingerprint check. He also ordered them to monitor Joshua Meister, whom he suspected was connected to Brown. Joshua, meanwhile, bought a round-trip ticket to Tokyo but had to settle for a flight the next morning to San Francisco due to no available seats. He was relieved the evening's rendezvous with Betsy was still on, avoiding any complications with her.

CHAPTER 32

Muqtar, anxious about his passports being flagged and fearing detection, left the nursing home and drove to the Costco next door. In the parking lot, he called Imam Rushi, hoping the man who had previously helped him with information about a drone strike might assist him again. Though he tried not to feel guilty about leaving his family behind, Muqtar's heart ached as he realized he was abandoning his son. The phone rang twice and then a male voice answered.

"Hello, this is Mohammed."

"Hello, Imam Mohammed. This is Muqtar. We spoke recently about a drone strike in my village."

There was a moment's hesitation then: "Yes. I remember you. I came to St. Louis to visit a mosque and if I recall correctly, you did not tell me your name was Muqtar. You said your name was Michael or something like that. Do I remember that correctly?"

Muqtar's head dropped, his chest tightening as a wave of heat rushed to his face. He felt deep shame for most everything he'd done since flunking out of NYU. The only exception was his love for his wife and son, who he was now leaving behind. He tried to justify his decision, telling himself they wouldn't survive the harsh life in northern Pakistan.

Muqtar couldn't stay in the U.S. any longer because his fake identity was about to be exposed; the guilt of leaving and the fear of being caught consumed him.

Finally, Muqtar spoke. "Yes, Imam. That is right. As I told you the other day, I have been living in the U.S. for several years now under a false identity."

Muqtar took a breath and continued. "But I have recently been found out, so I need to leave the country and go back home."

"Oh, OK," understood the Imam. "I presume the reason you are calling me is to get my help in doing so. Is that right? You are the same man who called me a few days ago requesting information about the missile strikes in a village in northern Pakistan, aren't you?"

"Yes, Imam. That is correct on both counts. I do need your help to get home and I desperately want to know what happened to my people at home. I have my passport from Pakistan, that is still valid but the student visa part is expired and I have my U.S. passport under my American name that is valid too. What do you think I should do?"

"I think you should drive to Los Angeles where we can discuss the matter in person."

Muqtar thought about this for a second. I guess I really do have to go, he realized.

"That sounds good. I will leave now and the trip will take me about twenty-four hours to get there, so I will call you about this time tomorrow."

"OK. Sounds good," was Imam Rushi's reply. "I will text you my address in L.A. Call or text me when you get close and have a safe trip."

"All right, thank you. Thank you very much, Imam, for your help."

After Muqtar hung up, he felt a small sense of liberation; liberation because soon he would no longer be living a lie. Michael Brown would once again be Muqtar Ashadi.

Muqtar wrote a note to Julie and decided to mail it to her when he had a chance. He then filled up his car on the outskirts of St. Louis, reflecting on the city he'd likely never see again. He was leaving to escape the unresolved murder in New York, where he was the prime suspect. Facing a lifetime in a hostile prison, he resolved it was better to run. His plan was to find the hydrogen bomb the Colonel dropped in Tokyo Bay at the end of WWII. Possessing it, Muqtar thought, could give him leverage to gain concessions for his homeland or even reunite him with his family. With his head now clear, he felt lighter as he drove through the night.

Joshua knocked on the door at Betsy's apartment. A couple of minutes later she opened the door wearing only a towel.

"Well, that looks inviting," Joshua gushed.

"I should hope so, big guy," was the enticing response. This comment made Joshua wonder whether she was referring to his physical size or to big J. No time to think about that distinction at that moment. Time for action.

"Well then, let's get this party started," was Joshua's comment as he shucked off his pants as fast as he could.

A couple of hours later, both were quite exhausted and content. "I'm just curious, Betsy. What made you decide to greet me in the wonderful way you did?"

"Well," Betsy answered. "I figured you would be going back to Japan pretty soon, so that we had to take full advantage of the time we had and what better way to spend our limited time together than the way we did. Don't you agree?" surmised Betsy. "And I figured no Asian woman was going to outdo me!"

"Okay, and there are no Japanese women waiting for me in Tokyo. I sure do think we spent the time the best way possible, Bets. Excellent plan, and I might add, even better execution!"

The two shared a pizza and passed out shortly thereafter. Joshua had set the alarm on his phone for 0500, and when the buzzer went off he jumped up and began hustling around the apartment.

Betsy lifted her head up and uttered in a dreamy voice: "Be safe on your trip, find the bomb and when you come back there will be some more of this waiting for you." She then lifted the covers to show Joshua her stairway to heaven.

"Okay, and you can count on me to be safe and I will definitely be back to partake in some more of that." Joshua replied, licking his lips and pointing at Betsy's gateway to heaven. With that he kissed Betsy gently and quietly let himself out the door, then down to the car and on to the airport.

Joshua relaxed on his flight from St. Louis to San Francisco, confident his trip to Japan would go smoothly. He had sent Bets a text asking her to see if there was a photo of the government visitor. After checking his bag through to Tokyo, he ate at a BBQ restaurant, anticipating there would be little of it in Japan. While waiting at the gate, Joshua received a surveillance photo of Agent Lozano from Betsy. Boarding the flight to Tokyo, Joshua asked for a drink and rethought his plan. Once in Japan, he would buy salvage balloons and straps with cash, rent a powerful boat with a steel transom, and attempt to tow the first hydrogen bomb ever built out of Tokyo Bay—an enormous and risky mission ahead.

Joshua smiled to himself, impressed by the weight—both literal and figurative—of his plan. After a moment, he dozed off. Hours later, he checked his watch to find four hours remaining until landing in Tokyo. When the flight attendant offered him another drink, Joshua declined, knowing it was best if he was fully alert for what lay ahead.

Day 6 in Japan

Joshua was slightly concerned but he cleared customs without issue and headed to the Hilton hotel where he had stayed before. In his room, he searched online for salvage operations but found nothing promising. He shifted his search to past storms in the bay, hoping to find references to sunken boats, but still came up empty. Joshua grimaced and decided to head to the bay around 2:00 p.m. He avoided the marina where he'd rented the boat before, not wanting to raise suspicion, though he still needed to retrieve his dive gear from Mr. Hosaki.

Hell, Joshua thought, the spook Lozano may already have notified the local authorities to be on the lookout for him given that the U.S. government would surely have tracked every purchase he had made in the past month. And, certainly, if the agency did check out Joshua's activities they would have spoken to Mr. Hosaki, too.

Joshua stopped at a place that rented mopeds, hopped on one and found he actually liked tooling around on his yellow Honda. Although his Japanese was bad, his ability to read Japanese characters was even worse. The only way to figure out where a sea salvage operation would be located was for him to see boats or barges with cranes or pulleys or something.

Joshua's once optimistic mood was changing. He looked and looked but saw nothing. He stopped the scooter and took a deep breath, looking deep inside himself for the strength and inspiration to keep on looking. He was about to throw in the towel when he finally spotted a promising lead: a gray metal building with boat hulls and shipping containers sitting outside. The sign, in both Japanese and Chinese, read "Ho and Son Salvage." Surprised to see Chinese characters in Tokyo, Joshua wondered if Ho and Son Salvage could be connected to his former girlfriend, Mei Lei Ho, from Hong Kong. Although he found the coincidence amusing, he couldn't recall what her family's business was. Laughing at himself, he approached the warehouse, still smiling at the rhyme of "Ho in Tokyo," but wincing at the memory of his last awkward conversation with Mei Lei.

Joshua heard voices speaking inside the almost pitch-black interior. Much to his pleasant surprise, they were speaking Mandarin Chinese, a language Joshua spoke well. He walked into the building, his eyes rapidly adjusting to the darkness.

"Hello," he called out in English. Nothing. He took a couple more steps, avoiding the big spools of coiled cable in front of him.

"Hello," Joshua called out again in English. Now being able to see pretty well, Joshua saw two men turn their heads to him.

"Hello," answered one of the men in English as the two came toward him.

"No speak English," Joshua thought he heard one of the men say.

Now standing about ten feet away from them, Joshua decided to go for broke.

"Hi, my name is Joshua and I have a sunken boat that I want to salvage," Joshua said in Chinese except for the word "salvage."

He could not quite remember how to say that word.

The men moved to stand right in front of Joshua. They both bowed politely and Joshua bowed more deeply in return.

Joshua spoke again in Chinese.

"Can you help me find a boat that sunk in the harbor?"

The men looked at each other.

"Sure, that is what we do. We salvage boats and equipment."

Now looking intently up at Joshua, the first man wanted to know: "How is it that you speak Chinese in Japan and how did you find us?"

"I went to the University of Michigan and that is where I learned to speak Chinese. I graduated in 2021."

The two Chinese men looked at each other. The one who had spoken earlier spoke again.

"We had a niece who studied at the University of Michigan around that time. Do you think you might have met her?"

Before answering, Joshua thought for a minute. There were more than fifty thousand students at Michigan while he was there, of which a good percentage were Asian. So the likelihood that he would know her was rather slim. But, what the hell, Joshua thought. Might as well go along with the program.

"It is possible. What is her name?"

"Her name is Mei Lei Ho."

Joshua took an involuntary step backward. Whoa what? Who? You could have knocked Joshua over with a feather.

"Mei Lei Ho," Joshua repeated. "Mei Lei Ho." He had not heard that name since he left Michigan and went to work for the CIA but for one very brief and cold recent conversation and one rude reference uttered by an FBI asshole.

"I am most surprised, but that is the name of the girl I studied with. She was a grad student studying international relations at the Ross School of Business."

Now it was the Chinese men's turn to be surprised. The first man pulled out his phone and began searching for photos. After a minute or so, he showed the phone to Joshua.

"Is this her?"

Joshua physically took another step back and the blood drained from his face. The photo was her, sure as shit. All he could muster was "Yes."

All three men were quiet for a moment. Then Joshua spoke again.

"I remember Mei Lei as a very bright and beautiful woman, and although she never told me her family business, Mei Lei did say the family had something to do with shipping."

Joshua and the two men, Ping and Wei Ho, quickly warmed up to each other and began discussing the family's salvage business, which operated in Hong Kong, the Philippines, Vietnam, and Japan. They mostly retrieved containers lost at sea, and after the Fukushima disaster, they set up operations in Japan. The Ho brothers ran the operation due to their knowledge of Japanese, and although Joshua's Chinese was rusty, they complimented him on his language skills. After a lengthy conversation, Joshua realized it was time to state his purpose for being there.

"Gentlemen, it is a joyful reunion for me to be here with Mei Lei's family. I almost feel like I have found family such a long way from home. But my business purpose is to perform a salvage operation in Tokyo Bay."

The men's attention sharpened.

"What is it, Joshua, that you wish to salvage?"

"I told you earlier that I wanted to salvage a boat. But really, I want to salvage a 10,000-pound cylinder that is submerged in

DAVID KENT

Tokyo Bay and is partially stuck in the mud."

"A 10,000-pound cylinder stuck in the mud in the bay?"

"Yes, sir. The cylinder is six feet in diameter and ten feet long, but the good news is that the cylinder has poles with holes in them welded on each end. My plan is to attach balloons to the poles and thereby float the cylinder up off the bottom and pull it out of the bay like an underwater barge."

"Your plan is to float the cylinder off the bottom and pull it out of the bay by yourself?" Wei asked incredulously.

"Yes, sir. That was my simple plan. Inflate some balloons that I will attach to the poles, float the cylinder up off the bottom and tow it out of the bay."

"Have you ever salvaged anything before? What is your experience?"

Joshua looked down at his shoes. "I have no experience, only a plan and hope. Oh, and there's one more thing I need to share with you. The object that I want to salvage is left over from World War II."

The men's eyes opened wide.

"What on earth is left over from World War II that is worth salvaging? An underwater mine or a container full of war relics?"

"No, gentlemen, far more important than that." Joshua announced in a quiet, serious tone of voice.

"Well, what then?" the men simultaneously asked, their curiosities piqued.

Joshua decided to throw caution to the side and tell the truth. "It is a huge bomb that my grandfather dropped three days before World War II ended. It didn't go off and landed in Tokyo Bay, where it has laid for almost eighty years."

"Okay," the men said, digesting what they had been told. "So why bother getting it now if the bomb has rested peacefully for so long?"

"Because, my newfound friends, it is not an ordinary bomb. It is . . ." Joshua hesitated but again decided to throw caution to the wind. "The first hydrogen bomb. More than one hundred times more powerful than the atomic bombs the U.S. dropped on Hiroshima and Nagasaki."

The two men were now in stunned silence, their mouths wide open.

"And you want to pick up this hydrogen bomb and ferry it out of Tokyo Bay?"

"Yes," Joshua answered simply. "Yes, I do. Ferry it out of the bay and drop it in the deep ocean."

The looks on the two men's faces told the whole story: part incredulous disbelief and part fear. One could have knocked them over with a feather, too. They moved away to talk between themselves. Although Joshua could not understand what was being said, he could tell by their exaggerated gestures that an animated, perhaps heated, discussion was being had.

After five minutes or so, they returned to where Joshua was standing. Ping spoke.

"If there is a bomb in Tokyo Bay, why don't you tell the Japanese government about it, or tell the United States government—your government—about it and let them deal with it?"

"Because to tell the Japanese government about the presence of a hydrogen bomb dropped at the end of World War II that landed in their harbor would generate great turmoil between the two countries, even now. The reason why revealing the bomb's existence would create havoc is because the bomb was destined to be dropped on the Japanese emperor's palace at a time when the United States government knew the Japanese were about to surrender, and in fact did surrender some three days after the bomb was dropped."

Ping and Wei nodded their heads.

Joshua explained further.

"The reason I cannot tell my U.S. government about the bomb is because they killed nearly all of the crew members who were on the airplane that day, and if the existence of the bomb was revealed, they would be greatly embarrassed for the same reason. So, my grandfather, who was the bombardier on the flight, and who wasn't killed because he was too popular of a war hero, would be killed. I would be killed, too, as would everyone who the government thinks might know the secret. My grandfather kept the location of where the bomb hit the water a secret until he shared the story with me about a week ago."

Joshua paused to allow the news to sink in, knowing that the revelation was a lot to absorb. Ping spoke again.

"We must carefully think about what you have said, given the danger and global implications of being involved in your plan. If we decide to help you, we will also have to think about how to communicate the task to the home office in Hong Kong without saying too much. All of our communications are monitored by government agents in Beijing. So go back to your hotel and wait. We will give you our decision in due time."

Joshua bowed twice, acknowledging that his fate now rested in the hands of Ping and Wei Ho, whom he'd met only an hour earlier. Though he was slightly reassured by his past connection with Mei Lei, he also feared that the Chinese government might use the revelation of a potential war crime to their political advantage. Pondering the meaning of "in due time," he left, his mind heavy with doubt.

On his way back to the hotel, Joshua thought of Mei Lei, wondering why she hadn't responded to his letters or emails in the past three and a half years. Despite their recent cold exchange, thoughts of her stirred something deep inside him.

Back at the hotel, Joshua reassured himself that no one was watching him but knew that his spy skills were de minimis; a realization that made him chuckle. Feeling liberated by having laid it on the line with Ping and Wei, he headed to the bar, contemplating that this might be his last drink as a free man. "Bottoms up!" as he raised his glass.

Wei and Ping went into their office after Joshua left. They discussed their options.

"The American seems very sincere," Wei observed.

"Yes, very sincere," agreed Ping.

"I believe his story that a big bomb left over from World War II is at the bottom of the bay."

"I do, too."

"I think we should call Mei Lei and ask her what she would wish for us to do."

"I do, too."

"You're not being very helpful, Ping."

"I'm not?"

"No, you're not!" was Wei's sharp retort. "I will call Mei Lei."

"Okay. Good."

After giving Ping a disgusted look and then after looking in his phone for a few minutes, Wei made the call.

"Hello, Mei Lei. This is your uncle Wei calling from Tokyo."

"Well, hello, uncle. Is everything okay?" Mei Lei asked, a bit concerned.

"Yes, everything is fine . . ." Wei hesitated. "Well, not everything is okay, not really."

"Okay, uncle. What isn't okay," Mei Lei inquired anxiously.

"Ping and I ran into a young American man earlier today and he wants us to do a salvage operation."

Now a bit relieved, Mei Lei stated, "Okay, that's fine. We can do salvage work for an American."

"Yes, thank you, Mei Lei. Our concern isn't doing salvage work for Americans. It is the work we are being asked to do and for whom we are being asked to do it."

"What?" Mei Lei did not understand. "What do you mean about the work and the American? What?"

"The situation is complicated. I will send you the proposal with the courier who is going to Hong Kong from here later today."

Now intrigued but annoyed that her uncle would not give her the details over the phone, Mei Lei confirmed, "Okay. So one of the workers is coming to Hong Kong from Tokyo on a flight tonight? Good enough. I will read the proposal and let you know what I think."

"Thank you, Mei Lei. Talk to you soon. *Zai jian.*"

Mei Lei was puzzled by the secrecy surrounding the conversation. Mei Lei furrowed her brow; she walked to her office window, her eyes rapidly moving from her desk to the window and back, a question hanging in the air. She tilted her head slightly, trying to catch a hint, but understanding the situation remained elusive, a mystery cloaked in something she couldn't quite place.

What could this possibly be? As she returned to her desk, her thoughts wandered to the past three years and her time at the University of Michigan, where she had fond memories of studying English, experiencing American culture, and spending time with her study buddy, Joshua Meister. Thinking of him stirred a mix of emotions—love, anger, longing, and sadness—

yet she had not heard from him in years until he recently called her.

During the first year after leaving Ann Arbor, Joshua had written her several letters and emails, which Mei Lei had kept and reread countless times. But she had never responded, though she still loved him. At the time, leaving him seemed like the right choice, given the strictness of her Chinese family and society. The authoritarian regime made her life difficult, but Mei Lei focused on her work, not politics.

When Mei Lei's father had offered her a position in the family salvage business, it was a way for her to express herself professionally in a way she couldn't in her personal life. Her boyfriend, Joshua, would never have fit into the rigid societal norms of Communist-controlled Hong Kong.

Mei Lei fondly remembered Joshua as a talented, fun-loving genius with the physique of a swimmer. She smiled as she recalled a Fourth of July when they were on a beach watching a fireworks display. A pontoon boat drifted away from the dock, and Joshua, without hesitation, dove into the water, swam 250 yards to reach the pontoon, tied a rope around his waist, and slowly swam back, pulling the boat behind him. His athletic ability and determination impressed her, as did the collective effort of others who had joined in to bring the boat back to shore.

Yay! was the shout from all the people at the party. Even Mei Lei in her reserved way stood up and clapped at Joshua's brave effort. Lots of people congratulated him as he made his way back up the beach, patting him on the back, tousling his hair, offering him beers.

For his part, Joshua was happy and joked with everyone on his way back to Mei Lei but kept walking up the beach. When he finally sat back down with Mei Lei, he looked at her and simply stated, "Well, someone had to do it."

Forgetting her non-contact upbringing for a moment, Mei Lei gave Joshua the biggest hug. Her hand brushed against his cheek, and without a word, she leaned in. Her lips met his softly, lingering for a brief moment, then pulling away, leaving a warmth between them that neither could quite explain. That was the first real kiss she had ever given anyone. Joshua definitely received the message as he had to shift around for a minute or two afterwards to hide his physical reaction to the kiss that was now prominently displayed in his wet swimsuit.

Ah, what a memory, thought Mei Lei. I wonder what Joshua is doing now. In one of his letters, Joshua had written that he had gone to work for the CIA. Mei Lei envisioned Joshua working as an undercover agent in some distant locale, ferreting out spies and terrorists. Probably married to some tall blonde American beauty with two kids, all destined to be tall, blonde, and beautiful, too.

Mei Lei wondered if Joshua ever thought about her or whether she was just a long-forgotten chapter of his life. She felt a bit bad for being so rude to him when he called a few days ago, but she couldn't afford to re-light that flame. That thought made her sad, but mad, too.

Mad at Joshua for not following her to Hong Kong and mad at herself for not writing back. Then she became even more angry that he had called her out of the blue, expecting her to jump at the chance to see him again. How rude—and definitely no. That he needed her help in Japan on a government mission? Right. Sure.

Mei Lei pushed thoughts of Joshua aside and focused on work. Just then, her maid called to inform her that her daughter, Li Li, was home and the English tutor was late. At two and a half years old, Li Li was already fluent in English and was learning Japanese and Vietnamese, much like Joshua. Mei Lei smiled at the thought of them speaking different languages together, though she knew they would never meet.

At nearly 8:00 p.m., after another long workday, Mei Lei gathered her things to go home and spend time with Li Li before bed. On her way out, she received an envelope from Tokyo. After settling into the car, she opened it, expecting nothing out of the ordinary. What she read, however, was a cruel joke. The letter mentioned Joshua Meister—her secret American boyfriend—and a bizarre plan to recover and ferry a bomb out of Tokyo Bay. Mei Lei couldn't believe it. She shook her head in dismay and bit her lip.

Amongst the information provided to Mei Lei in the note was the name of the hotel where Joshua was supposedly staying. Not being one to be shy or quiet, she decided to call the hotel. However, Mei Lei was wise and cautious, too, so she reached for the telephone that was not traceable.

Ring, ring.

"Hello. This is the Downtown Hilton, Tokyo, Japan. How may I help you?" the pleasant male voice answered in Japanese.

"Hello. Do you speak English?"

"Yes, ma'am. I do. How may I help you?"

"Do you have a guest named Joshua Meister staying with you?"

After a couple of seconds' delay, the voice responded, "Yes, we do. Would you like me to ring his room for you?"

Mei Lei hesitated for a moment then plunged ahead.

"Yes, I would. Please ring the room."

As the phone rang, Mei Lei's heart started pounding and she

shivered. Three and a half years. Three plus years since she had said goodbye in person to Joshua. Three years and so much had happened in those three years. Three years. Jesus Christ. What am I doing? But in spite of those reservations, Mei Lei did not hang up.

A deep male voice answered the phone.

"Hello."

"Hello. Is this the Joshua who attended the University of Michigan some years back?"

No response right away, then, "Yes, it is. Who is calling, please?" Upon hearing Mei Lei's voice Joshua nearly jumped out of his skin with excitement as he knew exactly who was calling.

Now was Mei Lei's turn to hesitate.

"This is Mei Lei Ho. We met at the University of Michigan in 2019."

With her heart now nearly pounding out of her chest, Mei Lei waited for Joshua to respond. He did, in Chinese.

"Hello, Mei Lei. Yes, it is me, Joshua. Thank you for calling me back. I'm here in Tokyo and quite by accident I met two of your relatives after you and I had our most recent telephone call."

"Yes, you did, indeed, Joshua. Is this proposal from you some kind of a joke?"

"Oh, no, Mei Lei. The proposal is not some kind of joke at all. It is dead serious."

Mei Lei did not respond right away.

"Without being more specific about the details, do you know what you are asking my company to do? What risk you are asking me to take?"

"Yes, I do, Mei Lei, and if you say no, I will completely understand."

"If I do what you ask and get caught, we will be kicked out of Japan, banned from the U.S. markets, and possibly face charges here in China, too."

"That's all true," conceded Joshua, "in a worst-case scenario. Best case is that your company performs this service and you will have helped avert a worldwide political crisis and averted the distinct possibility that many, many people could be hurt should someone else get to the prize first."

"Prize, huh? That is how you describe this object? Not a very good use of the word."

"True. In America we would probably call it a booby prize, which means a prize of no value, usually a mockery of a prize."

Mei Lei didn't quite understand the meaning of booby prize, but she understood enough to know that what was being discussed was an undesirable prize; not a prize at all.

Joshua continued: "There may be others who know the approximate location of the prize, which is why I took the chance and revealed my plan to your family."

"Oh, really," replied Mei Lei cuttingly, not sure whether Joshua was being honest with her or trying to manipulate her.

"Yes, really. There are two possible factions who are searching for the prize. Men from Pakistan who are bent on using the prize to cause great havoc in my country, bent on destroying a major coastal U.S. city and everyone in it."

"The everyone you describe would now also include me and my family in Hong Kong, right, Joshua?" was Mei Lei's strong retort.

"Yes, Mei Lei. That is true but unlikely because the Pakistanis are mad at the Americans for the ongoing drone strikes in their country, not the Chinese. The second faction is people from my country who will do anything to keep the existence of the prize a secret. And I am sad to say that you would be in the circle of those my government would likely seek to eliminate now that we have talked," was Joshua's apology. "But not if we pull this off because then there would be no point in doing anything. If the threat is eliminated, there would not be any reason for anyone to be eliminated."

Mei Lei considered this. Eliminated, eh? As in killed. Great. Then suddenly, "I will think about what to do, what is best for my company and my family. I will call you back soon."

"When?" Joshua wanted to know. "Do you want my number to call me directly?"

"Soon," was Mei Lei's brusque reply, "and I guess so."

Joshua gave Mei Lei the number of the burner phone he had purchased in St. Louis, then the line went dead. He knew "soon" could mean anything from an hour to a week, but at least it meant a response would come. Joshua could do nothing more to speed things up and began to think about his plan in case Mei Lei refused. If she kept quiet, he would figure out another way, but if she didn't, the authorities would soon intervene, ending his life as he knew it.

Mei Lei, meanwhile, was shaken by Joshua's reappearance. She had been in control of her life and business, but his unexpected return had thrown her off balance. She never expected to see or hear from him again, which was why she had ignored his attempts to contact her. His voice had stirred feelings she thought she had buried, bringing back a yearning she hadn't felt in years. Mei Lei was furious at herself for still being affected by him.

Ahh, how aggravating, thought an exasperated Mei Lei. She had built what she thought was a perfect world, and now, like Humpty Dumpty after the fall, her world was cracked beyond repair. Trying to force herself to think of what was best to do for her family business and for her, Mei Lei decided to go to Tokyo herself to sort out the situation and decide what to do when she arrived. So, Mei Lei sent Joshua a text: Be in Tokyo tomorrow.

When Joshua received the text confirming the meeting for tomorrow, he decided not to notify his grandfather just yet. He wouldn't update him until after the meeting with Mei Lei, knowing the outcome was not certain.

Joshua scanned his hotel room, wondering how Mei Lei had changed over the years—whether she was married, had gained weight, or altered her appearance. He felt the connection renewed, and from the depths of his soul the love and longing for Mei Lei came roaring back. As he prepared for the meeting, he hoped that upon seeing him again she would change her mind and that the two of them would be together. Despite the task at hand, memories of their time together took center stage in his mind.

Day 7 in Japan

Dawn brought a bright sunrise streaming through the shades Joshua had forgotten to close. He hurried to prepare for what could determine both the project's success and his own freedom. By 9:00 a.m., he sat in the hotel lobby with coffee, awaiting Mei Lei, whose flight had landed an hour earlier.

Only Joshua knew the actual location of an unexploded hydrogen bomb—and he was hoping to smuggle it past Japanese authorities. It was a reckless plan, but he was determined. Success would prevent a political scandal and, more importantly, keep the bomb from falling into the wrong hands—a disaster for humanity.

At 10:02, Mei Lei arrived. Just over five feet tall, she commanded attention not by her size but by her presence. Their eyes met, and they exchanged knowing smiles.

Joshua walked up to Mei Lei, not sure whether to bow, extend his hand, or hug her. He opted for a hug and was pleased and relieved that she accepted it.

"Hello, Mei Lei. It has been a long time."

Mei Lei stepped back a half step and looked at Joshua.

"Yes, it has. More than three years."

"Nearly four years have flown by, and you are even more beautiful now than you were when you left Michigan, Mei Lei."

Mei Lei blushed. She had not expected such a compliment.

"You are very kind, Joshua. Thank you. But the years have brought many changes to both of our lives, haven't they?" Mei Lei asked somewhat rhetorically as she looked around the room.

"Yes, the years have brought many changes to our lives," Joshua repeated. "But fate somehow chose for me to see a sign at a warehouse on Tokyo Bay that led me back to you. And despite the, shall I say, unusual circumstances that brought us together again, I am most happy to see you," Joshua declared, smiling, bowing slightly while looking directly into Mei Lei's eyes.

Mei Lei did not take her eyes away from Joshua's.

"I read the note the employee brought, but tell me, Joshua, tell me more about this mission of yours that could possibly end with all involved either jailed or killed?"

Joshua scanned the room to ensure no one was listening before speaking in Chinese. He recounted his grandfather Nathaniel's mysterious orders near the end of the war, his refusal to drop a hydrogen bomb on the Imperial Palace, the subsequent deaths of many of his crew, and his fear that both the U.S. government and a Pakistani nurse's aide might know about the location of the bomb and be after it too. He emphasized the urgency and danger of the mission.

Mei Lei listened intently, posing questions while weighing her options. Logic told her to immediately leave Tokyo and return to her business in Hong Kong. Yet, she felt drawn to the boldness and righteousness of Joshua's story—and her biracial daughter's safety added another layer of motivation. Despite her doubts, Mei Lei realized she both wanted to help and was capable of doing so.

Joshua sketched the bomb's dimensions on a napkin, and Mei Lei assessed the feasibility of the operation. Her company could float the bomb up from the bottom of the bay, lift it onto a barge, and discreetly remove it—routine logistics, save for the nature of the cargo. Success would demand absolute secrecy, and Mei Lei felt ready to take on the challenge.

Mei Lei wanted to know: "What likelihood is there that the bomb will explode when we move it?"

"Zero likelihood because the bomb was never armed as it fell into the ocean," was the response.

"What is the likelihood that the exterior of the bomb was breached by the impact so that there is radiation leaking?"

"Zero likelihood from what I have seen. I looked over the exterior that is exposed and it is not deformed at all."

"What likelihood is there that salt water has entered the casing and has armed the bomb somehow?"

"Unknown, but extremely unlikely because to set off the bomb two separate steps have to be followed in exact order. One of the steps is that a radio signal at a particular frequency has to be sent and received to arm the bomb. Then to set off the bomb, it has to be more than 3,500 feet in the air. Plus, all of the electrical connectors were made with gold, so salt water would not corrode them. Does that help?"

"Does it help? Does it help? Nothing will help me get out of the situation you put me in," Mei Lei snapped, sparks flying from her eyes as she spat out her words and stamped her foot. "And not only me. My business and my family are in danger now because you decided to suck me into this most dangerous affair for which I will never forgive you."

A long silence ensued. Joshua knew Mei Lei was right on every point she made, and obviously she was pissed. Mei Lei's back went rigid with anger as she flipped her hair back and crossed her arms. Joshua looked at her repeatedly, but Mei Lei only looked away.

"I'm sorry, Mei Lei, to have involved you in this mess. Forget I ever reached out to you. Forget the whole thing. This is my quest, my bomb quest. I will either figure it out on my own or I won't figure it out at all. OK?"

"No, it is not OK. Whether I say no or not, the whole mess, as you put it, cannot be forgotten. For as I am here talking with you, cameras are likely recording everything. If they track you down, they will come looking for me, too."

Joshua understood that "they" referred to the U.S. and Chinese governments. Both were relentless in uncovering plots, with the Communists being even more thorough. Guilt weighed heavily on him for agreeing to find the bomb and for dragging Mei Lei and her family into the ordeal. But she was right—her presence in Tokyo meant there was no turning back. Mei Lei, her family, and her company were now entangled in the mission.

After a tense silence filled with fear and frustration, Mei Lei finally spoke.

"Since you have left me no choice, I must join you on this stupid, dangerous venture. So, join you, I will, because the only way to avoid being killed is to succeed. That way, as you said, the U.S. will have no reason to kill me because the evidence will be 20,000 feet deep and out of everyone's reach."

"So," Mei Lei announced, turning and facing Joshua, looking directly into his eyes, "let's do it. I will make the necessary arrangements and pick you up here later today."

CHAPTER 33

Muqtar drove all night to San Francisco, motivated by fear and the angst of leaving his family. Around 5:00 p.m. the next afternoon, he found the address of the Imam and knocked on the door.

"Hello, who is it?" asked a pleasant-sounding female voice. "It's me, Muqtar Ashadi. I am here to see Imam Rushi."

"Oh, OK," was the reply. A minute later, the door swung open and the Imam's face appeared.

"Come in, son, come in. I'm glad to see you made it. Did you drive all night to get here?" welcomed the Imam as he stepped aside and gestured for Muqtar to come inside.

"Yes, Imam. I did. I drove all night to get here because I am afraid the authorities will soon be on my trail if they aren't already," was Muqtar's answer as he nervously scanned the neighborhood, looking to see if he had been followed.

"You must be exhausted from your travels," observed the Imam as he looked at Muqtar's bloodshot eyes with dark bags underneath and his overall drawn and bedraggled visage.

"Most definitely I am, Imam."

"Can I offer you some tea and dates, Muqtar?"

Muqtar's look of a starving dog was his reply as he began to shiver with fear.

"Honey, please make us some tea and bring some dates.

The Imam waved for Muqtar to sit on the couch, and he sat down next to him. Placing his hand on Muqtar's shoulder, the Imam asked, "Now, why would they be on your trail, Muqtar?"

Muqtar hung his head in shame. "Because I killed a man in New York over a drug deal, assumed a false identity, and moved to St. Louis."

Imam Rushi calmly nodded his head as he listened, barely raising an eyebrow. "How long ago did that happen, Muqtar?"

"That was nearly four years ago, Imam."

"So what makes you think they are after you now for something that happened four years ago, Muqtar?"

"Because murder cases stay open forever is what makes me think that, Imam. Additionally, the U.S. government is after me because I found out about the location of a lost U.S.-made hydrogen bomb."

"What?" was the Imam's incredulous response as he sat up and moved forward on the couch. "Please tell me about that."

Muqtar then proceeded to tell the Imam the entire story of the Colonel and the Google map and about the conversations he overheard between Nathaniel and Joshua. After taking all that in, the Imam spoke again.

"The New York situation is a problem, Muqtar, for sure. I agree that you need to leave the country, to go back to your village and start a new life there. Do you still have family there?"

"The last I knew I did, and I also had a beautiful girlfriend there," Muqtar recalled, lowering his face to look at the ground. "My guess is that she has moved on with her life or was killed in a drone strike."

"Maybe, maybe not, Muqtar. The only way to know is to go back and find her."

Changing the subject a bit, the Imam asked, "Do you have

both of your passports?"

"Yes, I do. I have my student visa from Pakistan, and I have my American passport as Michael Brown."

"Very good. Give them both to me and I will have a friend of mine check and see if either one of you is on the no-fly list," offered Imam Rushi, a concerned frown covering his forehead.

"You will stay here tonight, and we will make your trip plans tomorrow morning. For tonight, you will have a meal from back home to get you ready for your return to the mountains." Muqtar was so nervous and exhausted that he barely tasted his food, although the few bites he noticed were really good. Muqtar didn't think he would sleep, but he did—very heavily, until he awoke after hearing a light knock on the bedroom door. "Muqtar, are you awake? Breakfast will soon be ready," announced the Imam's wife cheerily.

Muqtar opened his eyes and looked around. His immediate reaction was abject fear—the result of being up for 36 hours before last night's sleep combined with his overall fear of being caught, plus guilt; extreme guilt to his core. Trying to put his negative thoughts aside, Muqtar saw the outline of a person that after a second or two he recognized as the Imam's wife.

"Good morning. Thank you," greeted Muqtar to the image in the doorway as she turned and began walking away.

"There is a towel and a facecloth in the guest bathroom for you to use, Muqtar. Once you are dressed, come downstairs as I am cooking breakfast. Coffee will be ready in a minute," she mentioned, her voice fading away as she descended the stairs.

Muqtar felt better that morning than he had since meeting the government agent—still exceedingly uneasy, but the morning felt promising. The aroma of coffee and cinnamon pushed him to start the day. He hoped for safe passage home, though his future remained uncertain.

A hot shower did little to ease his anxiety, though it refreshed him. As he descended the stairs, the guilt returned, in sharp focus now as he thought of Julie. Had she read his note? "I have to leave the country, darling, right away. Take care of yourself and my son. I'll contact you when I'm settled in Pakistan. All my love, Michael." He had intended to write her a letter and maybe he would once he returned to Pakistan, but this brief note was all he could come up with at the time.

"Good morning, again," Muqtar announced as cheerily as he could when he saw the Imam's wife standing in the kitchen.

"Good morning, Muqtar. Are you ready for some breakfast?"

"Yes, ma'am, I am, thank you," he replied as he sat down at the kitchen table. Muqtar looked up when he heard footsteps— footsteps that belonged to the Imam. He noticed that the Imam was carrying his prayer mat, and once again he felt ashamed. When was the last time he had prayed, Muqtar wondered, or had even thought about praying. Jesus, what a shithead I am. God, so many years had passed—probably since before he had left home to come to America—had Muqtar thought about his faith. Muqtar resolved that no matter what, he would once again pray on a regular basis. He knew his spiritual self had withered over the years, a victim of neglect, and now the only solace within reach was to redeem himself through prayer and devotion.

"Good morning," greeted the Imam.

"Good morning, Imam," returned Muqtar.

"I placed some phone calls and found out that your American passport has not been flagged, so you can leave the country using it. The only thing is that if you leave you can never come back to the United States, for if you do, you will most likely be detained and sent to New York to face criminal charges there."

"So, knowing that eventuality, what would you like to do?" questioned Mohammed. "I must go home, Imam. My heart aches and will always ache for what I will be leaving behind here—an American wife and a son—but for the safety of my American family and for me, I must go home."

"All right then. Home you will go. There is no time to waste. Who knows how long it will be before your cover identity is blown. Do you have money to buy an airline ticket?"

"Yes, Imam, I do."

With that decision having been made, Muqtar fired up the internet and purchased his ticket. Only one stop to change planes in Frankfurt, then home free . . . well, home at least, and yes, sort of free; maybe.

As the two men walked out the front door, Muqtar handed his car keys to the Imam. "Please sell the car and use the money for good, Imam. Will you do that for me?"

Before the Imam could answer, Muqtar continued. "The title is in the glove box, and the car should sell for fifteen or twenty thousand dollars, and I'm sure there are lots of people you know who could use a bit of help."

"That's true, Muqtar. But what of the needs of your American wife and son? What about them?"

"I have thought of them, too, Imam. I left my wife nearly all of the money I had saved for a rainy day."

The Imam seemed satisfied with this answer. "Okay, then. Let's go," agreed the Imam as he opened the driver's door and sat down behind the wheel.

Muqtar climbed into the car, his mind racing between fear

of being caught and the thrill of freedom. He felt both terrified and exhilarated at the prospect of returning home.

The ride to the airport was quiet. Muqtar gazed out the window, trying to imprint the urban landscape—the highways, tall buildings, and endless concrete—knowing the simplicity of his destination in Pakistan that awaited him.

As they neared the airport, he breathed a sigh of relief. The first hurdle was over. Security and then Islamabad were next, and he could hardly wait.

Outside the car, Muqtar handed the Imam a slip of paper.

"This is my wife's phone number and address in St. Louis. In about a week, please call her and let her know I'm in Pakistan and safe." He trusted the Imam would reach out to Julie.

"I will see to it," promised the Imam in his faint British-sounding accent. "Do you want me to tell her why you went to Pakistan?"

"No, Imam. Just that I am safe will suffice for now. And thank you very much for helping me."

"You're welcome, son. May Allah bless you in all you do. Do good works and you will be rewarded many multiples of what you give," pronounced the Imam, facing Muqtar with his hands on Muqtar's shoulders. The Imam embraced Muqtar, kissing him on both cheeks. Muqtar returned the gesture, then grabbed his backpack and headed toward the terminal without looking back, hiding the tears streaming down his face.

A sharp pang of guilt tightened in his chest, his thoughts swirling as the weight of regret settled in. After a moment or two more of self-pity, Muqtar refocused and approached the ticket counter. Handing over his American passport, he held his breath until the agent printed his ticket and checked his bag. Relieved, he headed to the gate with his boarding pass.

With over two hours until boarding, he sat and wrestled with thoughts of Julie and his son. Normally, he'd call them, but not this time—and likely never again.

What kind of man would his son grow up to be, Muqtar wondered? Then the end of a sharpened spear pierced his consciousness. What kind of man will be with my wife now that I am gone? The thought of Julie being with another man and raising his son caused Muqtar to bend forward in his seat, writhing in pain, holding back the urge to throw up. The brutal truth hit Muqtar square in the forehead. You don't get to decide what happens to them anymore, pendejo. You fucked that up when you murdered Allen and ran.

The CIA agent Lozano had exposed him while pursuing a different target: the Colonel and the bomb. Trying to lift himself up off the mat emotionally, Muqtar switched his thinking to what he believed the Colonel and his grandson were working together to do; that is, to recover the bomb dropped into Tokyo Bay. The stolen map coordinates confirmed its location, and Muqtar sensed the bomb would continue to shape his future.

His thoughts were interrupted by the boarding announcement. After passing through the gate and taking his seat, Muqtar exhaled deeply as the plane door closed. As the 777 lifted off, he thought, Home free—or almost. He drifted to sleep, relieved at last.

Returning to the retirement home the next morning, Alex wasn't surprised to learn that Michael Brown hadn't shown up for work. What did catch his attention was a group of nurses consoling a distraught colleague—Michael's wife. Alex made a mental note to question her later, but had other priorities at the moment. Today, he intended to interrogate Joshua Meister during his visit with his grandfather, confident his expertise in psychological manipulation would expose their plans.

Alex went to the administrative office, leaving instructions to be alerted when Joshua arrived. By 11:40 a.m., there was still no sign of him. Frustration turned to dread when Alex realized Joshua wasn't avoiding him—he had already left for Japan. A quick check of flights confirmed it: Joshua had departed that morning.

Cursing himself for not anticipating this move, Alex's mind galloped ahead. Joshua was now nearly 6,000 miles away. *Who at work could authorize an urgent trip to Tokyo with so little evidence?* Pissed off at himself, Alex muttered, *I should have seen this coming,* as he repeatedly pounded his right fist into his left palm.

Alex did not know anybody who would approve such an expensive trip without solid evidence anyhow. *How about Colonel Sanders? Oh hell no, he would fry me for letting the two prime subjects leave the U.S. Can't risk that.*

Crap! Fuck! Alex exploded. *I cannot let this smartass kid and the Paki get away with some plan to bomb Tokyo,* he vowed. *What to do? What to do,* he wondered as he literally walked about in circles.

Alex decided to take matters into his own hands. He decided to pursue his plan on the down low, using vacation days and paying out of pocket for a trip to Japan to track down Joshua and stop him—by any means necessary. To cover his tracks, Alex filed an inconclusive report, minimizing the significance of his investigation in St. Louis. *Never hurts to cover your ass,* he confirmed to himself.

To justify his trip, Alex would tell his supervisor he wanted to go fly-fishing in Japan, a plausible excuse given his boss's enthusiasm for the hobby. After checking flights, he booked one to Tokyo for Saturday, three days away, as same-day travel was too costly.

Before leaving the nursing home, Alex decided to make one last attempt to extract information from the Colonel. He knocked on the door.

"Hello? Who is it?" asked the voice behind the door.

"It is me, Alex Lozano. We met and spoke briefly yesterday. I have some matters I would like to discuss with you."

Silence. Then the door opened. Alex peeped inside the room but could not see the Colonel's face very well, as the sun was behind him and the bright light shone directly into Alex's eyes. Alex shielded his eyes and began to step into the room.

"I didn't say come in, did I?" the Colonel barked rudely.

Alex stopped in his tracks but did not stop dead in his tracks. "Why, no. You didn't say for me to come in," was Alex's sly response, trying to butter up the Colonel with the tone of his voice as he slowly sidled his way inside. "But may I?"

"Not no, but hell no, you may not come in," ordered the Colonel. "What do you want?"

"I want to know when your grandson will return because I want to talk to him," spoke Alex, getting down to business.

"No time soon," was the answer, followed by more uncomfortable silence.

"So do you know where he is?" was Alex's follow-up question, having confirmed via the Colonel's answer that Joshua had left St. Louis while already knowing that Joshua was on his way to Tokyo.

"No, I don't, and if I did I wouldn't tell you anyway."

Alex dropped his cheerful façade, adopting a stern, threatening tone. "This is a matter of national security, Colonel. Tell me where your grandson is and what he's doing, or I'll issue an all-points bulletin to detain him and have you arrested for treason."

Nathaniel laughed. "Listen, you sorry, sawed-off motherfucker. I'm 99 years old. After surviving Nazi captivity, there's nothing you or your threats can do to scare me. Waterboarding, pulling nails, crushing my nuts—you'll get nothing from me."

Furious and lower lip curling, Alex snarled, "Think you're tough? So did the camel jockeys at Guantanamo. They all broke eventually, and so will you."

Before Alex could continue, Nathaniel lunged and threw a punch at Alex that missed but caused him to stumble backwards. Luckily this time he didn't hit the back of his head on the opposite wall as staff members rushed into the hallway, drawn by the commotion.

Regaining his balance, Alex seethed. "This isn't over. When you're charged with treason, I'll be there to see you fry. And when I catch your grandson in Japan, he'll be begging for mercy."

"Oh, yeah?" sneered Nathaniel, having stepped into the hallway. "I may be old, but I am not dead and neither you nor any fucking scumbags like you that want to wrap yourselves in the American flag to justify torturing people will ever hear a peep out of me."

Nathaniel turned to the gathering crowd and declared, "Look at this little prick, threatening an old soldier with empty bullshit!" Pointing directly at Alex, he continued, "You're an embarrassment to this country. You, Cheney, and the others behind Guantanamo and Abu Ghraib should've been jailed decades ago for your war crimes. If you show your face here again, I'll do more than knock you on your ass, you sorry piece of shit."

With that, Nathaniel slammed the door. Alex glared at the onlookers, who quickly dispersed. Sweating, breathing hard, and fuming from humiliation, Alex vowed to bring both Nathaniel and Joshua to what he considered justice—extreme justice.

Inside his room, Nathaniel felt uneasy. Knowing Alex wouldn't back down, he called Joshua using the burner phone. Reaching voicemail, he left a message: "Joshua, this is your grandfather. That government guy came back today and was very rude and threatening. Keep your eyes peeled. Love you. Bye."

Later, Joshua turned on his phone and played the message, fixating on the final words, *Love you. Bye.* Nathaniel's words fueled his determination to complete his mission. Checking the time—8:30 p.m. back home—he decided it was too late to call.

With little else to do, Joshua scouted the area and noticed a Marriott across from the Hilton. He walked over and, from the lobby bar, identified the best vantage point to watch the Hilton's entrance, making a mental note for future use.

An hour later, Joshua returned to his room and decided to call his grandfather anyway.

"Grampa?"

"Hello. Yes?"

"Sorry for calling you so late, but everything is coming together over here."

"Really? Wow, grandson, that is great news, and I was awake anyway. What can you tell me?" Nathaniel asked in a surreptitious tone.

"I can tell you that I have successfully made arrangements

for help in acquiring the prize."

"What? Shit yes. Wow. I never dared think we would get this far."

"Well, we have. I am meeting with some people later today to figure out the exact logistics of the plan."

"Excellent, grandson. Excellent. Oh by the way, the nurse's aide has not been back to work since you left."

"Do you know where he went, Grampa?"

"From what I heard, he went to Pakistan. His wife, who is a nurse here, has been nonstop crying since."

"Fuck. That really worries me that he might be on his way over here from Pakistan to screw up our plans."

"You're right, Joshua. He could be on his way there. So keep your eyes open, okay? Oh, and more bad news; the little douche-bag said he was going to Japan too."

"Jesus; him too? Okay, Grampa. I will pay attention. Gotta go now. I love you, Grampa."

"Okay. Talk to you again soon."

Joshua waited for his grandfather to say *I love you* but nope, he didn't.

He looked at his watch: 10:50 a.m. local time. He expected a call from Mei Lei at 11:30, so Joshua had time to get ready but not enough time to call and check in with Betsy. Once show-ered, Joshua went to the hotel restaurant and ate as much as he could stand to eat. No telling how much time would pass before he ate again. Joshua avoided coffee. He would not need caffeine to get him going that day. He was plenty amped up.

Joshua looked at his watch again. It was now 11:25 and his phone rang.

"Hello, Joshua."

Joshua's heart leapt.

"Yes. Hello, Mei Lei."

"It is time to get going. Are you ready to go?"

"Yes, I am ready to go. What do you want me to do?"

"Meet me outside in 15 minutes. I will be in a red, four-door Honda."

"Okay," acknowledged Joshua as he hung up, so excited that his fingers crackled with electricity. Now standing outside the hotel in the cool early morning air, Joshua reflected on why he was so excited. *For the mission, for sure, but he was also most excited at the prospect of seeing Mei Lei again.* Then he felt a little guilty for blowing off Betsy, knowing that she wanted to talk to him. *And he wanted to talk to her too; just not right now.*

A red Honda pulled into the driveway, and Joshua waved as it approached. Mei Lei noticed and stopped, allowing him to get into the front passenger seat. "Good morning," Joshua greeted her.

Without much acknowledgment, Mei Lei muttered a quick "good morning," then focused on the road as she drove out of the driveway. Joshua found her cold and businesslike, a stark contrast to his own warm feelings toward her. He decided to stay quiet and see what the day would bring.

The ride was silent for about 40 minutes before Mei Lei finally spoke.

"I have arranged for a fishing boat at the public marina. It is fully equipped with scuba gear and everything we will need to check out the prize as you put it."

Joshua was impressed by how quickly Mei Lei had organized the next step, though he shouldn't have been—after all, she was the head of a global salvage operation.

At the marina, they boarded a boat where two Chinese men were waiting onboard. Without a word, one man started the engine while the other cast off the lines. Two minutes later, they were speeding across Tokyo Bay under the morning sun.

Joshua handed over the coordinates, and the helmsman inputted them into the GPS. About 15 minutes later, the boat slowed as they reached the exact location where the coordinates intersected.

"I suggest you throw down the anchor about 50 meters to the northwest so as to not give away the prize's true location," Joshua advised.

Fifty meters northwest, the men dropped anchor while Joshua and Mei Lei suited up. One man helped with their scuba gear, and they slipped into the dark water. Joshua swam southwest, Mei Lei following closely behind, both equalizing as they descended.

When Joshua didn't see the bomb where he expected, panic set in briefly, but then he spotted it about 20 feet away—big, ugly, and dangerous, half buried in the mud like a long piece of sewer pipe.

They circled the bomb, Mei Lei taking photos from all angles. Joshua pointed out the lifting poles, showing Mei Lei where to dig to find the other two. As time ran out, he signaled to ascend.

Once back on the boat, Mei Lei scrolled through the photos, examining each one carefully. Finally, she spoke.

"What happens if the exterior that's buried in the mud is compromised, J?"

Mei Lei called him J. Joshua liked that.

"Not likely because about half of the prize is exposed and it is not wrinkled or deformed along its leading edge. See?" explained Joshua, pointing out the top of the bomb in the photo to Mei Lei.

"Not likely, perhaps, but what if? Will everyone working nearby be exposed to nuclear radiation?"

"No, Mei Lei," assured Joshua. "The radioactive components are contained in their own separate spheres protected by two-inch-thick lead coatings. However, if you have access to a Geiger counter, we can measure the radioactivity levels to see if the lead shields have been breached."

Mei Lei decided to have a Geiger counter shipped by tomorrow. If the bomb wasn't leaking radiation, they'd begin excavation, using an underwater vacuum to minimize stress on the structure when lifting it.

Joshua remained silent, thinking, *Cool,* while feeling a mix of regret and selfish relief. Despite the danger, the mission was crucial, and he was more than glad to have Mei Lei's help.

The ride back to the hotel was quiet, and after a brief, unsentimental goodbye, Joshua headed to his room to call Betsy.

"Hi, Betsy. Sorry it is so late. But did I catch you at a good time?"

"Hi, Joshua. That's fine. I have been waiting to hear from you," she replied in a worried, sleepy voice.

"Everything is going really well, Bets. Much better than I could have hoped."

"Oh, that is great news."

"It looks like I will be here for about another week or so, then I will be back home."

"That is great news too," congratulated Betsy, then added, "I miss you."

"I miss you too, Betsy, and I will try to do better about calling you more often and earlier."

"That would be good so I won't worry as much."

"Okay. Bye for now."

"Okay, bye. Oh, before I let you go, Michael Brown disappeared and I heard he went to Pakistan."

"Huh. Okay. Thanks, sweetie. Bye."

"Bye."

"Shit," Joshua cursed to himself. *More affirmation that the motherfucker is surely coming to Tokyo to look for the bomb. Why else would he leave St. Louis? God damn it. I don't need that headache. Something else to look out for.*

Joshua had nothing to do for the rest of the day except worry. So he ate too much, drank too many cups of sake, and went to bed early.

Day 8 in Japan

The next morning, Joshua was up early and waiting outside the hotel at 6:00 a.m. Mei Lei arrived on time, and they drove off as before. Joshua greeted her with a "Good morning," but Mei Lei's blunt, somewhat rude reply surprised him.

"Is it Joshua?"

Her short response dashed his romantic fantasies about rekindling their relationship. He remained silent for the rest of the ride, taking in the sights of Tokyo. As they approached the warehouse, Mei Lei finally spoke again.

"The salvage ship we have here does not have strong enough lifting arms to pick up the prize once she breaches the surface of the bay, so I have ordered the ship we keep in Hong Kong to come over here to do the job."

"Okay. How long will it take to get here?"

"About three or four days, depending on the seas. Last night, when I realized how big and heavy the prize was, I ordered the ship to leave port in Hong Kong and begin the voyage to Tokyo."

"While we are waiting, we will have to come up with a reason to give the harbor authority as to what we are going to be doing in the bay. Do you have any ideas?"

Joshua thought for a moment because he had not even considered notifying anybody, thinking what was best was to keep the salvage operation a secret. Joshua offered, "I think it is best to work at night only and not tell anybody anything. Just bring in the ship without disclosing any particular plans to the port authority is my suggestion. What do you think about that?"

"Risky, is what I think about that. My company would be fined or kicked out if the port authorities realize we are working a salvage job without permits. Plus, parking a ship that far away from the rest of the ships in the harbor might draw attention."

"True, the plan is risky, but if we are found out, we are screwed anyway. If anyone finds out we are attempting to lift a hydrogen bomb off the bottom of the bay, a shit storm will surely ensue."

Now Mei Lei had to think about what to do. *True enough,* she thought, *being found out will spell doom for all involved.* Yet by not telling the authorities, Mei Lei felt they were most certainly going to attract the harbor master's attention. After all, the salvage ship was 50 meters long; not exactly something that no one would notice. And the Tokyo Bay coast guard policed the bay constantly.

"Joshua, we have to come up with a believable reason to have the salvage ship come from Hong Kong to Tokyo Bay, because once she enters the bay, the port authorities will inspect the paperwork and will be curious why the ship made such a long trip. So put your thinking cap on and come up with a legitimate reason why we are here. My thought is to tell the port authority we are only here for a short while then back out to sea to look for some lost containers."

Mei Lei knew they needed a permit to anchor in the harbor but wasn't sure what excuse to use. The one she suggested was the best she was able to come up with. She asked Joshua if he had any ideas. Joshua, considering the options, suggested two possibilities: testing for poisonous chemicals in the seabed or claiming a container ship had lost part of its load nearby, and the salvage ship was retrieving the load for a fee. Mei Lei, relieved to hear a plausible solution, considered Joshua's plan carefully before responding.

"The idea of testing the seabed will likely not work because who would hire a Chinese salvage ship to do such testing in Japanese waters. So, no to that idea. However, perhaps if we use the excuse that the big ship is here to salvage some lost containers and is waiting on crew and payment before she begins the work, the authorities will accept that. The idea makes sense because there was a loss about 250 kilometers to the east near one of the outer islands that has not been salvaged yet. I doubt the Japanese authorities will know that the lost containers were empty and therefore will not be salvaged."

Nodding her head in agreement with herself, Mei Lei continued.

"I think it will take about eight hours to extract the prize. We will run the vacuums at night and the sound will not likely attract attention. That would be a risk, but a small risk, and we will try to do it all in one night."

Mei Lei preferred his second option, the lost containers, which Joshua agreed with, admiring her sharp thinking and planning abilities. He realized that using their plan would avoid unnecessary questions from authorities and allow them to work discreetly. Mei Lei, sensing Joshua's excitement, briefly felt a pang of regret about what might have been between them, but quickly pushed the thought aside, focusing on the task at hand while grappling with the personal secret from their past.

"Joshua, I am ready to go forward with the plan we have created. I think it will work. I will notify the port authorities we have a salvage ship coming in to retrieve some containers, get supplies and crew, and while it is moored in the harbor, we will secretly extract the prize, sneak it out of the harbor and dispose of it safely once out to sea."

Now at the hotel, Joshua's face broke into a wide grin, his chest light, as a wave of excitement bubbled up inside him. He couldn't help but let out a short laugh, his motions quickening with a newfound energy. Joshua, feeling overjoyed, impulsively hugged Mei Lei. He was surprised when she hugged him back, even if just slightly. For a moment, he considered kissing her but quickly decided against pushing his luck.

CHAPTER 34

Muqtar touched down in Islamabad at 7:00 a.m. and breezed through customs without issue. Hearing his native language and being welcomed home filled him with relief. He felt liberated, knowing the Pakistani government would never extradite him to the U.S. Although he longed to call his mother, he had no way of reaching her, so he settled for a strong, sweet coffee and a date bar.

Yet, his thoughts lingered on the American wife and son he left behind. *Julie and Michael Junior must be devastated. Where is Daddy, Mommy? Is he coming home soon? He took a trip, son. He took a trip without us, Mommy? Yes, son, he had to go home to Pakistan. Where is Pakistan, Mommy?* He could almost hear the exchange as Julie's guts were ripped out trying to be brave in front of her son. He longed to rumple his son's hair and play horsey with him, but not to be—not now and not ever again. No Sunday mornings with his wife either.

Muqtar wanted to reach over the distance and hug them both, but realizing the futility in such thoughts, he turned to the hydrogen bomb he was determined to find. Muqtar believed the bomb existed based on the conversations he overheard and the coordinates from the old Colonel. His next move was to get to Japan and track down Joshua, the Colonel's grandson, who would lead him to the bomb. Energized, Muqtar headed to the bus terminal to begin his journey home.

Muqtar spent the day soaking in the sights and sounds of Pakistan, feeling a sense of welcome amidst the hustle and bustle. Yet he felt no inner comfort and knew he would never feel good about himself ever again. Muqtar would also have to explain his absence during the years he was supposed to be in college. When his bus arrived, Muqtar boarded and settled in for the long ride, enjoying a conversation with a young girl who offered him a piece of spice cake. As he ate, Muqtar estimated he'd be home in about nine hours.

After several stops, he finally arrived, greeted by the sight of snow-covered mountains and cool, fresh air. Though returning home as a failure, Muqtar hoped his family would forgive him; families are like that. His brothers would surely understand his falling for the lifestyle, and he could wow them with his stories of bravado and sexual conquest. His father, on the other hand, would not be so forgiving. After all, the family had sacrificed everything to pay for Muqtar's education along with all of their hopes and dreams riding on Muqtar's success; all of it was now a pile of burnt ashes.

Muqtar headed to the bakery owned by his former girlfriend's family, briefly pausing at the thought of possibly running into Alia. He assumed that if she had survived the drone strike, she would have already moved on and married someone else. With that thought in mind, Muqtar entered the bakery, also anxious to find out who in his family might have been killed in the strike.

"Hello, hello," Muqtar called out from just inside the door to the bakery, as no one was in the front. He examined the broken and covered windows and the cracked wall next to where the missile had hit. He heard movement, and then a female emerged from the shadows. It was Alia's mother; he recognized her right away.

"Hello, Mrs. Majed. It is I, Muqtar, having returned home from America."

She looked up at him, trying to recall who he was exactly.

"Oh, yes, Muqtar Ashadi. I remember you from a long time ago."

Then Muqtar heard another female voice from the back.

"Who is it, Mother? I recognize that voice."

Muqtar immediately recognized the second voice. The lyrical-sounding voice belonged to Alia, no doubt about it. His heart started pounding and his breaths started coming in short, rapid gulps. His head felt dizzy and he was afraid he was about to hyperventilate. Muqtar heard footsteps, and Alia appeared—still amazingly beautiful, but different.

"Alia, it is me, Muqtar. I have been gone a long time and now I have returned to my home."

"Oh, so it is you, Muqtar. I recognize your voice but I cannot see your face. I am blind."

Muqtar reached out and touched Alia's hands with his.

"Yes, Alia. It is me."

Alia's hands felt warm and soft as their fingers wove together. They stood that way for a while—hands clasped together over the bakery counter, each occupied with their own thoughts. Then Muqtar offered, "Alia, would you like to join me for a coffee?"

"Yes, I would. Mother, would that be okay if I left the bakery for a bit?"

"Yes, daughter. I will close the shop and come with you."

Muqtar stepped outside the shop and waited. Alia stepped out dressed in traditional Pakistani garb with a pretty blue scarf over her head, her mother close behind.

"You are as pretty as ever, Alia. As beautiful as the flowers that grow in the mountains in the spring."

Alia slipped her arm through his, knowing that because of her disability no one would shame her.

"And you, Muqtar, still say the nicest things."

The three walked the two blocks to the coffee shop silently, each still consumed with their own thoughts.

Muqtar helped Alia find a chair and she seated herself without assistance. Mrs. Majed sat down nearby.

"I see that you have become accustomed to your blindness, Alia. Tell me how this came to be, if you are willing."

"I will tell you what happened to me, Muqtar, but you must tell me first what happened to you. You left here five, almost six years ago, carrying with you the hopes of our entire village. Now you have returned completely out of the blue, having never answered a single one of my letters," scolded Alia.

"And I wrote you more than a hundred times before I gave up. What happened to you anyway?" demanded Alia.

Muqtar knew he had to be honest with Alia. Well, sort of honest.

"I got in trouble in New York because I was foolish. I began using and selling drugs, then I dropped out of college and ran away from New York. After many years of living on the run, I finally saved up enough money to buy a ticket home."

Alia thought about this explanation for a minute.

"You have returned home in shame, Muqtar, not in victory. I am very sorry for that, Muqtar, very sorry."

Muqtar hung his head.

"Yes, I am ashamed of myself, Alia, quite ashamed. But I have a plan that will make a lot of money; enough money to build a school in the village for girls."

Alia was skeptical.

"You, Muqtar, who has come home with no education and no career, have a plan that will make you a lot of money, huh? What about our plans, do you remember?" She reproached Muqtar, recalling how she had wasted her whole life waiting on him. And now here she was, blind and a burden—not a catch. She continued to hector him. "Surely such a plan has to involve something illegal or immoral or both. Given what you just told me, I'm sure it is both."

Turning in her chair to face him, and not believing him, Alia demanded, "So tell me, Muqtar, what is this fantastic plan of yours?"

Muqtar was torn whether to tell Alia the truth or not. He decided another half-truth was the way to go.

"I know where a container was buried just before the end of World War II that is most valuable."

"Most valuable, huh? How is it that you, a foreigner on the run, came to find out about buried treasure? Surely, you must be kidding." She scoffed.

"No, Alia, I am not kidding, however it could be dangerous for you to know the details. But believe me, what I am telling you is true."

Alia turned her head to the side.

"Oh yeah, right. The last time I believed you was when I believed that you would return in five years from America and marry me. And look what came of that promise," Alia raised up her arms, hesitated, and then spat out, "Nothing!"

Muqtar was silent, unable to deny Alia's words. He had let down everyone—his family, friends, Alia, and himself. He felt small as a heavy wave of shame washed over him. He took deep breaths, but the soil of his tainted past would not leave him.

"You're right, Alia. I'm a sorry piece of shit," Muqtar admitted. "But I swear I'll bring lots of money to the village one day."

"Money, Muqtar? Do you think that will fix everything?" Alia admonished, confirming her disbelief.

Muqtar struggled to explain. "Maybe not, but money is how we men value ourselves. It's all I have left—my hope for redemption. But enough about me. What about you?"

Alia, speaking slowly, began recounting her story.

Alia recounted her story: In the spring of 2021, while walking near the caves north of the village, she saw a group of armed men speaking Afghani arguing over an American soldier they had captured. Suddenly, two helicopters appeared, firing missiles, while American soldiers ambushed the Pashtuns. An explosion knocked her unconscious, and when she awoke, she was blind from shrapnel.

An American soldier, speaking Urdu, told her she had crossed over into Afghanistan but that she could regain her sight if taken to an American hospital. Alia knew the likelihood of that was slim. *No one here would raise money for me, a mere girl,* she commented, certain of her value. *I'll live the rest of my life blind and dependent on my mother, and when she's gone, I'll take my life.*

Muqtar, overwhelmed with grief and melted by her plight, felt responsible for her condition. He thought about how he had failed to return home to marry her, knowing that if he had, she would not be blind now.

"It's getting late," Alia announced, standing up. Muqtar silently admired her exquisite beauty and, while looking at her closely and despite her blindness, her eyes were most beautiful. He kept his thoughts to himself.

They began walking back to the bakery.

"Tell me, Alia, what of my family? My parents and my five brothers?"

Alia stopped walking.

"Oh, that's right. You have just returned so you don't know. Your father passed away about three years ago. He had some kind of blockage, and with no doctors in the village, he died before they could transport him to a hospital. But really, he died of a broken heart, and you know why." Muqtar knew exactly what she meant.

"Your mother is still alive," Alia continued. "She lives with your youngest brother and his family. I am sad to tell you that three of your brothers were killed in the recent drone strike that destroyed the building next to our bakery, and your oldest brother was fighting the Americans in Afghanistan before they left."

"What? My brother Rasheed is part of the Pashtun militants?"

"Yes, he became militarized some years ago when the drones from America began blowing up the cars and trucks that our friends across the border were driving. Many of the young men from the village left to fight the Americans."

"Does anyone have any idea where my brother Rasheed is?"

"No, not as far as I know. Perhaps still fighting somewhere, even though the Americans are gone. Your youngest brother may know. Oh yes, one more thing. As I said, three of your siblings were killed just a week ago when the American drones shot missiles that hit the village. You probably saw the crater to the left of the bakery."

"Yes, I did see the crater where my family home used to stand," replied Muqtar in a sad, resigned tone of voice, now having confirmed that the missile strike he had seen on the television had indeed showed the remains of the home where Muqtar had grown up.

Muqtar felt responsible for that too, while his shame turned to anger as he thought about his family's plight and Alia's suffering. His resolve to retrieve the bomb and bring wealth to his village, while exacting revenge on the Americans, solidified.

Determined, Muqtar decided to contact the man in Islamabad, whose name the Imam had given him. The man had the resources and connections he needed. But first, he would visit his mother and brother before heading to Islamabad.

As they walked back to the bakery, Muqtar reflected on the life he could have had if he had stuck to the original plan—an engineer, married, respected, with children. Alia was lost in her own thoughts, thinking about what could have been and now what would never be. They reached the bakery, and Alia could sense Muqtar staring at her.

Muqtar spoke: "I swear to you on my father's soul that I will avenge your loss of vision on those who perpetuated this crime. I swear it. I will also avenge the loss of my brothers' lives upon those who fired those missiles. I swear it."

Alia said nothing for a moment, then she replied.

"No amount of vengeance will restore my vision. No acts of vengeance will bring back to life those whose lives were lost. Vengeance will only bring the loss of your soul and perhaps your life, too. For one who is full of anger and hatred becomes consumed by it and sees nothing but it. If that is the path you have chosen, then walk it, but you will forever walk it alone."

Muqtar listened to Alia's words, knowing that pursuing vengeance would consume him, but the loss of his brothers and Alia's blindness fueled his rage.

As Alia and her mother entered the bakery, Muqtar turned to visit the site of his family's former home, anxious to see the damage from the missile strike. They parted in silence, the bond between them broken.

Muqtar thought about arranging another time to see Alia but thought the better of it. *Perhaps now is not the time to reopen old wounds any further.* He turned his focus to the mission—the bomb and his quest for revenge.

When he reached the ruins of his childhood home, memories flooded back, but the house was gone. Only a water-filled crater remained, a stark reminder of the chaos and loss. Muqtar stood there, overwhelmed by the senseless destruction and the unanswered question: why had his family been targeted?

Muqtar realized he might never find the answer, but he was determined to make those responsible suffer more than his family had. *A hydrogen bomb in Times Square,* he believed, *would dwarf the pain of 9/11 and balance the scales of loss.*

With most of his family dead and Alia blind, there was nothing left for Muqtar in the village. He decided to stay one more night, visit his mother in the morning, and then on to Islamabad to set his plan in motion. He stood in silence, his gaze distant, as if the world around him had blurred into nothingness. His hands rested motionless by his sides, limp, a hollow ache spreading through him, leaving him numb and adrift.

Feeling completely lost and empty, Muqtar resolved to sacrifice everything, even his own life, to exact his revenge.

CHAPTER 35

Alex was worried as he packed to return to Washington from St. Louis, dreading the criticism he'd likely face for his report on a possible Tokyo Bay bombing conspiracy. His investigation had led nowhere—three suspects, one silent and two gone. He knew the chances of getting approval for a trip to Japan were slim because he had no corroboration for his suspicions. But at least he wanted to track down where the grandson and nurse's aide were staying in Tokyo.

Arriving in DC around 4:00 p.m., Alex decided against going home and headed straight to the office. Inside the secure area, he felt at ease. Computer research was his strength, not field-work. After logging in, he typed in Joshua's name and found that he had arrived in Tokyo 18 hours earlier.

Alex ran a search for Michael Brown and found he had recently arrived in Islamabad, having no prior international travel, which struck him as odd. A deeper search revealed only one trip—four years ago, from New York to St. Louis. Even more strange, Brown's driver's license and passport history showed no prior records before age 20. That fit with his earlier finding that Michael Brown had not existed prior to 2019.

Alex's research skills kicked in as he found an address for Brown in New York City. Digging further, he discovered that Muqtar Ashadi was a former NYU student with ties to criminal investigations—drug sales and a homicide.

The murder victim was Allen Brown, a man with a criminal history, whose younger brother, Michael, had drowned in 2003. Muqtar Ashadi had also been an associate of Allen Brown. This all fit with the oddities Alex had observed in the nurse's aide's accent and behavior. The police file listed Muqtar Ashadi as a person of interest, but the file also showed that he had never been interviewed.

Alex considered the possibility that Muqtar, under the alias Michael Brown, might be a plant in the U.S., but it seemed more likely he was a Pakistani student who got involved in drugs. Alex speculated that Muqtar had killed the drug dealer Allen Brown, assumed his deceased brother's identity, and traveled west. Tracing Muqtar's NYU application, Alex learned he came from a village in northern Pakistan near Afghanistan, which had recently been hit by an accidental missile strike that killed many civilians. Alex wondered if Muqtar harbored a desire for revenge related to the strike.

Though the connection to the Tokyo bomb plot seemed tenuous, Alex couldn't dismiss the possibility that although Muqtar was probably not part of the Meister plan he may have overheard something about it in the nursing home. His final search revealed that after Muqtar's departure from New York, he came to St. Louis and no solid links to the Meisters were found, leaving Alex with more questions than answers.

Alex, feeling both stymied and satisfied, confirmed that Joshua was in Tokyo at the Hilton and placed tracers on his and Michael Brown's passports to track their movements. He also checked the set up for automatic recording for Joshua and the Colonel's cell phone numbers, along with the number of a nurse from the retirement home who was likely Muqtar's wife.

As Alex spun the top on his desk that defied gravity, he considered his next move. He could wait and see what came across the computer, ask for permission to go to Japan, or fund a trip there himself. Waiting didn't feel right to him—he wanted to act now to prevent a potential global crisis.

Alex again was certain his bosses wouldn't authorize a trip to Japan based on the limited information he had accumulated, so he again ruled out that option. Instead, he decided to pursue option 2 and request an immediate vacation, despite knowing it would raise eyebrows at the CIA. The weekend passed as he packed, buying fishing gear to support his cover story. He wrestled with the idea of going against protocol if his request was denied but ultimately decided not to jeopardize his pension. On Monday, Alex wrote his report, filling all four of the required four pages with pablum, downplaying his concerns to avoid scrutiny, and concluded there was no further action needed.

Taking a break from the stilted writing exercise for a minute, Alex accessed his inbox. The CIA inbox was where all the agents received emails, but it also was where the computer would download any telephone conversations, texts, or emails the agent was monitoring. He sifted through the mountains of useless emails and came upon another recorded conversation from Joshua's telephone.

Alex quivered with excitement. *I got you now, you son of a bitch,* he said to himself. He relished the thought of pounding sand up Joshua's ass and the old Colonel's too. What additional nuggets of information did this conversation contain, he wondered. He queued up the recording and sat up on the edge of his chair, anticipating. He listened closely, but didn't understand what they were saying because they were speaking Chinese. *Shit.* He routed the conversation through the translator on the computer.

"Hello, Mei Lei, it is Joshua. How is it going?"

"Fine, J. Why are you calling me?" the female voice replied curtly.

"Uh, sorry to bother you by calling, but I was feeling a bit bored and I thought I would reach out to you and check on status."

The female voice softened a little bit.

"The status is the same as it was two days ago. The ship will be in Japan in two days. She just left Hong Kong yesterday," reported the female voice.

"Oh, okay. I'm sorry for interrupting your workday. I'm just a bit anxious and like I said a minute ago, I have cabin fever."

"Cabin fever, J? What is cabin fever?"

"Oh. Okay, sorry. Cabin fever means a person is going stir crazy from being bored. Stir crazy and cabin fever mean the same thing," Joshua explained.

Silence for a few seconds.

"Okay, I understand. I will be back in Tokyo at about the same time the ship arrives. See you then, okay?"

"Okay, Mei Lei. Thank you. See you then."

Click. Alex's mind was in high gear now. *Who the fuck was Mei Lei and what fucking ship was going to Tokyo from Hong Kong?* Alex had to know. He clicked and clicked until he found Mei Lei's telephone number, her full name, and the name of the company associated with the phone. Alex discovered that she was the vice president of an ocean salvage operation based in Hong Kong that was the family business.

Alex now knew that a salvage ship from Hong Kong had left for Tokyo the day before, raising questions about its true purpose. Was it carrying explosives under the guise of salvage? Alex clapped his hands to his temples, anxiously looking around the room, searching the ethers for answers. He was stymied, not exactly knowing what the new information meant, if anything. The info certainly wasn't enough to get approval for a trip to Japan. He needed more information to justify going, but didn't have it. He calculated the ship's estimated arrival in Tokyo in about two days, making his decision to take vacation the only viable choice to investigate further.

Alex was unclear as to the purpose of the Chinese salvage ship heading to Tokyo, but he was certain something significant related to national security was about to happen in Tokyo Bay. With no other leads, Alex turned his focus to the Colonel. He dug into the Colonel's history, starting with his early love for flying, his rapid progression in the Army Air Force, and his unexpected assignment to be a bombardier instead of a pilot after Pearl Harbor. Alex wondered if the Colonel harbored resentment over this, though his family history showed no signs of personal loss to the Japanese.

Alex took a chance and emailed his superiors requesting a week's vacation starting Tuesday, planning to tell his fishing-enthusiast supervisor that a friend's canceled trip allowed him to take his place. With approval likely coming, Alex was set to go to Japan to ostensibly do some fly-fishing and enjoy the cherry blossoms, all while actually pursuing his investigation.

.

CHAPTER 36

Muqtar had $15,000 left—a small fortune in Pakistan. It was blood money, earned from killing an American, money he hadn't touched since fleeing New York. Now, he would use it to kill more Americans—people who deserved to die for what their country had done to his. His mother cried when he saw her, tears for her son's failure to become the man he could have been. She cried for the loss of her three sons and her husband.

The losses of his brothers and of Alia's eyesight stoked the burning fire of revenge that raged inside him. He wanted to cause blood to be shed and tears to flow as he filled his black heart with a plan. He bought a phone and dialed the number the Imam in America had given him. On the third ring, a male voice answered in Urdu. "Hello, who is calling?"

"Hello, this is Muqtar Ashadi. I am calling for Ali."

"This is Ali. How did you get this number?"

"I was given the number by Imam Omar. He said I could contact you if I needed any help."

"Oh, is that right? So exactly what kind of help do you need?"

"I need to talk to you in person, if you would be so kind."

"That can be arranged. Where are you now?"

"I am in my village in the mountains. I have the means to travel to wherever it would be convenient to meet."

"Okay. That is fine. You can come to Karachi. I will be there tomorrow. Can you make it to Karachi by tomorrow?"

"Yes, yes. I can most certainly travel to Karachi and be there by tomorrow afternoon."

"All right. Fine. Call me at this number when you get to Karachi," were Ali's final words, then click, the phone went silent.

Muqtar did his best to set aside thoughts of his American wife and family. He had a goal and a plan, with no time for distractions. His next stop: Karachi, where he hoped to find support for his trip to Japan. That evening, he boarded a bus, embarking on an 18-hour journey. After three bus changes and little sleep, he focused on how to present his plan to his connection. He needed men to help him in Japan, knowing he couldn't succeed alone.

As for the specifics of the mission, Muqtar had little—just a driver's license photograph of the American who had run into him, what he had overheard, and the coordinates from the Google Map. But that was enough; the prize—a U.S.-made hydrogen bomb—was worth the risk.

Muqtar wondered if he could convince others of the plan's chances of success. With four hours left before reaching Karachi, he tried—and failed—to sleep, his mind dancing with fear and excitement.

When the bus arrived at the Karachi station, Muqtar, unfamiliar with the city, followed the smell of food to a street-side restaurant. He ordered Lahore beef Karachi and fished for a cigarette, only to realize he was out of Marlboros. Settling for a pack of generic cigarettes from a vendor, he grimaced at the taste. *Note to self: Find a store selling American cigarettes.*

The city's vastness overwhelmed him. While he'd managed in New York, Karachi was different—chaotic, very few street signs, and bustling in a way he hadn't expected.

Muqtar devoured his food, recalling he hadn't eaten since boarding the bus. Two hours remained before making the call. A fleeting fear crossed his mind—*what if no one answered this time?* He pushed it aside too, knowing his trip could be wasted, but he had no other choice.

Ali was his only option—someone with connections in Japan and a shared hatred for Americans. Muqtar had no connections, only a common enemy. Checking his watch, he felt the time had come and dialed the number.

One ring.

Two rings.

Three rings.

Four rings.

Nothing.

Muqtar hung up the phone. Perhaps he had misdialed the number. That was impossible because he had simply redialed the number from the day before. *What the fuck?*

Muqtar banged his fist on the table. *Fuck,* he shouted in English. *No answer and a 20-hour bus ride for nothing. Now what? Shit.*

Ring. Muqtar's phone rang.

Ring.

"Hello, this is Muqtar. Who is calling?"

"It is me, Ali. Sorry I did not answer when you called a few minutes ago."

Muqtar felt a huge wave of relief flow through his body, and his tensed-up shoulders relaxed. *Yes! He had successfully made contact again. Yes!*

"Thank you for calling me back, Ali. I am near the downtown bus station."

"Okay, yes. Stay there, Muqtar. Someone will be by in about

30 minutes to collect you. What are you wearing?"

Muqtar described his attire and sat back to wait. Parts one and two of his plan had been accomplished. He had made the trip to Karachi and he had a meeting set up with someone who could help, who might help, who would hopefully help.

After a short while, Muqtar heard a car horn beeping and looked to his left. On the street a car had stopped, and a man was waving his hand out of the window, gesturing for Muqtar to come over.

Muqtar quickly rose to his feet and hustled over to the waiting car.

"Hello, I am Muqtar. Are you here to collect me?"

"Yes, yes," announced the man in the car. "Come and get in."

Muqtar sat in the front seat and began talking to the driver. Just two days back home and his Urdu was as good as if he had never left.

"Where are you taking me?" Muqtar wanted to know.

"I am taking you to meet Ali," was the response.

"How long will it take us to get to where he is?" followed up Muqtar.

"Not that long, sir," responded the driver, who shot an irritated look at Muqtar. "Why? Are you in a hurry or something?"

Now feeling a bit embarrassed, Muqtar meekly replied, "No, no, not at all. Just a bit curious."

The driver turned his head back to look at the traffic and said nothing more. Muqtar stared out the window. People, people everywhere.

After about 20 minutes, the driver pulled over and stopped. The driver pointed at a building and announced, "Ali is in there."

Realizing there was no point in speaking to the driver anymore, Muqtar exited the car and climbed the three steps to the building.

Before he could knock, the front door opened inward and a voice invited him to enter. The room was dimly lit, and Muqtar's eyes took a few seconds to adjust. He could make out four or five men sitting on the floor cross-legged, so he sat down too and waited.

"So, you are Muqtar Ashadi from a village in the mountains. Is that right?"

Muqtar recognized the voice as that of Ali's, so he turned his head in the direction of the sound and spoke.

"Yes, I am Muqtar Ashadi from the Shimsal Valley."

Muqtar wanted to continue talking but thought the better of speaking, given his conversation with the driver.

"Why are you here, Muqtar Ashadi?"

His eyes now having adjusted to the dimness, Muqtar told the story.

"I am here because I know where an unexploded U.S.-made hydrogen bomb is located and I want to go get it." Then he waited.

"There are many U.S.-made, unexploded hydrogen bombs, Muqtar."

Muqtar explained further.

"The bomb I am talking about is not within the U.S. military's control. It sits at the bottom of Tokyo Bay; lost since World War II."

Muqtar felt the men lean in close.

"Go on, Muqtar. Tell us the story," urged Ali.

"All right. After the U.S. dropped the atomic bombs on Hiroshima on 6 August 1945, then the second on Nagasaki on 9 August 1945, they had a third bomb, a hydrogen bomb 100 times more powerful than were the first two atomic bombs, that they attempted to drop on the Emperor's Palace on 12 August."

"Attempted, Muqtar? What do you mean by attempted?"

"Well, the Americans flew toward Tokyo with the hydrogen bomb on board, but before they reached their target, the bomb was dropped early and it landed in Tokyo Bay."

"So, the bomb never exploded," surmised Ali. "Why did it not explode?"

"That I do not know, sir. But I do know—I am certain—that the hydrogen bomb is sitting at the bottom of Tokyo Bay waiting to be recovered."

"And how can you be so certain, Muqtar, that the bomb is still there?"

"Because I overheard the American colonel who was on the bombing mission talk about it with his grandson, who is now in Japan trying to retrieve the bomb for himself."

"So the United States government is in Tokyo trying to retrieve the bomb? Is that right, Muqtar?"

"No, no. Not at all. The American government is not involved. The grandson is doing it on his own, trying to recover the bomb while keeping it a secret from his own government and from the Japanese, too."

"Well then, what is the American going to do with the bomb if he successfully retrieves it, Muqtar?"

"I am not exactly sure, but from what I overheard, I believe the grandson intends to take the bomb far out to sea and dispose of it."

The men in the room were taken aback by the revelation. Muqtar stayed quiet.

"What do you want from us?"

"To join me in the mission."

"Muqtar, could you leave us alone for a moment? We need to

talk amongst ourselves. Is your visa still valid?"

As Muqtar stood to leave the room, he replied, "Yes, Ali. My visa is still valid. I can easily travel to Japan." Then he walked out.

A few minutes later, Muqtar was invited to come back inside. Ali spoke: "We have decided to go along with your plan. We think it is a very long shot and very likely to fail for a variety of reasons, not the least of which is the very strong likelihood that there is no longer a hydrogen bomb at the bottom of Tokyo Bay, if there ever was one. Nonetheless, we think it is worth the risk to check it out, and we are going to send four men with you to Japan. When do you want to leave?"

"Tomorrow, Ali. The sooner, the better."

"Okay. Be at this location by 0700 tomorrow morning," ordered Ali, handing Muqtar a note. With that, the men in the room exited out the back, and Muqtar exited out the front.

Muqtar rented a small room in a locally owned, nondescript hotel in Karachi that did not have air conditioning, exhausted from the journey. He collapsed on the bed fully clothed. The next morning, he awoke covered in sweat to the call for prayers. Trying to be more faithful, he knelt and prayed, hoping for a sign of blessing for his mission, but none came. He felt guilty asking Allah for success in his plan to retrieve a hydrogen bomb for revenge rather than redemption.

Afterward, Muqtar left for a café near his meeting spot. The temperature was rising, signaling another hot day. He wondered how he'd blend in Japan, a place he'd never visited, and what story he'd tell customs. Checking his Pakistani visa, he was relieved to find it valid for two more years.

Muqtar heard his name and saw five men approaching. He stood to greet them, with Ali being the fifth. They discussed the plan to go to Japan, and the group seemed convinced it had merit.

Muqtar then asked, "What reason can we give Japanese customs for being there?"

One man offered, "My brother buys Japanese cars in Tokyo and ships them to Pakistan. We'll say we're going to look at cars to bring back. Very believable."

Muqtar nodded his head.

"That sounds like a very legitimate cover story. I doubt the Japanese authorities will even give us a second look. But I worry a little bit about so many of us showing up at the same time."

"No need to worry, Muqtar. The group will go on two separate flights. You and Abdul will leave today at noon, and the rest of the men will leave at 6:00 p.m.," planned Ali, pointing first at Abdul then at the other three.

"Will there be any issue that we are paying cash for our plane tickets? Will that create any scrutiny for us?" queried Muqtar.

"No, no, not at all. No need to worry about that, Muqtar," again answered Ali, placing his hand on Muqtar's cheek. "The tickets are being purchased on my mother's company credit card for you and Abdul and on my credit card for the other three. Not to worry," assured Ali.

Muqtar felt a sense of relief. The trip to Japan was organized, but how to find and acquire the bomb remained completely unknown, a flaw in the plan that made him nervous. A failed plan in Tokyo could cost him more than just his reputation—it could mean death or capture for him and his men.

Despite the risks, Muqtar had no choice but to press forward; the fire inside driving him. This was his chance for revenge, perhaps the only one he'd ever have to exact justice and make the Americans think twice about their interference with his people.

He announced, "I'm going to pack and head to the airport. Dress in Western clothes to blend in."

The men agreed, and Ali embraced Muqtar. "I pray for your success. If you succeed, we'll have a powerful bargaining chip to avenge our dead and strike back at the Americans."

Muqtar nodded, reflecting on how this mission reminded him of his drug-dealing days in New York—no one to call for help if things went wrong. With that thought, he bid his group farewell and headed to the airport. *Tokyo, here I come.*

CHAPTER 37

Alex woke up at 4:45 a.m., five hours before his flight to Los Angeles, then on to Tokyo. He had planned to sleep longer but knew it was pointless now. After a quick shower, he focused on his plan for Tokyo: stay at the Hilton where Joshua Meister was staying, stake it out, and follow Joshua when he appeared. Everything was set. Alex adjusted the thermostat, then called Uber on to the airport.

At the gate, he showed his boarding pass and made his way to seat 34B. An older man took the window seat and a young college student sat by the aisle. Alex exchanged pleasantries, then buried himself in *The Art of War*. As the plane took off, he reflected on the upcoming mission, trying to prepare for the difficult battle ahead.

A troubling thought crossed his mind—if the bomb was re-covered by Joshua, the U.S. government might think he was in-volved. The book's passage about ancient Chinese punishments for treason made him nervous. While he doubted the U.S. would chop off his head, he couldn't be sure what would happen if he were convicted of or even accused of treason.

Alex reflected on the U.S. government's history of silencing those who could expose sensitive information, like Lee Harvey Oswald and Sirhan Sirhan. It wasn't a comforting thought at the start of a mission he had undertaken out of love for America, even if it meant risking his life. *No need to be dramatic,* Alex cautioned himself. *The worst that could happen would be for me to lose my job and my pension. Ouchie! That is enough.*

Having landed at LAX, Alex assessed his surroundings, relieved to see no one watching. The first leg was over, and now he was on to Japan.

Once in Japan, Alex had no concrete plan beyond surveillance at the Hilton, where he hoped Joshua was still staying. He felt exposed, going out on this renegade mission solo, having not worked in the field for over a decade and lacking a support team. Fatigued, Alex fell asleep on the flight to Japan, waking just in time for the meal. He ate it all and resisted asking for a second.

At Tokyo International Airport, Alex felt disoriented, unsure of his next steps or if the CIA even had an office there. After taking a cab to his hotel, he called Joshua's room, hanging up before it was answered. He was certain he was on the right track now—Joshua was still staying there. After organizing his room, Alex headed to the hotel lobby, which was large and had multiple entry and exit points, making surveillance difficult. He needed to monitor Joshua without being seen, which posed a challenge.

Alex chose a seat with a clear view of the elevators and a partial view of the front door. Putting on a Pittsburgh Pirates cap, he opened his laptop and pretended to work. It was 10:00 a.m. local time, and he expected Joshua to appear soon. *What am I going to do if I see him,* considered Alex. *I can't arrest him, can't do anything really.*

Alex decided that if he saw something amiss that was solid, he would notify the local authorities and let them take over, thus protecting himself by so doing. Alex congratulated himself on his brilliant plan. However, unbeknownst to Alex, Joshua had already left the hotel earlier that morning, so seeing and possibly following Joshua was not going to happen.

As Alex waited, jet lag began to set in. Despite the exhaustion, he decided to stick it out until at least 1:00 p.m. The hours passed slowly, with Alex alternating between watching his screen and scanning the lobby. Finally, at 1:00 p.m., he returned to his room and collapsed into bed.

Muqtar felt pretty at ease on the plane, though he realized he was fully Westernized and could never return to a remote life on the Afghanistan border. He was focused on his mission and speculated that Karachi would be his future home.

As he waited to board, Muqtar stood in line with his new acquaintance Abdul, though they behaved as strangers. Once onboard, he flipped through *Road & Track*, dreaming of owning a Ferrari or Lamborghini. His mind wandered to his financial future, noting his limited job skills—driving a cab, working as a nurse's aide, and selling drugs—which wouldn't bring wealth. He then fantasized about the money he could make by selling a hydrogen bomb.

He first considered using the bomb to avenge his family by detonating it in the U.S. but also thought about selling it for millions. Recruiting a crew to retrieve the bomb was a huge struggle, so the logistics of transporting it to the U.S., figuring out how to detonate it, and actually doing so made him check his own bullshit. *Stay in your lane,* was what his internal voice recommended.

Nonetheless, the internal conflict weighed on him—revenge

versus profit. While part of him wanted to cause mass destruction, he also remembered his family and the struggles they were facing in St. Louis. Muqtar quickly pushed those thoughts aside, again convincing himself that he had to focus on his mission. Muqtar realized that if he had stayed behind in the U.S., he'd be locked up by now, probably facing murder charges.

Muqtar snapped out of his thoughts when the pilot's voice came over the intercom. He had a plan: follow the American who had the coordinates for the bomb's location in Tokyo Bay and steal it once it was recovered. Muqtar wasn't sure how the American would lift the bomb, but he assumed the extraction process would be difficult, and that the American had to have help.

Muqtar wondered what the American would do with the bomb—whether he planned to use it to extort the U.S. government or to cause destruction somewhere. Muqtar couldn't answer that, but he knew his own motives were very dark.

Twelve hours later, Muqtar and his team passed through immigration in Tokyo without drawing attention. They checked into rooms at the downtown Hilton, not knowing Joshua and Alex were also guests there, blending in as tourists/business travelers. Once settled, they gathered in the lobby, boarded a van Muqtar had rented, and headed to Tokyo Bay to begin their mission.

Once there, the group casually walked along looking at the container ships and the sights in general. Muqtar adjusted his telephone so the GPS would show their location in latitude and longitude. He looked out into the bay and tried to imagine where the line would intersect. No use; just open water.

Muqtar gathered the men to talk.

"Guys, look. I have the coordinates where I believe the hydrogen bomb landed in the bay. I have done research on the size of the earliest atomic bombs and of the hydrogen bombs that the U.S. designed and built. This bomb, which was built several years before the U.S. announced that a hydrogen bomb had been built, will be very large in size."

"How big is it?" asked one of the men.

"My best estimate is that it is around 3 to 4 meters long, cylindrical in shape, and about 2 meters in diameter."

"How much does it weigh?" another wanted to know.

"I'm not sure. My best guess is it weighs somewhere between 4,000 and 5,000 kilos," replied Muqtar.

The men were flabbergasted as they involuntarily drew back.

"Did you say 4 to 5,000 kilos, Muqtar?"

"Yes, 4 to 5,000 approximately."

"How are we going to lift such a heavy thing? We are only five men. There is no way we can lift anything weighing near that much, Muqtar. You have wasted our time and money with such a stupid plan," the men were disgusted.

"Hold on, hold on. We are not going to pick it up by hand, men. There are machines for that."

"Oh, yes," one of them shot back. "Where are we going to get such a machine? At the Toyota dealership?" was the derisive question delivered to Muqtar.

"Not to worry, men. Calm down," assuaged Muqtar. "We are not going to actually dig up the bomb from wherever it is stuck in the mud of Tokyo Bay. We are going to watch and wait for when the American gets here to do the excavation. Then once he retrieves it, we will snatch the bomb from him."

The men began to nod in understanding.

"So, once the American has retrieved the bomb, then our plan is to seize it from him."

"Exactly," specified Muqtar. "That is exactly our plan. We are going to post up here every day and every night until we see some unusual activity in the bay. Then we will strike as a unit and liberate the bomb from the American."

The men began to smile.

"We like the plan now, Muqtar. Good job. That will work," they communicated to one another.

"But Muqtar, we have no weapons, no guns, no nothing. How will we overpower the American?"

"Good question, Abdul. I have thought of that, too. Now this may sound strange, but some of you may know that no one except the police and the Yakuza have guns in Japan. And we are not friends with the police nor the Japanese mob. So," Muqtar continued, "we are going to buy souvenir knives and swords and use the element of surprise to overpower the American."

The group's mouths collectively dropped open.

"What? That sounds incredibly stupid, Muqtar, and two things come to mind in particular. First, none of us have ever used a sword, and second, Americans always have guns. So what happens if the American has guns?"

Muqtar thought for a minute.

"First of all, I find it unlikely that the American will have a gun because of what I just said. But if he does, we will have to rely on the advantage of surprise and hopefully catch him off guard, overpower him, and accomplish our goal that way," imagined Muqtar.

The men began murmuring amongst themselves, discontented by this latest revelation.

"Muqtar, we think it is most unlikely that the American will be alone. The bomb is too big and heavy for one man to maneuver, and as you have described it, the bomb is too big for

20 men to carry. So we are worried that the American will have a crew as big as our crew of five men; probably bigger. At the same time, Muqtar, if we confront them with Japanese samurai swords, they will not be scared. They will laugh at us."

Muqtar had no answer for this point on lack of adequate weaponry.

"That is a risk we will have to take unless someone knows a way to get guns smuggled to us here in Japan."

"I may know a way to get guns," spoke up Abdul. "My cousin, the car dealer, might know someone who can get us some guns."

"Okay, that's good news," responded Muqtar. "Leave now and check it out. The rest of us will continue to walk around like tourists to get a picture of how the bay looks to better be able to tell how it changes after the American arrives. But be sure," cautioned Muqtar, "to not disclose the reason why you want guns, for if the Yakuza find out our true purpose, they may kill us to get the bomb for themselves."

Off went Abdul. Muqtar turned to the remaining three men and spoke: "Okay, let's split up and begin walking around, taking in the sights while taking some photos. Be on the lookout for any Americans because the American may already be here. Is everybody's phone charged up?"

They all nodded and then split up.

Muqtar was right—Joshua was already in Tokyo, but he wasn't at the bay. After leaving the hotel early, he returned around 11:00 a.m., now anxiously awaiting a call from Mei Lei about the salvage ship's arrival. Bored and scared, Joshua felt trapped, knowing someone was likely searching for him. To keep a low profile, he began using the service elevator to avoid the lobby.

That morning, Joshua had seen the man from the photo Grandfather had sent to him sitting in the lobby, watching everything. Shocked and paranoid, he wondered if his plan had been compromised. *Should he confront the man or change hotels?* After retreating to his room, Joshua paced, considering abandoning the mission. But he decided against it—Mei Lei was involved, and the ship was on its way. He comforted himself with the thought that if the agent knew his room number, he would've already showed up. The agent was likely just doing reconnaissance; no doubt hoping to see Joshua.

During his surveillance, Joshua remembered the CIA agent's name: Alex Lozano. As he watched him, Lozano didn't make any calls or engage with anyone, which gave Joshua some comfort, but his anxiety remained high. Then, a text from Mei Lei confirmed the salvage ship would arrive the next evening, under the cover of darkness—a welcome development to avoid attention.

Joshua debated his next move: confront Lozano, leave through the lobby to see who was following, or sneak out through the kitchen. Exhausted from the stress, he decided to retreat to his room and take a nap.

Unbeknownst to Joshua, Alex was whipped from the travel and time change, and so soon after Joshua returned to his room, Alex had headed to his room, too.

Muqtar and his men spent the rest of the day surveilling Tokyo Bay, each taking cell phone pictures and mentally imprinting what was where in the bay. Abdul headed back downtown and called his cousin, who was in the Japanese car export business. After they exchanged pleasantries, Abdul obtained directions to his cousin's place and took a cab over there.

"Salutations, Abdul. God is good. How are you, cousin," greeted Noor.

"Salutations, Noor. God is good. How are you and your family," returned Abdul.

"Life is very good here, Abdul. I do not miss the heat and humidity from home, but I do miss our food."

Abdul laughed. "Of course, but you don't miss the madness of Karachi, cousin; no one does. But the smells of the food cooking everywhere on the street cannot be duplicated."

"Yes, that's true," agreed Noor, lifting his eyes to the left as he recalled the sights, sounds, and smells of home. "What brings you to Japan anyway? Are you looking for a car?"

"No, cousin, I am not looking for a car. I am looking for a bomb that was dropped near the end of World War II here in Japan," began Abdul.

"A bomb, really?" asked Noor. "Who cares about an old bomb?"

"I do, because it has some very modern technology inside that is most valuable. Four companions of mine have come here with me to find it and take it back home so that it can be examined and used somehow."

Noor was incredulous. "You're saying this bomb that was made more than 75 years ago has technology in it that is valuable today?"

"Yes, Noor, most valuable," assured Abdul. "And we are very serious about recovering it and taking it home."

Noor stared at Abdul for a moment and could tell Abdul was

not kidding. Then he spoke again: "OK, Abdul, what can I do to help you in this endeavor? Do you need a car or money or what?"

"I need guns, cousin. Guns because there are others who are coming or who may already be here who also seek to recover the bomb," was Abdul's explanation.

Noor was taken aback. "Guns? In Japan? No one except the police have guns in Japan, Abdul. No one."

"Are you sure, Noor? Someone must have a gun because I saw on the television where there was a shootout between rival Yakuza gangs."

Noor scoffed at Abdul's comment. "OK, sure. The Yakuza have guns, too, but you would have better luck getting guns from the police than from the Yakuza."

Abdul was discouraged by this response but was not giving up yet. "Surely, Noor, you must know someone who has some kind of underworld connection, don't you," pleaded Abdul.

Noor was thinking. "You know, Abdul, there is a Pakistani guy who buys cars from me from time to time—strictly high-end stuff. I think he may be involved in bringing drugs to Japan. If anybody would know how to get a gun, it would be him."

Abdul became excited. "Noor, I need five guns with ammunition, not just one. And I will pay a premium price for them."

"OK, OK. Well you may be in luck because he is supposed to come by today to pick up that luxury sedan over there," said Noor, pointing to a big, black four-door Mercedes.

"Excellent, Noor, excellent. Here is my cell phone number. Call me if your customer can help us out. And if he asks why we want them, tell him it is to take revenge against the American imperialists who bomb our villages and kill our women and children."

Noor thought for another second. "So the guns are not to be used against the Japanese people or the government here in Tokyo, is that correct, Abdul?"

"Yes, Noor, that is correct. We need the guns to protect ourselves against the Americans who are trying to retrieve the bomb for themselves; nothing against the Japanese people. In fact, once we get the bomb out of the country, a great threat to the Japanese people will be removed."

Noor's eyes widened with Abdul's last comment. *What on earth would be in a World War II relic that was so dangerous?* But Noor knew better than to ask any more questions because he did not want to know.

"Let's see what I can do, cousin. I will call you tonight."

As Abdul made his way back to the hotel, he pondered the likelihood of success of the plan, with or without guns. He realized the Americans would likely be prepared for any threat, especially given their affection for guns. He questioned whether he was willing to risk his life and freedom for the mission.

Once there, Abdul went straight to Muqtar's room and told him the news.

"Outstanding work, Abdul. You well could have found the answer to our dilemma."

"I am hoping so," was Abdul's response.

"When will you find out, Abdul?"

"Supposed to hear back from my cousin sometime tonight, Muqtar."

"That is most wonderful news, Abdul. With our own guns, we can surprise the Americans and hijack the bomb from them once they have retrieved it from the bottom of the bay."

"I agree, Muqtar, that should be our overall plan. But do you have a plan for how we position ourselves to surprise the Americans?"

"No, not yet, Abdul, because I don't know how the Americans plan to pull off the salvage operation. Obviously, boats will be involved given that the bomb is buried in Tokyo Bay. Once we see what they are doing and how they are doing it, we will make our plan and strike quickly. Hopefully, without gunfire."

Abdul nodded his head in understanding. "All right then, Muqtar. Nothing to do now but wait."

"Right, Abdul. Now we wait."

Joshua woke groggily from his nap at 5:00 p.m. and cautiously checked the hallway before heading to the elevator. On the mezzanine, he spotted a group of men in the lobby, one of whom he recognized was Michael Brown, a man he'd had an accident with and who worked at his grandfather's nursing home. Joshua was stunned and wondered if Brown was working with Lozano or separately. Deciding to stay cautious, he observed the men until they dispersed. They all looked to be Pakistani to him. He quickly packed, left his room, and made his way to the service elevator, careful not to be seen.

Joshua took a deep breath and held it as he waited for the elevator doors to open, hoping no one would be on the elevator who might recognize him. After all, Joshua did not know how many people were there with Lozano, nor did he know anything about four of the five men. The doors opened, and the elevator was empty, so Joshua exhaled and stepped on board.

Joshua rode the elevator down, his anxiety rising each time the doors opened and hotel employees joined him. Once on the ground floor, he let the others exit first, then slipped out through the kitchen to the back street. He circled around to the front and checked into the Marriott, across from the Hilton, with a view of the hotel's entrance. It was just before 7:00 p.m., and less than 24 hours until the salvage ship's arrival. After settling in, Joshua headed to the lobby bar, positioning himself where he could watch the Hilton from across the busy street.

Joshua contented himself with his position and sipped several little cups of Saki over the next two hours. At one point, he stood up and felt quite a strong head rush that staggered him.

"Whoo," Joshua exclaimed as he regained his balance. *Saki is powerful; have to watch that stuff in the future.* He glanced out at the front doors again and saw nothing notable across the street in the lobby of the Hilton. He then meandered toward the elevators, having to pay attention to his steps as he was having a difficult time walking in a straight line.

Back in his hotel room, Joshua found the burner phone. He picked it up and punched in his code. There he saw a message from Mei Lei: *Arrival time 6:15.* He was confused—whose arrival was it? Was it the ship's or Mei Lei's? Was it 6:15 a.m. or p.m.? Joshua figured the ship would arrive around 6:15 p.m. the next day, based on the original message mentioning evening. He knew better than to contact Mei Lei for clarification, so he decided to wait, though the uncertainty left him wondering and uneasy.

Good enough, thought Joshua. *I will just wait.* His semi-intoxicated brain was tapped out, no further thinking, and feeling somewhat satisfied, Joshua passed out cold.

Alex Lozano rose just before 11:00 p.m., disoriented and

hungry. He decided to go downstairs to the lobby bar, wolfing down noodles with fish. By midnight, he concluded that nothing would happen and returned to his room. He still had no solid plan, only the goal of finding Joshua and having him lead him to the bomb. He believed the boat would arrive the next day, but he wanted certainty. Alex tried calling Joshua's room, but after 12 rings and no answer, he became furious.

For fuck's sake! Alex slammed the phone down, exasperated, vowing to find Joshua. Despite his anger, he eventually fell asleep, setting his alarm to wake up before sunrise.

CHAPTER 38

The next morning, Muqtar woke up for prayers without waiting for the call to prayers, reflecting on how much life had changed in just seven days. A week ago, he was making pancakes for his wife and son; now he was praying. Muqtar felt compelled to pray, knowing the men he was with saw the mission as holy. *It couldn't hurt,* he thought, *maybe even help.* After finishing his prayers, he checked his watch—time to meet everyone downstairs. By the time they reached the bay, he figured the sun would be rising, just like the Japanese flag. *Ironic.*

Muqtar made his way to the lobby and found his mates in the breakfast restaurant. He joined them and could tell they had been talking amongst themselves.

"Good morning, men. How is everyone?"

"Fine, Muqtar, fine. How are you?"

"Also good. Thank you. Are we ready to go to the bay?"

"Go to the bay and do what, Muqtar?" Abdul wanted to know.

"Go to the bay as we had planned and find the boat or ship that the American is going to use to excavate the bomb," was Muqtar's testy reply.

"That seems like a long shot, Muqtar," observed Abdul as the other men nodded their heads in agreement.

"True enough, Abdul," Muqtar reminded them. "It is a long shot, but you all knew it was a long shot when you agreed to come over here."

"You're right, Muqtar. We all knew it was going to be difficult, but we did not realize that you had no idea of when, where, who, or how," spoke Abdul, emphasizing *how*. "You say you have the actual coordinates where the bomb hit the water, assuming that your story is true about the existence of a bomb in the first place."

"Assuming the story about the existence of the bomb is true in the first place," repeated Muqtar, who was getting pissed. "Did I misrepresent to any of you where the bomb hit the water?" snapped Muqtar, looking at each one of the men. "Did I?" his voice raising.

"No, no, you did not say that you knew exactly where the bomb is, that is true," was their collective reply. "But we thought we had a better chance of finding the bomb by finding the American rather than looking for something we don't even know exists by some means we have not identified."

"OK. Alright, then, fellows," declared Muqtar as he leaned back in his chair with his hands apart, palms up. "What do you all want to do? Go home, quit and go home?"

"Pretty much, yes, Muqtar. That is what we have decided to do," replied Abdul, with the others nodding their heads in agreement.

"Well, that fucking sucks a lot," was Muqtar's sharp retort. Then, looking at Abdul, he said, "Did you at least get me a gun? I will do this myself."

"Not yet, Muqtar. You know that if guns are available we are supposed to get them later today, and the day has just started."

Muqtar stood up to leave. "Then do me the favor of getting me a gun before you leave, if you would, please."

"We will do better than that, Muqtar. We will accompany

you on the wild goose chase for one more day, as the flights we booked do not leave until tomorrow."

Muqtar was completely disgusted. If he did not locate the ship or barge or boat today, the mission was off. Muqtar could not accept that. He would go on the mission alone if necessary, even though he knew he would most likely fail. Muqtar rose from his chair and ordered, "Everyone, meet me out front in 30 minutes. Let's not waste what little time we have sitting in this hotel."

Alex woke before his alarm, and after a shower he took the elevator down to the lobby. On his way through the lobby, he spotted a group of non-Japanese men exiting the restaurant, backs to him. They were definitely South Asian, but from where? Speaking what? Farsi? Urdu? He wasn't sure, but he knew Meister would know.

Then Alex recognized a voice. Straining to get a better look at the group, he realized they weren't just any men—they were the same dark-skinned, non-Arab men he'd seen the day before. *Could they be mercenaries or seamen Joshua had hired for the bomb retrieval?* The irony hit him hard. Curious, Alex followed them, and one man split off to use the bathroom. Alex lost track of the fifth man, whose voice Alex recognized as belonging to the nurse's aide, Michael Brown—who really was Muqtar Ashadi. *Damn,* he cursed to himself. *Missed that one.*

Alex made his way across the lobby toward the front door, doing his best to keep an eye on the group of men. About that time, the doors on the van opened up and the men piled in. *Who was the driver?* Alex wondered, as he tried to get a better look at him. But he did not have a clear look, and to try for a better look would have put him in their view, too. Although Alex couldn't see, he certainly believed the nurse's aide was the driver.

"Excuse me, sir. Do you speak English?" Alex inquired of the bellhop who had opened and shut the door to the van.

"No, not too much English; sorry," was the response.

The next bellboy overheard the exchange. "What can I help you with, sir? I speak English."

"I just want to know where the van is taking those men."

The second bellboy spoke to the first one and then turned back to Alex. "The driver said they were going to do sightseeing at Tokyo Bay."

"Any particular sight they want to see?" Alex wanted to know.

The two bellboys conversed again.

"No. Just go to Tokyo Bay."

"Thank you. Thank you very much," Alex responded as he dug in his pocket for some yen to give the bellboys.

What now? Alex thought. *Follow the men or head back to the room to gather my things?* After a brief hesitation, he opted for the latter. Better to be prepared. He returned to his room, packed his backpack with water, trail mix, Oreos, a jacket, hat, and binoculars, then headed back to the lobby. The second bellboy hailed him a cab, and Alex was off to the bay.

Arriving, Alex surveyed the area. The bay was vast, no sign of the men or Joshua. Walking around wouldn't help much, so he spotted a private marina nearby and decided to check it out, hoping to find a tour boat or skiff that would give him a better vantage point from the water.

Day 8 in Japan

Joshua woke up irritated with himself. He shouldn't have gone back to sleep. After splashing water on his face, he quickly left the room.

In the Marriott lobby, Joshua checked for any signs of trouble. Satisfied it was clear, he grabbed a cab to the bay. During the ride, he received a text from Mei Lei saying she'd be on a flight, arriving at 4:30 p.m. Joshua considered meeting her at the airport but, remembering their last terse exchange, decided to wait for her to reach out. He texted her his new room info and left it at that.

At Tokyo Bay, Joshua headed to the marina where he'd rented a boat, but didn't stop. He believed that Mr. Hosaki had probably been contacted by some government agents, so he kept walking until he reached the building where he had met the Chinese family.

Joshua went into the building and as his eyes adjusted to the semi-darkness inside, he recognized one of the men he had met previously as Mr. Chen.

"Hello, friend," greeted Joshua, bowing respectfully.

"Hello, friend," was the response from Mr. Chen.

"Have you heard from the salvage ship as to when they are going to arrive?"

"Yes. The ship notified me that they will arrive an hour ahead of schedule; 5:30 p.m. local time."

"Oh, that is great news," exclaimed Joshua.

"Is this great news, Joshua?" queried Chen. "Is it really?"

Joshua was taken aback by this frank comment. "Well, yes, I think it is. Don't you?"

"No, I do not. The bomb has rested peacefully on the bottom of the bay for almost eighty years, and now you come along and want to disturb the peace."

"That is true, Chen. That is true. But other people know about the bomb, and they will use it for very bad purposes if they get to the bomb first."

"And how do other people know about the bomb, Joshua? How did they find out?"

Joshua looked at the ground now, ashamed of himself.

"My big mouth was overheard when talking to my grandfather. That is how other people found out about the bomb. It is my fault."

"Yes, it is, Joshua. Yes, it is. And now our entire family is involved, including my favorite niece. Because of you, we are all risking our lives. Is your bomb worth it? Is my niece's safety worth it?"

Without hesitation, Joshua declared, "Yes, retrieving the bomb is worth the risk. It is worth all our futures, freedoms, and lives. Because the bomb is so big and so dangerous that it would instantly kill a million people if it were to explode in Tokyo, and another two and a half to three million would die of radiation poisoning eventually. Then Tokyo would be uninhabitable for many years. The same scenario would play out if the bomb were detonated in Hong Kong or New York. Because of that very real possibility, I am risking my life, my future, my everything," Joshua emphasized.

Chen turned away. "The wheels are in motion, Joshua, and you are responsible for whatever will happen. I pray all goes smoothly, but I fear it will not."

"I'm sorry, Chen. I'm sorry. I was chosen for this mission. I did not choose this quest for myself. And I am so sorry to involve your family and your favorite niece in the plan. I did not ask for this to be my fate. It was thrust upon me. I have no choice but to push forward, come hell or high water. And I will make sure Mei Lei is safe."

Chen turned back to face Joshua once more. "No, you did not have a choice, did you? But do you know why Mei Lei chose to help you when it is not her problem, not her quest, not her fate? And how can you guarantee that Mei Lei will be safe? Preposterous!"

Joshua was taken aback and puzzled by the question.

"No, I do not know why she chose to help me. Do you?"

Chen did not answer right away. He turned around and retreated toward his office. As he passed through the doorway, Chen looked over his shoulder and offered, "You might want to ask Mei Lei why she undertook this most dangerous and foolish mission."

Joshua watched Chen as he walked into his office and shut the door. Joshua was left with his thoughts and his confusion. He thought about telling Chen how he would assure Mei Lei's safety, but he knew his words were just that—hollow and meaningless. His shoulders slumped, weighed down by guilt.

God, what have I done, Joshua thought as he went outside. *And what am I about to do?*

The men opened the door of the van at the public marina and stepped out into the bright afternoon sunlight. The feelings of discontentment, disenchantment, discord, and all the other "dis" words were quite evident amongst the group. Muqtar spoke.

"Men, I know all of you have lives back home, and I know this mission may be dangerous. Don't be discouraged by the lack of a concrete plan. Stay with me. I know we will find the bomb somehow. I feel it. Allah will guide us along the path and will give us the vision to see what we need to see to attain our goal."

The men were all looking at Muqtar silently, and then Abdul spoke.

"Nice speech, Muqtar. Very inspiring. But as you know, today is the last day we are willing to spend in this country trying to capture smoke from the air. We have not even caught a glimpse of the American ghost. We don't even know if he is here, much less if there is actually a bomb. And look around, Muqtar," Abdul continued as he turned, gesturing toward the bay with his right arm extended. "Do you see any salvage ships in the bay?"

The men's eyes followed Abdul's gesture, five sets of eyes roaming the bay looking for a different type of vessel. No one saw anything remarkable. Abdul began again.

"So, the bottom line is, Muqtar, that we are here today until the sun goes down. If nothing shows up by then, we are going back to the hotel, then to the airport to catch the 9:00 p.m. flight back home."

"I thought the return flights were tomorrow?"

"The original flights we booked do depart tomorrow, but we found flights that leave tonight, so we changed our reservations."

Three of the five men nodded in agreement with Abdul. Only Muqtar did not. *Fucking great.* He gnashed his teeth and his neck was hurting, taut with tension. He looked at each man, searching for signs of faith and belief. The return looks were all blank and empty.

Muqtar begrudgingly accepted the reality that there was no further discussion to be had on the subject. Nothing he could say would make a difference. The crew had lost fire on the project; now it was time to return home. *Fuck. Oh well. I have failed.*

Muqtar began to pray for guidance, for success, praying in earnest for the first time since the unfortunate incident in New York, where he prayed he would get away. And he did escape that time. Perhaps Allah would answer his prayers once again. After all, asking Allah to answer two prayers in five years was not much to ask.

Now it was Muqtar's turn to speak.

"All right. I respect the decision you have made, but I promise you we will find the bomb today. I feel it. So, we need to prepare ourselves for the mission, to prepare ourselves for success. To that end, Abdul, let's find your cousin and get some guns."

Abdul picked his phone out of his pocket and sent a text to his cousin. After a few minutes, a response came back. Abdul smiled.

"We are in luck, men. My cousin will meet us in one hour at his boat, which should be about three kilometers to the west," Abdul announced, pointing with his hand at the marina.

Everyone's mood brightened as they began walking to the west. The day was sunny, no clouds in the sky, about eighteen degrees centigrade; a good day for a walk. They all saw the sign for the marina at about the same time, and everyone's mood brightened a bit more, their steps picking up pace. Once in the marina itself, Abdul began looking around for a large powerboat, one more than thirty feet long, capable of crossing the ocean.

There weren't too many boats of that size in the marina, and soon enough, they found the cousin's boat. It was named *Bad Habit,* a fitting name, thought Muqtar.

Abdul called out his cousin's name.

"Hello, Noor! Are you about?"

They heard footsteps and a man's head appeared from below.

"Hello, cousin! How are you," greeted Noor as he stepped up to the deck of the boat to hug Abdul.

"I am fine, Noor, and I am here to save the world," answered Abdul as he shot a glance at Muqtar.

After everyone was welcomed onboard the craft, Noor got down to business.

"You know how difficult it is to get guns in Japan? Practically no one sells them, so no one has them, and ammunition is just as hard to come by. But I," bragged Noor with a flourish and a big smile, "have a connection with some American soldiers, so I have weapons. Come and see."

With that, he led all the men downstairs and opened a cabinet. There were several 9-millimeter handguns stacked neatly on the shelves, with magazines and boxes of ammunition nearby.

Outstanding, thought Muqtar, as his own confidence began to rise. *The plan is going well now.*

All of the men grabbed 9 mils and began test-firing their weapons, fitting the guns in their pants, figuring out how to conceal them. After several minutes of playing with the weapons, Noor spoke.

"What's the plan, Muqtar? How do you intend to capture the bomb from the Americans? Where is the bomb anyway?"

All eyes turned to Muqtar once again.

"My plan is to steal the bomb from the Americans once they pluck it off the bottom of the bay and place it on a salvage ship or barge or something like that," explained Muqtar, as his voice sort of trailed off at the end.

Noor wrinkled his forehead and leaned back.

"That is it, Muqtar? That is your plan?" questioned Noor incredulously.

"Yes, Noor. That's my plan."

Noor looked around at the other men, and they all looked away.

"All of you came here to steal a bomb, and your plan is simply to steal it from the Americans?" Noor was astonished, and all the men, including Noor, fixed their stares at Muqtar.

"Yes, the simpler the plan the easier it is to pull it off," justified Muqtar. "We wait until the salvage ship gets here, watch as it retrieves the bomb, then storm the ship and steal the bomb."

"Storm the ship and steal the bomb," repeated Noor. "Don't you think the Americans will be on the lookout for such an attempt and will no doubt have their own guns to fend off such a threat?"

"Yes, they may be prepared for a potential hijacking, but we will have the element of surprise on our side. That will be the secret to our success; a quick strike without warning."

Noor contemplated this plan for a moment.

"You are correct that the element of surprise is your best asset, but how are you planning on sneaking up on a ship in the middle of Tokyo Bay?"

Muqtar shrugged his shoulders again.

"Allah will guide us on this holy mission. He will show us the way and we will succeed."

The men scoffed. Muqtar was doing his best to sound convincing, but no one was convinced, especially not Noor.

"I apologize for being negative, Muqtar, but that's a long shot at best, even with Allah's assistance. But I am here to help you in any way I can, so let's see what happens."

"OK, thank you, Noor. Is your boat equipped with GPS?"

"Yes, it is."

"All right, then if it is OK with you, let's take your boat to these coordinates that I believe reflect where the bomb lays at the bottom of the ocean," spelled out Muqtar as he handed Noor a slip of paper.

Noor took the paper and headed upstairs to the fly deck.

"Prepare to cast off, men," he called down below. A few minutes later, they were cruising out of the marina and headed toward the coordinates Muqtar had given Noor.

Alex stepped out of the cab at the public marina, scanning the vast bay. He did not know what he was looking for, per se, but was trying to convince himself that he would find it. He knew from the intercept that a salvage ship was supposed to arrive sometime late today, and Alex was counting on that to put all of the pieces together. Soon, he hoped he would know who was working with whom and for what purpose.

His next thought was, *well okay, if I figure out the plan, what am I going to do about it?* His inner bravado had originally planned to jump up like Superman and stop the dastardly devils dead in their tracks. But standing there by himself with no gun gave him pause as to the wisdom of his plan. Perhaps he would observe and then call the authorities to handle the situation. Still, how would he ever find anything here? He'd done his research, though, and knew what ship to look for. But after a thorough sweep with binoculars, he saw nothing resembling a salvage ship in the bay.

Shaking his head at the lack of making headway, Alex decided to follow his backup plan: head to the Tokyo Bay tour boat area. Maybe he'd spot something useful, like Joshua or the dark-skinned group. Two hours later, he returned with no new leads. Alex felt stupid for relying on unverified information—nothing had checked out, not even the brief glimpse of the foreign men he was sure included the nurse's aide from St. Louis.

Chastising himself for taking on this fool's errand, Alex resolved to wait out the day. He had nothing to lose. First, though, he needed food. He found a nearby restaurant, ordered noodles with fish and tea, and sat outside with a clear view of the bay. As he ate, Alex spent the time drinking tea and journaling, checking his watch; 5:15 p.m.

He drummed his fingers on the table, eyes scanning the room and the bay aimlessly. His shoulders slumped, and he let out a deep sigh, the minutes dragging on without end. Bored and vexed by the long, uneventful day, Alex debated returning to the hotel versus sticking it out to find the salvage ship—a ship that might never show. Just then, he spotted a ship entering the bay. Through his binoculars, Alex confirmed it was a salvage ship with Chinese markings, based in Hong Kong. Excited, Alex knew he was on the right track but still lacked solid proof. He decided not to notify the authorities yet.

Alex left the restaurant and headed to the commercial docks, keeping a discreet distance from other people as the ship anchored far out in the bay. He waited, watching for anyone to board or disembark. As it grew dark and fog rolled in, Alex checked his watch: 5:40 p.m. Having seen the ship, he was prepared to wait all night if necessary. A second ship came into view; much smaller than the salvage ship.

Alex watched as it circled the salvage ship, and he made

out several men, including the nurse's aide, on the deck. *What the hell? Are they going to board the ship?* Nope, that didn't happen, observed Alex as the smaller ship headed back toward the shore. *I'm going to head that way,* he decided. The smaller boat could hold a clue as to what was going to happen, Alex figured, a thought that buoyed his spirits.

Once they arrived at the coordinates Muqtar had provided, Noor lowered the anchor.

"The water is approximately 20 meters deep here," Noor announced.

Everyone nodded. Muqtar thought about making another inspirational speech but then thought better of any further speechifying. *That might be a good way to get thrown overboard,* was Muqtar's conclusion. And he was right. The men were pissed, disillusioned, and ready to go home. There was nothing to do now but wait. Wait and see.

Several hours went by and nothing was happening. Noor looked at his watch; the time was 5:15 p.m. The sun was going down in the west. He switched on his boat's running lights and started the engines. This drew everyone's attention as Muqtar made his way to the bridge.

When Muqtar arrived up top, he saw Noor raising the anchor via an electronic switch. Noor heard Muqtar come up to the bridge, and he turned around to see who was there.

"Oh. It is you, Muqtar."

"Yes, it is me, Noor. Are we going back to port now?"

"Yes, we are. We have been out here all day, and no one has seen anything. No point in wasting any more time. Sorry,

Muqtar, but it looks like nothing is going to come of your plan."

Muqtar sighed, realizing his plans had failed miserably. It was a failure that would tarnish his reputation with both his backers and those he'd convinced to join him in Japan. Staring at the late afternoon sun, Muqtar felt the weight of it all.

Then, he spotted an unfamiliar ship entering the harbor. "Noor, look! What's that?"

Noor, distracted, looked up. "That's not a typical ship, Muqtar. Let's check it out."

Muqtar instructed the men to move to the front of the boat. As the ship neared, its large hooks and booms became clear. Muqtar turned to the crew, excitement growing. "See? That's the ship here to retrieve the bomb."

The men agreed, their excitement palpable. Muqtar urged Noor to get as close as possible to assess how they could board undetected.

"Men, as we get closer, everyone check it out to see any possible ways to board her without being seen. I would like to snag the bomb from the Americans without firing a shot, if possible. Agreed?"

All the men nodded, now ready to do whatever was necessary to accomplish the goal, including killing everyone onboard if necessary. After all, each of the men had suffered a loss of life at the hands of the Americans. Yet they all also knew that gunfire would attract the Japanese authorities, and that would be bad for everyone.

The salvage ship appeared to be about 50 meters in length, equipped with giant claws on the starboard side big enough to grab a container. Alongside the claws were lifting booms, four of them, from which cables with looped ends hung.

Noor slowly floated past the starboard side of the ship and

saw only three men onboard. Muqtar came back up to the bridge.

"What do you think, Noor? Can we get on the boat without being seen?" Muqtar asked.

"Perhaps, Muqtar, perhaps. But let's say you do. And let's say further you overpower the Americans and take over the ship. Then what? What are you going to do with a very heavy bomb that is 3 meters long and 2 meters in diameter? How are you going to get it home or to wherever?"

Muqtar had not thought that far ahead. Muqtar had only planned the mission through grabbing the bomb from the Americans. *Shit. What the hell was I going to do with the bomb anyway? Not like I could call FedEx and have them come and pick the bomb up for delivery to New York.* Piss.

Then a thought came to him. Muqtar grabbed Noor by the arms and began to speak right in Noor's face.

"How about we put the bomb in a shipping container once we get it and ship it home? Huh? How about that, Noor? What do you think of that? Do you think that will work?"

"Calm down, Muqtar, and let go of my arms. Let me think for a minute. We could use the hooks to offload the bomb onto a barge then onto some dollies onshore and use a forklift to push it into a container. I load cars into containers all of the time when I export them to Pakistan. Hmmm, Muqtar. Your idea actually might work. I don't think the port authorities in Lahore scan incoming containers for radioactivity, so that may actually work," evaluated Noor, repeating himself as he considered the emerging plan.

"I think it will work," agreed Muqtar. "Now we just have to wait for the Americans to snatch the bomb up from the bottom of the bay and load it onto the ship. Then we will steal the bomb from them."

Noor turned his boat around and headed up the port side, looking for a ladder or rungs.

"Look there, Muqtar. On the port side near the stern, there is a ladder built into the side of the ship. I think that is the easiest and best way to access the ship, but for sure the Americans will guard that spot."

"I agree, Noor. They will monitor that spot, but perhaps we can set up some sort of diversion to attract their attention elsewhere and thereby sneak onboard and overpower them."

"Well, I will say the likelihood of success now looks a lot brighter than it did a half an hour ago," declared Noor again. "And look, Muqtar, there are containers on the deck of the ship."

"Excellent, and I couldn't agree more, Noor," Muqtar joyfully replied as he descended to the main deck to tell the men what the plan was.

The men listened carefully to the outline of the plan, and they all thought the plan could work. Muqtar showed them the ladder built near the stern and discussed how they would distract the Americans from the ladder to gain control of the ship.

"When do we move on the plan, Muqtar?" asked Abdul.

"As soon as we see them lift the bomb onboard, we will make our move. Noor will guide his boat near the ship, and we will take his little skiff to the back of the ship," Muqtar said. "Noor will distract them by cutting close in front of the ship and firing off a flare, during which time we will climb up the ladder and take over."

"Once we control the ship, we will put the bomb into one of the containers on the deck then make the captain head to the docks, where we will offload the container. Noor will see that the container is placed on a different ship as just another container bound for Lahore. We can then decide what to do with the bomb when we get it home," Muqtar concluded excitedly.

"Where will we get a container?"

"Look. There are containers on the deck," observed Muqtar. "We will load the bomb into one of them. Noor ships cars to Lahore all the time, so shipping another container there will not be noticed."

"How do we get the container down onto the dock?" another wanted to know.

"The salvage ship has booms that are designed for loading and unloading."

"None of us know how to do the unloading, Muqtar."

"Right. True enough. But the ship's hands know how to do it, and we will encourage them to do it," Muqtar explained, using his fingers to place air quotes around the word *encourage*.

The men smiled. Everyone now knew that the plan could work and that their trip to Japan had not been for naught.

Muqtar called upstairs. "Noor, take us to the marina. We have a plan."

And so they went.

Joshua anxiously counted the hours until 5:00 p.m., waiting for both the salvage ship and Mei Lei's arrival. At 4:00 p.m., Mei Lei texted to say she had landed and was heading to the marina. Excitement surged through Joshua as he quickly made his way back to the warehouse.

He checked his grandfather's aviation watch, eyes constantly on the clock. Finally, a cab pulled up, and Mei Lei stepped out. Even after all these years, she looked the same as when they were students in Ann Arbor. Joshua's heart nearly burst out of his chest as she approached.

Their eyes met, and time seemed to freeze—going back to their days together in Ann Arbor. Her look was one of love, and he burned it into his memory. But Mei Lei's expression shifted to all business, and Joshua smiled. She didn't smile back.

Mr. Chen, her uncle, greeted her with a formal bow, his face showing little emotion. Joshua knew better, though—he understood the depth of Uncle Chen's feelings, recalling his earlier harsh words to Joshua.

Now, with the mission at hand, they moved to a conference room where Mei Lei laid out her plan, and they all reviewed the photos of the bomb. As they quietly absorbed the details, it was clear Mei Lei's mind was working at lightning speed. Barely acknowledging Joshua, he resisted the urge to speak, choosing to remain quiet for now.

Finally, Mei Lei spoke again.

"OK, from what I see here, the salvage operation should take approximately four hours to suck away the sand and silt, then we will attach the hooks to the lifting poles on the prize. We will do that tonight. The actual lifting operation will take another two hours, then another hour or so to assemble a container around the item. Seven hours total. I radioed the ship to moor at the site. I have already cleared the anchor site with the harbor master."

"Fortunately, the area where the item is resting is in a spot of no naval traffic, so the ship will not be in anyone's way, which is also why the harbor master gave us permission to drop anchor there. Since we plan to pull off this operation tonight, we should be good," Mei Lei concluded.

Finally, she looked at Joshua, showing no emotion. "Do you

understand?"

"Yes, Mei Lei, I do understand, and I agree with everything you have said."

"I didn't ask you if you agreed, only if you understood," Mei Lei retorted.

Ouch. Mei Lei's sharp words stung, and Joshua almost stepped back, fighting the urge to snap back. He felt his face heat up, sure he was turning red, but forced himself to stay calm. He glanced at his watch—5:00 p.m. The ship would be arriving soon.

Then, something caught his eye—a large pleasure craft anchored near where the bomb was buried. He grabbed his binoculars and zoomed in. To his horror, *Bad Habit* was moored right above the bomb site.

Five men were on deck, and one was talking. Joshua's stomach sank and his jaw dropped at the realization. It was for sure Michael Brown. *What the hell was he doing here?* Joshua felt a pit in his stomach and abject fear overtake him as he now realized that for sure he wasn't the only one hunting for the bomb. He'd seen these guys leaving the Hilton, and now they were on a boat in the bay. *Great.*

Flummoxed and unsure as to what to do, Joshua's mind was spinning as he debated whether to inform Mei Lei and Chen, knowing he'd have to eventually. *But not now.* He scanned the harbor as *Bad Habit* began to move. Checking his watch, he saw it was 5:20 p.m., and he turned to see the salvage ship entering the harbor.

Then, to his surprise, *Bad Habit* wasn't where it had been. Joshua lowered the binoculars and saw it heading toward the front of the harbor, where the ship was arriving.

Oh, hell no. What the fuck are they doing? The fight-or-flight adrenaline was flowing, pounding through his body, interfering with his ability to think rationally. Breathing rapidly, almost to the point of hyperventilating, Joshua began to quake involuntarily. *Don't tell me Michael Brown and his comrades are going to blow up the pleasure boat next to the salvage ship like what had happened in Yemen to a U.S. Navy ship,* Joshua thought to himself. But as he watched and his breathing rate subsided a little, *Bad Habit* motored past the ship, then traveled around the stern and came back up the port side.

That's odd, was Joshua's first thought as he put down the binoculars and mulled over the situation. Then what was really happening hit him like a ton of bricks. *Those cocksuckers are scoping out the ship and are planning to hijack the bomb!* The more he considered it, the more certain he became.

He scanned the bay, locating the pleasure craft just as *Bad Habit* slipped into a private marina. Now he knew where they were, and he was sure they had no idea where he was. *But where was Lozano?* Joshua figured the little prick had probably made it to the bay, watching everything unfold just like he was.

Joshua was right. Alex had seen everything but was unsure what to make of it. The pleasure boat docked close to his position, and knowing its occupants would pass right by him, he moved to a better vantage point, less likely to be seen.

He overheard men talking as they walked up the pier, speaking the same language he had heard the other day. Alex didn't recognize them, but there were only three—two still on the boat. When the other two passed, speaking in English, Alex heard their plan to meet back at the pier at midnight. He was darned sure one of them was the nurse's aide from St. Louis—Muqtar Ashadi.

Back at midnight? Alex decided to stick to the plan. He trained his binoculars on the salvage ship, noticing it was anchored unusually far from the other commercial ships. It hit him: *that's where the bomb must be! Clever bastards.* But even with his binoculars, he couldn't make out any figures on the ship.

He waited, then thought he saw movement on deck, but couldn't tell who it was. The men from the pleasure boat must be part of the salvage plan—if that's what it was.

At 6:30 p.m., Alex glanced at his watch. Plenty of time to head back to the hotel without being spotted by the nurse's aide, then return to see what would unfold that night.

He didn't want to do anything that might scare off the bomb retrievers. Though he could notify the Japanese authorities or the CIA, Alex knew he had to be certain of the situation first—any mistake could end his career, or worse, his life.

As he rode back, Alex realized he was just one man against a group of Pakistanis and an American with connections in Tokyo. With no gun and limited physical skills—he'd been behind a desk for over ten years—his options were few. Waiting seemed the best choice. Once the bomb was retrieved, he'd make his move.

Chen, Mei Lei, and Joshua left the warehouse and boarded a speedboat heading toward the salvage ship. Joshua sat quietly in the back as they tied up near the stern, where a ladder led up to the deck of the ship. Once onboard, Mei Lei spoke with the crew away from Joshua. He noticed the ship seemed much larger up close than through binoculars.

Mei Lei conversed with four men, each bowing deeply when a fifth man appeared—likely the captain, Joshua thought, noting his age. Afterward, Mei Lei approached Joshua to speak with him.

"These men have been told about what we are going to do and have been informed of the danger of this project. They have all agreed to help."

"Thank you, Mei Lei. I could not have done this without you. I am deeply in your debt," offered Joshua sincerely while bowing.

"No need to thank me, Joshua. I undertook the project with my eyes wide open," was Mei Lei's quiet reply.

Joshua could not take the unknowing any longer. He had to ask Mei Lei why she was helping. Why she was being so fucking cold toward him. Her actions did not make sense. So, Joshua came out with it.

Mei Lei was standing about two feet away, turned partly to his left. Joshua reached out with his right hand and grasped her left arm, turning her to him.

"Why, Mei Lei? Why are you helping me?" Joshua had to know, looking straight into Mei Lei's eyes. She looked back.

"Because you gave me something and I owe you for it."

What, Joshua asked himself. *I owe her something, as I see it, but Mei Lei is saying she owes me,* thought Joshua, forehead wrinkled, trying to compute what was said, most perplexed. So, he spoke again.

"What did I give you, Mei Lei? What?"

Mei Lei shook Joshua's hand loose from her arm and did not reply immediately. Then she spoke.

"Something greater than you could comprehend, Joshua,"

was Mei Lei's oblique response.

Before Joshua could ask more, the captain of the crew came over and Mei Lei walked away with him.

Joshua stood there, completely befuddled and somewhat pissed at the inscrutable Chinese female who Joshua had to admit had stolen his heart a long time ago and who still had it.

Mei Lei returned.

"Are you ready for a night dive, Joshua? We need to get busy now in order to get the prize onboard before daylight."

"Yes, I'm ready, Mei Lei. And for whatever it is worth, after this mission is over, you and I will be even."

"No, we won't, Joshua, and I won't speak of it again," Mei Lei announced.

Joshua was given a wetsuit and scuba gear, and two crew members suited up as well. Each was provided with a powerful light, and Joshua noticed a large, flexible hose being lowered overboard, connected to a big machine. A few minutes later, the three men slipped into the dark water, with Joshua leading the way.

Mei Lei was left onboard. She tried to check her emotions as she had done so many times when it came to her feelings, her love for Joshua, but seeing him again released a flood thereof. Mei Lei's head was swimming with an uncontrollable longing for him. Her face flushed with sexual desire as she saw his long, lean swimmer's body strip down to his underwear before donning the wetsuit. She wanted to rub herself up against him like a cat in heat. Drops of perspiration formed on her neck and ran down her back in a river. She had to excuse herself to the bathroom to dry her brow and insert tissue into her panties to absorb the moistness. Mei Lei felt the magnetic attraction to Joshua that had made her give her virgin self to him the night before she left for Hong Kong. Her primeval self was demanding satisfaction. She had to have him penetrate her loins again as she fanned herself in a futile attempt to dissipate the animal heat.

All of this was unbeknownst to Joshua as he swam down to the bomb's location. He checked his compass and headed northwest. Soon, he spotted the bomb, exactly where he left it. Relieved, Joshua smiled at his earlier worry.

The men swam around the bomb, digging to expose the lifting poles. After testing the arms' sturdiness, they communicated with hand gestures. One crewman surfaced while the other held the hose. Joshua realized the machine was a giant vacuum, and as the crewman worked the hose back and forth, sand and silt were sucked away from the bomb.

Impressive, thought Joshua. *What a great way to free the bomb from its mud hole resting place of nearly 80 years.*

Joshua studied his dive watch. He had about fifteen minutes more oxygen before he had to return to the surface.

He was fascinated with the dirt removal process. With each pass back and forth, the size and shape of the bomb became more apparent. *God, this thing is big,* thought Joshua. *Really big.* He looked at the end of the bomb that was now completely exposed and shined his flashlight upon some handwriting he saw.

Sure enough, there were the remains of a stencil still visible on the end. It read:

> *United States Army*
> *Operation: Cherry Blossom*
> *PAYBACK*

PAYBACK, eh? I do understand, Joshua confirmed to himself. His grandfather had told Joshua the name of the mission and of the bomb too, and there it was, written on the side: *Operation: Cherry Blossom*. Not very impressive. *What did Joshua expect the lettering to say? Hydrogen bomb. First of its kind. Designed to pay back the Japanese for Pearl Harbor by killing the emperor of Japan and millions of innocent civilians when the U.S. knew they were about to announce their surrender. Yes, it was the big payback. Justified under the circumstances? Probably not. At least not in his grandfather's opinion at the time, nor Joshua's either as he thought about it.*

Just then Joshua saw the other crewman return and the first handed off the cleaning hose to the other after a few more hand gestures were exchanged. The second crewman began vacuuming where the first had stopped. Another glance at Joshua's dive watch: seven minutes of O_2 left. *Time to slowly ascend to the surface.* As Joshua swam around the fully exposed side of the bomb, he saw some more handwriting.

"*Target Tokyo*"
"*Kill the Emperor*"
"*Bomb's away*"

Wow. Shit. Just as his grandfather had told him, there were the exact words handwritten on the hydrogen bomb. Joshua ascended.

Once onboard the salvage ship, Joshua sought out the crewman he had been with on the bottom. He found him seated near the ladder still wearing his wetsuit.

"Hello. My name is Joshua."

The crewman nodded in Joshua's direction but did not speak.

"How long do you think it will take to fully expose the bomb using the vacuum hose?"

The crewman did not respond. Rather, he pointed at the ship's captain. Joshua understood the message, so he stood up and walked over to where the captain was.

"Sir, how long do you think it will take to vacuum the silt away from the prize?" Joshua was curious to know, using Mei Lei's term to describe the bomb.

"It will take as long as it takes," was the captain's stern response. In other words, the captain said, *Get the fuck out of my way, punk. I have work to do.*

Joshua realized he was of no value to any of the workers at this point; a point made obvious by the short, curt response issued by the captain. Having led the men to the location of the bomb, now it was Joshua's turn to wait.

Alex, back from the hotel, stood shivering, cold and alone by the marina, intently watching the salvage ship. He couldn't make out anyone clearly, but he was pretty sure the tallest figure was Joshua.

He considered his options:

First, he could storm the ship and try to detain everyone until U.S. authorities arrived. But he had no weapons, no backup, and no boat—his plan would only get him thrown overboard if somehow, he did find a way to the ship.

Second, he could do nothing and let events unfold. But that felt too risky, especially if the result was the destruction of an American city or Tokyo.

Third, he could try to sneak aboard, find a weapon, and take control—a long shot, but the best chance, though he still had no way to get to the ship.

And then there were the five men—the Pakis. They weren't on the ship but earlier had been circling it in a pleasure craft.

Alex's instincts told him they weren't allies of Joshua's group. He realized they were competitors, both vying for the bomb.

It all clicked. This was no simple operation. Both groups wanted the bomb, and Alex finally understood the stakes.

Alex wondered if Joshua knew about the Pakis. He figured the nurse's aide must have overheard something or deceived the Colonel into revealing the bomb's location.

His initial pride in solving the puzzle faded as he considered his next move. First, he had to choose a side. Reluctantly, he decided to back the American, putting aside the question of whether Joshua was a traitor for later.

The idea of putting both groups behind bars was tempting, but with no gun or transportation, it felt impossible at 11:00 p.m., sitting alone in the dark. Alex decided to act on instinct, striking when the opportunity came, hoping his instincts were correct.

He felt confident—he'd have the element of surprise. One way or another, Alex Lozano, CIA agent, would prevail. He felt like pounding his chest, brave undaunted American about to fight for American honor. Coming back to Earth, Alex knew that whatever was going to happen would occur before dawn.

CHAPTER 39

Back on the boat, the captain informed Joshua the excavation was nearly done and suggested he dive to check the progress. Without hesitation, Joshua was back in the water, heading down to the site.

He was stunned to see the bomb fully exposed. It was enormous, undamaged, and the lifting poles were clearly visible, perfect for the cranes to hook onto. But the ship was 200 feet away—too far for the cranes to reach.

As Joshua swam around the bomb, trying to figure out how they would lift it, he saw two Chinese sailors approaching with bundles under their arms. At first, he didn't understand their purpose. But soon, he realized they were inflatable bags being attached to each corner of the bomb. As they inflated the bags, the bomb began to rise off the ocean floor. This was exactly his plan now being executed by competent people.

Joshua felt a surge of pride and confidence as he watched the bomb float. Nice. The mission might actually succeed. The workers then attached a rope to the ship and the bomb slowly glided toward it. Amazing.

Joshua realized that soon they would be directly below the ship's booms and the bomb could then be lifted onto the waiting dollies. Afterwards the bomb would be pushed into a container, taken to the deepest part of the ocean and dropped to a resting place more than 20,000 feet deep. Amen. Quest completed! Mission accomplished! As soon as he thought those thoughts his inner voice checked him. Not so fast, big fella, don't shoot your wad too soon.

Joshua swam ahead of the ropes and climbed back onboard the ship. Mei Lei had reappeared in the meantime and he noticed that her cheeks were rosy red, but as usual, she looked away as she had no time for, and no apparent interest in him.

Alex's problem was getting to the ship. No water taxis were running past midnight, and he had not rented a boat himself. Damn it! If he was going to act, it had to be now, but how? Pacing back and forth, he wracked his brain trying to come up with a workable plan. Workable being the key, as in not being killed in the process of its execution.

Time to be bold, he told himself. He'd always claimed to be fearless, so why not take a reckless chance? Pumping himself up, he walked toward the private marina where he had seen *Bad Habit* enter. It took about fifteen minutes, and there it was—just as he'd suspected. He checked his watch: 1:00 a.m. The salvage ship hadn't moved, which meant he still had time.

From behind a power pole, Alex saw *Bad Habit*'s stern and a ladder hanging down. That was his way on, and no one was around—until he heard footsteps. Six men were approaching. He quickly hid, holding his breath as they passed and boarded the boat.

The men went upstairs. Now or never, Alex resolved, so he took his shoes off and slid into the cold water, no time to hesitate. He swam the forty feet to the ladder, heart pounding, freezing his ass off, knowing the window for action was closing fast.

Gripping the ladder, Alex heard the engines of *Bad Habit* roar to life. Perfect. The crew would be busy launching the boat, giving him a chance to sneak aboard. He peeked over the boat's stern and spotted a tarp on the deck. Ideal for hiding.

Just as he made his move, voices echoed nearby. Alex scrambled onto the boat, crawled under the tarp, and froze. He knew his wet footprints might give him away, but there was no turning back now.

He heard more voices, then felt the boat shift—*Bad Habit* was casting off. Alex resisted the urge to peek out, uncertain where the crew was. Meanwhile, Muqtar and his men had been watching the salvage ship for hours, noticing the booms starting to extend over the side.

"It is time we hatched our plan, men. From what I see, the booms are being readied to pick up the bomb. Once we see the bomb being lowered onto the deck, we will go near the ship in this boat, then we will take the skiff and sneak around to the back and then climb up onto the ship using the stern ladder. Noor will distract the ship's crew by shooting a flare over its bow and turning on his searchlight as we board her," Muqtar told the men.

"The distraction will give us time to board the ship and overpower the crew. Everyone understand?" Muqtar wanted to know.

Everyone nodded their heads in agreement. Noor idled out of the marina then opened up the throttle partway and began to make his way across the bay to the area where the salvage ship sat at anchor.

So far, so good, thought Joshua. The bomb was floating safely toward the ship, and now the real test would be lifting it aboard without triggering detonation. He watched as the crew positioned the bomb beneath the booms, attaching hooks to each corner. As the lifting cables strained, Joshua held his breath, silently praying the bomb wouldn't explode.

As the bomb breached the surface of the water, Joshua found himself instinctively making the sign of the cross. The bomb was nearly halfway out when the cables groaned under the weight. The crane motors revved, and with a creak, the bomb was slowly lifted entirely from the water. The cranes turned, and the bomb was now hovering above the ship.

Crew members swiftly positioned dollies and a forty-foot container to receive it. The bomb was carefully lowered, placed on the dollies, and secured with straps. Then a forklift moved in and gently began pushing the bomb toward its resting place inside the container.

Joshua watched as the forklift moved the bomb without issue, relieved that it wasn't deformed. Time was of the essence because who knew if the Japanese authorities would want to board the vessel and do an inspection or if the crew from the Hilton was going to try something nefarious. Joshua paced back and forth, electrical sparks of nervous energy shooting through his body. He couldn't tell if he was excited or scared or both—probably both.

His eyes darted from the container to the ocean and back, standing amidships as he looked at every shadow, intently suspicious that something was amiss. *"Paranoia will destroy ya"* is the chorus to the rock song that kept playing in his head. Thinking rationally as best he could, he watched intently as the bomb was secured inside the container, and therefore everything had to be fine. Right.

Just then, a flare shot into the night sky and landed on the foredeck. Everyone stopped, and Joshua's heart began to pound as he recognized the boat from earlier—*Bad Habit*. His gut twisted. The Pakis were using the flare as a distraction to hijack the bomb.

"Shit," Joshua shouted. Rushing to the foredeck, he hid behind a container and peeked around to see five armed men rounding up the crew, including Mei Lei. Sweating and shaking as panic set in, he knew he needed a weapon—FAST! He spied a four-foot pipe lying on the deck. Good enough, as it was his only choice anyway.

Joshua's mind was flying—could he take on five armed men with a pipe? No. The only choice was a banzai charge, hoping to distract the attackers long enough for the crew to act. It was a suicide mission, but Joshua was willing to risk it if it meant Mei Lei would be safe.

Joshua scanned the scene—the Pakis were herding Mei Lei and the crew into the open container doors, but there was still no clear way to act without getting killed. As the doors started to close, his heart started aching, but the world began to slow down despite his impotence at not being able to save her. Extreme clarity set in. Were they planning to offload the bomb with the crew inside or hijack the ship with the container still on board? Joshua quickly ruled out hijacking the ship—it would be too risky. The Pakis must be planning to unload the container onshore and transport it elsewhere.

Fuck that idea and fuck shutting Mei Lei and the crew into the container to die a slow death, were his brave thoughts. Free of fear now while thinking quickly and clearly, Joshua left his hiding place and ran to the back of the container that had the bomb inside. He stayed out of the view of the Pakis. There were ladder rungs on the back of the container that Joshua grabbed onto, and by using them Joshua climbed onto the top of the container. No one noticed. Good.

Joshua made his way to the front of the container and could overhear the captors talking amongst themselves below him, fortunately in English.

"Shit. That was easy, Abdul. We didn't even have to fire a shot." Joshua recognized that voice as being Michael Brown's.

"Yes, it was. Maybe too easy," replied another man, scanning the horizon.

"Why do you say that? We have the bomb and it is already secured in a container," Muqtar confirmed. "All we have to do is go to the dock, lift off the container and place it on a flatbed, then drive away."

"That all sounds easy, Muqtar, but how do we get to the pier to unload the container?"

"That is easy too, Abdul. The Chinese captain of the ship will cooperate because he will think we are going to let everyone go once we offload the bomb."

"And will we let everyone go once we have offloaded the container?"

"No, Abdul. We cannot take that chance. We will have to eliminate all of them to give us time to get away."

"And how do you propose to do that, Muqtar? Shoot them all?"

"No, not shoot them. We will lock all of them inside the container and nature will take care of them by the time the destination is reached."

"OK, so now what?" was Abdul's next question, but Muqtar did not have time to answer because a ruckus broke out at the stern. Joshua saw the CIA agent Alex climbing up onto the ship, but his foot was trapped in the ladder and he was stuck halfway on and halfway off the ship, screaming in agony.

Muqtar shouted for his men to get Alex, and as they ran toward him, Joshua saw his chance and seized it. He leapt down from the container, hitting Muqtar in the shoulders, crashing both of them to the ground and knocking the gun away. Joshua's left leg took the brunt of the impact, but he still gripped the pipe. Muqtar, dazed and hurt from the impact, scrambled for the gun. Joshua hobbled toward it, but before either man could reach it, they both saw Alex break free and charge at the men. Now glaring at each other, teeth bared, muscles tense, fists clenched, both Joshua and Muqtar knew it was going to be a fight to the death, and both were ready to die for their cause.

Muqtar grabbed the gun first, but Joshua swung the pipe, breaking Muqtar's arm with a loud crack. The gun flew free, and Muqtar collapsed, screaming in pain. Joshua quickly grabbed the gun as he turned towards the men who had heard the ruckus and were coming back his way, guns out. All the while Alex was running forward, screaming at the top of his lungs.

Joshua lifted the weapon, holding it with both hands, and carefully aimed it at the first man who was charging toward him. He barely heard the reports of gunfire as bullets whizzed past him. He was 100% focused on his target.

Bam! The first man dropped after Joshua's shot hit his chest, spun him around, and down he went. The other three dropped to the deck of the boat and continued firing. Muqtar, hurt but still moving, limped toward the stern. Joshua quickly ducked inside the container and partially shut a door for cover, feeling and hearing the bullets ricochet off the metal. The firing paused for a second as the attackers retreated with their wounded comrade.

Joshua peeked out and saw one of them with his gun pointed at Alex's head. He had tripped and fallen and was lying on his back, clutching his knee with his free hand up in front of his face, pleading for mercy. Their eyes met, both knowing Alex was doomed. Without hesitation and not bothering to aim this time, Joshua fired three shots. The third struck the attacker, sending him spinning to the ground.

Fuck you, motherfucker! Shoot a helpless man when he is down. I'll show you! Joshua's anger had overcome his fear. Then more bullets came Joshua's way as the Pakis started firing at him again as they retreated to the stern, carrying the two men Joshua had hit.

Joshua heard Alex screaming and saw him firing at the retreating attackers, having grabbed the gun from the second man Joshua had shot. During the chaos, Joshua had lost track of Muqtar and the first attacker, but when he looked again, they were all gone.

He hurried to the railing, peering over. Seeing the skiff leaving, he considered firing more shots but decided to conserve his ammo, unsure if they might come back.

Joshua felt weak in the knees and emotionally drained, his breath ragged from the exertion as his leg pain returned. He heard a noise and wheeled in that direction, raising his gun, ready to fire.

With his hands in the air: "It's me, Joshua. Alex Lozano. Don't shoot."

"I won't," answered Joshua, seeing Alex limp toward him as

he lowered the handgun. "Are you OK, Alex?"

"Well, I'm alive, thanks to you. But I tore up my knee trying to get on the ship."

"Yeah, my right leg hurts like hell now too from jumping off the top of the container. But you're right. We are alive and more or less uninjured, thank goodness."

Joshua peeked inside the container and told the crew the attackers were gone. They slowly emerged from the container, eyes and mouths wide open, looking all around. Mei Lei was the last to come out. Several of the men had tears streaming down their faces—from gratitude or fear, Joshua didn't know which. They each came up and touched Joshua's hand and bowed deeply. Two of them had large wet spots on their pants and another had vomit covering his shirt.

When it appeared for sure that the threat was gone, the men's demeanors lightened. No longer wincing and bent over, they began to smile and breathe deep breaths. The three who had had accidents disappeared to change clothes, and everyone kept a watchful eye on the stern, still afraid the attackers would return. Their faces were now lit up at having been saved, and their relieved expressions showed how terrified they'd been. The men were deeply grateful to Joshua for the courage he had displayed under fire. Everyone kept bowing, and the captain pumped his hand vigorously.

Mei Lei, though thankful, stayed in the background. Joshua eventually sought her out, and when she finally did look his way, she gave him a sharp look, aware that Joshua had also put them in danger, that they all could have been killed. Her mind was swirling. In the past twenty minutes she had had amorous thoughts about Joshua, thought she was going to die, was proud of Joshua's heroism, and was pissed at him because, as she had forecasted, the task he had induced her to undertake was fraught with danger. Trying to balance all of her emotions, Mei Lei stood in front of Joshua and spoke to him face-to-face.

"Thank you for saving all of our lives. We surely would have perished inside the container had you not acted so bravely and come to our rescue." Mei Lei bowed. Joshua bowed in return.

Mei Lei continued. "However, had you not reached out to me, my men, my ship, and I would not have been put in danger in the first place."

Joshua knew she was right, of course, but he had heard enough.

"That is true, Mei Lei, and you are welcome. What you and your men have accomplished will never be written in the history books. No tales of bravery will ever be told. But by helping remove this bomb away from a densely populated area, each and every one of you," Joshua expounded, gesturing toward everyone with his right hand, "is a hero, and I thank you." Joshua finished by bowing in turn to each member of the crew.

Alex, not following the conversation in Chinese, spoke. "What's the plan now, Joshua? What are you going to do with the bomb?"

"The plan is the same as it has always been. We're going to take the bomb out to the deepest part of the Pacific Ocean and drop it overboard."

"Oh. Your intention is not to use the bomb in some terrorist plot to threaten the U.S.?" a relieved Alex inquired.

"No, of course not, Alex," scoffed Joshua. "You have read my file and my grandfather's file. We are not terrorists. We are patriots. I undertook this mission to remove a threat from getting into the hands of our Pakistani friends," Joshua said, pointing in the direction of the fleeing skiff.

"What do you want to do about the authorities, Joshua? Surely, they will ask questions."

"Surely they will, Alex," agreed Joshua, looking at everyone. "We will tell them some Chinese fireworks accidentally went off and that everything is fine."

"And how will we explain our presence on this ship, Joshua?" Alex wanted to know.

"We won't, Alex. We will get off the ship now and leave it to the crew to explain."

Joshua turned to the crew and explained to them in Chinese what his plan was. They all nodded, and Joshua turned to Mei Lei.

"Let's go now, Mei Lei."

"Yes, we should go now," she agreed. Turning to the captain, Mei Lei ordered, "Captain, follow the plan Joshua has outlined. I will be back after daylight to finish up here."

"Yes, Mei Lei," replied the captain as he bowed to his boss.

With Alex's knee and Joshua's injured leg, it was a struggle to climb down the ladder onto Mei Lei's boat. Flashing lights and sirens from the harbor patrol were closing in. Once onboard, Mei Lei started the engine, quickly pulling away from the salvage ship without turning on any lights.

CHAPTER 40

At last, Alex, Joshua, and Mei Lei were a safe distance away from the ship, and all breathed a sigh of relief.

"That was a close one," declared Alex.

"Far too close," agreed Joshua. "What are you going to do now that you know there is a hydrogen bomb on the loose?"

"Joshua, you saved my life, and for that I'll be eternally grateful. I learned something while lying there, about to be shot. When you're staring down the barrel of a gun, nothing matters except survival. No thoughts of country, right or wrong—just 'Please, let me make it through this.'"

Alex paused, then added, "I'm not going to do anything with the info I have. I came to Japan for a vacation and ended up with a twisted knee. But I'll say this: what you did was damned brave. You stuck your neck out and took out the guy who was going to kill me. Good shooting, too. If you ever need anything, anything at all, I'm your man, fifty grand!"

Joshua smiled. What a turn of events. Everything worked out, except for his non-relationship with Mei Lei. They rode in silence to the marina, where they dropped Alex off.

Just the two of them remained. Mei Lei expertly docked the boat, and as they tied it up, her phone rang. She listened, then said, *"Shay shay"*—Chinese for "thank you"—before hanging up.

"The port authorities came onboard and were told the story

of fireworks. They were satisfied with the explanation and left," Mei Lei reported.

"That is good news, Mei Lei. Very good news. Now we can complete the mission as planned. Have you told the men where to go and what to do?"

"Yes, they understand completely."

"Well, good then. And what of you, Mei Lei? What will you do now?"

"I am going to take the trip back to Hong Kong on the ship. I like to do that every now and then, and I want to see for myself that the prize goes to its final resting place," Mei Lei announced.

"OK, Mei Lei. OK. That sounds like a good plan to me, especially now that it is safe. And what of us, Mei Lei? Seeing you again has made me realize that I still love you." Joshua put his heart out there and waited.

Mei Lei's eyes were misty as she looked up into Joshua's eyes.

"Love, Joshua? Love is something I did not and do not have time for; only work." Stone cold.

Joshua definitely had had enough by now.

"Mei Lei, that is the same line of shit you fed me when we were in college. Yet you gave yourself to me the night before you left. Explain that. And while you are at it, please explain why you never responded to a single letter or email that I sent you, and I sent you close to a hundred," Joshua insisted.

"I cannot explain why I did what I did, Joshua, nor can I explain why I didn't do what I didn't do," Mei Lei responded in her inscrutable way. "I'm sorry I hurt you then, but that was then and we have no future now."

"That is cold, Mei Lei. Ice cold. And you are lying to yourself and to me by stating that we have no future, because we do. I can see that you love me; it is all over your face. All we have to do is try and I am willing to try," Joshua begged.

Mei Lei cut him off mid-sentence, her hand raised in a firm, silent gesture. Her eyes locked on his, cutting through his words before he could finish.

"I am not willing to try, Joshua. Not at all. I cannot. Now it's time to say goodbye forever, for the reason for us to have seen each other will soon be disposed of at sea."

"So that is that, Mei Lei? It is over now?" was Joshua's question, not believing what he was hearing.

"Yes, Joshua, that's that. Your quest has been completed and so has mine," replied Mei Lei, softly reaching her hand up to touch his cheek.

Joshua sighed again, the sigh emanating from the deepest depths of his soul as tears welled up in his eyes. He emitted a second anguished sigh of resignation and sadness as Joshua desperately searched for some way to change her mind, while knowing there was nowhere to go and nothing to say.

"OK, Mei Lei. You go and live your life alone." Joshua could not resist the shot. "And so will I."

Mei Lei took her hand down and began to turn away. But Joshua had to say more, because he couldn't bear the thought of losing Mei Lei again without one more attempt.

"Enjoy the trip back home alone, Mei Lei," mocked Joshua. "You will have plenty of time to think. And when you realize that you and I together is the best thing that could ever happen to both of us, you will contact me."

Mei Lei turned back around to face Joshua. "No, Joshua, I will not. I will only contact you to let you know the container is safely resting at the bottom of the sea," affirmed Mei Lei, her heart quaking, her head pounding, a dark blanket of grief enveloping her entire being. She knew she could change the outcome, that she could have Joshua in her life. But no, not to be, not now and not ever. A deep wave of sadness and despair rose up from the depths of her soul too.

Joshua dug his heels into the deck, his gaze fixed down, the third deep sigh escaping him involuntarily. His chest was heavy, every breath an effort, the weight of disappointment pressing in as he ran a hand through his hair, knowing he was about to lose something he'd hoped to get back, that he wanted more than anything.

Joshua did his best to put on a good face. "All right, Mei Lei. I accept that, and I will sleep well knowing that the bomb has been safely disposed of and that you are safe."

"Will I be safe now, Joshua? Will I?"

THE END

ABOUT THE AUTHOR

David Kent, based in Houston, Texas, was a member of the
South Texas Law Review and was a mock trial champion;
graduating magna cum laude in 1988.David has served the
community primarily as a personal jury lawyer; having
represented thousands of people in the last 35 years. He has
tried to verdict more than 300 cases of all kinds and is eligible
to be board certified as a personal injury lawyer, a civil trial
lawyer, a criminal defense lawyer, a family lawyer and an
appellate lawyer.David was recently elected to be a member of
ABOTA.

ABOUT THE PUBLISHER

Di Angelo Publications was founded in 2008 by Sequoia Schmidt—at the age of seventeen. The modernized publishing firm's creative headquarters is in Los Angeles, California. In 2020, Di Angelo Publications made a conscious decision to move all printing and production for domestic distribution of its books to the United States. The firm is comprised of eleven imprints, and the featured imprint, Reverie, was inspired by the long-lasting legacy of fiction and adult literature.